Everyman, I will go with thee,
and be thy guide

Thomas Hardy

THE LIFE AND DEATH OF
THE MAYOR OF
CASTERBRIDGE

A STORY OF A MAN OF
CHARACTER

Edited by
PAMELA NORRIS

EVERYMAN
J.M. DENT · LONDON
CHARLES E. TUTTLE
VERMONT

This title first published in Everyman 1983
This edition first published 1993

J.M. Dent
Orion Publishing Group, Orion House
5 Upper St Martin's Lane London WC2H 9EA
and
Charles E. Tuttle
28, South Main Street, Rutland, Vermont
05701, USA

Typeset by Deltatype Ltd, Ellesmere Port, Cheshire
Printed in Great Britain by
The Guernsey Press Co. Ltd
Guernsey, C.I.

ISBN 0 460 87279 6

CONTENTS

A NOTE ON THE AUTHOR AND EDITOR

Thomas Hardy was born on 2 June 1840 in Higher Bockhampton near Dorchester, the son of a stonemason and builder, and a former domestic servant, Jemima Hand. After an education that included Latin, French and mathematics, Hardy was articled at sixteen to a Dorchester architect and in 1862 went to work in London. He pursued a programme of self-education with a view to entering the church, but by 1863 was already considering becoming a writer. He returned to Dorset in 1867 and began his first (unpublished) novel, *The Poor Man and the Lady*. In 1870 he went to St Juliot in Cornwall to survey the church and met Emma Lavinia Gifford, the rector's sister-in-law. The publication of *Desperate Remedies* (1871), *Under the Greenwood Tree* (1872) and *A Pair of Blue Eyes* (serialised from September 1872) encouraged Hardy to give up architecture for writing, and the success of *Far from the Madding Crowd* in 1874 enabled him to marry Emma.

After a number of moves between London and Dorset, the Hardys finally settled in 1885 at Max Gate near Dorchester, where Hardy continued to write novels and short stories, but the harsh reviews of *Jude the Obscure* (1895) encouraged him to relinquish fiction for poetry. *Wessex Poems* appeared in 1898. Although their marriage was unhappy, Emma inspired some of Hardy's most memorable verse, written after her death in 1912. He married Florence Dugdale in 1914. By Hardy's death in 1928 he had written over 900 poems, and had also published a vast epic drama, *The Dynasts*. He was awarded the Order of Merit in 1910, and was buried at Westminster Abbey.

Pamela Norris read English at Bristol University and spent several years teaching abroad, before working in publishing as a commissioning editor. In 1990 she completed an MA at London University. Previous publications include editions of Jane Austen's *Pride and Prejudice* and *Mansfield Park* for Everyman, and *Sound the Deep Waters*, an anthology of Victorian women poets.

A CHRONOLOGY OF HARDY'S LIFE

Year	Age	Life
1840		Thomas Hardy born, first child of Thomas and Jemima (Hand) Hardy, in Higher Bockhampton, Dorset, 2 June
1841–56		Birth of siblings: Mary (1841), Henry (1851), Katharine (1856)
1848	8	Starts school at Stinsford National (i.e. Church of England) School
1850	10	To Isaac Last's British School in Dorchester
1853–6	13–16	Attends Isaac Last's independent 'commercial academy', where he studies Latin, maths, and technical studies; also takes private lessons in French
1856	16	Articled to John Hicks, a Dorchester architect. Witnesses public execution of Martha Browne. Pursuing programme of self-education
1857	17	By 1857, establishes close friendship with the scholar Horace Moule
1860	20	Completes articles with Hicks (extended by a year); employed as an assistant
1862	21–2	Travels to London and finds employment as 'Gothic draughtsman' with Arthur Blomfield. Elected member of Architectural Association in November
1863	22	Wins two architectural prizes. Considers undertaking literary journalism
1863–7	22–7	Relationship with Eliza Nicholls
1867	27	Returns to Dorset in July to work for Hicks; begins first (unpublished) novel *The Poor Man and the Lady*
1868–9	28–9	Manuscript of *The Poor Man and the Lady* rejected by four publishers

A CHRONOLOGY OF HIS TIMES

Year	Literary context[1]	Historical and cultural context[1]
1840		Queen Victoria m. Prince Albert
1846	Lear: *A Book of Nonsense*	Corn Laws repealed
1847	Charlotte Brontë: *Jane Eyre*	
1848	Thackeray: *Vanity Fair*	Revolutions in Europe
1850	Tennyson: *In Memoriam*	Tennyson: Poet Laureate
1853	Dickens: *Bleak House*	
1854	Patmore: *The Angel in the House* (I)	Crimean War
1855	Trollope: *The Warden*	
1857	Hughes: *Tom Brown's Schooldays*	Matrimonial Causes Act Indian Mutiny
1860	George Eliot: *The Mill on the Floss*	
1861	Dickens: *Great Expectations*	American Civil War
1862	M. Braddon: *Lady Audley's Secret* C. Rossetti: *Goblin Market and Other Poems*	Hugo: *Les Misérables*
1863	Kingsley: *The Water-Babies*	Huxley: *Evidence as to Man's Place in Nature*
1864	Browning: *Dramatis Personae*	
1867		Second Parliamentary Reform Act: extends male franchise Marx: *Das Kapital* (I)
1868		Last public hangings in England

[1] Dates of novels refer to publication in book form. The list of works is necessarily selective.

[1] Including foreign literature

Year	Age	Life
1869	28–9	Working in Weymouth; writing *Desperate Remedies*
1870	29	Meets Emma Gifford while surveying church in St Juliot, North Cornwall
1871	30	*Desperate Remedies* published in March by William Tinsley; Hardy pays £75 towards the costs
1872	32	*Under the Greenwood Tree* published by Tinsley, who paid £30 for the copyright. *A Pair of Blue Eyes* serialised in *Tinsleys' Magazine* (from September)
1873	32–3	3-volume edition of *A Pair of Blue Eyes*; Horace Moule commits suicide
1874	33–4	*Far from the Madding Crowd* serialised in *The Cornhill Magazine* (edited by Leslie Stephen); 2-volume edition published by Smith, Elder; marriage to Emma in September
1875	35	*The Hand of Ethelberta* serialised in the *Cornhill*; the Hardys move from London to Dorset
1878	37–8	Move to Tooting. *The Return of the Native* serialised in *Belgravia*; 3-volume edition published
1880	39–40	*The Trumpet-Major* serialised in *Good Words*; 3-volume edition published. Hardy seriously ill, winter 1880–1
1881	40–1	*A Laodicean* published in *Harper's New Monthly Magazine*; and 3-volume edition. Move to Wimborne, Dorset
1882	41–2	*Two on a Tower* serialised in *Atlantic Monthly*; 3-volume edition
1883	43	Move to Dorchester
1885	45	Move to his final home: Max Gate, designed by Hardy

Year	Literary context	Historical and cultural context
1869	R. D. Blackmore: *Lorna Doone*	Flaubert: *L'Éducation sentimentale*
	Arnold: *Culture and Anarchy*	Tolstoy: *War and Peace*
1870	D. G. Rossetti: *Poems*	Married Women's Property Act
1871	Macdonald: *At the Back of the North Wind*	Trade Union Act: unions legalised
		Darwin: *The Descent of Man*
1872	Butler: *Erewhon*	
	George Eliot: *Middlemarch*	
1873	Arnold: *Literature and Dogma*	Death of Livingstone in central Africa
	Bridges: *Poems*	
1874	Thomson: 'The City of Dreadful Night'	Factory Act: 56-hour working week
		First Impressionist exhibition in Paris
1876	Carroll: *The Hunting of the Snark*	Queen Victoria: Empress of India
1878		Whistler v. Ruskin libel case
1879	Meredith: *The Egoist*	Zulu War
	Henry James: *Daisy Miller*	Ibsen: *A Doll's House*
1880		Dostoevsky: *The Brothers Karamazov*
1881	Henry James: *Portrait of a Lady*	
1882	Swinburne: *Tristram of Lyonesse and Other Poems*	Phoenix Park murders in Dublin
1883	O. Schreiner: *The Story of an African Farm*	
1885	R. L. Stevenson: *A Child's Garden of Verses*	Criminal Law Amendment Act: age of consent raised

Year	Age	Life
1886	45–6	*The Mayor of Casterbridge* serialised in the *Graphic* and published in 2-volume edition. Serialisation of *The Woodlanders* begins in *Macmillan's Magazine*
1887	46	3-volume edition of *The Woodlanders* published
1888	47	2-volume edition of *Wessex Tales*, Hardy's first collection of short stories
1890	50	*A Group of Noble Dames* published in the *Graphic*
1891	50–1	Hardy elected to Athenaeum Club for his 'distinguished merit' in literature. Volume edition of *A Group of Noble Dames*, with four additional stories. Serialisation of *Tess of the d'Urbervilles* in the *Graphic*; 3-volume edition
1892	52	Death of Hardy's father. *The Pursuit of the Well-Beloved* serialised in the *Illustrated London News*
1893	52–3	Hardy forms an apparently unreciprocated romantic attachment for Mrs Florence Henniker
1894	53–4	Publication of *Life's Little Ironies*, a third volume of short stories. Serialisation of *Jude the Obscure* begins in *Harper's* in December
1895	55	Publication of *Jude the Obscure*; receives hostile reviews
1895–7	55–6	Osgood, McIlvaine edition of the 'Wessex novels'
1897	56	Publication of *The Well-Beloved*, the last of Hardy's novels to appear in book form
1898	58	Publication of *Wessex Poems and Other Verses*, illustrated by Hardy, to mixed reviews. Deepening estrangement with Emma
1901	61	Publication of *Poems of the Past and the Present*
1902	61–2	Final change of publishers to Macmillan
1904	63	First part of verse drama, *The Dynasts*, published. Jemima, Hardy's beloved mother, dies
1905	65	Meets his future second wife, Florence Dugdale

Year	Literary context	Historical and cultural context
1886	H. Rider Haggard: *King Solomon's Mines*	Defeat of Gladstone's Irish Home Rule Bill
1887		'Bloody Sunday' riots in Trafalgar Square
1888	Mrs Humphry Ward: *Robert Elsmere*	Match girls strike in East London
1890		Parnell resigns over O'Shea divorce case
1891	Gissing: *New Grub Street*	US Copyright Bill
1892	Wilde: *Lady Windermere's Fan*	Franco-Russian threat in Mediterranean
1893	Pinero: *The Second Mrs Tanqueray*	Independent Labour Party founded
1894	George Moore: *Esther Waters* Kipling: *The Jungle Book* (I)	
1895	Grant Allen: *The Woman Who Did*	Jameson Raid: invasion of Transvaal
1896	Housman: *A Shropshire Lad*	*Daily Mail* on sale
1897	Henry James: *What Maisie Knew*	Havelock Ellis: *Studies in the Psychology of Sex* (I)
1898	H. G. Wells: *The War of the Worlds*	Peking Convention: British 99-year lease of territory
1899		Boer War
1901	Beatrix Potter: *The Tale of Peter Rabbit*	Victoria dies: succeeded by Edward VII
1902	Kipling: *Just So Stories*	
1904	Henry James: *The Golden Bowl*	Dogger Bank incident: war with Russia averted
1905		Major disturbances in Russia

Year	Age	Life
1906	65	Publication of second part of *The Dynasts*
1908	67–8	Publication of third part of *The Dynasts*. Publication of the *Select Poems of William Barnes*, edited by Hardy
1909	69	Covent Garden performance of Baron d'Erlanger's opera *Tess*. Publication of third volume of poems, *Time's Laughingstocks*, to good reviews
1910	70	Hardy receives Order of Merit. Florence Dugdale: Hardy's literary 'handyman'
1912–13	71–2	April 1912 – early 1913 Macmillan's definitive Wessex Edition of Hardy's work. Emma Hardy dies in November 1912
1913	73	Final collection of short stories, *A Changed Man*
1914	73–4	Marries Florence Dugdale. Publication of *Satires of Circumstance*, including 'Poems of 1912–13' about his relationship with Emma
1915	75	Hardy's beloved sister, Mary, dies in November
1916	76	*Selected Poems of Thomas Hardy*
1917	77	*Moments of Vision*. Hardy and Florence begin work on the 2-volume 'biography' of Hardy eventually published under Florence's name
1919–20	78–80	Macmillan's Mellstock Edition: 37-volume *de luxe* edition of Hardy's work
1922	81	*Late Lyrics and Earlier*: includes Hardy's 'Apology' in which he expressed his resentment against critics who had attacked the form and content of his poetry
1923	83	*The Famous Tragedy of the Queen of Cornwall*, a poetic drama
1924	84	Dramatisation of *Tess* in Dorchester with Gertrude Bugler, a talented local actress, as Tess
1925	85	*Human Shows Far Phantasies Songs and Trifles*
1928	87	Hardy dies on 11 January. *Winter Words* published posthumously

Year	Literary context	Historical and cultural context
1906	Galsworthy: *The Man of Property*	
1908	Bennett: *The Old Wives' Tale* Grahame: *The Wind in the Willows*	Annexation of Bosnia-Herzegovina by Austria-Hungary
1910	E. M. Forster: *Howards End*	Edward VII dies; succeeded by George V
1912	*Georgian Poetry* (I)	Sinking of the *Titantic* Balkan Wars
1913	Lawrence: *Sons and Lovers*	'Cat and Mouse Act'
1914	Joyce: *Dubliners*	Ulster crisis over Home Rule Archduke Franz Ferdinand assassinated in Sarajevo
1914–18		First World War
1915	V. Woolf: *The Voyage Out*	
1917	T. S. Eliot: *Prufrock and Other Observations* Yeats: *The Wild Swans at Coole*	
1919		Treaty of Versailles
1922	K. Mansfield: *The Garden Party, and Other Stories* Joyce: *Ulysses* (UK 1936) T. S. Eliot: *The Waste Land*	Mussolini: Prime Minister of Italy
1923		Matrimonial Causes Act: equal rights in divorce suits
1924	Shaw: *Saint Joan*	Ramsay MacDonald: first Labour PM
1925	V. Woolf: *Mrs Dalloway*	Chinese civil war begins
1928	Waugh: *Decline and Fall* Yeats: *The Tower*	Equal Franchise Act: vote for women of 21 and over

INTRODUCTION

The tradition that fed Hardy's greatest work, the six 'Wessex' novels and his poetry, was rural and oral. He was born in the village of Higher Bockhampton in Dorset, the son and grandson of earlier Thomas Hardys, both master masons, and the eldest and most delicate child of Jemima Hand, a former domestic servant whose childhood poverty had forced her into paid work at an early age. Hardy's beginnings were reputedly unpropitious – after a difficult labour, the child was at first cast aside as dead – and his early fragility may have encouraged the tendency to introspection and bleak realism that characterises his mature work. Lacking robust health, 'Tommy', as he liked to call himself, was particularly vulnerable to his family environment, a domestic circle dominated by the strong and aspiring personality of Jemima. In the intimate female gatherings of Hardy and Hand relatives, young Thomas Hardy heard the country songs, legends and gossip that he recreated to such good effect in novels, stories and finally poetry, a rich stock of rural narrative in which domestic and social relations were imaginatively explored and superstition respected. From his handsome and apparently charming and fun-loving father, Thomas inherited the responsiveness to music he later attributed to Michael Henchard: '. . . with Henchard music was of regal power. The merest trumpet or organ tone was enough to move him.'

Despite Hardy's reluctance to grow up, recorded in his poem 'Childhood among the Ferns', Jemima's ambition secured for her son an adequate education, enabling him to train as an architect. However, experience of architectural practice in London suggested to Hardy that he lacked the social skills and connections essential to success, and his relationship with the scholar Horace Moule led him to consider a career in the church. Like Jude Fawley in *Jude the Obscure*, he pursued an industrious programme of self-education with the hope of eventually obtaining a university education for the ministry. At the same time he wondered about becoming an art critic, whilst dabbling in journalism. But the impulse towards fiction was strong, and once he had experienced the excitement of having his first novel, *The Poor Man and the Lady*, seriously considered (albeit rejected) by publishers, Hardy became determined to succeed as a writer.

Hardy's second novel, *Desperate Remedies*, was published to mixed reviews in 1871; *Under the Greenwood Tree, A Pair of Blue Eyes* and *Far from the Madding Crowd* rapidly followed, establishing Hardy's reputation as a writer of talent, and enabling him to marry Emma Gifford in 1874. The couple moved between London and Dorset while Hardy continued to write novels for serialisation in the *Cornhill, Belgravia, Good Words* and other magazines both in England and America, and for subsequent volume publication. *The Mayor of Casterbridge* was his tenth published novel, written when preparing to settle finally in Max Gate, the house Hardy designed and had built for himself and Emma near Dorchester. The move to Max Gate in 1885 enabled him to devote himself increasingly to his work as a novelist and then to writing the hundreds of poems that were published in a series of collections from *Wessex Poems* in 1898 to the posthumous *Winter Words*. Characteristic of his poetry as well as the best of his fiction is a detailed observation and understanding of the natural world, specifically in his native Dorset, an intense interest in life's ambiguities and ironies, and a response to rural superstition. Hardy's work, and the series of passionate attachments he felt for kindly disposed but ultimately unavailable women, testify to his sensitivity to the romantic possibilities of love. His real-life failure to establish a happy marriage with either of his two wives may have been due in part to the influence of the dominant Jemima. What is clear is that, for Hardy, the dreams and imaginings of his interior world took precedence over reality, to the benefit of his readers but with painful consequences for the two women who married him.

Today Hardy's reputation as a novelist centres around six key works, the 'Wessex' novels: *Far from the Madding Crowd* (1874), *The Return of the Native* (1878), *The Mayor of Casterbridge* (1886), *The Woodlanders* (1886–7), *Tess of the d'Urbervilles* (1891) and *Jude the Obscure* (1894–5). His complete corpus, however, covers a wider variety of genre and experiment, and is worth exploring. In planning his novels, Hardy took a strong commercial interest in meeting the requirements of his publishers, and his selection of material was further influenced by the serialisation of most of his novels in magazines intended for a family audience. Serialisation required complex plots with plenty of incident, 'cliff-hanging' endings to sections, and the avoidance of sexually explicit material. The careful re-working of *The Mayor of Casterbridge* was a response to the differing demands of magazine and book publication, although Hardy was later to express concern that he had somewhat over-egged this particular pudding (see Note on the Text), a view that was not shared by either his public or subsequent critics.

Hardy's six major novels are set in the fictional territory that he designated as Wessex and which in fact incorporates much of Dorset (see Notes, p. 294), and carefully observed descriptions of nature frequently act as background or commentary on the plot. The novels examine the often subtle gradations in social rank in rural communities, and the effects of social and intellectual aspiration on marriage alliances and personal happiness. The working-out of the plot is the subject of lively comment by an often articulate group of local 'rustics', and irony, coincidence, and the apparent malevolence of fate are consistent features of the complex action. The texts contain evidence of the influences on Hardy's work – the Bible, folk tales and songs, his reading of local newspapers and records, and the novelists, poets, philosophers and religious thinkers whom he studied through the course of his life, often in specific preparation for his writing. What does change through the course of the six novels is the focus of the plots, and in the character of Michael Henchard, Hardy begins that detailed study of an individual fate and its interactions with society that was to be central in *Tess* and *Jude*. In all three cases, the temperament of the central character brings about conflict with social laws and works against his or her aspirations with ultimately tragic consequences. In investigating the histories of Michael, Tess and Jude, Hardy drew extensively on the rural tradition he had absorbed in childhood, and exposed its rules to a critical scrutiny that was at times daringly unconventional and testified to his willingness to criticise Victorian moral codes. The innovation of his attitudes can be attributed to wide reading and a questioning intelligence, but perhaps, also, to his perception of the discrepancy between real and prescribed sexual behaviour in the rural communities that he knew.

The full title of the novel, *The Life and Death of The Mayor of Casterbridge: A Story of a Man of Character*, suggests a number of entry points to the basic question: What is the novel about? It gives Michael Henchard's death as much weight as his life, confirms his history as the main focus of the novel, and declares Henchard to be a man of character. The structure of the book is also instructive: the novel begins with Henchard's auction of his wife and child when Henchard is twenty-one, and then skips more than eighteen years to the return of Susan with Elizabeth-Jane to Weydon-Priors in search of the erstwhile hay-trusser. From the time of Susan's arrival in Casterbridge with her daughter, Henchard's fortunes, already past their zenith, wane to a point that takes him full circle beyond the resumption of his relatively lowly occupation at the beginning of the novel to his lonely death with one faithful attendant. We know nothing of Henchard's origins, but this isolated moment at the departure of life recalls the ritual seclusion of birth. The plot structure makes it clear that the key events in Henchard's history revolve around his (failed) relationship with his wife and child; the interim period, which advances him through his own hard effort and energy from a jobbing labourer to a prosperous corn-factor and the prestigious role of Mayor of Casterbridge, is barely sketched in – and its few details are only revealed retrospectively through the history of another botched emotional encounter, Henchard's apparently brief and rather prosaic love affair with Lucetta.

The personality of the 'Man of Character' is established in the first scene of the novel. We learn that he is moody, aspiring, self-centred and impulsive. He married at eighteen, but feels no pleasure in his wife and child, and claims that his family is an impediment to his worldly success. The question of his own responsibility for the alliance is not addressed. He is no stranger to alcohol, careless of its uninhibiting effects, and indeed takes advantage of the laced furmity to shed his unwanted commitments. His shame when sober over the sale of Susan drives him to the 'fetichistic' vow of abstinence, which he keeps by a powerful act of will, but as soon as the set time has elapsed, because things have begun to go wrong for him, he 'busts out drinking' as if no moral lesson had been learnt.

Henchard has the energy and brute force of the sledge-hammer with which Hardy compares him, and he is as repetitive in his actions. Seen again after the lapse of nearly twenty years, we are aware that there has been little significant change in his character. Hardy presents him positioned like Christ at the Last Supper in a Renaissance painting, the central figure at a dinner table, framed by the spacious bow-window of the King's Arms. But this is no inspired leader of men. Heavy, commanding, coarse-bodied, with the florid complexion of a choleric personality, the Mayor claims attention by his exaggerated laugh and his old-fashioned but ostentatiously ornate dinner-dress. It is no wonder that his effect on Susan is overpowering and that her first impulse is to run away: 'I have seen him, and it is enough for me! Now I only want to go – pass away – die.' Henchard's initial search for his wife had been motivated as much by guilt and social anxiety as by affection; now he is determined to make reparation to Susan, but there is little heart in the act. Although he is a man 'to whom some human object for pouring out his heat upon – were it emotive or were it choleric – was almost a necessity', his emotion at this time is impulsively poured out on Farfrae, his surrogate brother – or son – until he too disappoints him. Henchard's feeling for Elizabeth-Jane is based on a possessive paternity: his belief that he is her father, and his wish to 'provide a comfortable home for [her] under his paternal eye'. When reality challenges Henchard's romantic affections – for Farfrae, Elizabeth-Jane and Lucetta – requiring him to look beyond his own childish wants and to act in a way that acknowledges the other person's needs, he veers off, and is unable to judge the goodness of others' intentions or their moral character. Given his own lack of moral and emotional stability and his 'introspective inflexibility', this is unsurprising. What makes Henchard interesting and even sympathetic is the force of his character: the energy that brings him wealth and status – and then secures his downfall, his openness and honesty, however ill-judged, and the consistency that makes him act first and reflect later. Unable to learn from his mistakes, he does not flinch from the suffering that his behaviour causes him.

Some critics see a development in Henchard as a result of adversity and Elizabeth-Jane's 'softening' influence, and he does indeed feel, on his return to the scene of the auction at the end of the novel, 'the bitterness of a man who finds, in looking back upon an ambitious course, that what he has sacrificed in sentiment was worth as much as what he has gained in substance . . . He had been sorry for all this long ago; but his attempts to replace ambition by love had been as fully foiled as his ambition itself.'

But the responsibility for his failed hopes lies with himself, in the repetitiveness with which he seeks his own harm, even to the last meeting with Elizabeth-Jane when he proudly says not a word in his own defence. Pride and a powerful sense of isolation consistently inhibit Henchard from sharing his humanity with people who would have been glad to help and succour him, and the document he leaves pinned to the head of his death-bed perpetuates this sense of his own separateness beyond the grave.

The Mayor of Casterbridge, however, refuses to be read in isolation; it demands recognition and understanding of the texts that have fed it. The novel is littered with reminders of a literary tradition that goes back to the Greeks (invoked by Hardy when he compares the *carrefour* in front of Lucetta's house with 'the regulation Open Place in spectacular dramas'), and there is a running sub-text of comparison with Bible stories – the conflict between Saul and David, Jacob getting the better of Laban, the trials of Job – that stretch meaning and, for the Bible-literate audience of the late nineteenth century, would have significantly enhanced their reading of the story. Hardy specifically invites comparison with the morality tale – Henchard breaks a social taboo by auctioning his wife and is ultimately punished for it – by linking Henchard's loss of prosperity to Fall literature. Character, he points out, is Fate, and he compares Henchard with Faust, 'a vehement gloomy being who had quitted the ways of vulgar men, without light to guide him on a better way', thus suggesting that Henchard has, like Faust, dared to challenge God and because of his refusal to mend his ways must be bruised and finally broken. Henchard himself feels a link with the prototypical social outcast, Cain, but whereas Cain protests at his punishment, Henchard takes full responsibility for his actions: 'I – Cain – go alone as I deserve – an outcast and a vagabond. But my punishment is *not* greater than I can bear!'

The history of Michael Henchard is in part the story of his interaction with a particular time and place, and the setting and period of The Mayor of Casterbridge are significant. By focusing the action on Casterbridge/Dorchester, Hardy was able to explore a tightly knit community which was both socially and economically interdependent. Hardy had been at school in Dorchester and was living there during the gestation of The Mayor of Casterbridge, and the novel reveals his close observation of life in the town.

The importance of agriculture and the surrounding countryside to Casterbridge are immediately apparent when Susan and her daughter arrive in the town and pass shop windows full of agricultural and pastoral implements: 'Scythes, reap-hooks, sheep-shears, bill-hooks, spades, mattocks, and hoes at the ironmonger's'. Hardy emphasises this a few pages later when he describes Elizabeth-Jane's perambulations to find Henchard's house:

> Casterbridge lived by agriculture at one remove further from the fountain-head than the adjoining villages – no more. The townsfolk understood every fluctuation in the rustic's condition, for it affected their receipts as much as the labourer's . . . And even at the dinner-parties of the professional families the subjects of discussion were corn, cattle-disease, sowing and reaping, fencing and planting;

In this close relationship with its environs, Casterbridge differed 'from the many manufacturing towns which are as foreign bodies set down, like boulders on a plain, in a green world with which they have nothing in common.' Even the natural world treats the town as its own domain:

> Bees and butterflies in the cornfields at the top of the town, who desired to get to the meads at the bottom, took no circuitous course, but flew straight down High Street without any apparent consciousness that they were traversing strange latitudes.

The community is also socially closely integrated, a factor which the 'outsider' Lucetta fails to appreciate when she plays down Henchard's influence in her husband's success during the visit of the Royal Personage. Both Henchard and Farfrae achieve high civic status and considerable business prestige after humble beginnings, and when the furmity-seller challenges Michael Henchard as being no better than she is, Henchard's early struggles in the town are sufficiently well-remembered for her words to carry weight. The initial cause of his downfall, the sale of corrupted wheat, affects everyone in the community: bread is a staple of everyday life. When Henchard leaves his prestigious house in the centre of town, the move to Jopp's poor cottage by the Priory Mill represents a substantial drop in status, but it is something of a nine-days' wonder (Henchard is accepted as workmate and drinking companion by the men he used to command, and even Farfrae begins to see him in the same light as the rest of his workers), and in geographical terms the distance is not great.

The contrast between Farfrae and Henchard gives dramatic expression to the conflict that was still being experienced in mid-nineteenth-century England between an ancient agricultural tradition and the incursions of mechanism. Hardy records rather than judges, using the economic revolution as a vehicle for exploring the effects of change on the (backward) Casterbridge community and to reveal the personalities of Henchard and his manager. Henchard himself points out the difference between his approach and Farfrae's: 'In my business, 'tis true that strength and bustle build up a firm. But judgment and knowledge are what keep it established. Unluckily, I am bad at science, Farfrae; bad at figures – a rule o' thumb sort of man. You are just the reverse – I can see that.' Later the man of science, Farfrae, introduces the (garish) horse-drill, a new and more efficient kind of sowing-machine than the labourers customarily still employed in that region, but Henchard is now hostile to science and criticises Farfrae's innovation, and even the sensible Elizabeth-Jane mourns the lost 'romance of the sower'. When Farfrae takes over from the bankrupt Henchard, 'scales and steelyards began to be busy where guess-work had formerly been the rule.' The placing of the novel in the period just prior to the repeal of the Corn Laws lends credibility to Henchard's almost overnight ruin; speculation resulting from the restrictions on imports of foreign wheat made dealers particularly susceptible to poor weather and their own ability to judge likely harvest yields. Henchard was not the only businessman, fictitious or real, to be ruined by miscalculation, and it is Farfrae's ability to play the market that confirms his commercial success – evidence of his cooler brains and more phlegmatic personality.

The Mayor of Casterbridge is not a romantic novel in the traditional sense, but love and marriage are central themes. None of the relationships, however, are free from strain. Henchard's marriage to Susan is so irksome that he impulsively auctions her to a stranger. Their subsequent re-marriage and his courtship of Lucetta when she comes to Casterbridge is for the sake of making reparation rather than from any strong feeling for either woman. Lucetta, another impulsive character, compromises herself with Henchard and feels obliged to marry him. When she falls in love with Farfrae, her happiness is shadowed by anxiety that he will find out about Henchard, and when the truth is revealed it kills her and the child she carries. Newson's care of Susan and her child is insufficient to overcome her scruples about the illegality of their marriage and she is not only relieved to hear of his death, but then feels impelled for the sake of her daughter to seek out the husband who had humiliated her. Elizabeth-Jane's nascent feeling for Farfrae is finally rewarded by marriage, but only after she has been rejected for the more glamorous Lucetta, and the brief description of her married life that closes the novel suggests a cautious contentment that contrasts with Lucetta's earlier doting delight in her young husband.

The contrast between Lucetta and Elizabeth-Jane provides an essential dynamic in the novel. But Susan Henchard, probably one of the least regarded of Hardy's 'heroines', also plays a major role. Described by an early critic as 'so colourless as to be almost imperceptible' (*Saturday Review*, 29 May 1886), and nicknamed 'The Ghost' by the Casterbridge boys, Susan's self-effacing presence nevertheless exerts a powerful influence over events. There are hints from the beginning that she could be described as a 'Woman of Character': her personality is as strong and inflexible as her first husband's. In the furmity tent, she calls Henchard's bluff not only by standing up to allow herself to be auctioned, but also by leaving with Newson once the transaction has been concluded. Her decision, based on a close look at the sailor's face as he invites her to bring the child, proves to have been percipient. Newson never makes much money while Susan is living with him, but his behaviour suggests that he is a man of unusual tact and great kindness. Despite their poverty, they seem to have been happy in Canada, where Susan 'worked as hard as any woman could to keep their cottage cheerful and well-provided', and initially on their return to England.

When Susan discovers that the auction had not altered her legal status as Henchard's wife, Newson relieves her anguish by quietly disappearing, apparently lost at sea. Susan then takes the momentous decision, for her daughter's sake, to seek out her lost husband, from whom she had had 'nothing but temper'. Although already suffering from ill-health, she makes the long journey to Weydon-Priors and then to Casterbridge, only to be overwhelmed by the sight of Henchard in his position of authority at the public dinner. She is rallied, however, by the more sanguine Elizabeth-Jane, and manages to make contact with Henchard, and to play with dignity her part in his courtship and subsequent marriage of Newson's 'genteel widow'. Once married, she quietly fends off Henchard's attempt to persuade Elizabeth-Jane to take his name, tries to stage-manage a romance between her daughter and Farfrae, and salves her conscience at the deception over Elizabeth-Jane's parentage by leaving a letter for Henchard to be read once Elizabeth-Jane has found a husband to take care of her. In this 'poor fragile woman', there is a will of steel.

Unable, finally, to control events from the grave, Susan's influence continues to be felt in the personality of her daughter. Just as Elizabeth-Jane's face in repose reveals the 'buried genealogical facts, ancestral curves, dead men's traits' that mark her as Richard Newson's child, so her nature has derived an essential imprint from her mother. When Farfrae treats her coldly after he has fallen in love with Lucetta, 'Susan Henchard's daughter bore up against the frosty ache of the treatment'. The reference to Susan in this context is striking. Her death has been the occasion of Lucetta's arrival in Casterbridge and hence of Elizabeth-Jane's loss of Farfrae, but her daughter's fortitude when faced with a hostile environment is a direct inheritance from the woman who, although '[a]bsolutely helpless', successfully managed her 'marriage' to Newson and the re-establishment of social propriety with Henchard.

What ultimately undermines Susan's manipulations is the same obsession that destroys the more flamboyant Henchard and Lucetta. Susan shares with her husband and his one-time lover the passionate desire to keep a secret that is, nevertheless, eventually revealed with catastrophic consequences. Henchard's youthful sale of his wife, Lucetta's sexual intimacy with Henchard, and the truth about Elizabeth-Jane's parentage are all laid open despite frantic attempts to suppress information and destroy the evidence. The 'survivors' in the novel – Elizabeth-Jane, Newson and Donald Farfrae – are those protagonists who (apparently) have nothing to hide.

The Mayor of Casterbridge is a dark and often claustrophobic novel of frustrated hopes and stifled impulses towards good. Henchard's heroic attempt to wrestle life into his own mould leads to disappointment, loss and an isolated death, and the secret of his step-daughter's eventual domestic happiness lies in her modest ability to make 'limited opportunities endurable', hard-won knowledge that she generously shares with 'the narrow-lived ones around her' in Casterbridge. Henchard's energetic striving for civic status and commercial success is obversely reflected in Elizabeth-Jane's feeling that 'she could perceive no great personal difference between being respected in the nether parts of Caster-bridge and glorified at the uppermost end of the social world', and the novel ends with her quiet reflections on the random nature of human experience, and 'the persistence of the unforeseen'.

Pamela Norris, 1993

NOTE ON THE TEXT

The Mayor of Casterbridge was written in 1884–5, and Hardy immediately revised it to make it more exciting for serial publication, which required a steady stream of incidents to keep the reader's interest. Hardy was later to say, in the person of his wife Florence: 'It was a story which Hardy fancied he had damaged more recklessly as an artistic whole, in the interest of the newspaper in which it appeared serially, than perhaps any other of his novels, his aiming to get an incident into almost every week's part causing him in his own judgment to add events to the narrative somewhat too freely' (Florence Emily Hardy, *The Early Life of Thomas Hardy*, London, 1928, p. 235).

The novel was serialised in twenty parts in the *Graphic*, and in *Harper's Weekly* in the United States, from 2 January to 15 May 1886. Hardy made further revisions for its publication in two volumes by Smith, Elder and Co. on 10 May 1886, and again for the Sampson Low one-volume edition in 1887. For the 1895 uniform edition of his novels by Osgood, McIlvaine and Co., Hardy again revised the text, and made more alterations for Macmillan's definitive Wessex Edition of Hardy's works in 1912. A few further corrections were made for the Mellstock Edition in 1919–20, again published by Macmillan. Revisions included the pruning of extraneous action, modifications in the relationship between Henchard and Lucetta, and the reinstatement of a substantial part of Chapter 44 (see Notes, pp. 293–4).

The text of this edition is based on that of the Wessex Edition of 1912, incorporating alterations made by Hardy for the Mellstock Edition and later printings of the Wessex Edition.

AUTHOR'S PREFACE

Readers of the following story who have not yet arrived at middle age are asked to bear in mind that, in the days recalled by the tale,* the home Corn Trade, on which so much of the action turns, had an importance that can hardly be realized by those accustomed to the sixpenny loaf of the present date, and to the present indifference of the public to harvest weather.*

The incidents narrated arise mainly out of three events, which chanced to range themselves in the order and at or about the intervals of time here given, in the real history of the town called Casterbridge* and the neighbouring country. They were the sale of a wife by her husband,* the uncertain harvests which immediately preceded the repeal of the Corn Laws,* and the visit of a Royal personage to the aforesaid part of England.*

The present edition of the volume, like the previous one, contains nearly a chapter which did not at first appear in any English copy, though it was printed in the serial issue of the tale, and in the American edition. The restoration was made at the instance of some good judges across the Atlantic, who strongly represented that the home edition suffered from the omission.* Some shorter passages and names, omitted or altered for reasons which no longer exist, in the original printing of both English and American editions, have also been replaced or inserted.

The story is more particularly a study of one man's deeds and character than, perhaps, any other of those included in my Exhibition of Wessex life.* Objections have been raised to the Scotch language of Mr Farfrae, the second character; and one of his fellow-countrymen went so far as to declare that men beyond the Tweed did not and never could say 'warrld', 'cannet', 'advairrtisment', and so on. As this gentleman's pronunciation in correcting me seemed to my Southron* ear an exact repetition of what my spelling implied, I was not struck with the truth of his remark, and somehow we did not get any forwarder in the matter. It must be remembered that the Scotchman of the tale is represented not as he would appear to other Scotchmen, but as he would appear to people of outer regions. Moreover, no attempt is made herein to reproduce his entire pronunciation phonetically, any more than that of the Wessex speakers. I should add, however, that this new edition of the book has had the accidental advantage of a critical overlooking by a professor of the tongue in question* – one of undoubted authority: – in fact he is a gentleman who adopted it for ugent personal reasons in the first year of his existence.

Furthermore, a charming non-Scottish lady, of strict veracity and admitted penetration, the wife of a well-known Caledonian, came to the writer shortly after the story was first published, and inquired if Farfrae were not drawn from her husband, for he seemed to her to be the living portrait of that (doubtless) happy man. It happened that I had never thought of her husband in constructing Farfrae. I trust therefore that Farfrae may be allowed to pass, if not as a Scotchman to Scotchmen, as a Scotchman to Southerners.

The novel was first published complete, in two volumes, in May 1886.

February 1895 – May 1912*   T.H.

THE MAYOR OF CASTERBRIDGE

Chapter 1

One evening of late summer, before the nineteenth century had reached one-third of its span, a young man and woman, the latter carrying a child, were approaching the large village of Weydon-Priors,* in Upper Wessex, on foot. They were plainly but not ill clad, though the thick hoar of dust which had accumulated on their shoes and garments from an obviously long journey lent a disadvantageous shabbiness to their appearance just now.

The man was of fine figure, swarthy and stern in aspect; and he showed in profile a facial angle so slightly inclined as to be almost perpendicular. He wore a short jacket of brown corduroy, newer than the remainder of his suit, which was a fustian* waistcoat with white horn buttons, breeches of the same, tanned leggings, and a straw hat overlaid with black glazed canvas. At his back he carried by a looped strap a rush basket, from which protruded at one end the crutch of a hay-knife, a wimble for hay-bonds* being also visible in the aperture. His measured, springless walk was the walk of the skilled countryman as distinct from the desultory shamble of the general labourer; while in the turn and plant of each foot there was, further, a dogged and cynical indifference personal to himself, showing its presence even in the regularly interchanging fustian folds, now in the left leg, now in the right, as he paced along.

What was really peculiar, however, in this couple's progress, and would have attracted the attention of any casual observer otherwise disposed to overlook them, was the perfect silence they preserved. They walked side by side in such a way as to suggest afar off the low, easy, confidential chat of people full of reciprocity; but on closer view it could be discerned that the man was reading, or pretending to read, a ballad sheet* which he kept before his eyes with some difficulty by the hand that was passed through the basket strap. Whether this apparent cause were the real cause, or whether it were an assumed one to escape an intercourse that would have been irksome to him, nobody but himself could have said precisely; but his taciturnity was unbroken, and the woman enjoyed no society whatever from his presence. Virtually she walked the highway alone, save for the child she bore. Sometimes the man's bent elbow almost touched her shoulder, for she kept as close to his side as was possible without actual contact; but she seemed to have no idea of taking his arm, nor he of offering it; and far from exhibiting surprise at his ignoring silence she appeared to receive it as a natural thing. If any word at all were uttered by the little group, it was an occasional whisper of the woman to the child – a tiny girl in short clothes and blue boots of knitted yarn – and the murmured babble of the child in reply.

The chief – almost the only – attraction of the young woman's face was its mobility. When she looked down sideways to the girl she became pretty, and even handsome, particularly that in the action her features caught slantwise the rays of the strongly coloured sun, which made transparencies of her eyelids and nostrils and set fire on her lips. When she plodded on in the shade of the hedge, silently thinking, she had the hard, half-apathetic expression of one who deems anything possible at the hands of Time and Chance except, perhaps, fair play.* The first phase was the work of Nature, the second probably of civilization.

That the man and woman were husband and wife, and the parents of the girl in arms, there could be little doubt. No other than such relationship would have accounted for the atmosphere of stale familiarity which the trio carried along with them like a nimbus* as they moved down the road.

The wife mostly kept her eyes fixed ahead, though with little interest – the scene for that matter being one that might have been matched at almost any spot in any county in England at this time of the year; a road neither straight nor crooked, neither level nor hilly, bordered by hedges, trees, and other vegetation, which had entered the blackened-green stage of colour that the doomed leaves pass through on their way to dingy, and yellow, and red. The grassy margin of the bank, and the nearest hedgerow boughs, were powdered by the dust that had been stirred over them by hasty vehicles, the same dust as it lay on the road deadening their footfalls like a carpet; and this, with the aforesaid total absence of conversation, allowed every extraneous sound to be heard.

For a long time there was none, beyond the voice of a weak bird singing a trite old evening song that might doubtless have been heard on the hill at the same hour, and with the self-same trills, quavers and breves,* at any sunset of that season for centuries untold. But as they approached the village sundry distant shouts and rattles reached their ears from some elevated spot in that direction, as yet screened from view by foliage. When the outlying houses of Weydon-Priors could just be descried, the family group was met by a turnip-hoer with his hoe on his shoulder, and his dinner-bag suspended from it. The reader promptly glanced up.

'Any trade doing here?' he asked phlegmatically, designating the village in his van by a wave of the broadsheet. And thinking the labourer did not understand him, he added, 'Anything in the hay-trussing line?'

The turnip-hoer had already begun shaking his head. 'Why, save the man, what wisdom's in him that 'a should come to Weydon for a job of that sort this time o' year?'

'Then is there any house to let – a little small new cottage just a-builded, or such like?' asked the other.

The pessimist still maintained a negative. 'Pulling down is more the nater* of Weydon. There were five houses cleared away last year, and three this; and the volk* nowhere to go – no, not so much as a thatched hurdle;* that's the way o' Weydon-Priors.'

The hay-trusser, which he obviously was, nodded with some superciliousness. Looking towards the village, he continued, 'There is something going on here, however, is there not?'

'Ay. 'Tis Fair Day. Though what you hear now is little more than the clatter and scurry of getting away the money o' children and fools, for the real business is done earlier than this. I've been working within sound o't all day, but I didn't go up – not I. 'Twas no business of mine.'

The trusser and his family proceeded on their way, and soon entered the Fair-field, which showed standing-places and pens where many hundreds of horses and sheep had been exhibited and sold in the forenoon, but were now in great part taken away. At present, as their informant had observed, but little real business remained on hand, the chief being the sale by auction of a few inferior animals, that could not otherwise be disposed of, and had been absolutely refused by the better class of traders, who came and went early. Yet the crowd was denser now than during the morning hours, the frivolous contingent of visitors, including journeymen* out for a holiday, a stray soldier or two home on furlough, village shopkeepers, and the like, having latterly flocked in; persons whose activities found a congenial field among the peep-shows, toy-stands, waxworks, inspired monsters, disinterested medical men who travelled for the public good, thimble-riggers,* nick-nack vendors, and readers of Fate.

Neither of our pedestrians had much heart for these things, and they looked around for a refreshment tent among the many which dotted the down. Two, which stood nearest to them in the ochreous haze of expiring sunlight, seemed almost equally inviting. One was formed of new, milk-hued canvas, and bore red flags on its summit; it announced 'Good Home-brewed Beer, Ale, and Cyder'. The other was less new; a little iron stove-pipe came out of it at the back, and in front appeared the placard, 'Good Furmity* Sold Hear'. The man mentally weighed the two inscriptions, and inclined to the former tent.

'No – no – the other one,' said the woman. 'I always like furmity; and so does Elizabeth-Jane; and so will you. It is nourishing after a long day.'

'I've never tasted it,' said the man. However, he gave way to her representations, and they entered the furmity booth forthwith.

A rather numerous company appeared within, seated at the long narrow tables that ran down the tent on each side. At the upper end stood a stove, containing a charcoal fire, over which hung a large three-legged crock, sufficiently polished round the rim to show that it was made of bell-metal.* A haggish creature of about fifty presided, in a white apron, which, as it threw an air of respectability over her as far as it extended, was made so wide as to reach nearly round her waist. She slowly stirred the contents of the pot. The dull scrape of her large spoon was audible throughout the tent as she thus kept from burning the mixture of corn in the grain, flour, milk, raisins, currants, and what not, that composed the antiquated slop in which she dealt. Vessels holding the separate ingredients stood on a white-clothed table of boards and trestles close by.

The young man and woman ordered a basin each of the mixture, steaming hot, and sat down to consume it at leisure. This was very well so far, for furmity, as the woman had said, was nourishing, and as proper a food as could be obtained within the four seas; though, to those not accustomed to it, the grains of wheat swollen as large as lemon-pips, which floated on its surface, might have a deterrent effect at first.

But there was more in that tent than met the cursory glance; and the man, with the instinct of a perverse character, scented it quickly. After a mincing attack on his bowl, he watched the hag's proceedings from the corner of his eye, and saw the game she played. He winked to her, and passed up his basin in reply to her nod; when she took a bottle from under the table, slily measured out a quantity of its contents, and tipped the same into the man's furmity. The liquor poured in was rum. The man as slily sent back money in payment.

He found the concoction, thus strongly laced, much more to his satisfaction than it had been in its natural state. His wife had observed the proceeding with much uneasiness; but he persuaded her to have hers laced also, and she agreed to a milder allowance after some misgiving.

The man finished his basin, and called for another, the rum being signalled for in yet stronger proportion. The effect of it was soon apparent in his manner, and his wife but too sadly perceived that in strenuously steering off the rocks of the licensed liquor-tent she had only got into maelstrom depths* here amongst the smugglers.*

The child began to prattle impatiently, and the wife more than once said to her husband, 'Michael, how about our lodging? You know we may have trouble in getting it if we don't go soon.'

But he turned a deaf ear to those bird-like chirpings. He talked loud to the company. The child's black eyes, after slow, round, ruminating gazes at the candles when they were lighted, fell together; then they opened, then shut again, and she slept.

At the end of the first basin the man had risen to serenity; at the second he was jovial; at the third, argumentative; at the fourth, the qualities signified by the shape of his face, the occasional clench of his mouth, and the fiery spark of his dark eye, began to tell in his conduct; he was overbearing – even brilliantly quarrel-some.

The conversation took a high turn, as it often does on such occasions. The ruin of good men by bad wives, and, more particularly, the frustration of many a promising youth's high aims and hopes and the extinction of his energies by an early imprudent marriage, was the theme.

'I did for myself that way thoroughly,' said the trusser, with a contemplative bitterness that was well-nigh resentful. 'I married at eighteen, like the fool that I was; and this is the consequence o't.' He pointed at himself and family with a wave of the hand intended to bring out the penuriousness of the exhibition.

The young woman his wife, who seemed accustomed to such

remarks, acted as if she did not hear them, and continued her intermittent private words on tender trifles to the sleeping and waking child, who was just big enough to be placed for a moment on the bench beside her when she wished to ease her arms. The man continued –

'I haven't more than fifteen shillings in the world, and yet I am a good experienced hand in my line. I'd challenge England to beat me in the fodder business; and if I were a free man again* I'd be worth a thousand pound before I'd done o't. But a fellow never knows these little things till all chance of acting upon 'em is past.'

The auctioneer selling the old horses in the field outside could be heard saying, 'Now this is the last lot – now who'll take the last lot for a song? Shall I say forty shillings? 'Tis a very promising brood-mare, a trifle over five years old, and nothing the matter with the hoss at all, except that she's a little holler* in the back and had her left eye knocked out by the kick of another, her own sister, coming along the road.'

'For my part I don't see why men who have got wives and don't want 'em, shouldn't get rid of 'em as these gipsy fellows do their old horses,' said the man in the tent. 'Why shouldn't they put 'em up and sell 'em by auction to men who are in need of such articles? Hey? Why, begad, I'd sell mine this minute if anybody would buy her!'

'There's them that would do that,' some of the guests replied, looking at the woman, who was by no means ill-favoured.

'True,' said a smoking gentleman, whose coat had the fine polish about the collar, elbows, seams, and shoulder-blades that long-continued friction with grimy surfaces will produce, and which is usually more desired on furniture than on clothes. From his appearance he had possibly been in former time groom or coachman to some neighbouring county family. 'I've had my breedings in as good circles, I may say, as any man,' he added, 'and I know true cultivation, or nobody do; and I can declare she's got it – in the bone, mind ye, I say – as much as any female in the fair – though it may want a little bringing out.' Then, crossing his legs, he resumed his pipe with a nicely-adjusted gaze at a point in the air.

The fuddled young husband stared for a few seconds at this unexpected praise of his wife, half in doubt of the wisdom of his own attitude towards the possessor of such qualities. But he speedily lapsed into his former conviction, and said harshly –

'Well, then, now is your chance; I am open to an offer for this gem o' creation.'

She turned to her husband and murmured, 'Michael, you have talked this nonsense in public places before. A joke is a joke, but you may make it once too often, mind!'

'I know I've said it before; I meant it. All I want is a buyer.'

At the moment a swallow, one among the last of the season, which had by chance found its way through an opening into the upper part of the tent, flew to and fro in quick curves above their heads, causing all eyes to follow it absently. In watching the bird till it made its escape the assembled company neglected to respond to the workman's offer, and the subject dropped.

But a quarter of an hour later the man, who had gone on lacing his furmity more and more heavily, though he was either so strong-minded or such an intrepid toper that he still appeared fairly sober, recurred to the old strain, as in a musical fantasy the instrument fetches up the original theme. 'Here – I am waiting to know about this offer of mine. The woman is no good to me. Who'll have her?'

The company had by this time decidedly degenerated, and the renewed inquiry was received with a laugh of appreciation. The woman whispered; she was imploring and anxious: 'Come, come, it is getting dark, and this nonsense won't do. If you don't come along, I shall go without you. Come!'

She waited and waited; yet he did not move. In ten minutes the man broke in upon the desultory conversation of the furmity drinkers with, 'I asked this question, and nobody answered to 't. Will any Jack Rag or Tom Straw among ye buy my goods?'

The woman's manner changed, and her face assumed the grim shape and colour of which mention has been made.

'Mike, Mike,' said she; 'this is getting serious. O! – too serious!'

'Will anybody buy her?' said the man.

'I wish somebody would,' said she firmly. 'Her present owner is not at all to her liking!'

'Nor you to mine,' said he. 'So we are agreed about that. Gentlemen, you hear? It's an agreement to part. She shall take the girl if she wants to, and go her ways. I'll take my tools, and go my ways. 'Tis simple as Scripture history. Now then, stand up, Susan, and show yourself.'

'Don't, my chiel,'* whispered a buxom staylace* dealer in

voluminous petticoats, who sat near the woman; 'yer good man don't know what he's saying.'

The woman, however, did stand up. 'Now, who's auctioneer?' cried the hay-trusser.

'I be,' promptly answered a short man, with a nose resembling a copper knob, a damp voice, and eyes like button-holes. 'Who'll make an offer for this lady?'

The woman looked on the ground, as if she maintained her position by a supreme effort of will.

'Five shillings,' said some one, at which there was a laugh.

'No insults,' said her husband. 'Who'll say a guinea?'

Nobody answered; and the female dealer in staylaces interposed.

'Behave yerself moral, good man, for Heaven's love! Ah, what a cruelty is the poor soul married to! Bed and board is dear at some figures, 'pon my 'vation* 'tis!'

'Set it higher, auctioneer,' said the trusser.

'Two guineas!' said the auctioneer; and no one replied.

'If they don't take her for that, in ten seconds they'll have to give more,' said the husband. 'Very well. Now, auctioneer, add another.'

'Three guineas – going for three guineas!' said the rheumy man.

'No bid?' said the husband. 'Good Lord, why she's cost me fifty times the money, if a penny. Go on.'

'Four guineas!' cried the auctioneer.

'I'll tell ye what – I won't sell her for less than five,' said the husband, bringing down his fist so that the basins danced. 'I'll sell her for five guineas to any man that will pay me the money, and treat her well; and he shall have her for ever, and never hear aught o' me. But she shan't go for less. Now then – five guineas – and she's yours. Susan, you agree?'

She bowed her head with absolute indifference.

'Five guineas,' said the auctioneer, 'or she'll be withdrawn. Do anybody give it? The last time. Yes or no?'

'Yes,' said a loud voice from the doorway.

All eyes were turned. Standing in the triangular opening which formed the door of the tent was a sailor, who, unobserved by the rest, had arrived there within the last two or three minutes. A dead silence followed his affirmation.

'You say you do?' asked the husband, staring at him.

'I say so,' replied the sailor.

'Saying is one thing, and paying is another. Where's the money?'

The sailor hesitated a moment, looked anew at the woman, came in, unfolded five crisp pieces of paper, and threw them down upon the table-cloth. They were Bank-of-England notes for five pounds. Upon the face of this he chinked down the shillings severally – one, two, three, four, five.

The sight of real money in full amount, in answer to a challenge for the same till then deemed slightly hypothetical, had a great effect upon the spectators. Their eyes became riveted upon the faces of the chief actors, and then upon the notes as they lay, weighted by the shillings, on the table.

Up to this moment it could not positively have been asserted that the man, in spite of his tantalizing declaration, was really in earnest. The spectators had indeed taken the proceedings throughout as a piece of mirthful irony carried to extremes; and had assumed that, being out of work, he was, as a consequence, out of temper with the world, and society, and his nearest kin. But with the demand and response of real cash the jovial frivolity of the scene departed. A lurid colour seemed to fill the tent, and change the aspect of all therein. The mirth-wrinkles left the listeners' faces, and they waited with parting lips.

'Now,' said the woman, breaking the silence, so that her low dry voice sounded quite loud, 'before you go further, Michael, listen to me. If you touch that money, I and this girl go with the man. Mind, it is a joke no longer.'

'A joke? Of course it is not a joke!' shouted her husband, his resentment rising at her suggestion. 'I take the money: the sailor takes you. That's plain enough. It has been done elsewhere – and why not here?'

' 'Tis quite on the understanding that the young woman is willing,' said the sailor blandly. 'I wouldn't hurt her feelings for the world.'

'Faith, nor I,' said her husband. 'But she is willing, provided she can have the child. She said so only the other day when I talked o't!'

'That you swear?' said the sailor to her.

'I do,' said she, after glancing at her husband's face and seeing no repentance there.

'Very well, she shall have the child, and the bargain's complete,' said the trusser. He took the sailor's notes and deliberately folded them, and put them with the shillings in a high remote pocket, with an air of finality.

The sailor looked at the woman and smiled. 'Come along!' he said kindly. 'The little one too – the more the merrier!' She paused for an instant, with a close glance at him. Then dropping her eyes again, and saying nothing, she took up the child and followed him as he made towards the door. On reaching it, she turned, and pulling off her wedding-ring, flung it across the booth in the hay-trusser's face.

'Mike,' she said, 'I've lived with thee a couple of years, and had nothing but temper! Now I'm no more to 'ee; I'll try my luck elsewhere. 'Twill be better for me and Elizabeth-Jane, both. So good-bye!'

Seizing the sailor's arm with her right hand, and mounting the little girl on her left, she went out of the tent sobbing bitterly.

A stolid look of concern filled the husband's face, as if, after all, he had not quite anticipated this ending; and some of the guests laughed.

'Is she gone?' he said.

'Faith, ay; she's gone clane* enough,' said some rustics near the door.

He rose and walked to the entrance with the careful tread of one conscious of his alcoholic load. Some others followed, and they stood looking into the twilight. The difference between the peacefulness of inferior nature and the wilful hostilities of mankind was very apparent at this place. In contrast with the harshness of the act just ended within the tent was the sight of several horses crossing their necks and rubbing each other lovingly as they waited in patience to be harnessed for the homeward journey. Outside the fair, in the valleys and woods, all was quiet. The sun had recently set, and the west heaven was hung with rosy cloud, which seemed permanent, yet slowly changed. To watch it was like looking at some grand feat of stagery from a darkened auditorium. In presence of this scene after the other there was a natural instinct to abjure man as the blot on an otherwise kindly universe; till it was remembered that all terrestrial conditions were intermittent, and that mankind might some night be innocently sleeping when these quiet objects were raging loud.*

'Where do the sailor live?' asked a spectator, when they had vainly gazed around.

'God knows that,' replied the man who had seen high life. 'He's without doubt a stranger here.'

'He came in about five minutes ago,' said the furmity woman, joining the rest with her hands on her hips. 'And then 'a stepped back, and then 'a looked in again. I'm not a penny the better for him.'

'Serves the husband well be-right,' said the staylace vendor. 'A comely respectable body like her – what can a man want more? I glory in the woman's sperrit. I'd ha' done it myself – od send if I wouldn't, if a husband behaved so to me! I'd go, and 'a might call, and call, till his keacorn* was raw; but I'd never come back – no, not till the great trumpet,* would I!'

'Well, the woman will be better off,' said another of a more deliberative turn. 'For seafaring natures be very good shelter for shorn lambs, and the man do seem to have plenty of money, which is what she's not been used to lately, by all showings.'

'Mark me – I'll not go after her!' said the trusser, returning doggedly to his seat. 'Let her go! If she's up to such vagaries she must suffer for 'em. She'd no business to take the maid – 'tis my maid; and if it were the doing again she shouldn't have her!'

Perhaps from some little sense of having countenanced an indefensible proceeding, perhaps because it was late, the customers thinned away from the tent shortly after this episode. The man stretched his elbows forward on the table, leant his face upon his arms, and soon began to snore. The furmity seller decided to close for the night, and after seeing the rum-bottles, milk, corn, raisins, etc., that remained on hand, loaded into the cart, came to where the man reclined. She shook him, but could not wake him. As the tent was not to be struck that night, the fair continuing for two or three days, she decided to let the sleeper, who was obviously no tramp, stay where he was, and his basket with him. Extinguishing the last candle, and lowering the flap of the tent, she left it, and drove away.

Chapter 2

The morning sun was streaming through the crevices of the canvas when the man awoke. A warm glow pervaded the whole atmosphere of the marquee, and a single big blue fly buzzed musically round and round it. Besides the buzz of the fly there was not a sound. He looked about – at the benches – at the table supported by trestles – at his basket of tools – at the stove where the furmity had been boiled – at the empty basins – at some shed grains of wheat – at the corks which dotted the grassy floor. Among the odds and ends he discerned a little shining object, and picked it up. It was his wife's ring.

A confused picture of the events of the previous evening seemed to come back to him, and he thrust his hand into his breast-pocket. A rustling revealed the sailor's bank-notes thrust carelessly in.

This second verification of his dim memories was enough; he knew now they were not dreams. He remained seated, looking on the ground for some time. 'I must get out of this as soon as I can,' he said deliberately at last, with the air of one who could not catch his thoughts without pronouncing them. 'She's gone – to be sure she is – gone with that sailor who bought her, and little Elizabeth-Jane. We walked here, and I had the furmity, and rum in it – and sold her. Yes, that's what's happened, and here am I. Now, what am I to do – am I sober enough to walk, I wonder?' He stood up, found that he was in fairly good condition for progress, unencumbered.* Next he shouldered his tool basket, and found he could carry it. Then lifting the tent door he emerged into the open air.

Here the man looked around with gloomy curiosity. The freshness of the September morning inspired and braced him as he stood. He and his family had been weary when they arrived the night before, and they had observed but little of the place; so that he now beheld it as a new thing. It exhibited itself as the top of an open down, bounded on one extreme by a plantation, and approached by a winding road. At the bottom stood the village which lent its name to the upland and the annual fair that was held thereon. The spot stretched downward into valleys, and onward to other uplands, dotted with barrows, and trenched with the remains of prehistoric forts. The whole scene lay under the rays of a newly risen sun, which had not as yet dried a single blade of the heavily dewed grass, whereon the shadows of the yellow and red vans were projected far away, those thrown by the felloe* of each wheel being elongated in shape to the orbit of a comet. All the gipsies and showmen who had remained on the ground lay snug within their carts and tents, or wrapped in horse-cloths under them, and were silent and still as death, with the exception of an occasional snore that revealed their presence. But the Seven Sleepers had a dog;* and dogs of the mysterious breeds that vagrants own, that are as much like cats as dogs and as much like foxes as cats, also lay about here. A little one started up under one of the carts, barked as a matter of principle, and quickly lay down again. He was the only positive spectator of the hay-trusser's exit from the Weydon Fair-field.

This seemed to accord with his desire. He went on in silent thought, unheeding the yellowhammers which flitted about the hedges with straws in their bills, the crowns of the mushrooms, and the tinkling of local sheep-bells, whose wearers had had the good fortune not to be included in the fair. When he reached a lane, a good mile from the scene of the previous evening, the man pitched his basket and leant upon a gate. A difficult problem or two occupied his mind.

'Did I tell my name to anybody last night, or didn't I tell my name?' he said to himself; and at last concluded that he did not. His general demeanour was enough to show how he was surprised and nettled that his wife had taken him so literally – as much could be seen in his face, and in the way he nibbled a straw which he pulled from the hedge. He knew that she must have been somewhat excited to do this; moreover, she must have believed that there was some sort of binding force in the transaction. On this latter point he felt almost certain, knowing her freedom from levity of character, and the extreme simplicity of her intellect. There may, too, have been enough recklessness and resentment beneath her ordinary placidity to make her stifle any momentary doubts. On a previous occasion when he had declared during a fuddle that he would dispose of her as he had done, she had replied that she would not hear him say that many times more before it happened, in the resigned tones of a fatalist . . . 'Yet she knows I am not in my senses when I do that!' he exclaimed. 'Well, I must walk about till I find her . . . Seize her, why didn't she know better than bring me into this disgrace!' he roared out. 'She wasn't queer if I was. 'Tis like Susan to show some idiotic simplicity. Meek – that meekness has done me more harm than the bitterest temper!'

When he was calmer he turned to his original conviction that he must somehow find her and his little Elizabeth-Jane, and put up with the shame as best he could. It was of his own making, and he ought to bear it. But first he resolved to register an oath, a greater oath than he had ever sworn before: and to do it properly he required a fit place and imagery; for there was something fetichistic* in this man's beliefs.

He shouldered his basket and moved on, casting his eyes inquisitively round upon the landscape as he walked, and at the distance of three or four miles perceived the roofs of a village and the tower of a church. He instantly made towards the latter object. The village was quite still, it being that motionless hour of rustic daily life which fills the interval between the departure of the field-labourers to their work, and the rising of their wives and daughters to prepare the breakfast for their return. Hence he reached the church without observation, and the door being only latched he entered. The hay-trusser deposited his basket by the font, went up the nave till he reached the altar-rails, and opening the gate entered the sacrarium,* where he seemed to feel a sense of the strangeness for a moment; then he knelt upon the foot-pace.* Dropping his head upon the clamped book which lay on the Communion-table, he said aloud –

'I, Michael Henchard, on this morning of the sixteenth of September, do take an oath before God here in this solemn place that I will avoid all strong liquors for the space of twenty-one years to come, being a year for every year that I have lived. And this I swear upon the book before me; and may I be strook* dumb, blind, and helpless, if I break this my oath!'

When he had said it and kissed the big book, the hay-trusser arose, and seemed relieved at having made a start in a new direction. While standing in the porch a moment he saw a thick jet of wood smoke suddenly start up from the red chimney of a cottage near, and knew that the occupant had just lit her fire. He went round to the door, and the housewife agreed to prepare him some breakfast for a trifling payment, which was done. Then he started on the search for his wife and child.

The perplexing nature of the undertaking became apparent soon enough. Though he examined and inquired, and walked hither and thither day after day, no such characters as those he described had anywhere been seen since the evening of the fair. To add to the difficulty he could gain no sound of the sailor's name. As money was short with him he decided, after some hesitation, to spend the sailor's money in the prosecution of this search; but it was equally in vain. The truth was that a certain shyness of revealing his conduct prevented Michael Henchard from following up the investigation with the loud hue-and-cry such a pursuit demanded to render it effectual; and it was probably for this reason that he obtained no clue, though everything was done by him that did not involve an explanation of the circumstances under which he had lost her.

Weeks counted up to months, and still he searched on, maintaining himself by small jobs of work in the intervals. By this time he had arrived at a seaport, and there he derived intelligence that persons answering somewhat to his description had emigrated a little time before. Then he said he would search no longer, and that he would go and settle in the district which he had had for some time in his mind. Next day he started, journeying southwestward, and did not pause, except for nights' lodgings, till he reached the town of Casterbridge, in a far distant part of Wessex.

Chapter 3

The highroad into the village of Weydon-Priors was again carpeted with dust. The trees had put on as of yore their aspect of dingy green, and where the Henchard family of three had once walked along, two persons not unconnected with that family walked now.

The scene in its broad aspect had so much of its previous character, even to the voices and rattle from the neighbouring village down, that it might for that matter have been the afternoon following the previously recorded episode. Change was only to be observed in details; but here it was obvious that a long procession of years had passed by. One of the two who walked the road was she who had figured as the young wife of Henchard on the previous occasion; now her face had lost much of its rotundity; her skin had undergone a textural change; and though her hair had not lost colour it was considerably thinner than heretofore. She was dressed in the mourning clothes of a widow. Her companion, also in black, appeared as a well-formed young woman about eighteen, completely possessed of that ephemeral precious essence youth, which is itself beauty, irrespective of complexion or contour.

A glance was sufficient to inform the eye that this was Susan Henchard's grown-up daughter. While life's middle summer had set its hardening mark on the mother's face, her former spring-like specialities were transferred so dexterously by Time to the second figure, her child, that the absence of certain facts within her mother's knowledge from the girl's mind would have seemed for the moment, to one reflecting on those facts, to be a curious imperfection in Nature's powers of continuity.

They walked with joined hands, and it could be perceived that this was the act of simple affection. The daughter carried in her outer hand a withy basket* of old-fashioned make; the mother a blue bundle, which contrasted oddly with her black stuff gown.*

Reaching the outskirts of the village they pursued the same track as formerly, and ascended to the fair. Here, too, it was evident that the years had told. Certain mechanical improvements might have been noticed in the roundabouts and highfliers, machines for testing rustic strength and weight, and in the erections devoted to shooting for nuts. But the real business of the fair had considerably dwindled. The new periodical great markets of neighbouring towns were beginning to interfere seriously with the trade carried on here for centuries. The pens for sheep, the tie-ropes for horses, were about half as long as they had been. The stalls of tailors, hosiers, coopers,* linen-drapers, and other such trades had almost disappeared, and the vehicles were far less numerous. The mother and daughter threaded the crowd for some little distance, and then stood still.

'Why did we hinder our time by coming in here? I thought you wished to get onward?' said the maiden.

'Yes, my dear Elizabeth-Jane,' explained the other. 'But I had a fancy for looking up here.'

'Why?'

'It was here I first met with Newson – on such a day as this.'

'First met with father here? Yes, you have told me so before. And now he's drowned and gone from us!' As she spoke the girl drew a card from her pocket and looked at it with a sigh. It was edged with black, and inscribed within a design resembling a mural tablet were the words, 'In affectionate memory of Richard Newson, mariner, who was unfortunately lost at sea, in the month of November 184–,* aged forty-one years.'

'And it was here,' continued her mother, with more hesitation, 'that I last saw the relation we are going to look for – Mr Michael Henchard.'

'What is his exact kin to us, mother? I have never clearly had it told me.'

'He is, or was – for he may be dead – a connection by marriage,' said her mother, deliberately.

'That's exactly what you have said a score of times before!' replied the young woman, looking about her inattentively. 'He's not a near relation, I suppose?'

'Not by any means.'

'He was a hay-trusser, wasn't he, when you last heard of him?'

'He was.'

'I suppose he never knew me?' the girl innocently continued.

Mrs Henchard paused for a moment, and answered uneasily, 'Of course not, Elizabeth-Jane. But come this way.' She moved on to another part of the field.

'It is not much use inquiring here for anybody, I should think,' the daughter observed, as she gazed round about. 'People at fairs change like the leaves of trees; and I daresay you are the only one here to-day who was here all those years ago.'

'I am not so sure of that,' said Mrs Newson, as she now called herself, keenly eyeing something under a green bank a little way off. 'See there.'

The daughter looked in the direction signified. The object pointed out was a tripod of sticks stuck into the earth, from which hung a three-legged crock, kept hot by a smouldering wood fire beneath. Over the pot stooped an old woman, haggard, wrinkled, and almost in rags. She stirred the contents of the pot with a large spoon, and occasionally croaked in a broken voice, 'Good furmity sold here!'

It was indeed the former mistress of the furmity tent – once thriving, cleanly, white-aproned, and chinking with money – now tentless, dirty, owning no tables or benches, and having scarce any customers except two small whity-brown boys, who came up and asked for 'A ha'p'orth, please – good measure', which she served in a couple of chipped yellow basins of commonest clay.

'She was here at that time,' resumed Mrs Newson, making a step as if to draw nearer.

'Don't speak to her – it isn't respectable!' urged the other.

'I will just say a word – you, Elizabeth-Jane, can stay here.'

The girl was not loth, and turned to some stalls of coloured prints while her mother went forward. The old woman begged for the latter's custom as soon as she saw her, and responded to Mrs Henchard-Newson's request for a pennyworth with more alacrity than she had shown in selling sixpennyworths in her younger days. When the *soi-disant** widow had taken the basin of thin poor slop that stood for the rich concoction of the former time, the hag opened a little basket behind the fire, and looking up slily, whispered, 'Just a thought o' rum in it? – smuggled, you know – say two penn'orth – 'twill make it slip down like cordial!'

Her customer smiled bitterly at this survival of the old trick, and shook her head with a meaning the old woman was far from translating. She pretended to eat a little of the furmity with the leaden spoon offered, and as she did so said blandly to the hag, 'You've seen better days?'

'Ah, ma'am – well ye may say it!' responded the old woman, opening the sluices of her heart forthwith. 'I've stood in this fair-ground, maid, wife, and widow, these nine-and-thirty year, and in that time have known what it was to do business with the richest stomachs in the land! Ma'am you'd hardly believe that I was once the owner of a great pavilion-tent that was the attraction of the fair. Nobody could come, nobody could go, without having a dish of Mrs Goodenough's furmity. I knew the clergy's taste, the dandy gent's taste; I knew the town's taste, the country's taste. I even knowed the taste of the coarse shameless females. But Lord's my life – the world's no memory; straightforward dealings don't bring profit – 'tis the sly and the underhand that get on in these times!'

Mrs Newson glanced round – her daughter was still bending over the distant stalls. 'Can you call to mind,' she said cautiously to the old woman, 'the sale of a wife by her husband in your tent eighteen years ago to-day?'

The hag reflected, and half shook her head. 'If it had been a big thing I should have minded it in a moment,' she said. 'I can mind every serious fight o' married parties, every murder, every manslaughter, even every pocket-picking – leastwise large ones – that't has been my lot to witness. But a selling? Was it done quiet-like?'

'Well, yes. I think so.'

The furmity woman half shook her head again. 'And yet,' she said, 'I do. At any rate, I can mind a man doing something o' the sort – a man in a cord jacket, with a basket of tools; but, Lord bless ye, we don't gi'e it head-room, we don't, such as that. The only reason why I can mind the man is that he came back here to the next year's fair, and told me quite private-like that if a woman ever asked for him I was to say he had gone to – where? – Casterbridge – yes – to Casterbridge, said he. But, Lord's my life, I shouldn't ha' thought of it again!'

Mrs Newson would have rewarded the old woman as far as her small means afforded had she not discreetly borne in mind that it was by that unscrupulous person's liquor her husband had been degraded. She briefly thanked her informant, and rejoined Elizabeth, who greeted her with, 'Mother, do let's go on – it was hardly respectable for you to buy refreshments there. I see none but the lowest do.'

'I have learned what I wanted, however,' said her mother quietly. 'The last time our relative visited this fair he said he was living at Casterbridge. It is a long, long way from here, and it was many years ago that he said it; but there I think we'll go.'

With this they descended out of the fair, and went onward to the village, where they obtained a night's lodging.

Chapter 4

Henchard's wife acted for the best, but she had involved herself in difficulties. A hundred times she had been upon the point of telling her daughter Elizabeth-Jane the true story of her life, the tragical crisis of which had been the transaction at Weydon Fair, when she was not much older than the girl now beside her. But she had refrained. An innocent maiden had thus grown up in the belief that the relations between the genial sailor and her mother were the ordinary ones that they had always appeared to be. The risk of endangering a child's strong affection by disturbing ideas which had grown with her growth was to Mrs Henchard too fearful a thing to contemplate. It had seemed, indeed, folly to think of making Elizabeth-Jane wise.

But Susan Henchard's fear of losing her dearly loved daughter's heart by a revelation had little to do with any sense of wrong-doing on her own part. Her simplicity – the original ground of Henchard's contempt for her – had allowed her to live on in the conviction that Newson had acquired a morally real and justifiable right to her by his purchase – though the exact bearings and legal limits of that right were vague. It may seem strange to sophisticated minds that a sane young matron could believe in the seriousness of such a transfer; and were there not numerous other instances of the same belief the thing might scarcely be credited. But she was by no means the first or last peasant woman who had religiously adhered to her purchaser, as too many rural records show.

The history of Susan Henchard's adventures in the interim can be told in two or three sentences. Absolutely helpless she had been taken off to Canada, where they had lived several years without any great worldly success, though she worked as hard as any woman could to keep their cottage cheerful and well-provided. When Elizabeth-Jane was about twelve years old the three returned to England, and settled in Falmouth, where Newson made a living for a few years as boatman and general handy shoreman.

He then engaged in the Newfoundland trade, and it was during this period that Susan had an awakening. A friend to whom she confided her history ridiculed her grave acceptance of her position; and all was over with her peace of mind. When Newson came home at the end of one winter he saw that the delusion he had so carefully sustained had vanished for ever.

There was then a time of sadness, in which she told him her doubts if she could live with him longer. Newson left home again on the Newfoundland trade when the season came round. The vague news of his loss at sea a little later on solved a problem which had become torture to her meek conscience. She saw him no more.

Of Henchard they heard nothing. To the liege subjects of Labour,* the England of those days was a continent, and a mile a geographical degree.

Elizabeth-Jane developed early into womanliness. One day, a month or so after receiving intelligence of Newson's death off the Bank of Newfoundland, when the girl was about eighteen, she was sitting on a willow chair in the cottage they still occupied, working twine nets for the fishermen. Her mother was in a back corner of the same room, engaged in the same labour; and dropping the heavy wood needle she was filling* she surveyed her daughter thoughtfully. The sun shone in at the door upon the young woman's head and hair, which was worn loose, so that the rays streamed into its depths as into a hazel copse. Her face, though somewhat wan and incomplete, possessed the raw materials of beauty in a promising degree. There was an under-handsomeness in it, struggling to reveal itself through the provisional curves of immaturity, and the casual disfigurements that resulted from the straitened circumstances of their lives. She was handsome in the bone, hardly as yet handsome in the flesh. She possibly might never be fully handsome, unless the carking* accidents of her daily existence could be evaded before the mobile parts of her countenance had settled to their final mould.

The sight of the girl made her mother sad – not vaguely, but by logical inference. They both were still in that strait-waistcoat of poverty from which she had tried so many times to be delivered for the girl's sake. The woman had long perceived how zealously and constantly the young mind of her companion was struggling for enlargement; and yet now, in her eighteenth year, it still remained but little unfolded. The desire – sober and repressed – of Elizabeth-Jane's heart was indeed to see, to hear, and to understand. How could she become a woman of wider knowledge, higher repute – 'better', as she termed it – this was her constant inquiry of her mother. She sought further into things than other girls in her position ever did, and her mother groaned as she felt she could not aid in the search.

The sailor, drowned or no, was probably now lost to them; and Susan's staunch, religious adherence to him as her husband in principle, till her views had been disturbed by enlightenment, was demanded no more. She asked herself whether the present moment, now that she was a free woman again, were not as opportune a one as she would find in a world where everything had been so inopportune, for making a desperate effort to advance Elizabeth. To pocket her pride and search for the first husband seemed, wisely or not, the best initiatory step. He had possibly drunk himself into his tomb. But he might, on the other hand, have had too much sense to do so; for in her time with him he had been given to bouts only, and was not a habitual drunkard.

At any rate, the propriety of returning to him, if he lived, was unquestionable. The awkwardness of searching for him lay in enlightening Elizabeth, a proceeding which her mother could not endure to contemplate. She finally resolved to undertake the search without confiding to the girl her former relations with

Henchard, leaving it to him if they found him to take what steps he might choose to that end. This will account for their conversation at the fair and the half-informed state in which Elizabeth was led onward.

In this attitude they proceeded on their journey, trusting solely to the dim light afforded of Henchard's whereabouts by the furmity woman. The strictest economy was indispensable. Sometimes they might have been seen on foot, sometimes on farmers' waggons, sometimes in carriers' vans; and thus they drew near to Casterbridge. Elizabeth-Jane discovered to her alarm that her mother's health was not what it had once been, and there was ever and anon in her talk that renunciatory tone which showed that, but for the girl, she would not be very sorry to quit a life she was growing thoroughly weary of.

It was on a Friday evening, near the middle of September, and just before dusk, that they reached the summit of a hill within a mile of the place they sought. There were high-banked hedges to the coach-road here, and they mounted upon the green turf within, and sat down. The spot commanded a full view of the town and its environs.

'What an old-fashioned place it seems to be!' said Elizabeth-Jane, while her silent mother mused on other things than topography. 'It is huddled all together; and it is shut in by a square wall of trees, like a plot of garden ground by a box-edging.'

Its squareness was, indeed, the characteristic which most struck the eye in this antiquated borough, the borough of Casterbridge – at that time, recent as it was, untouched by the faintest sprinkle of modernism. It was compact as a box of dominoes. It had no suburbs – in the ordinary sense. Country and town met at a mathematical line.

To birds of the more soaring kind Casterbridge must have appeared on this fine evening as a mosaic-work of subdued reds, browns, greys, and crystals, held together by a rectangular frame of deep green. To the level eye of humanity it stood as an indistinct mass behind a dense stockade of limes and chestnuts, set in the midst of miles of rotund down and concave field. The mass became gradually dissected by the vision into towers, gables, chimneys, and casements, the highest glazings shining bleared and bloodshot with the coppery fire they caught from the belt of sunlit cloud in the west.

From the centre of each side of this tree-bound square ran

avenues east, west, and south into the wide expanse of corn-land and coomb* to the distance of a mile or so. It was by one of these avenues that the pedestrians were about to enter. Before they had risen to proceed two men passed outside the hedge, engaged in argumentative conversation.

'Why, surely,' said Elizabeth, as they receded, 'those men mentioned the name of Henchard in their talk – the name of our relative?'

'I thought so too,' said Mrs Newson.

'That seems to hint to us that he is still here.'

'Yes.'

'Shall I run after them, and ask them about him –'

'No, no, no! Not for the world just yet. He may be in the workhouse, or in the stocks, for all we know.'

'Dear me – why should you think that, mother?'

' 'Twas just something to say – that's all! But we must make private inquiries.'

Having sufficiently rested they proceeded on their way at evenfall. The dense trees of the avenue rendered the road dark as a tunnel, though the open land on each side was still under a faint daylight; in other words, they passed down a midnight between two gloamings. The features of the town had a keen interest for Elizabeth's mother, now that the human side came to the fore. As soon as they had wandered about they could see that the stockade of gnarled trees which framed in Casterbridge was itself an avenue, standing on a low green bank or escarpment, with a ditch yet visible without. Within the avenue and bank was a wall more or less discontinuous, and within the wall were packed the abodes of the burghers.

Though the two women did not know it these external features were but the ancient defences of the town, planted as a promenade.

The lamplights now glimmered through the engirdling trees, conveying a sense of great snugness and comfort inside, and rendering at the same time the unlighted country without strangely solitary and vacant in aspect, considering its nearness to life. The difference between burgh and champaign* was in-creased, too, by sounds which now reached them above others – the notes of a brass band. The travellers returned into the High Street, where there were timber houses with overhanging stories, whose small-paned lattices were screened by dimity* curtains on a drawing-string, and under whose barge-boards* old cobwebs waved in the breeze. There were houses of brick-nogging,* which derived their chief support from those adjoining. There were slate roofs patched with tiles, and tile roofs patched with slate, with occasionally a roof of thatch.[1]

The agricultural and pastoral character of the people upon whom the town depended for its existence was shown by the class of objects displayed in the shop windows. Scythes, reap-hooks, sheep-shears, bill-hooks, spades, mattocks, and hoes at the iron-monger's; bee-hives, butter-firkins, churns, milking stools and pails, hay-rakes, field-flagons, and seed-lips at the cooper's; cart-ropes and plough-harness at the saddler's; carts, wheel-barrows, and mill-gear at the wheelwright's and machinist's; horse-embrocations at the chemist's; at the glover's and leather-cutter's, hedging-gloves, thatchers' knee-caps, ploughmen's leggings, villagers' pattens and clogs.*

They came to a grizzled church, whose massive square tower rose unbroken into the darkening sky, the lower parts being illuminated by the nearest lamps sufficiently to show how completely the mortar from the joints of the stonework had been nibbled out by time and weather, which had planted in the crevices thus made little tufts of stone-crop and grass almost as far up as the very battlements. From this tower the clock struck eight, and thereupon a bell began to toll with a peremptory clang. The curfew* was still rung in Casterbridge, and it was utilized by the inhabitants as a signal for shutting their shops. No sooner did the deep notes of the bell throb between the house-fronts than a clatter of shutters arose from the whole length of the High Street. In a few minutes business at Caster-bridge was ended for the day.

Other clocks struck eight from time to time — one gloomily from the gaol, another from the gable of an almshouse, with a preparative creak of machinery, more audible than the note of the bell; a row of tall, varnished case-clocks from the interior of a clock-maker's shop joined in one after another just as the shutters were enclosing them, like a row of actors delivering their final speeches before the fall of the curtain; then chimes were heard stammering out the Sicilian Mariners' Hymn;[2]*

---

[1] Most of these old houses have now been pulled down (1912).

[2] These chimes, like those of other country churches, have been silenced for many years.

so that chronologists of the advanced school were appreciably on their way to the next hour before the whole business of the old one was satisfactorily wound up.

In an open space before the church walked a woman with her gown-sleeves rolled up so high that the edge of her under-linen was visible, and her skirt tucked up through her pocket hole. She carried a loaf under her arm from which she was pulling pieces of bread, and handing them to some other women who walked with her; which pieces they nibbled critically. The sight reminded Mrs Henchard-Newson and her daughter that they had an appetite; and they inquired of the woman for the nearest baker's.

'Ye may as well look for manna-food* as good bread in Casterbridge just now,' she said, after directing them. 'They can blare their trumpets and thump their drums, and have their roaring dinners' — waving her hand towards a point further along the street, where the brass band could be seen standing in front of an illuminated building — 'but we must needs be put-to for want of a wholesome crust. There's less good bread than good beer in Casterbridge now.'

'And less good beer than swipes,'* said a man with his hands in his pockets.

'How does it happen there's no good bread?' asked Mrs Henchard.

'Oh, 'tis the corn-factor* — he's the man that our millers and bakers all deal wi', and he has sold 'em growed wheat,* which they didn't know was growed, so they *say*, till the dough ran all over the ovens like quicksilver; so that the loaves be as flat as toads, and like suet pudden* inside. I've been a wife, and I've been a mother, and I never see such unprincipled bread in Casterbridge as this before. — But you must be a real stranger here not to know what's made all the poor volks' insides plim like blowed bladders* this week?'

'I am,' said Elizabeth's mother shyly.

Not wishing to be observed further till she knew more of her future in this place, she withdrew with her daughter from the speaker's side. Getting a couple of biscuits at the shop indicated as a temporary substitute for a meal, they next bent their steps instinctively to where the music was playing.

Chapter 5

A few score yards brought them to the spot where the town band was now shaking the window-panes with the strains of 'The Roast Beef of Old England'.*

The building before whose doors they had pitched their music-stands was the chief hotel in Casterbridge – namely, the King's Arms. A spacious bow-window projected into the street over the main portico, and from the open sashes came the babble of voices, the jingle of glasses, and the drawing of cords. The blinds, moreover, being left unclosed, the whole interior of this room could be surveyed from the top of a flight of stone steps to the road-waggon office opposite, for which reason a knot of idlers had gathered there.

'We might, perhaps, after all, make a few inquiries about – our relation Mr Henchard,' whispered Mrs Newson who, since her entry into Casterbridge, had seemed strangely weak and agitated, 'And this, I think, would be a good place for trying it – just to ask, you know, how he stands in the town – if he is here, as I think he must be. You, Elizabeth-Jane, had better be the one to do it. I'm too worn out to do anything – pull down your fall* first.'

She sat down upon the lowest step, and Elizabeth-Jane obeyed her directions and stood among the idlers.

'What's going on to-night?' asked the girl, after singling out an old man and standing by him long enough to acquire a neigh-bourly right of converse.

'Well, ye must be a stranger sure,' said the old man, without taking his eyes from the window. 'Why, 'tis a great public dinner of the gentle-people and such like leading volk – wi' the Mayor in the chair. As we plainer fellows bain't invited, they leave the winder-shutters open that we may get jist a sense o't out here. If you mount the steps you can see 'em. That's Mr Henchard, the Mayor, at the end of the table, a facing ye; and that's the Council men right and left . . . Ah, lots of them when they begun life were no more than I be now!'

'Henchard!' said Elizabeth-Jane, surprised, but by no means suspecting the whole force of the revelation. She ascended to the top of the steps.

Her mother, though her head was bowed, had already caught from the inn-window tones that strangely riveted her attention, before the old man's words, 'Mr Henchard, the Mayor', reached her ears. She arose, and stepped up to her daughter's side as soon as she could do so without showing exceptional eagerness.

The interior of the hotel dining-room was spread out before her, with its tables, and glass, and plate, and inmates. Facing the window, in the chair of dignity, sat a man about forty years of age; of heavy frame, large features, and commanding voice; his general build being rather coarse than compact. He had a rich complexion, which verged on swarthiness, a flashing black eye, and dark, bushy brows and hair. When he indulged in an occasional loud laugh at some remark among the guests, his large mouth parted so far back as to show to the rays of the chandelier a full score or more of the two-and-thirty sound white teeth that he obviously still could boast of.

That laugh was not encouraging to strangers; and hence it may have been well that it was rarely heard. Many theories might have been built upon it. It fell in well with conjectures of a temperament which would have no pity for weakness, but would be ready to yield ungrudging admiration to greatness and strength. Its producer's personal goodness, if he had any, would be of a very fitful cast – an occasional almost oppressive generosity rather than a mild and constant kindness.

Susan Henchard's husband – in law, at least – sat before them, matured in shape, stiffened in line, exaggerated in traits; disciplined, thought-marked – in a word, older. Elizabeth, encumbered with no recollections as her mother was, regarded him with nothing more than the keen curiosity and interest which the discovery of such unexpected social standing in the long-sought relative naturally begot. He was dressed in an old-fashioned evening suit, an expanse of frilled shirt showing on his broad breast; jewelled studs, and a heavy gold chain. Three glasses stood at his right hand, but, to his wife's surprise, the two for wine were empty, while the third, a tumbler, was half full of water.

When last she had seen him he was sitting in a corduroy jacket, fustian waistcoat and breeches, and tanned leather leggings, with a basin of hot furmity before him. Time, the magician, had wrought much here. Watching him, and thus thinking of past days, she became so moved that she shrank back against the jamb of the waggon-office doorway to which the steps gave access, the shadow from it conveniently hiding her features. She forgot her daughter till a touch from Elizabeth-Jane aroused her. 'Have you seen him, mother?' whispered the girl.

'Yes, yes,' answered her companion hastily. 'I have seen him, and it is enough for me! Now I only want to go – pass away – die.'

'Why – O what?' She drew closer, and whispered in her mother's ear, 'Does he seem to you not likely to befriend us? I thought he looked a generous man. What a gentleman he is, isn't he? and how his diamond studs shine! How strange that you should have said he might be in the stocks, or in the workhouse, or dead! Did ever anything go more by contraries! Why do you feel so afraid of him? I am not at all; I'll call upon him – he can but say he don't own such remote kin.'

'I don't know at all – I can't tell what to set about. I feel so down.'

'Don't be that, mother, now we have got here and all! Rest there where you be a little while – I will look on and find out more about him.'

'I don't think I can ever meet Mr Henchard. He is not how I thought he would be – he overpowers me! I don't wish to see him any more.'

'But wait a little time and consider.'

Elizabeth-Jane had never been so much interested in anything in her life as in their present position, partly from the natural elation she felt at discovering herself akin to a coach;* and she gazed again at the scene. The younger guests were talking and eating with animation; their elders were searching for titbits, and sniffing and grunting over their plates like sows nuzzling for acorns. Three drinks seemed to be sacred to the company – port, sherry, and rum; outside which old-established trinity few or no palates ranged.

A row of ancient rummers* with ground figures on their sides, and each primed with a spoon, was now placed down the table, and these were promptly filled with grog at such high temperatures as to raise serious considerations for the articles exposed to its vapours. But Elizabeth-Jane noticed that, though this filling went on with great promptness up and down the table, nobody filled the Mayor's glass, who still drank large quantities of water from the tumbler behind the clump of crystal vessels intended for wine and spirits.

'They don't fill Mr Henchard's wine-glasses,' she ventured to say to her elbow acquaintance, the old man.

'Ah, no; don't ye know him to be the celebrated abstaining worthy of that name? He scorns all tempting liquors; never touches nothing. O yes, he've strong qualities that way. I have heard tell that he sware a gospel oath in by-gone times, and has bode by it ever since. So they don't press him, knowing it would be unbecoming in the face of that; for yer gospel oath is a serious thing.'

Another elderly man, hearing this discourse, now joined in by inquiring, 'How much longer have he got to suffer from it, Solomon Longways?'

'Another two year, they say. I don't know the why and the wherefore of his fixing such a time, for 'a never has told anybody. But 'tis exactly two calendar years longer, they say. A powerful mind to hold out so long!'

'True . . . But there's great strength in hope. Knowing that in four-and-twenty months' time ye'll be out of your bondage, and able to make up for all you've suffered, by partaking without stint – why, it keeps a man up, no doubt.'

'No doubt, Christopher Coney, no doubt. And 'a must need such reflections – a lonely widow man,' said Longways.

'When did he lose his wife?' asked Elizabeth.

'I never knowed her. 'Twas afore he came to Casterbridge,' Solomon Longways replied with terminative emphasis, as if the fact of his ignorance of Mrs Henchard were sufficient to deprive her history of all interest. 'But I know that 'a's a banded tee-totaller,* and that if any of his men be ever so little overtook by a drop he's down upon 'em as stern as the Lord upon the jovial Jews.'*

'Has he many men, then?' said Elizabeth-Jane.

'Many! Why, my good maid, he's the powerfullest member of the Town Council, and quite a principal man in the country round besides. Never a big dealing in wheat, barley, oats, hay, roots, and such-like but Henchard's got a hand in it. Ay, and he'll go into other things too; and that's where he makes his mistake. He worked his way up from nothing when 'a came here; and now he's a pillar of the town. Not but what he's been shaken a little to-year about this bad corn he has supplied in his contracts. I've seen the sun rise over Durnover Moor* these nine-and-sixty year, and though Mr Henchard has never cussed me unfairly ever since I've worked for'n, seeing I be but a little small man, I must say that I have never before tasted such rough bread as has been made from

Henchard's wheat lately. 'Tis that growed out that ye could a'most call it malt, and there's a list* at bottom o' the loaf as thick as the sole of one's shoe.'

The band now struck up another melody, and by the time it was ended the dinner was over, and speeches began to be made. The evening being calm, and the windows still open, these orations could be distinctly heard. Henchard's voice arose above the rest; he was telling a story of his hay-dealing experiences, in which he had outwitted a sharper who had been bent upon outwitting him.

'Ha-ha-ha!' responded his audience at the upshot of the story; and hilarity was general till a new voice arose with, 'This is all very well; but how about the bad bread?'

It came from the lower end of the table, where there sat a group of minor tradesmen who, although part of the company, appeared to be a little below the social level of the others; and who seemed to nourish a certain independence of opinion and carry on discussions not quite in harmony with those at the head; just as the west end of a church is sometimes persistently found to sing out of time and tune with the leading spirits in the chancel.

This interruption about the bad bread afforded infinite satisfaction to the loungers outside, several of whom were in the mood which finds its pleasure in others' discomfiture; and hence they echoed pretty freely, 'Hey! How about the bad bread, Mr Mayor?' Moreover, feeling none of the restraints of those who shared the feast, they could afford to add, 'You rather ought to tell the story o' that, sir!'

The interruption was sufficient to compel the Mayor to notice it.

'Well, I admit that the wheat turned out badly,' he said. 'But I was taken in in buying it as much as the bakers who bought it o' me.'

'And the poor folk who had to eat it whether or no,' said the inharmonious man outside the window.

Henchard's face darkened. There was temper under the thin bland surface – the temper which, artificially intensified, had banished a wife nearly a score of years before.

'You must make allowances for the accidents of a large business,' he said. 'You must bear in mind that the weather just at the harvest of that corn was worse than we have known it for years. However, I have mended my arrangements on account o't. Since I have found my business too large to be well looked after by myself alone, I have advertised for a thorough good man as manager of the corn department. When I've got him you will find these mistakes will no longer occur – matters will be better looked into.'

'But what are you going to do to repay us for the past?' inquired the man who had before spoken, and who seemed to be a baker or miller. 'Will you replace the grown flour we've still got by sound grain?'

Henchard's face had become still more stern at these interruptions, and he drank from his tumbler of water as if to calm himself or gain time. Instead of vouchsafing a direct reply, he stiffly observed –

'If anybody will tell me how to turn grown wheat into wholesome wheat I'll take it back with pleasure. But it can't be done.'

Henchard was not to be drawn again. Having said this, he sat down.

Chapter 6

Now the group outside the window had within the last few minutes been reinforced by new arrivals, some of them respectable shopkeepers and their assistants, who had come out for a whiff of air after putting up the shutters for the night; some of them of a lower class. Distinct from either there appeared a stranger – a young man of remarkably pleasant aspect – who carried in his hand a carpet-bag of the smart floral pattern prevalent in such articles at that time.

He was ruddy and of a fair countenance,* bright-eyed, and slight in build. He might possibly have passed by without stopping at all, or at most for half a minute to glance in at the scene, had not his advent coincided with the discussion on corn and bread; in which event this history had never been enacted. But the subject seemed to arrest him, and he whispered some inquiries of the other bystanders, and remained listening.

When he heard Henchard's closing words, 'It can't be done', he smiled impulsively, drew out his pocket-book, and wrote down a few words by the aid of the light in the window. He tore out the leaf, folded and directed it, and seemed about to throw it in through the open sash upon the dining-table; but, on second thoughts, edged himself through the loiterers, till he reached the door of the hotel, where one of the waiters who had been serving inside was now idly leaning against the door-post.

'Give this to the Mayor at once,' he said, handing in his hasty note.

Elizabeth-Jane had seen his movements and heard the words, which attracted her both by their subject and by their accent – a strange one for those parts. It was quaint and northerly.

The waiter took the note, while the young stranger continued –

'And can ye tell me of a respectable hotel that's a little more moderate than this?'

The waiter glanced indifferently up and down the street.

'They say the Three Mariners,* just below here, is a very good place,' he languidly answered; 'but I have never stayed there myself.'

The Scotchman, as he seemed to be, thanked him, and strolled on in the direction of the Three Mariners aforesaid, apparently more concerned about the question of an inn than about the fate of his note, now that the momentary impulse of writing it was over. While he was disappearing slowly down the street the waiter left the door, and Elizabeth-Jane saw with some interest the note brought into the dining-room and handed to the Mayor.

Henchard looked at it carelessly, unfolded it with one hand, and glanced it through. Thereupon it was curious to note an unexpected effect. The nettled, clouded aspect which had held possession of his face since the subject of his corn-dealings had been breached, changed itself into one of arrested attention. He read the note slowly, and fell into thought, not moody, but fitfully intense, as that of a man who has been captured by an idea.

By this time toasts and speeches had given place to songs, the wheat subject being quite forgotten. Men were putting their heads together in twos and threes, telling good stories, with pantomimic laughter which reached convulsive grimace. Some were beginning to look as if they did not know how they had come there, what they had come for, or how they were going to get home again; and provisionally sat on with a dazed smile. Square-built men showed a tendency to become hunchbacks; men with a dignified presence lost it in a curious obliquity of figure, in which their features grew disarranged and one-sided; whilst the heads of a few who had dined with extreme thoroughness were somehow sinking into their shoulders, the corners of their mouth and eyes being bent upwards by the subsidence. Only Henchard did not conform to these flexuous* changes; he remained stately and vertical, silently thinking.

The clock struck nine. Elizabeth-Jane turned to her companion. 'The evening is drawing on, mother,' she said. 'What do you propose to do?'

She was surprised to find how irresolute her mother had become. 'We must get a place to lie down in,' she murmured. 'I have seen – Mr Henchard; and that's all I wanted to do.'

'That's enough for to-night, at any rate,' Elizabeth-Jane replied soothingly. 'We can think to-morrow what is best to do about him. The question now is – is it not? – how shall we find a lodging?'

As her mother did not reply Elizabeth-Jane's mind reverted to the words of the waiter, that the Three Mariners was an inn of moderate charges. A recommendation good for one person was probably good for another. 'Let's go where the young man has gone to,' she said. 'He is respectable. What do you say?'

Her mother assented, and down the street they went.

In the meantime the Mayor's thoughtfulness, engendered by the note as stated, continued to hold him in abstraction; till, whispering to his neighbour to take his place, he found opportunity to leave the chair. This was just after the departure of his wife and Elizabeth.

Outside the door of the assembly-room he saw the waiter, and beckoning to him asked who brought the note which had been handed in a quarter of an hour before.

'A young man, sir – a sort of traveller. He was a Scotchman seemingly.'

'Did he say how he had got it?'

'He wrote it himself, sir, as he stood outside the window.'

'Oh – wrote it himself . . . Is the young man in the hotel?'

'No, sir. He went to the Three Mariners, I believe.'

The Mayor walked up and down the vestibule of the hotel with his hands under his coat tails, as if he were merely seeking a cooler atmosphere than that of the room he had quitted. But there could be no doubt that he was in reality still possessed to the full by the new idea, whatever that might be. At length he went back to the door of the dining-room, paused, and found that the songs, toasts, and conversation were proceeding quite satisfactorily without his presence. The Corporation, private residents, and major and minor tradesmen had in fact gone in for comforting beverages to such an extent that they had quite forgotten, not only the Mayor, but all those vast political, religious, and social differences which they felt necessary to maintain in the daytime, and which separated them like iron grills. Seeing this the Mayor took his hat, and when the waiter had helped him on with a thin holland overcoat,* went out and stood under the portico.

Very few persons were now in the street; and his eyes, by a sort of attraction, turned and dwelt upon a spot about a hundred yards further down. It was the house to which the writer of the note had gone – the Three Mariners – whose two prominent Elizabethan gables, bow-window, and passage-light could be seen from where he stood. Having kept his eyes on it for a while he strolled in that direction.

This ancient house of accommodation for man and beast, now, unfortunately, pulled down, was built of mellow sandstone, with mullioned* windows of the same material, markedly out of perpendicular from the settlement of foundations. The bay window projecting into the street, whose interior was so popular among the frequenters of the inn, was closed with shutters, in each of which appeared a heart-shaped aperture, somewhat more attenuated in the right and left ventricles than is seen in Nature. Inside these illuminated holes, a distance of about three inches, were ranged at this hour, as every passer knew, the ruddy polls* of Billy Wills the glazier, Smart the shoe-maker, Buzzford the general dealer, and others of a secondary set of worthies, of a grade somewhat below that of the diners at the King's Arms, each with his yard of clay.*

A four-centred Tudor arch* was over the entrance, and over the arch the signboard, now visible in the rays of an opposite lamp. Hereon the Mariners, who had been represented by the artist as persons of two dimensions only – in other words, flat as a shadow – were standing in a row in paralysed attitudes. Being on the sunny side of the street the three comrades had suffered largely from warping, splitting, fading, and shrinkage, so that they were but a half-invisible film upon the reality of the grain, and knots, and nails, which composed the signboard. As a matter of fact, this state of things was not so much owing to Stannidge the landlord's neglect, as from the lack of a painter in

Casterbridge who would undertake to reproduce the features of men so traditional.

A long, narrow, dimly-lit passage gave access to the inn, within which passage the horses going to their stalls at the back, and the coming and departing human guests, rubbed shoulders indiscriminately, the latter running no slight risk of having their toes trodden upon by the animals. The good stabling and the good ale of the Mariners, though somewhat difficult to reach on account of there being but this narrow way to both, were nevertheless perseveringly sought out by the sagacious old heads who knew what was what in Casterbridge.

Henchard stood without the inn for a few instants; then lowering the dignity of his presence as much as possible by buttoning the brown holland coat over his shirt-front, and in other ways toning himself down to his ordinary everyday appearance, he entered the inn door.

Chapter 7

Elizabeth-Jane and her mother had arrived some twenty minutes earlier. Outside the house they had stood and considered whether even this homely place, though recommended as moderate, might not be too serious in its prices for their light pockets. Finally, however, they had found courage to enter, and duly met Stannidge the landlord; a silent man, who drew and carried frothing measures to this room and to that, shoulder to shoulder with his waiting-maids – a stately slowness, however, entering into his ministrations by contrast with theirs, as became one whose service was somewhat optional. It would have been altogether optional but for the orders of the landlady, a person who sat in the bar, corporeally motionless, but with a flitting eye and quick ear, with which she observed and heard through the open door and hatchway the pressing needs of customers whom her husband overlooked though close at hand. Elizabeth and her mother were passively accepted as sojourners, and shown to a small bedroom under one of the gables, where they sat down.

The principle of the inn seemed to be to compensate for the antique awkwardness, crookedness, and obscurity of the passages, floors, and windows, by quantities of clean linen spread about everywhere, and this had a dazzling effect upon the travellers.

''Tis too good for us – we can't meet it!' said the elder woman, looking round the apartment with misgiving as soon as they were left alone.

'I fear it is, too,' said Elizabeth. 'But we must be respectable.'

'We must pay our way even before we must be respectable,' replied her mother. 'Mr Henchard is too high for us to make ourselves known to him, I much fear; so we've only our own pockets to depend on.'

'I know what I'll do,' said Elizabeth-Jane after an interval of waiting, during which their needs seemed quite forgotten under the press of business below. And leaving the room, she descended the stairs and penetrated to the bar.

If there was one good thing more than another which characterized this single-hearted girl it was a willingness to sacrifice her personal comfort and dignity to the common weal.

'As you seem busy here to-night, and mother's not well off, might I take out part of our accommodation by helping?' she asked of the landlady.

The latter, who remained as fixed in the arm-chair as if she had been melted into it when in a liquid state, and could not now be unstuck, looked the girl up and down inquiringly, with her hands on the chair-arms. Such arrangements as the one Elizabeth proposed were not uncommon in country villages; but, though Casterbridge was old-fashioned, the custom was well-nigh obsolete here. The mistress of the house, however, was an easy woman to strangers, and she made no objection. Thereupon Elizabeth, being instructed by nods and motions from the taciturn landlord as to where she could find the different things, trotted up and down stairs with materials for her own and her parent's meal.

While she was doing this the wood partition in the centre of the house thrilled to its centre with the tugging of a bell-pull upstairs. A bell below tinkled a note that was feebler in sound than the twanging of wires and cranks that had produced it.

''Tis the Scotch gentleman,' said the landlady omnisciently; and turning her eyes to Elizabeth, 'Now then, can you go and see if his supper is on the tray? If it is you can take it up to him. The front room over this.'

Elizabeth-Jane, though hungry, willingly postponed serving

herself awhile, and applied to the cook in the kitchen, whence she brought forth the tray of supper viands, and proceeded with it upstairs to the apartment indicated. The accommodation of the Three Mariners was far from spacious, despite the fair area of ground it covered. The room demanded by intrusive beams and rafters, partitions, passages, staircases, disused oven, settles,* and four-posters, left comparatively small quarters for human beings. Moreover, this being at a time before home-brewing was abandoned by the smaller victuallers, and a house in which the twelve-bushel strength* was still religiously adhered to by the landlord in his ale, the quality of the liquor was the chief attraction of the premises, so that everything had to make way for utensils and operations in connection therewith. Thus Elizabeth found that the Scotchman was located in a room quite close to the small one that had been allotted to herself and her mother.

When she entered nobody was present but the young man himself – the same whom she had seen lingering without the windows of the King's Arms Hotel. He was now idly reading a copy of the local paper, and was hardly conscious of her entry, so that she looked at him quite coolly, and saw how his forehead shone where the light caught it, and how nicely his hair was cut, and the sort of velvet-pile or down that was on the skin at the back of his neck, and how his cheek was so truly curved as to be part of a globe, and how clearly drawn were the lids and lashes which hid his bent eyes.

She set down the tray, spread his supper, and went away without a word. On her arrival below the landlady, who was as kind as she was fat and lazy, saw that Elizabeth-Jane was rather tired, though in her earnestness to be useful she was waiving her own needs altogether. Mrs Stannidge thereupon said with a considerate peremptoriness that she and her mother had better take their own suppers if they meant to have any.

Elizabeth fetched their simple provisions, as she had fetched the Scotchman's, and went up to the little chamber where she had left her mother, noiselessly pushing open the door with the edge of the tray. To her surprise her mother, instead of being reclined on the bed where she had left her, was in an erect position, with lips parted. At Elizabeth's entry she lifted her finger.

The meaning of this was soon apparent. The room allotted to the two women had at one time served as a dressing-room to the Scotchman's chamber, as was evidenced by signs of a door of communication between them – now screwed up and pasted over with the wall paper. But, as is frequently the case with hotels of far higher pretensions than the Three Mariners, every word spoken in either of these rooms was distinctly audible in the other. Such sounds came through now.

Thus silently conjured Elizabeth deposited the tray, and her mother whispered as she drew near, ''Tis he.'

'Who?' said the girl.

'The Mayor.'

The tremors in Susan Henchard's tone might have led any person but one so perfectly unsuspicious of the truth as the girl was, to surmise some closer connection than the admitted simple kinship as a means of accounting for them.

Two men were indeed talking in the adjoining chamber, the young Scotchman and Henchard, who, having entered the inn while Elizabeth-Jane was in the kitchen waiting for the supper, had been deferentially conducted upstairs by host Stannidge himself. The girl noiselessly laid out their meal, and beckoned to her mother to join her, which Mrs Henchard mechanically did, her attention being fixed on the conversation through the door.

'I merely strolled in on my way home to ask you a question about something that has excited my curiosity,' said the Mayor, with careless geniality. 'But I see you have not finished supper.'

'Ay, but I will be done in a little! Ye needn't go, sir. Take a seat. I've almost done, and it makes no difference at all.'

Henchard seemed to take the seat offered, and in a moment he resumed: 'Well, first I should ask, did you write this?' A rustling of paper followed.

'Yes, I did,' said the Scotchman.

'Then,' said Henchard, 'I am under the impression that we have met by accident while waiting for the morning to keep an appointment with each other? My name is Henchard; ha'n't you replied to an advertisement for a corn-factor's manager that I put into the paper – ha'n't you come here to see me about it?'

'No,' said the Scotchman, with some surprise.

'Surely you are the man,' went on Henchard insistingly, 'who arranged to come and see me? Joshua, Joshua, Jipp – Jopp – what was his name?'

'You're wrong!' said the young man. 'My name is Donald Farfrae. It is true I am in the corren trade – but I have replied to no advairrtisment, and arranged to see no one. I am on my way to

Bristol – from there to the other side of the warrld, to try my fortune in the great wheat-growing districts of the West! I have some inventions useful to the trade, and there is no scope for developing them heere.'

'To America – well, well,' said Henchard, in a tone of disappointment, so strong as to make itself felt like a damp atmosphere. 'And yet I could have sworn you were the man!'

The Scotchman murmured another negative, and there was a silence, till Henchard resumed: 'Then I am truly and sincerely obliged to you for the few words you wrote on that paper.'

'It was nothing, sir.'

'Well, it has a great importance for me just now. This row about my grown wheat, which I declare to Heaven I didn't know to be bad till the people came complaining, has put me to my wits' end. I've some hundreds of quarters* of it on hand; and if your renovating process will make it wholesome, why, you can see what a quag* 'twould get me out of. I saw in a moment there might be truth in it. But I should like to have it proved; and of course you don't care to tell the steps of the process sufficiently for me to do that, without my paying ye well for't first.'

The young man reflected a moment or two. 'I don't know that I have any objection,' he said. 'I'm going to another country, and curing bad corn is not the line I'll take up there. Yes, I'll tell ye the whole of it – you'll make more out of it heere than I will in a foreign country. Just look heere a minute, sir. I can show ye by a sample in my carpet-bag.'

The click of a lock followed, and there was a sifting and rustling; then a discussion about so many ounces to the bushel, and drying, and refrigerating, and so on.

'These few grains will be sufficient to show ye with,' came in the young fellow's voice; and after a pause, during which some operation seemed to be intently watched by them both, he exclaimed, 'There, now, do you taste that.'

'It's complete! – quite restored, or – well – nearly.'

'Quite enough restored to make good seconds* out of it,' said the Scotchman. 'To fetch it back entirely is impossible; Nature won't stand so much as that, but heere you go a great way towards it. Well, sir, that's the process; I don't value it, for it can be but of little use in countries where the weather is more settled than in ours; and I'll be only too glad if it's of service to you.'

'But hearken to me,' pleaded Henchard. 'My business, you

know, is in corn and in hay; but I was brought up as a hay-trusser simply, and hay is what I understand best, though I now do more in corn than in the other. If you'll accept the place, you shall manage the corn branch entirely, and receive a commission in addition to salary.'

'You're liberal – very liberal; but no, no – I cannet!' the young man still replied, with some distress in his accents.

'So be it!' said Henchard conclusively. 'Now – to change the subject – one good turn deserves another; don't stay to finish that miserable supper. Come to my house; I can find something better for 'ee than cold ham and ale.'

Donald Farfrae was grateful – said he feared he must decline – that he wished to leave early next day.

'Very well,' said Henchard quickly, 'please yourself. But I tell you, young man, if this holds good for the bulk, as it has done for the sample, you have saved my credit, stranger though you be. What shall I pay you for this knowledge?'

'Nothing at all, nothing at all. It may not prove necessary to ye to use it often, and I don't value it at all. I thought I might just as well let ye know, as you were in a difficulty, and they were harrd upon ye.'

Henchard paused. 'I shan't soon forget this,' he said. 'And from a stranger! . . . I couldn't believe you were not the man I had engaged! Says I to myself "He knows who I am, and recommends himself by this stroke." And yet it turns out, after all, that you are not the man who answered my advertisement, but a stranger!'

'Ay, ay; that's so,' said the young man.

Henchard again suspended his words, and then his voice came thoughtfully: 'Your forehead, Farfrae, is something like my poor brother's – now dead and gone; and the nose, too, isn't unlike his. You must be, what – five foot nine, I reckon? I am six foot one and a half out of my shoes. But what of that? In my business, 'tis true that strength and bustle build up a firm. But judgment and knowledge are what keep it established. Unluckily, I am bad at science, Farfrae; bad at figures – a rule o' thumb sort of man. You are just the reverse – I can see that. I have been looking for such as you these two year, and yet you are not for me. Well, before I go, let me ask this: Though you are not the young man I thought you were, what's the difference? Can't ye stay just the same? Have you really made up your mind about this American notion? I won't mince matters. I feel you would be invaluable to me – that needn't be said – and if you will bide and be my manager, I will make it worth your while.'

'My plans are fixed,' said the young man, in negative tones. 'I have formed a scheme, and so we need na say any more about it. But will you not drink with me, sir? I find this Casterbridge ale warreming to the stomach.'

'No, no; I fain would, but I can't,' said Henchard gravely, the scraping of his chair informing the listeners that he was rising to leave. 'When I was a young man I went in for that sort of thing too strong – far too strong – and was well-nigh ruined by it! I did a deed on account of it which I shall be ashamed of to my dying day. It made such an impression on me that I swore, there and then, that I'd drink nothing stronger than tea for as many years as I was old that day. I have kept my oath; and though, Farfrae, I am sometimes that dry in the dog days* that I could drink a quarter-barrel to the pitching,* I think o' my oath, and touch no strong drink at all.'

'I'll no' press ye, sir – I'll no' press ye. I respect your vow.'

'Well, I shall get a manager somewhere, no doubt,' said Henchard, with strong feeling in his tones. 'But it will be long before I see one that would suit me so well!'

The young man appeared much moved by Henchard's warm convictions of his value. He was silent till they reached the door. 'I wish I could stay – sincerely I would like to,' he replied. 'But no – it cannet be! it cannet! I want to see the warrld.'

Chapter 8

Thus they parted; and Elizabeth-Jane and her mother remained each in her thoughts over their meal, the mother's face being strangely bright since Henchard's avowal of shame for a past action. The quivering of the partition to its core presently denoted that Donald Farfrae had again rung his bell, no doubt to have his supper removed; for humming a tune, and walking up and down, he seemed to be attracted by the lively bursts of conversation and melody from the general company below. He sauntered out upon the landing, and descended the staircase.

When Elizabeth-Jane had carried down his supper tray, and

also that used by her mother and herself, she found the bustle of serving to be at its height below, as it always was at this hour. The young woman shrank from having anything to do with the ground-floor serving, and crept silently about observing the scene – so new to her, fresh from the seclusion of a seaside cottage. In the general sitting-room, which was large, she remarked the two or three dozen strong-backed chairs that stood round against the wall, each fitted with its genial occupant; the sanded floor; the black settle which, projecting endwise from the wall within the door, permitted Elizabeth to be a spectator of all that went on without herself being particularly seen.

The young Scotchman had just joined the guests. These, in addition to the respectable master-tradesmen occupying the seats of privilege in the bow-window and its neighbourhood, included an inferior set at the unlighted end, whose seats were mere benches against the wall, and who drank from cups instead of from glasses. Among the latter she noticed some of those personages who had stood outside the windows of the King's Arms.

Behind their backs was a small window, with a wheel ventilator in one of the panes, which would suddenly start off spinning with a jingling sound, as suddenly stop, and as suddenly start again.

While thus furtively making her survey the opening words of a song greeted her ears from the front of the settle, in a melody and accent of peculiar charm. There had been some singing before she came down; and now the Scotchman had made himself so soon at home that, at the request of some of the master-tradesmen, he, too, was favouring the room with a ditty.

Elizabeth-Jane was fond of music; she could not help pausing to listen; and the longer she listened the more she was enraptured. She had never heard any singing like this; and it was evident that the majority of the audience had not heard such frequently, for they were attentive to a much greater degree than usual. They neither whispered, nor drank, nor dipped their pipe-stems in their ale to moisten them, nor pushed the mug to their neighbours. The singer himself grew emotional, till she could imagine a tear in his eye as the words went on:—

> It's hame, and it's hame, hame fain would I be,
> O hame, hame, hame to my ain countree!
> There's an eye that ever weeps, and a fair face will be fain,
> As I pass through Annan Water with my bonnie bands again;

When the flower is in the bud, and the leaf upon the tree,
The lark shall sing me hame to my ain countree!*

There was a burst of applause, and a deep silence which was even more eloquent than the applause. It was of such a kind that the snapping of a pipe-stem too long for him by old Solomon Longways, who was one of those gathered at the shady end of the room, seemed a harsh and irreverent act. Then the ventilator in the window-pane spasmodically started off for a new spin, and the pathos of Donald's song was temporarily effaced.

''Twas not amiss − not at all amiss!' muttered Chistopher Coney, who was also present. And removing his pipe a finger's breadth from his lips, he said aloud, 'Draw on the next verse, young gentleman, please.'

'Yes. Let's have it again, stranger,' said the glazier, a stout, bucket-headed man, with a white apron rolled up round his waist. 'Folks don't lift up their hearts like that in this part of the world.' And turning aside, he said in undertones, 'Who is the young man? − Scotch, d'ye say?'

'Yes, straight from the mountains of Scotland, I believe,' replied Coney.

Young Farfrae repeated the last verse. It was plain that nothing so pathetic had been heard at the Three Mariners for a considerable time. The difference of accent, the excitability of the singer, the intense local feeling, and the seriousness with which he worked himself up to a climax, surprised this set of worthies, who were only too prone to shut up their emotions with caustic words.

'Danged if our country down here is worth singing about like that!' continued the glazier, as the Scotchman again melodized with a dying fall, 'My ain countree!' 'When you take away from among us the fools and the rogues, and the lammigers,* and the wanton hussies, and the slatterns, and such like, there's cust few left to ornament a song with in Casterbridge, or the country round.'

'True,' said Buzzford, the dealer, looking at the grain of the table. 'Casterbridge is a old, hoary place o' wickedness, by all account. 'Tis recorded in history that we rebelled against the King* one or two hundred years ago, in the time of the Romans, and that lots of us was hanged on Gallows Hill, and quartered, and our different jints sent about the country like butcher's meat; and for my part I can well believe it.'

'What did ye come away from yer own country for, young

maister, if ye be so wownded* about it?' inquired Christopher Coney, from the background, with the tone of a man who preferred the original subject. 'Faith, it wasn't worth your while on our account, for, as Maister Billy Wills says, we be bruckle* folk here – the best o' us hardly honest sometimes, what with hard winters, and so many mouths to fill, and God-a'mighty sending his little taties so terrible small to fill 'em with. We don't think about flowers and fair faces, not we – except in the shape o' cauliflowers and pigs' chaps.'*

'But no!' said Donald Farfrae, gazing round into their faces with earnest concern; 'the best of ye hardly honest – not that surely? None of ye has been stealing what didn't belong to him?'

'Lord! no, no!' said Solomon Longways, smiling grimly. 'That's only his random way o' speaking. 'A was always such a man of under-thoughts.' (And reprovingly towards Christopher): 'Don't ye be so over-familiar with a gentleman that ye know nothing of – and that's travelled a'most from the North Pole.'

Christopher Coney was silenced, and as he could get no public sympathy, he mumbled his feelings to himself: 'Be dazed, if I loved my country half as well as the young feller do, I'd live by claning* my neighbour's pigsties afore I'd go away! For my part I've no more love for my country than I have for Botany Bay!'

'Come,' said Longways; 'let the young man draw onward with his ballet, or we shall be here all night.'

'That's all of it,' said the singer apologetically.

'Soul of my body, then we'll have another!' said the general dealer.

'Can you turn a strain to the ladies, sir?' inquired a fat woman with a figured purple apron, the waist-string of which was overhung so far by her sides as to be invisible.

'Let him breathe – let him breathe, Mother Cuxsom. He hain't got his second wind yet,' said the master glazier.

'O yes, but I have!' exclaimed the young man; and he at once rendered 'O Nannie'* with faultless modulations, and another or two of the like sentiment, winding up at their earnest request with 'Auld Lang Syne'.

By this time he had completely taken possession of the hearts of the Three Mariners' inmates, including even old Coney. Notwithstanding an occasional odd gravity which awoke their sense of the ludicrous for the moment, they began to view him through a golden haze which the tone of his mind seemed to raise around him. Casterbridge had sentiment – Casterbridge had romance; but this stranger's sentiment was of differing quality. Or rather, perhaps, the difference was mainly superficial; he was to them like the poet of a new school who takes his contemporaries by storm; who is not really new, but is the first to articulate what all his listeners have felt, though dumbly till then.

The silent landlord came and leant over the settle while the young man sang; and even Mrs Stannidge managed to unstick herself from the framework of her chair in the bar and get as far as the door-post, which movement she accomplished by rolling herself round, as a cask is trundled on the chine* by a drayman without losing much of its perpendicular.

'And are you going to bide in Casterbridge, sir?' she asked.

'Ah – no!' said the Scotchman, with melancholy fatality in his voice, 'I'm only passing thirrough! I am on my way to Bristol, and on frae there to foreign parts.'

'We be truly sorry to hear it,' said Solomon Longways. 'We can ill afford to lose tuneful wynd-pipes like yours when they fall among us. And verily, to mak' acquaintance with a man a-come from so far, from the land o' perpetual snow, as we may say, where wolves and wild boars and other dangerous animalcules be as common as blackbirds hereabout – why, 'tis a thing we can't do every day; and there's good sound information for bide-at-homes like we when such a man opens his mouth.'

'Nay, but ye mistake my country,' said the young man, looking round upon them with tragic fixity, till his eye lighted up and his cheek kindled with a sudden enthusiasm to right their errors. 'There are not perpetual snow and wolves at all in it! – except snow in winter, and – well – a little in summer just sometimes, and a "gaberlunzie"* or two stalking about here and there, if ye may call them dangerous. Eh, but you should take a summer jarreny to Edinboro', and Arthur's Seat, and all round there, and then go on to the lochs, and all the Highland scenery – in May and June – and you would never say 'tis the land of wolves and perpetual snow!'

'Of course not – it stands to reason,' said Buzzford. ''Tis barren ignorance that leads to such words. He's a simple home-spun man, that never was fit for good company – think nothing of him, sir.'

'And do ye carry your flock bed, and your quilt, and your crock, and your bit of chiney? or do ye go in bare bones, as I may say?' inquired Christopher Coney.

'I've sent on my luggage – though it isn't much; for the voyage is long.' Donald's eyes dropped into a remote gaze as he added: 'But I said to myself, "Never a one of the prizes of life will I come by unless I undertake it!" and I decided to go.'

A general sense of regret, in which Elizabeth-Jane shared not least, made itself apparent in the company. As she looked at Farfrae from the back of the settle she decided that his statements showed him to be no less thoughtful than his fascinating melodies revealed him to be cordial and impassioned. She admired the serious light in which he looked at serious things. He had seen no jest in ambiguities and roguery, as the Casterbridge toss-pots had done; and rightly not – there was none. She disliked those wretched humours of Christopher Coney and his tribe; and he did not appreciate them. He seemed to feel exactly as she felt about life and its surroundings – that they were a tragical rather than a comical thing; that though one could be gay on occasion, moments of gaiety were interludes, and no part of the actual drama. It was extraordinary how similar their views were.

Though it was still early the young Scotchman expressed his wish to retire, whereupon the landlady whispered to Elizabeth to run upstairs and turn down his bed. She took a candlestick and proceeded on her mission, which was the act of a few moments only. When, candle in hand, she reached the top of the stairs on her way down again, Mr Farfrae was at the foot coming up. She could not very well retreat; they met and passed in the turn of the staircase.

She must have appeared interesting in some way – notwith-standing her plain dress – or rather, possibly, in consequence of it, for she was a girl characterized by earnestness and soberness of mien, with which simple drapery accorded well. Her face flushed, too, at the slight awkwardness of the meeting, and she passed him with her eyes bent on the candle-flame that she carried just below her nose. Thus it happened that when confronting her he smiled; and then, with the manner of a temporarily light-hearted man, who has started himself on a flight of song whose momentum he cannot readily check, he softly tuned an old ditty that she seemed to suggest –

> As I came in by my bower door,
>   As day was waxin' wearie,
> Oh wha came tripping down the stair
>   But bonnie Peg my dearie.*

Elizabeth-Jane, rather disconcerted, hastened on; and the Scotchman's voice died away, humming more of the same within the closed door of his room.

Here the scene and sentiment ended for the present. When, soon after, the girl rejoined her mother, the latter was still in thought – on quite another matter than a young man's song.

'We've made a mistake,' she whispered (that the Scotchman might not overhear). 'On no account ought ye to have helped serve here to-night. Not because of ourselves, but for the sake of *him*. If he should befriend us, and take us up, and then find out what you did when staying here, 'twould grieve and wound his natural pride as Mayor of the town.'

Elizabeth, who would perhaps have been more alarmed at this than her mother had she known the real relationship, was not much disturbed about it as things stood. Her 'he' was another man than her poor mother's. 'For myself,' she said, 'I didn't at all mind waiting a little upon him. He's so respectable, and educated – far above the rest of 'em in the inn. They thought him very simple not to know their grim broad way of talking about themselves here. But of course he didn't know – he was too refined in his mind to know such things!' Thus she earnestly pleaded.

Meanwhile, the 'he' of her mother was not so far away as even they thought. After leaving the Three Mariners he had sauntered up and down the empty High Street, passing and repassing the inn in his promenade. When the Scotchman sang his voice had reached Henchard's ears through the heart-shaped holes in the window-shutters, and had led him to pause outside them a long while.

'To be sure, to be sure, how that fellow does draw me!' he had said to himself. 'I suppose 'tis because I'm so lonely. I'd have given him a third share in the business to have stayed!'

Chapter 9

When Elizabeth-Jane opened the hinged casement next morning the mellow air brought in the feel of imminent autumn almost as distinctly as if she had been in the remotest hamlet. Casterbridge was the complement of the rural life around; not its urban opposite. Bees and butterflies in the cornfields at the top of the town, who desired to get to the meads at the bottom, took no circuitous course, but flew straight down High Street without any apparent consciousness that they were traversing strange latitudes. And in autumn airy spheres of thistledown floated into the same street, lodged upon the shop fronts, blew into drains, and innumerable tawny and yellow leaves skimmed along the pavement, and stole through people's doorways into their passages with a hesitating scratch on the floor, like the skirts of timid visitors.

Hearing voices, one of which was close at hand, she withdrew her head and glanced from behind the window-curtains. Mr Henchard – now habited no longer as a great personage, but as a thriving man of business – was pausing on his way up the middle of the street, and the Scotchman was looking from the window adjoining her own. Henchard, it appeared, had gone a little way past the inn before he had noticed his acquaintance of the previous evening. He came back a few steps, Donald Farfrae opening the window further.

'And you are off soon, I suppose?' said Henchard upwards.

'Yes – almost this moment, sir,' said the other. 'Maybe I'll walk on till the coach makes up on me.'

'Which way?'

'The way ye are going.'

'Then shall we walk together to the top o' town?'

'If ye'll wait a minute,' said the Scotchman.

In a few minutes the latter emerged, bag in hand. Henchard looked at the bag as at an enemy. It showed there was no mistake about the young man's departure. 'Ah, my lad,' he said, 'you should have been a wise man, and have stayed with me.'

'Yes, yes – it might have been wiser,' said Donald, looking microscopically at the houses that were furthest off. 'It is only telling ye the truth when I say my plans are vague.'

They had by this time passed on from the precincts of the inn, and Elizabeth-Jane heard no more. She saw that they continued in conversation, Henchard turning to the other occasionally, and emphasizing some remark with a gesture. Thus they passed the King's Arms Hotel, the Market House, St Peter's churchyard wall, ascending to the upper end of the long street till they were small as two grains of corn; when they bent suddenly to the right into the Bristol Road, and were out of view.

'He was a good man – and he's gone,' she said to herself. 'I was nothing to him, and there was no reason why he should have wished me good-bye.'

The simple thought, with its latent sense of slight, had moulded itself out of the following little fact: when the Scotchman came out at the door he had by accident glanced up at her; and then he had looked away again without nodding, or smiling, or saying a word.

'You are still thinking, mother,' she said, when she turned inwards.

'Yes; I am thinking of Mr Henchard's sudden liking for that young man. He was always so. Now, surely, if he takes so warmly to people who are not related to him at all, may he not take as warmly to his own kin?'

While they debated this question a procession of five large waggons went past, laden with hay up to the bedroom windows. They came in from the country, and the steaming horses had probably been travelling a great part of the night. To the shaft of each hung a little board, on which was painted in white letters, 'Henchard, corn-factor and hay-merchant'. The spectacle renewed his wife's conviction that, for her daughter's sake, she should strain a point to rejoin him.

The discussion was continued during breakfast, and the end of it was that Mrs Henchard decided, for good or for ill, to send Elizabeth-Jane with a message to Henchard, to the effect that his relative Susan, a sailor's widow, was in the town; leaving it to him to say whether or not he would recognize her. What had brought her to this determination were chiefly two things. He had been described as a lonely widower; and he had expressed shame for a past transaction of his life. There was promise in both.

'If he says no,' she enjoined, as Elizabeth-Jane stood, bonnet on, ready to depart; 'if he thinks it does not become the good position he has reached to in the town, to own – to let us call on him as – his distant kinsfolk, say, "Then, sir, we would rather not intrude; we will leave Casterbridge as quietly as we have come, and go back to our own country." . . . I almost feel that I would rather he did say so, as I have not seen him for so many years, and we are so – little allied to him!'

'And if he say yes?' inquired the more sanguine one.

'In that case,' answered Mrs Henchard cautiously, 'ask him to write me a note, saying when and how he will see us – or *me*.'

Elizabeth-Jane went a few steps towards the landing. 'And tell him,' continued her mother, 'that I fully know I have no claim upon him – that I am glad to find he is thriving; that I hope his life may be long and happy – there, go.' Thus with a half-hearted willingness, a smothered reluctance, did the poor forgiving woman start her unconscious daughter on this errand.

It was about ten o'clock, and market-day, when Elizabeth paced up the High Street, in no great hurry; for to herself her position was only that of a poor relation deputed to hunt up a rich one. The front doors of the private houses were mostly left open at this warm autumn time, no thought of umbrella stealers disturbing the minds of the placid burgesses. Hence, through the long, straight entrance passages thus unclosed could be seen, as through tunnels, the mossy gardens at the back, glowing with nasturtiums, fuchsias, scarlet geraniums, 'bloody warriors',* snapdragons, and dahlias, this floral blaze being backed by crusted grey stone-work remaining from a yet remoter Casterbridge than the venerable one visible in the street. The old-fashioned fronts of these houses, which had older than old-fashioned backs, rose sheer from the pavement, into which the bow-windows protruded like bastions, necessitating a pleasing *chassez-déchassez** movement to the time-pressed pedestrian at every few yards. He was bound also to evolve other Terpsichorean* figures in respect of door-steps, scrapers, cellar-hatches, church buttresses, and the overhanging angles of walls which, originally unobtrusive, had become bow-legged and knock-kneed.

In addition to these fixed obstacles which spoke so cheerfully of individual unrestraint as to boundaries, movables occupied the path and roadway to a perplexing extent. First the vans of the carriers in and out of Casterbridge, who hailed from Mellstock, Weatherbury, The Hintocks, Sherton-Abbas, Kingsbere, Over-combe,* and many other towns and villages round. Their owners were numerous enough to be regarded as a tribe, and had almost distinctiveness enough to be regarded as a race. Their vans had just arrived, and were drawn up on each side of the street in close file, so as to form at places a wall between the pavement and the roadway. Moreover every shop pitched out half its contents upon trestles and boxes on the kerb, extending the display each week a little further and further into the roadway, despite the expostulations of the two feeble old constables,* until there remained but a tortuous defile for carriages down the centre of the street, which afforded fine opportunities for skill with the reins. Over the pavement on the sunny side of the way hung shopblinds so constructed as to give the passenger's hat a smart buffet off his head, as from the unseen hands of Cranstoun's Goblin Page,* celebrated in romantic lore.

Horses for sale were tied in rows, their forelegs on the pavement, their hind legs in the street, in which position they occasionally nipped little boys by the shoulder who were passing to school. And any inviting recess in front of a house that had been modestly kept back from the general line was utilized by pig-dealers as a pen for their stock.[1]

The yeomen, farmers, dairymen, and townsfolk, who came to transact business in these ancient streets, spoke in other ways than by articulation. Not to hear the words of your interlocutor in metropolitan centres is to know nothing of his meaning. Here the face, the arms, the hat, the stick, the body throughout spoke equally with the tongue. To express satisfaction the Casterbridge market-man added to his utterance a broadening of the cheeks, a crevicing of the eyes, a throwing back of the shoulders, which was intelligible from the other end of the street. If he wondered, though all Henchard's carts and waggons were rattling past him, you knew it from perceiving the inside of his crimson mouth, and a target-like circling of his eyes. Deliberation caused sundry attacks on the moss of adjoining walls with the end of his stick, a change of his hat from the horizontal to the less so; a sense of tediousness announced itself in a lowering of the person by spreading the knees to a lozenge-shaped aperture and contorting the arms. Chicanery, subterfuge, had hardly a place in the streets of this honest borough to all appearance; and it was said that the lawyers in the Court House hard by occasionally threw in strong arguments for the other side out of pure generosity (though apparently by mischance) when advancing their own.

Thus Casterbridge was in most respects but the pole, focus, or nerve-knot of the surrounding country life; differing from the many manufacturing towns which are as foreign bodies set down, like boulders on a plain, in a green world with which they have nothing in common. Casterbridge lived by agriculture at one remove further from the fountain-head than the adjoining villages

---

[1] The reader will scarcely need to be reminded that time and progress have obliterated from the town that suggested these descriptions many or most of the old-fashioned features here enumerated.

– no more. The townsfolk understood every fluctuation in the rustic's condition, for it affected their receipts as much as the labourer's; they entered into the troubles and joys which moved the aristocratic families ten miles round – for the same reason. And even at the dinner-parties of the professional families the subjects of discussion were corn, cattle-disease, sowing and reaping, fencing and planting; while politics were viewed by them less from their own standpoint of burgesses with rights and privileges than from the standpoint of their county neighbours.

All the venerable contrivances and confusions which delighted the eye by their quaintness, and in a measure reasonableness, in this rare old market-town, were metropolitan novelties to the unpractised eyes of Elizabeth-Jane, fresh from netting fish-seines* in a seaside cottage. Very little inquiry was necessary to guide her footsteps. Henchard's house was one of the best, faced with dull red-and-grey old brick. The front door was open, and, as in other houses, she could see through the passage to the end of the garden – nearly a quarter of a mile off.

Mr Henchard was not in the house, but in the store-yard. She was conducted into the mossy garden, and through a door in the wall, which was studded with rusty nails speaking of generations of fruit-trees that had been trained there. The door opened upon the yard, and here she was left to find him as she could. It was a place flanked by hay-barns, into which tons of fodder, all in trusses, were being packed from the waggons she had seen pass the inn that morning. On other sides of the yard were wooden granaries on stone staddles,* to which access was given by Flemish ladders,* and a store-house several floors high. Wherever the doors of these places were open, a closely packed throng of bursting wheat-sacks could be seen standing inside, with the air of awaiting a famine that would not come.

She wandered about this place, uncomfortably conscious of the impending interview, till she was quite weary of searching; she ventured to inquire of a boy in what quarter Mr Henchard could be found. He directed her to an office which she had not seen before, and knocking at the door she was answered by a cry of 'Come in'.

Elizabeth turned the handle; and there stood before her, bending over some sample-bags on a table, not the corn-merchant, but the young Scotchman Mr Farfrae – in the act of pouring some grains of wheat from one hand to the other. His hat hung on a peg behind him, and the roses of his carpet-bag glowed from the corner of the room.

Having toned her feelings and arranged words on her lips for Mr Henchard, and for him alone, she was for the moment confounded.

'Yes, what is it?' said the Scotchman, like a man who permanently ruled there.

She said she wanted to see Mr Henchard.

'Ah, yes; will you wait a minute? He's engaged just now,' said the young man, apparently not recognizing her as the girl at the inn. He handed her a chair, bade her sit down, and turned to his sample-bags again. While Elizabeth-Jane sits waiting in great amaze at the young man's presence we may briefly explain how he came there.

When the two new acquaintances had passed out of sight that morning towards the Bath and Bristol road they went on silently, except for a few commonplaces, till they had gone down an avenue on the town walls called the Chalk Walk, leading to an angle where the North and West escarpments met. From this high corner of the square earthworks a vast extent of country could be seen. A footpath ran steeply down the green slope, conducting from the shady promenade on the walls to a road at the bottom of the scarp. It was by this path the Scotchman had to descend.

'Well, here's success to 'ee,' said Henchard, holding out his right hand and leaning with his left upon the wicket which protected the descent. In the act there was the inelegance of one whose feelings are nipped and wishes defeated. 'I shall often think of this time, and of how you came at the very moment to throw a light upon my difficulty.'

Still holding the young man's hand he paused, and then added deliberately: 'Now I am not the man to let a cause be lost for want of a word. And before ye are gone for ever I'll speak. Once more, will ye stay? There it is, flat and plain. You can see that it isn't all selfishness that makes me press 'ee; for my business is not quite so scientific as to require an intellect entirely out of the common. Others would do for the place without doubt. Some selfishness perhaps there is, but there is more; it isn't for me to repeat what. Come bide with me – and name your own terms. I'll agree to 'em willingly and 'ithout a word of gainsaying; for, hang it, Farfrae, I like thee well!'

The young man's hand remained steady in Henchard's for a

moment or two. He looked over the fertile country that stretched beneath them, then backward along the shaded walk reaching to the top of the town. His face flushed.

'I never expected this – I did not!' he said. 'It's Providence! Should any one go against it? No; I'll not go to America; I'll stay and be your man!'

His hand, which had lain lifeless in Henchard's, returned the latter's grasp.

'Done,' said Henchard.

'Done,' said Donald Farfrae.

The face of Mr Henchard beamed forth a satisfaction that was almost fierce in its strength. 'Now you are my friend!' he exclaimed. 'Come back to my house; let's clinch it at once by clear terms, so as to be comfortable in our minds.' Farfrae caught up his bag and retraced the North-West Avenue in Henchard's company as he had come. Henchard was all confidence now.

'I am the most distant fellow in the world when I don't care for a man,' he said. 'But when a man takes my fancy he takes it strong. Now I am sure you can eat another breakfast? You couldn't have eaten much so early, even if they had anything at that place to gi'e thee, which they hadn't; so come to my house and we will have a solid, staunch tuck-in, and settle terms in black-and-white if you like; though my word's my bond. I can always make a good meal in the morning. I've got a splendid cold pigeon-pie going just now. You can have some home-brewed if you want to, you know.'

'It is too airly in the morning for that,' said Farfrae with a smile.

'Well, of course, I didn't know. I don't drink it because of my oath; but I am obliged to brew for my work-people.'

Thus talking they returned, and entered Henchard's premises by the back way or traffic entrance. Here the matter was settled over the breakfast, at which Henchard heaped the young Scotchman's plate to a prodigal fulness. He would not rest satisfied till Farfrae had written for his luggage from Bristol, and despatched the letter to the post-office. When it was done this man of strong impulses declared that his new friend should take up his abode in his house – at least till some suitable lodgings could be found.

He then took Farfrae round and showed him the place, and the stores of grain, and other stock; and finally entered the offices where the younger of them has already been discovered by Elizabeth.

Chapter 10

While she still sat under the Scotchman's eyes, a man came up to the door, reaching it as Henchard opened the door of the inner office to admit Elizabeth. The new-comer stepped forward like the quicker cripple at Bethesda,* and entered in her stead. She could hear his words to Henchard: 'Joshua Jopp, sir – by appointment – the new manager.'

'The new manager! – he's in his office,' said Henchard bluntly.

'In his office!' said the man, with a stultified air.

'I mentioned Thursday,' said Henchard; 'and as you did not keep your appointment, I have engaged another manager. At first I thought he must be you. Do you think I can wait when business is in question?'

'You said Thursday or Saturday, sir,' said the new-comer, pulling out a letter.

'Well, you are too late,' said the corn-factor. 'I can say no more.'

'You as good as engaged me,' murmured the man.

'Subject to an interview,' said Henchard. 'I am sorry for you – very sorry indeed. But it can't be helped.'

There was no more to be said, and the man came out, encountering Elizabeth-Jane in his passage. She could see that his mouth twitched with anger, and that bitter disappointment was written in his face everywhere.

Elizabeth-Jane now entered, and stood before the master of the premises. His dark pupils – which always seemed to have a red spark of light in them, though this could hardly be a physical fact – turned indifferently round under his dark brows until they rested on her figure. 'Now then, what is it, my young woman?' he said blandly.

'Can I speak to you – not on business, sir?' said she.

'Yes – I suppose.' He looked at her more thoughtfully.

'I am sent to tell you, sir,' she innocently went on, 'that a distant relative of yours by marriage, Susan Newson, a sailor's widow, is in the town; and to ask whether you would wish to see her.'

The rich *rouge-et-noir** of his countenance underwent a slight change. 'Oh – Susan is – still alive?' he asked with difficulty.

'Yes, sir.'

'Are you her daughter?'

'Yes sir – her only daughter.'

'What – do you call yourself – your Christian name?'

'Elizabeth-Jane, sir.'

'Newson?'

'Elizabeth-Jane Newson.'

This at once suggested to Henchard that the transaction of his early married life at Weydon Fair was unrecorded in the family history. It was more than he could have expected. His wife had behaved kindly to him in return for his unkindness, and had never proclaimed her wrong to her child or to the world.

'I am – a good deal interested in your news,' he said. 'And as this is not a matter of business, but pleasure, suppose we go indoors.'

It was with a gentle delicacy of manner, surprising to Elizabeth, that he showed her out of the office and through the outer room, where Donald Farfare was overhauling bins and samples with the inquiring inspection of a beginner in charge. Henchard preceded her through the door in the wall to the suddenly changed scene of the garden and flowers, and onward into the house. The dining-room to which he introduced her still exhibited the remnants of the lavish breakfast laid for Farfrae. It was furnished to profusion with heavy mahogany furniture of the deepest red-Spanish hues. Pembroke tables,* with leaves hanging so low that they well-nigh touched the floor, stood against the walls on legs and feet shaped like those of an elephant, and on one lay three huge folio volumes – a Family Bible, a 'Josephus',* and a 'Whole Duty of Man'.* In the chimney corner was a fire-grate with a fluted semicircular back, having urns and festoons cast in relief thereon; and the chairs were of the kind which, since that day, has cast lustre upon the names of Chippendale and Sheraton,* though, in point of fact, their patterns may have been such as those illustrious carpenters never saw or heard of.

'Sit down – Elizabeth-Jane – sit down,' he said, with a shake in his voice as he uttered her name; and sitting down himself he allowed his hands to hang between his knees, while he looked upon the carpet. 'Your mother, then, is quite well?'

'She is rather worn out, sir, with travelling.'

'A sailor's widow – when did he die?'

'Father was lost last spring.'*

Henchard winced at the word 'father', thus applied. 'Do you and she come from abroad – America or Australia?' he asked.

'No. We have been in England some years. I was twelve when we came here from Canada.'

'Ah; exactly.' By such conversation he discovered the circumstances which had enveloped his wife and her child in such total obscurity that he had long ago believed them to be in their graves. These things being clear, he returned to the present. 'And where is your mother staying?'

'At the Three Mariners.'

'And you are her daughter Elizabeth-Jane?' repeated Henchard. He arose, came close to her, and glanced in her face. 'I think,' he said, suddenly turning away with a wet eye, 'you shall take a note from me to your mother. I should like to see her . . . She is not left very well off by her late husband?' His eye fell on Elizabeth's clothes, which, though a respectable suit of black, and her very best, were decidedly old-fashioned even to Casterbridge eyes.

'Not very well,' she said, glad that he had divined this without her being obliged to express it.

He sat down at the table and wrote a few lines; next taking from his pocket-book a five-pound note, which he put in the envelope with the letter, adding to it, as by an after-thought, five shillings. Sealing the whole up carefully, he directed it to 'Mrs Newson, Three Mariners Inn,' and handed the packet to Elizabeth.

'Deliver it to her personally, please,' said Henchard. 'Well, I am glad to see you here, Elizabeth-Jane – very glad. We must have a long talk together – but not just now.'

He took her hand at parting, and held it so warmly that she, who had known so little friendship, was much affected, and tears rose to her aerial-grey eyes. The instant that she was gone Henchard's state showed itself more distinctly; having shut the door he sat in his dining-room stiffly erect, gazing at the opposite wall as if he read his history there.

'Begad!' he suddenly exclaimed, jumping up. 'I didn't think of that. Perhaps these are impostors – and Susan and the child dead after all!'

However, a something in Elizabeth-Jane soon assured him that, as regarded her, at least, there could be little doubt. And a few hours would settle the question of her mother's identity; for he had arranged in his note to see her that evening.

'It never rains but it pours!' said Henchard. His keenly excited interest in his new friend the Scotchman was now eclipsed by this event; and Donald Farfrae saw so little of him during the rest of the day that he wondered at the suddenness of his employer's moods.

In the meantime Elizabeth had reached the inn. Her mother, instead of taking the note with the curiosity of a poor woman expecting assistance, was much moved at sight of it. She did not read it at once, asking Elizabeth to describe her reception, and the very words Mr Henchard used, Elizabeth's back was turned when her mother opened the letter. It ran thus:—

> Meet me at eight o'clock this evening, if you can, at the Ring on the Budmouth road. The place is easy to find. I can say no more now. The news upsets me almost. The girl seems to be in ignorance. Keep her so till I have seen you.
>
> M.H.

He said nothing about the enclosure of five guineas. The amount was significant; it may tacitly have said to her that he bought her back again. She waited restlessly for the close of the day, telling Elizabeth-Jane that she was invited to see Mr Henchard; that she would go alone. But she said nothing to show that the place of meeting was not at his house, nor did she hand the note to Elizabeth.

Chapter 11

The Ring at Casterbridge* was merely the local name of one of the finest Roman Amphitheatres, if not the very finest, remaining in Britain.

Casterbridge announced old Rome in every street, alley, and precinct. It looked Roman, bespoke the art of Rome, concealed dead men of Rome. It was impossible to dig more than a foot or two deep about the town fields and gardens without coming upon some tall soldier or other of the Empire, who had lain there in his silent unobtrusive rest for a space of fifteen hundred years. He was mostly found lying on his side, in an oval scoop in the chalk, like a chicken in its shell; his knees drawn up to his chest; sometimes with the remains of his spear against his arm; a fibula* or brooch of bronze on his breast or forehead; an urn at his knees, a jar at his throat, a bottle at his mouth; and mystified conjecture pouring down upon him from the eyes of Casterbridge street boys and men, who had turned a moment to gaze at the familiar spectacle as they passed by.

Imaginative inhabitants, who would have felt an unpleasantness at the discovery of a comparatively modern skeleton in their gardens, were quite unmoved by these hoary shapes. They had lived so long ago, their time was so unlike the present, their hopes and motives were so widely removed from ours, that between them and the living there seemed to stretch a gulf too wide for even a spirit to pass.

The Amphitheatre was a huge circular enclosure, with a notch at opposite extremities of its diameter north and south. From its sloping internal form it might have been called the spittoon of the Jötuns.* It was to Casterbridge what the ruined Coliseum is to modern Rome, and was nearly of the same magnitude. The dusk of evening was the proper hour at which a true impression of this suggestive place could be received. Standing in the middle of the arena at that time there by degrees became apparent its real vastness, which a cursory view from the summit at noon-day was apt to obscure. Melancholy, impressive, lonely, yet accessible from every part of the town, the historic circle was the frequent spot for appointments of a furtive kind. Intrigues were arranged there; tentative meetings were there experimented after divisions and feuds. But one kind of appointment – in itself the most common of any – seldom had place in the Amphitheatre: that of happy lovers.

Why, seeing that it was pre-eminently an airy, accessible, and sequestered spot for interviews, the cheerfullest form of those occurrences never took kindly to the soil of the ruin, would be a curious inquiry. Perhaps it was because its associations had about them something sinister. Its history proved that. Apart from the sanguinary nature of the games originally played therein, such incidents attached to its past as these: that for scores of years the town-gallows had stood at one corner; that in 1705 a woman who had murdered her husband* was half-strangled and then burnt there in the presence of ten thousand spectators. Tradition reports that at a certain stage of the burning her heart burst and leapt out of her body, to the terror of them all, and that not one of those ten thousand people ever cared particularly for hot roast after that. In addition to these old tragedies, pugilistic encounters almost to the death had come off down to recent dates in that secluded arena, entirely invisible to the outside world save by climbing to the top of the enclosure, which few townspeople in the daily round of their lives ever took the trouble to do. So that, though close to the turnpike-road, crimes might be perpetrated there unseen at mid-day.

Some boys had latterly tried to impart gaiety to the ruin by using the central arena as a cricket-ground. But the game usually languished for the aforesaid reason – the dismal privacy which the earthen circle enforced, shutting out every appreciative passer's vision, every commendatory remark from outsiders – everything, except the sky; and to play at games in such circumstances was like acting to an empty house. Possibly, too, the boys were timid, for some old people said that at certain moments in the summer time, in broad daylight, persons sitting with a book or dozing in the arena had, on lifting their eyes, beheld the slopes lined with a gazing legion of Hadrian's* soldiery as if watching the gladiatorial combat; and had heard the roar of their excited voices; that the scene would remain but a moment, like a lightning flash, and then disappear.

It was related that there still remained under the south entrance excavated cells for the reception of the wild animals and athletes who took part in the games. The arena was still smooth and circular, as if used for its original purpose not so very long ago. The sloping pathways by which spectators had ascended to their seats were pathways yet. But the whole was grown over with grass, which now, at the end of summer, was bearded with withered bents* that formed waves under the brush of the wind, returning to the attentive ear Æolian* modulations, and detaining for moments the flying globes of thistledown.

Henchard had chosen this spot as being the safest from observation which he could think of for meeting his long-lost wife, and at the same time as one easily to be found by a stranger after nightfall. As Mayor of the town, with a reputation to keep up, he could not invite her to come to his house till some definite course had been decided on.

Just before eight he approached the deserted earthwork, and entered by the south path which descended over the *débris* of the former dens. In a few moments he could discern a female figure creeping in by the great north gap, or public gateway. They met in the middle of the arena. Neither spoke just at first – there was no necessity for speech – and the poor woman leant against Henchard, who supported her in his arms.

'I don't drink,' he said in a low, halting, apologetic voice. 'You hear, Susan? – I don't drink now – I haven't since that night.' Those were his first words.

He felt her bow her head in acknowledgement that she understood. After a minute or two he again began:

'If I had known you were living, Susan! But there was every reason to suppose you and the child were dead and gone. I took every possible step to find you – travelled – advertised. My opinion at last was that you had started for some colony with that man, and had been drowned on your voyage out. Why did you keep silent like this?'

'O Michael! because of him – what other reason could there be? I thought I owed him faithfulness to the end of one of our lives – foolishly I believed there was something solemn and binding in the bargain; I thought that even in honour I dared not desert him when he had paid so much for me in good faith. I meet you now only as his widow – I consider myself that, and that I have no claim upon you. Had he not died I should never have come – never! Of that you may be sure.'

'Ts-s-s! How could you be so simple?'

'I don't know. Yet it would have been very wicked – if I had not thought like that!' said Susan, almost crying.

'Yes – yes – so it would. It is only that which makes me feel 'ee an innocent woman. But – to lead me into this!'

'What, Michael?' she asked, alarmed.

'Why, this difficulty about our living together again, and Elizabeth-Jane. She cannot be told all – she would so despise us both that – I could not bear it!'

'That was why she was brought up in ignorance of you. I could not bear it either.'

'Well – we must talk of a plan for keeping her in her present belief, and getting matters straight in spite of it. You have heard I am in a large way of business here – that I am Mayor of the town, and churchwarden, and I don't know what all?'

'Yes,' she murmured.

'These things, as well as the dread of the girl discovering our disgrace, make it necessary to act with extreme caution. So that I don't see how you two can return openly to my house as the wife and daughter I once treated badly, and banished from me; and there's the rub o't.'

'We'll go away at once. I only came to see –'

'No, no, Susan; you are not to go – you mistake me!' he said, with kindly severity. 'I have thought of this plan: that you and Elizabeth take a cottage in the town as the widow Mrs Newson and her daughter; that I meet you, court you, and marry you, Elizabeth-Jane coming to my house as my step-daughter. The thing is so natural and easy that it is half done in thinking o't. This would leave my shady, headstrong, disgraceful life as a young man absolutely unopened; the secret would be yours and mine only; and I should have the pleasure of seeing my own only child under my roof, as well as my wife.'

'I am quite in your hands, Michael,' she said meekly. 'I came here for the sake of Elizabeth; for myself, if you tell me to leave again tomorrow morning, and never come near you more, I am content to go.'

'Now, now; we don't want to hear that,' said Henchard gently. 'Of course you won't leave again. Think over the plan I have proposed for a few hours; and if you can't hit upon a better one we'll adopt it. I have to be away for a day or two on business, unfortunately; but during that time you can get lodgings – the only ones in the town fit for you are those over the china-shop in High Street – and you can also look for a cottage.'

'If the lodgings are in High Street they are dear, I suppose?'

'Never mind – you *must* start genteel if our plan is to be carried out. Look to me for money. Have you enough till I come back?'

'Quite,' said she.

'And are you comfortable at the inn?'

'O yes.'

'And the girl is quite safe from learning the shame of her case and ours? – that's what makes me most anxious of all.'

'You would be surprised to find how unlikely she is to dream of the truth. How could she ever suppose such a thing?'

'True!'

'I like the idea of repeating our marriage,' said Mrs Henchard, after a pause. 'It seems the only right course, after all this. Now I think I must go back to Elizabeth-Jane, and tell her that our kinsman, Mr Henchard, kindly wishes us to stay in the town.'

'Very well – arrange that yourself. I'll go some way with you.'

'No, no. Don't run any risk!' said his wife anxiously. 'I can find my way back – it is not late. Please let me go alone.'

'Right,' said Henchard. 'But just one word. Do you forgive me, Susan?'

She murmured something; but seemed to find it difficult to frame her answer.

'Never mind – all in good time,' said he. 'Judge me by my future works – good-bye!'

He retreated, and stood at the upper side of the Amphitheatre while his wife passed out through the lower way, and descended under the trees to the town. Then Henchard himself went homeward, going so fast that by the time he reached his door he was almost upon the heels of the unconscious woman from whom he had just parted. He watched her up the street, and turned into his house.

Chapter 12

On entering his own door after watching his wife out of sight, the Mayor walked on through the tunnel-shaped passage into the garden, and thence by the back door towards the stores and granaries. A light shone from the office-window, and there being no blind to screen the interior Henchard could see Donald Farfrae still seated where he had left him, initiating himself into the managerial work of the house by overhauling the books. Henchard entered, merely observing, 'Don't let me interrupt you, if ye will stay so late.'

He stood behind Farfrae's chair, watching his dexterity in clearing up the numerical fogs which had been allowed to grow so thick in Henchard's books as almost to baffle even the Scotchman's perspicacity. The corn-factor's mien was half admiring, and yet it was not without a dash of pity for the tastes of any one who could care to give his mind to such finnikin details. Henchard himself was mentally and physically unfit for grubbing subtleties from soiled paper; he had in a modern sense received the education of Achilles,* and found penmanship a tantalizing art.

'You shall do no more to-night,' he said at length, spreading his great hand over the paper. 'There's time enough to-morrow. Come indoors with me and have some supper. Now you shall! I am determined on't.' He shut the account-books with friendly force.

Donald had wished to get to his lodgings; but he already saw that his friend and employer was a man who knew no moderation in his requests and impulses, and he yielded gracefully. He liked

Henchard's warmth, even if it inconvenienced him; the great difference in their characters adding to the liking.

They locked up the office, and the young man followed his companion through the private little door which, admitting directly into Henchard's garden, permitted a passage from the utilitarian to the beautiful at one step. The garden was silent, dewy, and full of perfume. It extended a long way back from the house, first as lawn and flower-beds, then as fruit-garden, where the long-tied espaliers,* as old as the old house itself, had grown so stout, and cramped, and gnarled that they had pulled their stakes out of the ground and stood distorted and writhing in vegetable agony, like leafy Laocoöns.* The flowers which smelt so sweetly were not discernible; and they passed through them into the house.

The hospitalities of the morning were repeated, and when they were over Henchard said, 'Pull your chair round to the fireplace, my dear fellow, and let's make a blaze – there's nothing I hate like a black grate, even in September.' He applied a light to the laid-in fuel, and a cheerful radiance spread around.

'It is odd,' said Henchard, 'that two men should meet as we have done on a purely business ground, and that at the end of the first day I should wish to speak to 'ee on a family matter. But, damn it all, I am a lonely man, Farfrae: I have nobody else to speak to; and why shouldn't I tell it to 'ee?'

'I'll be glad to hear it, if I can be of any service,' said Donald, allowing his eyes to travel over the intricate wood-carvings of the chimney-piece, representing garlanded lyres, shields, and quivers, on either side of a draped ox-skull, and flanked by heads of Apollo and Diana in low relief.

'I've not been always what I am now,' continued Henchard, his firm deep voice being ever so little shaken. He was plainly under that strange influence which sometimes prompts men to confide to the new-found friend what they will not tell to the old. 'I began life as a working hay-trusser, and when I was eighteen I married on the strength o' my calling. Would you think me a married man?'

'I heard in the town that you were a widower.'

'Ah, yes – you would naturally have heard that. Well, I lost my wife nineteen years ago or so – by my own fault . . . This is how it came about. One summer evening I was travelling for employment, and she was walking at my side, carrying the baby, our only child. We came to a booth in a country fair. I was a drinking man at that time.'

Henchard paused a moment, threw himself back so that his elbow rested on the table, his forehead being shaded by his hand, which, however, did not hide the marks of introspective inflexibility on his features as he narrated in fullest detail the incidents of the transaction with the sailor. The tinge of indifference which had at first been visible in the Scotchman now disappeared.

Henchard went on to describe his attempts to find his wife; the oath he swore; the solitary life he led during the years which followed. 'I have kept my oath for nineteen years,' he went on; 'I have risen to what you see me now.'

'Ay!'

'Well – no wife could I hear of in all that time; and being by nature something of a woman-hater, I have found it no hardship to keep mostly at a distance from the sex. No wife could I hear of, I say, till this very day. And now – she has come back.'

'Come back, has she!'

'This morning – this very morning. And what's to be done?'

'Can ye no' take her and live with her, and make some amends?'

'That's what I've planned and proposed. But, Farfrae,' said Henchard gloomily, 'by doing right with Susan I wrong another innocent woman.'

'Ye don't say that?'

'In the nature of things, Farfrae, it is almost impossible that a man of my sort should have the good fortune to tide through twenty years o' life without making more blunders than one. It has been my custom for many years to run across to Jersey in the way of business, particularly in the potato and root season. I do a large trade wi' them in that line. Well, one autumn when stopping there I fell quite ill, and in my illness I sank into one of those gloomy fits I sometimes suffer from, on account o' the loneliness of my domestic life, when the world seems to have the blackness of hell, and, like Job, I could curse the day that gave me birth.'*

'Ah, no, I never feel like it,' said Farfrae.

'Then pray to God that you never may, young man. While in this state I was taken pity on by a woman – a young lady I should call her, for she was of good family, well bred, and well educated –the daughter of some harum-scarum military officer who had got into difficulties, and had his pay sequestrated.* He was dead now, and her mother too, and she was as lonely as I. This young creature was staying at the boarding-house where I happened to have my lodging; and when I was pulled down she took upon herself to nurse me. Heaven knows why, for I wasn't worth it. But being together in the same house, and her feelings warm, we got naturally intimate. I won't go into particulars of what our relations were. It is enough to say that we honestly meant to marry. There arose a scandal, which did me no harm, but was of course ruin to her. Though, Farfrae, between you and me, as man and man, I solemnly declare that philandering with womankind has neither been my vice nor my virtue. She was terribly careless of appearances, and I was perhaps more, because o' my dreary state; and it was through this that the scandal arose. At last I was well and came away. When I was gone she suffered much on my account, and didn't forget to tell me so in letters one after another; till, latterly, I felt I owed her something, and thought that, as I had not heard of Susan for so long, I would make this other one the only return I could make, and ask her if she would run the risk of Susan being alive (very slight as I believed) and marry me, such as I was. She jumped for joy, and we should no doubt soon have been married – but, behold, Susan appears!'

Donald showed his deep concern at a complication so far beyond the degree of his simple experiences.

'Now see what injury a man may cause around him! Even after that wrong-doing at the fair when I was young, if I had never been so selfish as to let this giddy girl devote herself to me over at Jersey, to the injury of her name, all might now be well. Yet, as it stands, I must bitterly disappoint one of these women; and it is the second. My first duty is to Susan – there's no doubt about that.'

'They are both in a very melancholy position, and that's true!' murmured Donald.

'They are! For myself I don't care – 'twill all end one way. But these two.' Henchard paused in reverie. 'I feel I should like to treat the second, no less than the first, as kindly as a man can in such a case.'

'Ah, well, it cannet be helped!' said the other, with philosophic woefulness. 'You mun write to the young lady, and in your letter you must put it plain and honest that it turns out she cannet be your wife, the first having come back; that ye cannet see her more; and that – ye wish her weel.'

'That won't do, 'Od seize it, I must do a little more than that! I must – though she did always brag about her rich uncle or rich aunt, and her expectations from 'em – I must send a useful sum of money to her, I suppose – just as a little recompense, poor girl . . . Now, will you help me in this, and draw up an explanation to her of all I've told ye, breaking it as gently as you can? I'm so bad at letters.'

'And I will.'

'Now, I haven't told you quite all yet. My wife Susan has my daughter with her – the baby that was in her arms at the fair; and this girl knows nothing of me beyond that I am some sort of relation by marriage. She has grown up in the belief that the sailor to whom I made over her mother, and who is now dead, was her father, and her mother's husband. What her mother has always felt, she and I together feel now – that we can't proclaim our disgrace to the girl by letting her know the truth. Now what would you do? – I want your advice.'

'I think I'd run the risk, and tell her the truth. She'll forgive ye both.'

'Never!' said Henchard. 'I am not going to let her know the truth. Her mother and I be going to marry again; and it will not only help us to keep our child's respect, but it will be more proper. Susan looks upon herself as the sailor's widow, and won't think o' living with me as formerly without another religious ceremony – and she's right.'

Farfrae thereupon said no more. The letter to the young Jersey woman was carefully framed by him, and the interview ended, Henchard saying, as the Scotchman left, 'I feel it a great relief, Farfrae, to tell some friend o' this! You see now that the Mayor of Casterbridge is not so thriving in his mind as it seems he might be from the state of his pocket.'

'I do. And I'm sorry for ye!' said Farfrae.

When he had gone Henchard copied the letter, and, enclosing a cheque, took it to the post-office, from which he walked back thoughtfully.

'Can it be that it will go off so easily!' he said. 'Poor thing – God knows! Now then, to make amends to Susan!'

Chapter 13

The cottage which Michael Henchard hired for his wife Susan under her name of Newson – in pursuance of their plan – was in the upper or western part of the town, near the Roman wall, and the avenue which overshadowed it. The evening sun seemed to shine more yellowly there than anywhere else this autumn – stretching its rays, as the hours grew later, under the lowest sycamore boughs, and steeping the ground-floor of the dwelling, with its green shutters, in a substratum of radiance which the foliage screened from the upper parts. Beneath these sycamores on the town walls could be seen from the sitting-room the tumuli* and earth forts of the distant uplands; making it altogether a pleasant spot, with the usual touch of melancholy that a past-marked prospect lends.

As soon as the mother and daughter were comfortably installed, with a white-aproned servant and all complete, Henchard paid them a visit, and remained to tea. During the entertainment Elizabeth was carefully hoodwinked by the very general tone of the conversation that prevailed – a proceeding which seemed to afford some humour to Henchard, though his wife was not particularly happy in it. The visit was repeated again and again with business-like determination by the Mayor, who seemed to have schooled himself into a course of strict mechanical rightness towards this woman of prior claim, at any expense to the later one and to his own sentiments.

One afternoon the daughter was not indoors when Henchard came, and he said drily, 'This is a very good opportunity for me to ask you to name the happy day, Susan.'

The poor woman smiled faintly; she did not enjoy pleasantries on a situation into which she had entered solely for the sake of her girl's reputation. She liked them so little, indeed, that there was room for wonder why she had countenanced deception at all, and had not bravely let the girl know her history. But the flesh is weak;* and the true explanation came in due course.

'O Michael!' she said, 'I am afraid all this is taking up your time and giving trouble – when I did not expect any such thing!' And she looked at him and at his dress as a man of affluence, and at the furniture he had provided for the room – ornate and lavish to her eyes.

'Not at all,' said Henchard, in rough benignity. 'This is only a cottage – it costs me next to nothing. And as to taking up my time' – here his red and black visage* kindled with satisfaction – 'I've a splendid fellow to superintend by business now – a man whose like I've never been able to lay hands on before. I shall soon be able to leave everything to him, and have more time to call my own than I've had for these last twenty years.'

Henchard's visits here grew so frequent and so regular that it soon became whispered, and then openly discussed, in Caster-bridge that the masterful, coercive Mayor of the town was captured and enervated by the genteel widow Mrs Newson. His well-known haughty indifference to the society of womankind, his silent avoidance of converse with the sex, contributed a piquancy to what would otherwise have been an unromantic matter enough. That such a poor fragile woman should be his choice was inexplicable, except on the ground that the engage-ment was a family affair in which sentimental passion had no place; for it was known that they were related in some way. Mrs Henchard was so pale that the boys called her 'The Ghost'. Sometimes Henchard overheard this epithet when they passed together along the Walks – as the avenues on the walls were named – at which his face would darken with an expression of destructiveness towards the speakers ominous to see; but he said nothing.

He pressed on the preparations for his union, or rather reunion, with this pale creature in a dogged, unflinching spirit which did credit to his conscientiousness. Nobody would have conceived from his outward demeanour that there was no amatory fire or pulse of romance acting as stimulant to the bustle going on in his gaunt, great house; nothing but three large resolves – one, to make amends to his neglected Susan; another, to provide a comfortable home for Elizabeth-Jane under his paternal eye; and a third, to castigate himself with the thorns which these restitu-tory acts brought in their train; among them the lowering of his dignity in public opinion by marrying so comparatively humble a woman.

Susan Henchard entered a carriage for the first time in her life when she stepped into the plain brougham* which drew up at the door on the wedding-day to take her and Elizabeth-Jane to church. It was a windless morning of warm November rain, which floated down like meal, and lay in a powdery form on the nap of hats and coats. Few people had gathered round the church door though they were all well packed within. The Scotchman, who assisted as groomsman, was of course the only one present, beyond the chief actors, who knew the true situation of the contracting parties. He, however, was too inexperienced, too thoughtful, too judicial, too strongly conscious of the serious side of the business, to enter into the scene in its dramatic aspect. That required the special genius of Christopher Coney, Solomon Longways, Buzzford, and their fellows. But they knew nothing of the secret; though, as the time for coming out of church drew on, they gathered on the pavement adjoining, and expounded the subject according to their lights.

' 'Tis five-and-forty years since I had my settlement in this here town,' said Coney; 'but daze me if ever I see a man wait so long before to take so little! There's a chance even for thee after this, Nance Mockridge.' The remark was addressed to a woman who stood behind his shoulder – the same who had exhibited Henchard's bad bread in public when Elizabeth and her mother entered Casterbridge.

'Be cust if I'd marry any such as he, or thee either,' replied that lady. 'As for thee, Christopher, we know what ye be, and the less said the better. And as for he – well, there – (lowering her voice) 'tis said 'a was a poor parish 'prentice – I wouldn't say it for all the world – but 'a was a poor parish 'prentice, that began life wi' no more belonging to 'en than a carrion crow.'

'And now he's worth ever so much a minute,' murmured Longways. 'When a man is said to be worth so much a minute, he's a man to be considered!'

Turning, he saw a circular disc reticulated with creases, and recognized the smiling countenance of the fat woman who had asked for another song at the Three Mariners. 'Well, Mother Cuxsom,' he said, 'how's this? Here's Mrs Newson, a mere skellinton, has got another husband to keep her, while a woman of your tonnage have not.'

'I have not. Nor another to beat me . . . Ah, yes, Cuxsom's gone, and so shall leather breeches!'*

'Yes; with the blessing of God leather breeches shall go.'

' 'Tisn't worth my old while to think of another husband,' continued Mrs Cuxsom. 'And yet I'll lay my life I'm as respectable born as she.'

'True; your mother was a very good woman – I can mind her.

She were rewarded by the Agricultural Society* for having begot the greatest number of healthy children without parish assistance, and other virtuous marvels.'

' 'Twas that that kept us so low upon ground – that great hungry family.'

'Ay. Where the pigs be many the wash* runs thin.'

'And dostn't mind how mother would sing, Christopher?' continued Mrs Cuxsom, kindling at the retrospection; 'and how we went with her to the party at Mellstock, do ye mind? – at old Dame Ledlow's, farmer Shiner's aunt, do ye mind? – she we used to call Toad-skin, because her face were so yaller and freckled, do ye mind?'

'I do, hee-hee, I do!' said Christopher Coney.

'And well do I – for I was getting up husband-high at that time – one half girl, and t'other half woman, as one may say. And canst mind' – she prodded Solomon's shoulder with her finger-tip, while her eyes twinkled between the crevices of their lids – 'canst mind the sherry-wine, and the zilver-snuffers,* and how Joan Dummett was took bad when we were coming home, and Jack Griggs was forced to carry her through the mud; and how 'a let her fall in Dairyman Sweetapple's cow-barton,* and we had to clane her gown wi' grass – never such a mess as 'a were in?'

'Ay – that I do – hee-hee, such doggery as there was in them ancient days, to be sure! Ah, the miles I used to walk then; and now I can hardly step over a furrow!'

Their reminiscences were cut short by the appearance of the reunited pair – Henchard looking round upon the idlers with that ambiguous gaze of his, which at one moment seemed to mean satisfaction, and at another fiery disdain.

'Well – there's a difference between 'em, though he do call himself a teetotaller,' said Nance Mockridge. 'She'll wish her cake dough* afore she's done of him. There's a bluebeardy* look about 'en; and 'twill out in time.'

'Stuff – he's well enough! Some folk want their luck buttered. If I had a choice as wide as the ocean sea I wouldn't wish for a better man. A poor twanking* woman like her – 'tis a godsend for her, and hardly a pair of jumps* or night-rail* to her name.'

The plain little brougham drove off in the mist, and the idlers dispersed. 'Well, we hardly know how to look at things in these times!' said Solomon. 'There was a man dropped down dead yesterday, not so very many miles from here; and what wi' that, and this moist weather, 'tis scarce worth one's while to begin any work o' consequence to-day. I'm in such a low key with drinking nothing but small table ninepenny* this last week or two that I shall call and warm up at the Mar'ners as I pass along.'

'I don't know but that I may as well go with 'ee, Solomon,' said Christopher; 'I'm as clammy as a cockle-snail.'*

Chapter 14

A Martinmas summer* of Mrs Henchard's life set in with her entry into her husband's large house and respectable social orbit; and it was as bright as such summers well can be. Lest she should pine for deeper affection than he could give he made a point of showing some semblance of it in external action. Among other things he had the iron railings, that had smiled sadly in dull rust for the last eighty years, painted a bright green, and the heavy-barred, small-paned Georgian sash windows enlivened with three coats of white. He was as kind to her as a man, mayor, and churchwarden could possibly be. The house was large, the rooms lofty, and the landings wide; and the two unassuming women scarcely made a perceptible addition to its contents.

To Elizabeth-Jane the time was a most triumphant one. The freedom she experienced, the indulgence with which she was treated, went beyond her expectations. The reposeful, easy, affluent life to which her mother's marriage had introduced her was, in truth, the beginning of a great change in Elizabeth. She found she could have nice personal possessions and ornaments for the asking, and, as the mediæval saying puts it, 'Take, have, and keep, are pleasant words.' With peace of mind came development, and with development beauty. Knowledge – the result of great natural insight – she did not lack; learning, accomplishments – those, alas, she had not; but as the winter and spring passed by her thin face and figure filled out in rounder and softer curves; the lines and contractions upon her young brow went away; the muddiness of skin which she had looked upon as her lot by nature departed with a change to abundance of good things, and a bloom came upon her cheek. Perhaps, too, her grey, thoughtful eyes revealed an arch gaiety sometimes; but this was infrequent; the sort of wisdom which looked from their pupils did not readily keep company with these lighter moods. Like all people who have known rough times, light-heartedness seemed to her too irrational and inconsequent to be indulged in except as a reckless dram now and then; for she had been too early habituated to anxious reasoning to drop the habit suddenly. She felt none of those ups and downs of spirit which beset so many people without cause; never – to paraphrase a recent poet* – never a gloom in Elizabeth-Jane's soul but she well knew how it came there; and her present cheerfulness was fairly proportionate to her solid guarantees for the same.

It might have been supposed that, given a girl rapidly becoming good-looking, comfortably circumstanced, and for the first time in her life commanding ready money, she would go and make a fool of herself by dress. But no. The reasonableness of almost everything that Elizabeth did was nowhere more conspicuous than in this question of clothes. To keep in the rear of opportunity in matters of indulgence is as valuable a habit as to keep abreast of opportunity in matters of enterprise. This unsophisticated girl did it by an innate perceptiveness that was almost genius. Thus she refrained from bursting out like a water-flower that spring, and clothing herself in puffings and knick-knacks, as most of the Casterbridge girls would have done in her circumstances. Her triumph was tempered by circumspection; she had still that fieldmouse fear of the coulter* of destiny despite fair promise, which is common among the thoughtful who have suffered early from poverty and oppression.

'I won't be too gay on any account,' she would say to herself. 'It would be tempting Providence to hurl mother and me down, and afflict us again as He used to do.'

We now see her in a black silk bonnet, velvet mantle or silk spencer,* dark dress, and carrying a sunshade. In this latter article she drew the line at fringe, and had it plain edged, with a little ivory ring for keeping it closed. It was odd about the necessity for that sunshade. She discovered that with the clarification of her complexion and the birth of pink cheeks her skin had grown more sensitive to the sun's rays. She protected those cheeks forthwith, deeming spotlessness part of womanliness.

Henchard had become very fond of her, and she went out with him more frequently than with her mother now. Her appearance one day was so attractive that he looked at her critically.

'I happened to have the ribbon by me, so I made it up,' she faltered, thinking him perhaps dissatisfied with some rather bright trimming she had donned for the first time.

'Ay – of course – to be sure,' he replied in his leonine* way. 'Do as you like – or rather as your mother advises ye. 'Od send – I've nothing to say to't!'

Indoors she appeared with her hair divided by a parting that arched like a white rainbow from ear to ear. All in front of this line was covered with a thick encampment of curls; all behind was dressed smoothly, and drawn to a knob.

The three members of the family were sitting at breakfast one day, and Henchard was looking silently, as he often did, at this head of hair, which in colour was brown – rather light than dark. 'I thought Elizabeth-Jane's hair – didn't you tell me that Elizabeth-Jane's hair promised to be black when she was a baby?' he said to his wife.

She looked startled, jerked her foot warningly, and murmured, 'Did I?'

As soon as Elizabeth was gone to her own room Henchard resumed. 'Begad, I nearly forgot myself just now! What I meant was that the girl's hair certainly looked as if it would be darker, when she was a baby.'

'It did; but they alter so,' replied Susan.

'Their hair gets darker, I know – but I wasn't aware it lightened ever?'

'O yes.' And the same uneasy expression came out on her face, to which the future held the key. It passed as Henchard went on:

'Well, so much the better. Now, Susan, I want to have her called Miss Henchard – not Miss Newson. Lots o' people do it already in carelessness – it is her legal name – so it may as well be made her usual name – I don't like t'other name at all for my own flesh and blood. I'll advertise it in the Casterbridge paper – that's the way they do it. She won't object.'

'No. O no. But –'

'Well, then, I shall do it,' said he, peremptorily. 'Surely, if she's willing, you must wish it as much as I?'

'O yes – if she agrees let us do it by all means,' she replied.

Then Mrs Henchard acted somewhat inconsistently; it might have been called falsely, but that her manner was emotional and full of the earnestness of one who wishes to do right at great hazard. She went to Elizabeth-Jane, whom she found sewing in her own sitting-room upstairs, and told her what had been proposed about her surname. 'Can you agree – is it not a slight upon Newson – now he's dead and gone?'

Elizabeth reflected. 'I'll think of it, mother,' she answered.

When, later in the day, she saw Henchard, she adverted to the matter at once, in a way which showed that the line of feeling started by her mother had been persevered in. 'Do you wish this change so very much, sir?' she asked.

'Wish it? Why, my blessed fathers, what an ado you women make about a trifle! I proposed it – that's all. Now, 'Lizabeth-Jane, just please yourself. Curse me if I care what you do. Now, you understand, don't 'ee go agreeing to it to please me.'

Here the subject dropped, and nothing more was said, and nothing was done, and Elizabeth still passed as Miss Newson, and not by her legal name.

Meanwhile the great corn and hay traffic conducted by Henchard throve under the management of Donald Farfrae as it had never thriven before. It had formerly moved in jolts; now it went on oiled castors. The old crude *vivâ voce** system of Henchard, in which everything depended upon his memory, and bargains were made by the tongue alone, was swept away. Letters and ledgers took the place of 'I'll do't', and 'you shall hae't'; and, as in all such cases of advance, the rugged picturesqueness of the old method disappeared with its inconveniences.

The position of Elizabeth-Jane's room – rather high in the house, so that it commanded a view of the hay-stores and granaries across the garden – afforded her opportunity for accurate observation of what went on there. She saw that Donald and Mr Henchard were inseparables. When walking together Henchard would lay his arm familiarly on his manager's shoulder, as if Farfrae were a younger brother, bearing so heavily that his slight figure bent under the weight. Occasionally she would hear a perfect cannonade of laughter from Henchard, arising from something Donald had said, the latter looking quite innocent and not laughing at all. In Henchard's somewhat lonely life he evidently found the young man as desirable for comradeship as he was useful for consultations. Donald's brightness of intellect maintained in the corn-factor the admiration it had won at the first hour of their meeting. The poor opinion, and but ill-concealed, that he entertained of the slim Farfrae's physical girth, strength, and dash was more than counterbalanced by the immense respect he had for his brains.

Her quiet eye discerned that Henchard's tigerish* affection for the younger man, his constant liking to have Farfrae near him, now and then resulted in a tendency to domineer, which, however, was checked in a moment when Donald exhibited marks of real offence. One day, looking down on their figures from on high, she heard the latter remark, as they stood in the doorway between the garden and yard, that their habit of walking and driving about together rather neutralized Farfrae's value as a second pair of eyes, which should be used in places where the principal was not. ' 'Od damn it,' cried Henchard, 'what's all the world! I like a fellow to talk to. Now come along and hae some supper, and don't take too much thought about things, or ye'll drive me crazy.'

When she walked with her mother, on the other hand, she often beheld the Scotchman looking at them with a curious interest. The fact that he had met her at the Three Mariners was insufficient to account for it, since on the occasions on which she had entered his room he had never raised his eyes. Besides, it was at her mother more particularly than at herself that he looked, to Elizabeth-Jane's half-conscious, simple-minded, perhaps pardonable, disappointment. Thus she could not account for this interest by her own attractiveness, and she decided that it might be apparant only – a way of turning his eyes that Mr Farfrae had.

She did not divine the ample explanation of his manner, without personal vanity, that was afforded by the fact of Donald being the depositary of Henchard's confidence in respect of his past treatment of the pale, chastened mother who walked by her side. Her conjectures on that past never went further than faint ones based on things casually heard and seen – mere guesses that Henchard and her mother might have been lovers in their younger days, who had quarrelled and parted.

Casterbridge, as has been hinted, was a place deposited in the block upon a corn-field. There was no suburb in the modern sense, or transitional intermixture of town and down. It stood, with regard to the wide fertile land adjoining, clean-cut and distinct, like a chess-board on a green table-cloth. The farmer's boy could sit under his barley-mow* and pitch a stone into the office-window of the town-clerk; reapers at work among the sheaves nodded to acquaintances standing on the pavement-corner; the red-robed judge, when he condemned a sheep-stealer, pronounced sentence to the tune of Baa, that floated in at the window from the remainder of the flock browsing hard by; and at executions the waiting crowd stood in a meadow immediately before the drop, out of which the cows had been temporarily driven to give the spectators room.

The corn grown on the uplands side of the borough was garnered by farmers who lived in an eastern purlieu called Durnover. Here wheat-ricks overhung the old Roman street, and thrust their eaves against the church tower; green-thatched barns, with doorways as high as the gates of Solomon's temple,* opened directly upon the main thoroughfare. Barns indeed were so numerous as to alternate with every half-dozen houses along the way. Here lived burgesses who daily walked the fallow; shepherds in an intra-mural squeeze. A street of farmers' homesteads – a street ruled by a mayor and corporation, yet echoing with the thump of the flail, the flutter of the winnowing-fan, and the purr of the milk into the pails – a street which had nothing urban in it whatever – this was the Durnover end of Casterbridge.

Henchard, as was natural, dealt largely with this nursery or bed of small farmers close at hand – and his waggons were often down that way. One day, when arrangements were in progress for getting home corn from one of the aforesaid farms, Elizabeth-Jane received a note by hand, asking her to oblige the writer by coming at once to a granary on Durnover Hill. As this was the granary whose contents Henchard was removing, she thought the request had something to do with his business, and proceeded thither as soon as she had put on her bonnet. The granary was just within the farm-yard, and stood on stone staddles,* high enough for persons to walk under. The gates were open, but nobody was within. However, she entered and waited. Presently she saw a figure approaching the gate – that of Donald Farfrae. He looked up at the church clock, and came in. By some unaccountable shyness, some wish not to meet him there alone, she quickly ascended the step-ladder leading to the granary door, and entered it before he had seen her. Farfrae advanced, imagining himself in solitude; and a few drops of rain beginning to fall he moved and stood under the shelter where she had just been standing. Here he leant against one of the staddles, and gave himself up to patience. He, too, was plainly expecting some one; could it be herself? if so, why? In a few minutes he looked at his watch, and then pulled out a note, a duplicate of the one she had herself received.

The situation began to be very awkward, and the longer she waited the more awkward it became. To emerge from a door just above his head and descend the ladder, and show she had been in hiding there, would look so very foolish that she still waited on. A winnowing machine stood close beside her, and to relieve her suspense she gently moved the handle; whereupon a cloud of wheat husks flew out into her face, and covered her clothes and bonnet, and stuck into the fur of her victorine.* He must have heard the slight movement for he looked up, and then ascended the steps.

'Ah – it's Miss Newson,' he said as soon as he could see into the granary. 'I didn't know you were there. I have kept the appointment, and am at your service.'

'O Mr Farfrae,' she faltered; 'so have I. But I didn't know it was you who wished to see me, otherwise I –'

'I wished to see you? O no – at least, that is, I am afraid there may be a mistake.'

'Didn't you ask me to come here? Didn't you write this?' Elizabeth held out her note.

'No. Indeed, at no hand would I have thought of it! And for you – didn't you ask me? This is not your writing?' And he held up his.

'By no means.'

'And is that really so! Then it's somebody wanting to see us both. Perhaps we would do well to wait a little longer.'

Acting on this consideration they lingered, Elizabeth-Jane's face being arranged to an expression of preternatural composure, and the young Scot, at every footstep in the street without, looking from under the granary to see if the passer were about to enter and declare himself their summoner. They watched individual drops of rain creeping down the thatch of the opposite rick – straw after straw – till they reached the bottom; but nobody came, and the granary roof began to drip.

'The person is not likely to be coming,' said Farfrae. 'It's a trick perhaps, and if so, it's a great pity to waste our time like this, and so much to be done.'

' 'Tis a great liberty,' said Elizabeth.

'It's true, Miss Newson. We'll hear news of this some day, depend on't, and who it was that did it. I wouldn't stand for it hindering myself; but you, Miss Newson –'

'I don't mind – much,' she replied.

'Neither do I.'

They lapsed again into silence. 'You are anxious to get back to Scotland, I suppose, Mr Farfrae?' she inquired.

'O no, Miss Newson. Why should I be?'

'I only supposed you might be from the song you sang at the Three Mariners – about Scotland and home, I mean – which you seemed to feel so deep down in your heart; so that we all felt for you.'

'Ay – and I did sing there – I did – But, Miss Newson' – and Donald's voice musically undulated between two semitones, as it always did when he became earnest – 'it's well you feel a song for a few minutes, and your eyes they get quite tearful; but you finish it, and for all you felt you don't mind it or think of it again for a long while. O no, I don't want to go back! Yet I'll sing the song to you wi' pleasure whenever you like. I could sing it now, and not mind at all?'

'Thank you, indeed. But I fear I must go – rain or no.'

'Ay! Then, Miss Newson, ye had better say nothing about this hoax, and take no heed of it. And if the person should say anything to you, be civil to him or her, as if you did not mind it – so you'll take the clever person's laugh away.' In speaking his eyes became fixed upon her dress, still sown with wheat husks. 'There's husks and dust on you. Perhaps you don't know it?' he said, in tones of extreme delicacy. 'And it's very bad to let rain come upon clothes when there's chaff on them. It washes in and spoils them. Let me help you – blowing is the best.'

As Elizabeth neither assented nor dissented Donald Farfrae began blowing her back hair, and her side hair, and her neck, and the crown of her bonnet, and the fur of her victorine, Elizabeth saying, 'O, thank you,' at every puff. At last she was fairly clean, though Farfrae, having got over his first concern at the situation, seemed in no manner of hurry to be gone.

'Ah – now I'll go and get ye an umbrella,' he said.

She declined the offer, stepped out and was gone. Farfrae walked slowly after, looking thoughtfully at her diminishing figure, and whistling in undertones, 'As I came down through Cannobie'.*

Chapter 15

At first Miss Newson's budding beauty was not regarded with much interest by anybody in Casterbridge. Donald Farfrae's gaze, it is true, was now attracted by the Mayor's so-called step-daughter, but he was only one. The truth is that she was but a poor illustrative instance of the prophet Baruch's sly definition:* 'The virgin that loveth to go gay'.

When she walked abroad she seemed to be occupied with an inner chamber of ideas, and to have slight need for visible objects. She formed curious resolves on checking gay fancies in the matter of clothes, because it was inconsistent with her past life to blossom gaudily the moment she had become possessed of money. But nothing is more insidious than the evolution of wishes from mere fancies, and of wants from mere wishes. Henchard gave Elizabeth-Jane a box of delicately-tinted gloves one spring day. She wanted to wear them to show her appreciation of his kindness, but she had no bonnet that would harmonize. As an artistic indulgence she thought she would have such a bonnet. When she had a bonnet that would go with the gloves she had no dress that would go with the bonnet. It was now absolutely necessary to finish; she ordered the requisite article, and found that she had no sunshade to go with the dress. In for a penny in for a pound; she bought the sunshade, and the whole structure was at last complete.

Everybody was attracted, and some said that her bygone simplicity was the art that conceals art, the 'delicate imposition' of Rochefoucauld;* she had produced an effect, a contrast, and it had been done on purpose. As a matter of fact this was not true, but it had its result; for as soon as Casterbridge thought her artful it thought her worth notice. 'It is the first time in my life that I have been so much admired,' she said to herself; 'though perhaps it is by those whose admiration is not worth having.'

But Donald Farfrae admired her, too; and altogether the time was an exciting one; sex had never before asserted itself in her so strongly, for in former days she had perhaps been too imperson-ally human to be distinctively feminine. After an unprecedented success one day she came indoors, went upstairs, and leant upon her bed face downwards, quite forgetting the possible creasing and damage. 'Good Heaven,' she whispered, 'can it be? Here am I setting up as the town beauty!'

When she had thought it over, her usual fear of exaggerating appearances engendered a deep sadness. 'There is something wrong in all this,' she mused. 'If they only knew what an unfinished girl I am – that I can't talk Italian, or use globes, or show any of the accomplishments they learn at boarding-schools, how they would despise me! Better sell all this finery and buy myself grammar-books and dictionaries and a history of all the philosophies!'

She looked from the window and saw Henchard and Farfrae in the hay-yard talking, with that impetuous cordiality on the Mayor's part, and genial modesty on the younger man's, that was now so generally observable in their intercourse. Friendship between man and man; what a rugged strength there was in it, as evinced by these two. And yet the seed that was to lift the foundation of this friendship was at that moment taking root in a chink of its structure.

It was about six o'clock; the men were dropping off homeward one by one. The last to leave was a round shouldered, blinking young man of nineteen or twenty, whose mouth fell ajar on the slightest provocation, seemingly because there was no chin to support it. Henchard called aloud to him as he went out of the gate. 'Here – Abel Whittle!'

Whittle turned, and ran back a few steps. 'Yes, sir,' he said, in breathless deprecation, as if he knew what was coming next.

'Once more – be in time to-morrow morning. You see what's to be done, and you hear what I say, and you know I'm not going to be trifled with any longer.'

'Yes, sir.' Then Abel Whittle left, and Henchard and Farfrae; and Elizabeth saw no more of them.

Now there was good reason for this command on Henchard's part. Poor Abel, as he was called, had an inveterate habit of oversleeping himself and coming late to his work. His anxious will was to be among the earliest; but if this comrades omitted to pull the string that he always tied round his great toe and left hanging out of the window for that purpose, his will was as wind. He did not arrive in time.

As he was often second hand at the hay-weighing, or at the crane which lifted the sacks, or was one of those who had to accompany the waggons into the country to fetch away stacks that had been purchased, this affliction of Abel's was productive of much inconvenience. For two mornings in the present week he had kept the others waiting nearly an hour; hence Henchard's threat. It now remained to be seen what would happen tomorrow.

Six o'clock struck, and there was no Whittle. At half-past six Henchard entered the yard; the waggon was horsed that Abel was to accompany; and the other man had been waiting twenty minutes. Then Henchard swore, and Whittle coming up breathless at that instant, the corn-factor turned on him, and declared with an oath that this was the last time; that if he were behind once more, by God, he would come and drag him out o' bed.

'There is sommit wrong in my make, your worshipful!' said Abel, 'especially in the inside, whereas my poor dumb brain gets as dead as a clot afore I've said my few scrags* of prayers. Yes – it came on as a stripling, just afore I'd got man's wages, whereas I never enjoy my bed at all, for no sooner do I lie down than I be asleep, and afore I be awake I be up. I've fretted my gizzard green* about it, maister, but what can I do? Now last night, afore I went to bed, I only had a scantling* o' cheese and –'

'I don't want to hear it!' roared Henchard. 'To-morrow the waggons must start at four, and if you're not here, stand clear. I'll mortify thy flesh for thee!'

'But let me clear up my points, your worshipful –'

Henchard turned away.

'He asked me and he questioned me, and then 'a wouldn't hear my points!' said Abel, to the yard in general. 'Now, I shall twitch like a moment-hand* all night to-night for fear o' him!'

The journey to be taken by the waggons next day was a long one into Blackmoor Vale,* and at four o'clock lanterns were moving about the yard. But Abel was missing. Before either of the other men could run to Abel's and warn him, Henchard appeared in the garden doorway. 'Where's Abel Whittle? Not come after all I've said? Now I'll carry out my word, by my blessed fathers – nothing else will do him any good! I'm going up that way.'

Henchard went off, entered Abel's house, a little cottage in Back Street, the door of which was never locked because the inmates had nothing to lose. Reaching Whittle's bedside the corn-factor shouted a bass note so vigorously that Abel started up instantly, and beholding Henchard standing over him, was galvanized into spasmodic movements which had not much relation to getting on his clothes.

'Out of bed, sir, and off to the granary, or you leave my employ to-day! 'Tis to teach ye a lesson. March on; never mind your breeches!'

The unhappy Whittle threw on his sleeve waistcoat, and managed to get into his boots at the bottom of the stairs, while Henchard thrust his hat over his head. Whittle then trotted on down Back Street, Henchard walking sternly behind.

Just at this time Farfrae, who had been to Henchard's house to look for him, came out of the back gate, and saw something white fluttering in the morning gloom, which he soon perceived to be the part of Abel's shirt that showed below his waistcoat.

'For maircy's sake, what object's this?' said Farfrae, following Abel into the yard, Henchard being some way in the rear by this time.

'Ye see, Mr Farfrae,' gibbered Abel with a resigned smile of terror, 'he said he'd mortify my flesh if so be I didn't get up sooner, and now he's a-doing on't! Ye see it can't be helped, Mr Farfrae; things do happen queer sometimes! Yes – I'll go to Blackmoor Vale half naked as I be, since he do command; but I shall kill myself afterwards; I can't outlive the disgrace; for the women-folk will be looking out of their winders at my mortification all the way along, and laughing me to scorn as a man 'ithout breeches! You know how I feel such things, Maister Farfrae, and how forlorn thoughts get hold upon me. Yes – I shall do myself harm – I feel it coming on!'

'Get back home, and slip on your breeches, and come to wark like a man! If ye go not, you'll ha'e your death standing there!'

'I'm afeard I mustn't! Mr Henchard said –'

'I don't care what Mr Henchard said, nor anybody else! 'Tis simple foolishness to do this. Go and dress yourself instantly, Whittle.'

'Hullo, hullo!' said Henchard, coming up behind. 'Who's sending him back?'

All the men looked toward Farfrae.

'I am,' said Donald. 'I say this joke has been carried far enough.'

'And I say it hasn't! Get up in the waggon, Whittle.'

'Not if I am manager,' said Farfrae. 'He either goes home, or I march out of this yard for good.'

Henchard looked at him with a face stern and red. But he paused for a moment, and their eyes met. Donald went up to him, for he saw in Henchard's look that he began to regret this.

'Come,' said Donald quietly, 'a man o' your position should ken better, sir! It is tyrannical and no worthy of you.'

' 'Tis not tyrannical!' murmured Henchard, like a sullen boy. 'It is to make him remember!' He presently added, in a tone of one bitterly hurt: 'Why did you speak to me before them like that, Farfrae? You might have stopped till we were alone. Ah – I know why! I've told ye the secret o' my life – fool that I was to do't – and you take advantage of me!'

'I had forgot it,' said Farfrae simply.

Henchard looked on the ground, said nothing more, and turned away. During the day Farfrae learnt from the men that Henchard had kept Abel's old mother in coals and snuff all the previous winter, which made him less antagonistic to the corn-factor. But Henchard continued moody and silent, and when one of the men inquired of him if some oats should be hoisted to an upper floor or not, he said shortly, 'Ask Mr Farfrae. He's master here!'

Morally he was; there could be no doubt of it. Henchard, who had hitherto been the most admired man in his circle, was the most admired no longer. One day the daughters of a deceased farmer in Durnover wanted an opinion on the value of their haystack, and sent a messenger to ask Mr Farfrae to oblige them with one. The messenger, who was a child, met in the yard not Farfrae, but Henchard.

'Very well,' he said. 'I'll come.'

'But please will Mr Farfrae come?' said the child.

'I am going that way . . . Why Mr Farfrae?' said Henchard, with the fixed look of thought. 'Why do people always want Mr Farfrae?'

'I suppose because they like him so – that's what they say.'

'Oh – I see – that's what they say – hey? They like him because he's cleverer than Mr Henchard, and because he knows more; and in short, Mr Henchard can't hold a candle to him – hey?'

'Yes – that's just it, sir – some of it.'

'Oh, there's more? Of course there's more! What besides? Come, here's sixpence for a fairing.'*

' "And he's better-tempered, and Henchard's a fool to him," they say. And when some of the women were a-walking home they said. "He's a diment* – he's a chap o' wax* – he's the best – he's the horse for my money," says they. And they said, "He's the most understanding man o' them two by long chalks. I wish he was the master instead of Henchard," they said.'

'They'll talk any nonsense,' Henchard replied with covered gloom. 'Well, you can go now. And *I* am coming to value the hay, d'ye hear? – I.' The boy departed, and Henchard murmured, 'Wish he was master here, do they?'

He went towards Durnover. On his way he overtook Farfrae. They walked on together, Henchard looking mostly on the ground.

'You're no yoursel' the day?' Donald inquired.

'Yes, I am very well,' said Henchard.

'But ye are a bit down – surely ye are down? Why, there's nothing to be angry about! 'Tis splendid stuff that we've got from Blackmoor Vale. By the by, the people in Durnover want their hay valued.'

'Yes. I am going there.'

'I'll go with ye.'

As Henchard did not reply Donald practised a piece of music *sotto voce*,* till, getting near the bereaved people's door, he stopped himself with –

'Ah, as their father is dead I won't go on with such as that. How could I forget?'

'Do you care so very much about hurting folks' feelings?' observed Henchard with a half sneer. 'You do, I know – especially mine!'

'I am sorry if I have hurt yours, sir,' replied Donald, standing still, with a second expression of the same sentiment in the regretfulness of his face. 'Why should you say it – think it?'

The cloud lifted from Henchard's brow, and as Donald finished the corn-merchant turned to him, regarding his breast rather than his face.

'I have been hearing things that vexed me,' he said. ' 'Twas that made me short in my manner – made me overlook what you really are. Now, I don't want to go in here about this hay – Farfrae, you can do it better than I. They sent for 'ee, too. I have to attend a meeting of the Town Council at eleven, and 'tis drawing on for't.'

They parted thus in renewed friendship, Donald forbearing to ask Henchard for meanings that were not very plain to him. On Henchard's part there was now again repose; and yet, whenever he thought of Farfrae, it was with a dim dread; and he often regretted that he had told the young man his whole heart, and confided to him the secrets of his life.

Chapter 16

On this account Henchard's manner towards Farfrae insensibly became more reserved. He was courteous – too courteous – and Farfrae was quite surprised at the good breeding which now for the first time showed itself among the qualities of a man he had hitherto thought undisciplined, if warm and sincere. The corn-factor seldom or never again put his arm upon the young man's shoulder so as to nearly weigh him down with the pressure of mechanized friendship. He left off coming to Donald's lodgings and shouting into the passage, 'Hoy, Farfrae, boy, come and have some dinner with us! Don't sit here in solitary confinement!' But in the daily routine of their business there was little change.

Thus their lives rolled on till a day of public rejoicing was suggested to the country at large in celebration of a national event* that had recently taken place.

For some time Casterbridge, by nature slow, made no response. Then one day Donald Farfrae broached the subject to Henchard by asking if he would have any objection to lend some rick-cloths* to himself and a few others, who contemplated getting up an entertainment of some sort on the day named, and required a shelter for the same, to which they might charge admission at the rate of so much a head.

'Have as many cloths as you like,' Henchard replied.

When his manager had gone about the business Henchard was fired with emulation. It certainly had been very remiss of him, as Mayor, he thought, to call no meeting ere this, to discuss what should be done on this holiday. But Farfrae had been so cursed quick in his movements as to give old-fashioned people in authority no chance of the initiative. However, it was not too late; and on second thoughts he determined to take upon his own shoulders the responsibility of organizing some amusements, if the other Councilmen would leave the matter in his hands. To this they quite readily agreed, the majority being fine old crusted characters who had a decided taste for living without worry.

So Henchard set about his preparations for a really brilliant thing – such as should be worthy of the venerable town. As for Farfrae's little affair, Henchard nearly forgot it; except once now and then when, on it coming into his mind, he said to himself, 'Charge admission at so much a head – just like a Scotchman! –

who is going to pay anything a head?' The diversions which the Mayor intended to provide were to be entirely free.

He had grown so dependent upon Donald that he could scarcely resist calling him in to consult. But by sheer self-coercion he refrained. No, he thought, Farfrae would be suggesting such improvements in his damned luminous way that in spite of himself he, Henchard, would sink to the position of second fiddle, and only scrape harmonies to his manager's talents.

Everybody applauded the Mayor's proposed entertainment, especially when it became known that he meant to pay for it all himself.

Close to the town was an elevated green spot surrounded by an ancient square earthwork – earthworks square, and not square, were as common as blackberries hereabout – a spot whereon the Casterbridge people usually held any kind of merry-making, meeting, or sheep-fair that required more space than the streets would afford. On one side it sloped to the river Froom, and from any point a view was obtained of the country round for many miles. This pleasant upland was to be the scene of Henchard's exploit.

He advertised about the town, in long posters of a pink colour, that games of all sorts would take place here; and set to work a little battalion of men under his own eye. They erected greasy-poles for climbing, with smoked hams and local cheeses at the top. They placed hurdles in rows for jumping over; across the river they laid a slippery pole, with a live pig of the neighbourhood tied at the other end, to become the property of the man who could walk over and get it. There were also provided wheelbarrows for racing, donkeys for the same, a stage for boxing, wrestling, and drawing blood generally; sacks for jumping in. Moreover, not forgetting his principles, Henchard provided a mammoth tea, of which everybody who lived in the borough was invited to partake without payment. The tables were laid parallel with the inner slope of the rampart, and awnings were stretched overhead.

Passing to and fro the Mayor beheld the unattractive exterior of Farfrae's erection in the West Walk, rick-cloths of different sizes and colours being hung up to the arching trees without any regard to appearance. He was easy in his mind now, for his own preparations far transcended these.

The morning came. The sky, which had been remarkably clear down to within a day or two, was overcast, and the weather threatening, the wind having an unmistakable hint of water in it. Henchard wished he had not been quite so sure about the continuance of a fair season. But it was too late to modify or postpone, and the proceedings went on. At twelve o'clock the rain began to fall, small and steady, commencing and increasing so insensibly that it was difficult to state exactly when dry weather ended or wet established itself. In an hour the slight moisture resolved itself into a monotonous smiting of earth by heaven, in torrents to which no end could be prognosticated.

A number of people had heroically gathered in the field, but by three o'clock Henchard discerned that his project was doomed to end in failure. The hams at the top of the poles dripped watered smoke in the form of a brown liquor, the pig shivered in the wind, the grain of the deal tables showed through the sticking table-cloths, for the awning allowed the rain to drift under at its will, and to enclose the sides at this hour seemed a useless undertaking. The landscape over the river disappeared; the wind played on the tent-cords in Æolian* improvisations; and at length rose to such a pitch that the whole erection slanted to the ground, those who had taken shelter within it having to crawl out on their hands and knees.

But towards six the storm abated, and a drier breeze shook the moisture from the grass bents. It seemed possible to carry out the programme after all. The awning was set up again; the band was called out from its shelter, and ordered to begin, and where the tables had stood a place was cleared for dancing.

'But where are the folk?' said Henchard, after the lapse of half-an-hour, during which time only two men and a woman had stood up to dance. 'The shops are all shut. Why don't they come?'

'They are at Farfrae's affair in the West Walk,' answered a Councilman who stood in the field with the Mayor.

'A few, I suppose. But where are the body o' 'em?'

'All out of doors are there.'

'Then the more fools they!'

Henchard walked away moodily. One or two young fellows gallantly came to climb the poles, to save the hams from being wasted; but as there were no spectators, and the whole scene presented the most melancholy appearance, Henchard gave orders that the proceedings were to be suspended, and the entertainment closed, the food to be distributed among the poor people of the town. In a short time nothing was left in the field but a few hurdles, the tents, and the poles.

Henchard returned to his house, had tea with his wife and daughter, and then walked out. It was now dusk. He soon saw that the tendency of all promenaders was towards a particular spot in the Walks, and eventually proceeded thither himself. The notes of a stringed band came from the enclosure that Farfrae had erected – the pavilion as he called it – and when the Mayor reached it he perceived that a gigantic tent had been ingeniously constructed without poles or ropes. The densest point of the avenue of sycamores had been selected, where the boughs made a closely interlaced vault overhead; to these boughs the canvas had been hung, and a barrel roof was the result. The end towards the wind was enclosed, the other end was open. Henchard went round and saw the interior.

In form it was like the nave of a cathedral with one gable removed, but the scene within was anything but devotional. A reel or fling of some sort was in progress; and the usually sedate Farfrae was in the midst of the other dancers in the costume of a wild Highlander, flinging himself about and spinning to the tune. For a moment Henchard could not help laughing. Then he perceived the immense admiration for the Scotchman that revealed itself in the women's faces; and when this exhibition was over, and a new dance proposed, and Donald had disappeared for a time to return in his natural garments, he had an unlimited choice of partners, every girl in a coming-on disposition towards one who so thoroughly understood the poetry of motion as he.

All the town crowded to the Walk, such a delightful idea of a ballroom never having occurred to the inhabitants before. Among the rest of the onlookers were Elizabeth and her mother – the former thoughtful yet much interested, her eyes beaming with a longing lingering light, as if Nature had been advised by Correggio* in their creation. The dancing progressed with unabated spirit, and Henchard walked and waited till his wife should be disposed to go home. He did not care to keep in the light, and when he went into the dark it was worse, for there he heard remarks of a kind which were becoming too frequent:

'Mr Henchard's rejoicings couldn't say good morning to this,' said one. 'A man must be a headstrong stunpoll* to think folk would go up to that bleak place to-day.'

The other answered that people said it was not only in such things as those that the Mayor was wanting. 'Where would his business be if it were not for this young fellow? 'Twas verily

Fortune sent him to Henchard. His accounts were like a bramble-wood when Mr Farfrae came. He used to reckon his sacks by chalk strokes all in a row like garden-palings, measure his ricks by stretching with his arms, weigh his trusses by a lift, judge his hay by a chaw,* and settle the price with a curse. But now this accomplished young man does it all by ciphering and mensuration. Then the wheat – that sometimes used to taste so strong o' mice when made into bread that people could fairly tell the breed – Farfrae has a plan for purifying, so that nobody would dream the smallest four-legged beast had walked over it once. O yes, everybody is full of him, and the care Mr Henchard has to keep him, to be sure!' concluded this gentleman.

'But he won't do it for long, good-now,' said the other.

'No!' said Henchard to himself behind the tree. 'Or if he do, he'll be honeycombed* clean out of all the character and standing that he's built up in these eighteen year!'

He went back to the dancing pavilion. Farfrae was footing a quaint little dance with Elizabeth-Jane – an old country thing, the only one she knew, and though he considerately toned down his movements to suit her demurer gait, the pattern of the shining little nails in the soles of his boots became familiar to the eyes of every bystander. The tune had enticed her into it; being a tune of a busy, vaulting, leaping sort – some low notes on the silver string of each fiddle, then a skipping on the small, like running up and down ladders – 'Miss M'Leod of Ayr'* was its name, so Mr Farfrae had said, and that it was very popular in his own country.

It was soon over, and the girl looked at Henchard for approval; but he did not give it. He seemed not to see her. 'Look here, Farfrae,' he said, like one whose mind was elsewhere, 'I'll go to Port-Bredy Great Market to-morrow myself. You can stay and put things right in your clothes-box, and recover strength to your knees after your vagaries.' He planted on Donald an antagonistic glare that had begun as a smile.

Some other townsmen came up, and Donald drew aside. 'What's this, Henchard,' said Alderman Tubber, applying his thumb to the corn-factor like a cheese-taster. 'An opposition randy* to yours, eh? Jack's as good as his master, eh? Cut ye out quite, hasn't he?'

'You see, Mr Henchard,' said the lawyer, another good-natured friend, 'where you made the mistake was in going so far afield. You should have taken a leaf out of his book, and have had your sports in a sheltered place like this. But you didn't think of it, you see; and he did, and that's where he's beat you.'

'He'll be top-sawyer soon of you two, and carry all afore him,' added jocular Mr Tubber.

'No,' said Henchard gloomily. 'He won't be that, because he's shortly going to leave me.' He looked towards Donald, who had again come near. 'Mr Farfrae's time as my manager is drawing to a close – isn't it, Farfrae?'

The young man, who could now read the lines and folds of Henchard's strongly-traced face as if they were clear verbal inscriptions, quietly assented; and when people deplored the fact, and asked why it was, he simply replied that Mr Henchard no longer required his help.

Henchard went home, apparently satisfied. But in the morning, when his jealous temper had passed away, his heart sank within him at what he had said and done. He was the more disturbed when he found that this time Farfrae was determined to take him at his word.

Chapter 17

Elizabeth-Jane had perceived from Henchard's manner that in assenting to dance she had made a mistake of some kind. In her simplicity she did not know what it was till a hint from a nodding acquaintance enlightened her. As the Mayor's step-daughter, she learnt, she had not been quite in her place in treading a measure amid such a mixed throng as filled the dancing pavilion.

Thereupon her ears, cheeks, and chin glowed like live coals at the dawning of the idea that her tastes were not good enough for her position, and would bring her into disgrace.

This made her very miserable, and she looked about for her mother; but Mrs Henchard, who had less idea of conventionality than Elizabeth herself, had gone away, leaving her daughter to return at her own pleasure. The latter moved on into the dark dense old avenues, or rather vaults of living woodwork, which ran along the town boundary, and stood reflecting.

A man followed in a few minutes, and her face being towards the shine from the tent he recognized her. It was Farfrae – just come from the dialogue with Henchard which had signified his dismissal.

'And it's you, Miss Newson? – and I've been looking for ye everywhere!' he said, overcoming a sadness imparted by the estrangement with the corn-merchant. 'May I walk on with you as far as your street-corner?'

She thought there might be something wrong in this, but did not utter any objection. So together they went on, first down the West Walk, and then into the Bowling Walk, till Farfrae said, 'It's like that I'm going to leave you soon.'

She faltered 'Why?'

'Oh – as a mere matter of business – nothing more. But we'll not concern ourselves about it – it is for the best. I hoped to have another dance with you.'

She said she could not dance – in any proper way.

'Nay, but you do! It's the feeling for it rather than the learning of steps that makes pleasant dancers . . . I fear I offend your father by getting up this! And now, perhaps, I'll have to go to another part o' the warrld altogether!'

This seemed such a melancholy prospect that Elizabeth-Jane breathed a sigh – letting it off in fragments that he might not hear her. But darkness makes people truthful, and the Scotchman went on impulsively – perhaps he had heard her after all:

'I wish I was richer, Miss Newson; and your stepfather had not been offended; I would ask you something in a short time – yes, I would ask you to-night. But that's not for me!'

What he would have asked her he did not say, and instead of encouraging him she remained incompetently silent. Thus afraid one of another they continued their promenade along the walls till they got near the bottom of the Bowling Walk; twenty steps further and the trees would end, and the street-corner and lamps appear. In consciousness of this they stopped.

'I never found out who it was that sent us to Durnover granary on a fool's errand that day,' said Donald, in his undulating tones. 'Did ye ever know yourself, Miss Newson?'

'Never,' said she.

'I wonder why they did it!'

'For fun, perhaps.'

'Perhaps it was not for fun. It might have been that they thought they would like us to stay waiting there, talking to one another? Ay, well! I hope you Casterbridge folk will not forget me if I go.'

'That I'm sure we won't!' she said earnestly. 'I – wish you wouldn't go at all.'

They had got into the lamplight. 'Now, I'll think over that,' said Donald Farfrae. 'And I'll not come up to your door; but part from you here; lest it make your father more angry still.'

They parted, Farfrae returning into the dark Bowling Walk, and Elizabeth-Jane going up the street. Without any consciousness of what she was doing she started running with all her might till she reached her father's door. 'O dear me – what am I at?' she thought, as she pulled up breathless.

Indoors she fell to conjecturing the meaning of Farfrae's enigmatic words about not daring to ask her what he fain would. Elizabeth, that silent observing woman, had long noted how he was rising in favour among the townspeople; and knowing Henchard's nature now she had feared that Farfrae's days as manager were numbered; so that the announcement gave her little surprise. Would Mr Farfrae stay in Casterbridge despite his words and her father's dismissal? His occult breathings to her might be solvable by his course in that respect.

The next day was windy – so windy that walking in the garden she picked up a portion of the draft of a letter on business in Donald Farfrae's writing, which had flown over the wall from the office. The useless scrap she took indoors, and began to copy the caligraphy, which she much admired. The letter began 'Dear Sir', and presently writing on a loose slip 'Elizabeth-Jane', she laid the latter over 'Sir', making the phrase 'Dear Elizabeth-Jane'. When she saw the effect a quick red ran up her face and warmed her through, though nobody was there to see what she had done. She quickly tore up the slip, and threw it away. After this she grew cool and laughed at herself, walked about the room, and laughed again; not joyfully, but distressfully rather.

It was quickly known in Casterbridge that Farfrae and Henchard had decided to dispense with each other. Elizabeth-Jane's anxiety to know if Farfrae were going away from the town reached a pitch that disturbed her, for she could no longer conceal from herself the cause. At length the news reached her that he was not going to leave the place. A man following the same trade as Henchard, but on a very small scale, had sold his business to Farfrae, who was forthwith about to start as corn and hay merchant on his own account.

Her heart fluttered when she heard of this step of Donald's, proving that he meant to remain; and yet, would a man who cared one little bit for her have endangered his suit by setting up a business in opposition to Mr Henchard's? Surely not; and it must have been a passing impulse only which had led him to address her so softly.

To solve the problem whether her appearance on the evening of the dance were such as to inspire a fleeting love at first sight, she dressed herself up exactly as she had dressed then – the muslin, the spencer, the sandals, the parasol – and looked in the mirror. The picture glassed back was, in her opinion, precisely of such a kind as to inspire that fleeting regard, and no more – 'just enough to make him silly, and not enough to keep him so,' she said luminously; and Elizabeth thought, in a much lower key, that by this time he had discovered how plain and homely was the informing spirit of that pretty outside.

Hence, when she felt her heart going out to him, she would say to herself with a mock pleasantry that carried an ache with it, 'No, no, Elizabeth-Jane – such dreams are not for you!' She tried to prevent herself from seeing him, and thinking of him; succeeding fairly well in the former attempt, in the latter not so completely.

Henchard, who had been hurt at finding that Farfrae did not mean to put up with his temper any longer, was incensed beyond measure when he learnt what the young man had done as an alternative. It was in the town-hall, after a council meeting, that he first became aware of Farfrae's *coup* for establishing himself independently in the town; and his voice might have been heard as far as the town-pump expressing his feelings to his fellow councilmen. Those tones showed that, though under a long reign of self-control he had become Mayor and churchwarden and what not, there was still the same unruly volcanic stuff beneath the rind of Michael Henchard as when he had sold his wife at Weydon Fair.

'Well, he's a friend of mine, and I'm a friend of his – or if we are not, what are we?' Od send, if I've not been his friend, who has, I should like to know? Didn't he come here without a sound shoe to his voot?* Didn't I keep him here – help him to a living? Didn't I help him to money, or whatever he wanted? I stuck out for no terms – I said "Name your own price." I'd have shared my last crust with that young fellow at one time, I liked him so well. And now he's defied me! But damn him, I'll have a tussle with him now – at fair buying and selling, mind – at fair buying and selling! And if I can't overbid such a stripling as he, then I'm not wo'th a varden!* We'll show that we know our business as well as one here and there!'

His friends of the Corporation did not specially respond. Henchard was less popular now than he had been when, nearly two years before, they had voted him to the chief magistracy on account of his amazing energy. While they had collectively profited by this quality of the corn-factor's they had been made to wince individually on more than one occasion. So he went out of the hall and down the street alone.

Reaching home he seemed to recollect something with a sour satisfaction. He called Elizabeth-Jane. Seeing how he looked when she entered she appeared alarmed.

'Nothing to find fault with,' he said, observing her concern. 'Only I want to caution you, my dear. That man, Farfrae – it is about him. I've seen him talking to you two or three times – he danced with 'ee at the rejoicings, and came home with 'ee. Now, now, no blame to you. But just hearken: Have you made him any foolish promise? Gone the least bit beyond sniff and snaff* at all?'

'No. I have promised him nothing.'

'Good. All's well that ends well. I particularly wish you not to see him again.'

'Very well, sir.'

'You promise?'

She hesitated for a moment, and then said –

'Yes, if you much wish it.'

'I do. He's an enemy to our house!'

When she had gone he sat down, and wrote in a heavy hand to Farfrae thus:—

> SIR, – I make request that henceforth you and my step-daughter be as strangers to each other. She on her part has promised to welcome no more addresses from you; and I trust, therefore, you will not attempt to force them upon her.

> M. HENCHARD

One would almost have supposed Henchard to have had policy to see that no better *modus vivendi** could be arrived at with Farfrae than by encouraging him to become his son-in-law. But such a scheme for buying over a rival had nothing to recommend it to the Mayor's headstrong faculties. With all domestic *finesse* of that kind he was hopelessly at variance. Loving a man or hating him, his diplomacy was as wrongheaded as a buffalo's; and his wife had not ventured to suggest the course which she, for many reasons, would have welcomed gladly.

Meanwhile Donald Farfrae had opened the gates of commerce on his own account at a spot on Durnover Hill – as far as possible from Henchard's stores, and with every intention of keeping clear of his former friend and employer's customers. There was, it seemed to the younger man, room for both of them and to spare. The town was small, but the corn and hay-trade was proportionately large, and with his native sagacity he saw opportunity for a share of it.

So determined was he to do nothing which should seem like trade-antagonism to the Mayor that he refused his first customer – a large farmer of good repute – because Henchard and this man had dealt together within the preceding three months.

'He was once my friend,' said Farfrae, 'and it's not for me to take business from him. I am sorry to disappoint you, but I cannot hurt the trade of a man who's been so kind to me.'

In spite of this praiseworthy course the Scotchman's trade increased. Whether it were that his northern energy was an overmastering force among the easy-going Wessex worthies, or whether it was sheer luck, the fact remained that whatever he touched he prospered in. Like Jacob in Padan-Aram,* he would no sooner humbly limit himself to the ringstraked-and-spotted exceptions of trade than the ringstraked-and-spotted would multiply and prevail.

But most probably luck had little to do with it. Character is Fate, said Novalis,* and Farfrae's character was just the reverse of Henchard's, who might not inaptly be described as Faust* has been described – as a vehement gloomy being who had quitted the ways of vulgar men, without light to guide him on a better way.

Farfrae duly received the request to discontinue attentions to Elizabeth-Jane. His acts of that kind had been so light that the request was almost superfluous. Yet he had felt a considerable interest in her, and after some cogitation he decided that it would be as well to enact no Romeo part just then – for the young girl's sake no less than his own. Thus the incipient attachment was stifled down.

A time came when, avoid collision with his former friend as he might, Farfrae was compelled, in sheer self-defence, to close with Henchard in mortal commercial combat. He could no longer parry the fierce attacks of the latter by simple avoidance. As soon as their war of prices began everybody was interested, and some few guessed the end. It was, in some degree, Northern insight matched against Southron doggedness – the dirk against the cudgel – and Henchard's weapon was one which, if it did not deal ruin at the first or second stroke, left him afterwards well-nigh at his antagonist's mercy.

Almost every Saturday they encountered each other amid the crowd of farmers which thronged about the market-place in the weekly course of their business. Donald was always ready, and even anxious, to say a few friendly words; but the Mayor invariably gazed stormfully past him, like one who had endured and lost on his account, and could in no sense forgive the wrong; nor did Farfrae's snubbed manner of perplexity at all appease him. The large farmers, corn-merchants, millers, auctioneers, and others had each an official stall in the corn-market room, with their names painted thereon; and when to the familiar series of 'Henchard', 'Everdene', 'Shiner', 'Darton', and so on, was added one inscribed 'Farfrae', in staring new letters, Henchard was stung into bitterness; like Bellerophon,* he wandered away from the crowd, cankered in soul.

From that day Donald's Farfrae's name was seldom mentioned in Henchard's house. If at breakfast or dinner Elizabeth-Jane's mother inadvertently alluded to her favourite's movements, the girl would implore her by a look to be silent; and her husband would say, 'What – are you, too, my enemy?'

Chapter 18

There came a shock which had been foreseen for some time by Elizabeth, as the box passenger* foresees the approaching jerk from some channel across the highway.

Her mother was ill – too unwell to leave her room. Henchard, who treated her kindly, except in moments of irritation, sent at once for the richest, busiest doctor, whom he supposed to be the best. Bedtime came, and they burnt a light all night. In a day or two she rallied.

Elizabeth, who had been staying up, did not appear at breakfast on the second morning, and Henchard sat down alone. He was startled to see a letter for him from Jersey in a writing he knew too well, and had expected least to behold again. He took it up in his hands and looked at it as at a picture, a vision, a vista of past enactments; and then he read it as an unimportant finale to conjecture.

The writer said that she at length perceived how impossible it would be for any further communications to proceed between them now that his re-marriage had taken place. That such reunion had been the only straightforward course open to him she was bound to admit.

'On calm reflection, therefore,' she went on, 'I quite forgive you for landing me in such a dilemma, remembering that you concealed nothing before our ill-advised acquaintance; and that you really did set before me in your grim way the fact of there being a certain risk in intimacy with you, slight as it seemed to be after fifteen or sixteen years of silence on your wife's part. I thus look upon the whole as a misfortune of mine, and not a fault of yours.

'So that, Michael, I must ask you to overlook those letters with which I pestered you day after day in the heat of my feelings. They were written whilst I thought your conduct to me cruel; but now I know more particulars of the position you were in I see how inconsiderate my reproaches were.

'Now you will, I am sure, perceive that the one condition which will make any future happiness possible for me is that the past connection between our lives be kept secret outside this isle. Speak of it I know you will not; and I can trust you not to write of it. One safeguard more remains to be mentioned – that no writings of mine, or trifling articles belonging to me, should be left in your possession through neglect or forgetfulness. To this end may I request you to return to me any such you may have, particularly the letters written in the first abandonment of feeling.

'For the handsome sum you forwarded to me as a plaster to the wound I heartily thank you.

'I am now on my way to Bristol, to see my only relative. She is rich, and I hope will do something for me. I shall return through Casterbridge and Budmouth, where I shall take the packet-boat.* Can you meet me with the letters and other trifles? I shall be in the coach which changes horses at the Antelope Hotel at half-past five Wednesday evening; I shall be wearing a Paisley shawl with a red centre, and thus may easily be found. I should prefer this plan of receiving them to having them sent. – I remain still, yours ever,

'LUCETTA'

Henchard breathed heavily. 'Poor thing – better you had not known me! Upon my heart and soul, if ever I should be left in a position to carry out that marriage with thee, I *ought* to do it – I ought to do it, indeed!'

The contingency that he had in his mind was, of course, the death of Mrs Henchard.

As requested, he sealed up Lucetta's letters, and put the parcel aside till the day she had appointed; this play of returning them by hand being apparently a little *ruse* of the young lady for exchanging a word or two with him on past times. He would have preferred not to see her; but deeming that there could be no great harm in acquiescing thus far, he went at dusk and stood opposite the coach-office.

The evening was chilly, and the coach was late. Henchard crossed over to it while the horses were being changed; but there was no Lucetta inside or out. Concluding that something had happened to modify her arrangements he gave the matter up and went home, not without a sense of relief.

Meanwhile Mrs Henchard was weakening visibly. She could not go out of doors any more. One day, after much thinking which seemed to distress her, she said she wanted to write something. A desk was put upon her bed with pen and paper, and at her request she was left alone. She remained writing for a short time, folded her paper carefully, called Elizabeth-Jane to bring a taper and wax, and then, still refusing assistance, sealed up the sheet, directed it, and locked it in her desk. She had directed it in these words:—

'*Mr Michael Henchard. Not to be opened till Elizabeth-Jane's wedding-day.*'

The latter sat up with her mother to the utmost of her strength night after night. To learn to take the universe seriously there is no quicker way than to watch – to be a 'waker', as the country-people call it. Between the hours at which the last toss-pot went by and the first sparrow shook himself, the silence in Casterbridge – barring the rare sound of the watchman – was broken in Elizabeth's ear only by the time-piece in the bedroom ticking frantically against the clock on the stairs; ticking harder and harder till it seemed to clang like a gong; and all this while the subtle-souled girl asking herself why she was born, why sitting in a room, and blinking at the candle; why things around her had taken the shape they wore in preference to every other possible shape. Why they stared at her so helplessly, as if waiting for the touch of some wand that should release them from terrestrial constraint; what that chaos called consciousness, which spun in her at this moment like a top, tended to, and began in. Her eyes fell together; she was awake, yet she was asleep.

A word from her mother roused her. Without preface, and as the continuation of a scene already progressing in her mind, Mrs Henchard said: 'You remember the note sent to you and Mr Farfrae – asking you to meet some one in Durnover Barton – and that you thought it was a trick to make fools of you?'

'Yes.'

'It was not to make fools of you – it was done to bring you together. 'Twas I did it.'

'Why?' said Elizabeth, with a start.

'I – wanted you to marry Mr Farfrae.'

'O mother!' Elizabeth-Jane bent down her head so much that she looked quite into her own lap. But as her mother did not go on, she said, 'What reason?'

'Well, I had a reason. 'Twill out one day. I wish it could have been in my time! But there – nothing is as you wish it! Henchard hates him.'

'Perhaps they'll be friends again,' murmured the girl.

'I don't know – I don't know.' After this her mother was silent, and dozed; and she spoke on the subject no more.

Some little time later on Farfrae was passing Henchard's house on a Sunday morning, when he observed that the blinds were all down. He rang the bell so softly that it only sounded a single full note and a small one; and then he was informed that Mrs Henchard was dead – just dead – that very hour.

At the town-pump there were gathered when he passed a few old inhabitants, who came there for water whenever they had, as at present, spare time to fetch it, because it was purer from that original fount than from their own wells. Mrs Cuxsom, who had been standing there for an indefinite time with her pitcher, was describing the incidents of Mrs Henchard's death, as she had learnt them from the nurse.

'And she was as white as marble-stone,' said Mrs Cuxsom. 'And likewise such a thoughtful woman, too – ah, poor soul – that a' minded every little thing that wanted tending. "Yes," says she, "when I'm gone, and my last breath's blowed, look in the top drawer o' the chest in the back room by the window, and you'll find all my coffin clothes; a piece of flannel – that's to put under me, and the little piece is to put under my head; and my new stockings for my feet – they are folded alongside, and all my other things. And there's four ounce pennies,* the heaviest I could find, a-tied up in bits of linen, for weights – two for my right eye and two for my left," she said. "And when you've used 'em, and my eyes don't open no more, bury the pennies, good souls, and don't ye go spending 'em, for I shouldn't like it. And open the windows as soon as I am carried out, and make it as cheerful as you can for Elizabeth-Jane." '

'Ah, poor heart!'

'Well, and Martha did it, and buried the ounce pennies in the garden. But if ye'll believe words, that man, Christopher Coney, went and dug 'em up, and spent 'em at the Three Mariners. "Faith," he said, "why should death rob life o' fourpence? Death's not of such good report that we should respect 'en to that extent," says he.'

' 'Twas a cannibal deed!' deprecated her listeners.

'Gad, then, I won't quite ha'e it,' said Solomon Longways. 'I say it to-day, and 'tis a Sunday morning, and I wouldn't speak wrongfully for a zilver zixpence at such a time. I don't see noo harm in it. To respect the dead is sound doxology;* and I wouldn't sell skellintons – leastwise respectable skellintons – to be varnished for 'natomies,* except I were out o' work. But money is scarce, and throats get dry. Why *should* death rob life o' four pence? I say there was no treason in it.'

'Well, poor soul; she's helpless to hinder that or anything now,' answered Mother Cuxsom. 'And all her shining keys will be took from her, and her cupboards opened; and little things a' didn't wish seen, anybody will see; and her wishes and ways will all be as nothing!'*

Chapter 19

Henchard and Elizabeth sat conversing by the fire. It was three weeks after Mrs Henchard's funeral; the candles were not lighted, and a restless, acrobatic flame, poised on a coal, called from the shady walls the smiles of all shapes that could respond – the old pier-glass,* with gilt columns and huge entablature,* the picture-frames, sundry knobs and handles, and the brass rosette at the bottom of each riband bell-pull on either side of the chimney-piece.

'Elizabeth, do you think much of old times?' said Henchard.

'Yes, sir; often,' said she.

'Who do you put in your pictures of 'em?'

'Mother and father – nobody else hardly.'

Henchard always looked like one bent on resisting pain when Elizabeth-Jane spoke of Richard Newson as 'father'. 'Ah! I am out of all that, am I not?' he said . . . 'Was Newson a kind father?'

'Yes, sir; very.'

Henchard's face settled into an expression of stolid loneliness which gradually modulated into something softer. 'Suppose I had been your real father?' he said. 'Would you have cared for me as much as you cared for Richard Newson?'

'I can't think it,' she said quickly. 'I can think of no other as my father, except my father.'

Henchard's wife was dissevered from him by death; his friend and helper Farfrae by estrangement; Elizabeth-Jane by ignorance. It seemed to him that only one of them could possibly be recalled, and that was the girl. His mind began vibrating between the wish to reveal himself to her and the policy of leaving well alone, till he could no longer sit still. He walked up and down, and then he came and stood behind her chair, looking down upon the top of her head. He could no longer restrain his impulse. 'What did your mother tell you about me – my history?' he asked.

'That you were related by marriage.'

'She should have told more – before you knew me! Then my task would not have been such a hard one . . . Elizabeth, it is I who am your father, and not Richard Newson. Shame alone prevented your wretched parents from owning this to you while both of 'em were alive.'

The back of Elizabeth's head remained still, and her shoulders did not denote even the movements of breathing. Henchard went on: 'I'd rather have your scorn, your fear, anything than your ignorance; 'tis that I hate. Your mother and I were man and wife when we were young. What you saw was our second marriage. Your mother was too honest. We had thought each other dead – and – Newson became her husband.'

This was the nearest approach Henchard could make to the full truth. As far as he personally was concerned he would have screened nothing; but he showed a respect for the young girl's sex and years worthy of a better man.

When he had gone on to give details which a whole series of slight and unregarded incidents in her past life strangely corroborated; when, in short, she believed his story to be true, she became greatly agitated, and turning round to the table flung her face upon it weeping.

'Don't cry – don't cry!' said Henchard, with vehement pathos, 'I can't bear it, I won't bear it. I am your father; why should you cry? Am I so dreadful, so hateful to 'ee? Don't take against me, Elizabeth-Jane!' he cried, grasping her wet hand. 'Don't take against me – though I was a drinking man once, and used your mother roughly – I'll be kinder to you than *he* was! I'll do anything, if you will only look upon me as your father!'

She tried to stand up and confront him trustfully; but she could not; she was troubled at his presence, like the brethren at the avowal of Joseph.*

'I don't want you to come to me all of a sudden,' said Henchard in jerks, and moving like a great tree in a wind. 'No, Elizabeth, I don't. I'll go away and not see you till to-morrow, or when you like; and then I'll show 'ee papers to prove my words. There, I am gone, and won't disturb you any more . . . 'Twas I that chose your name, my daughter; your mother wanted it Susan. There, don't forget 'twas I gave you your name!' He went out at the door and shut her softly in, and she heard him go away into the garden. But he had not done. Before she had moved, or in any way recovered from the effect of his disclosure, he reappeared.

'One word more, Elizabeth,' he said. 'You'll take my surname now – hey? Your mother was against it; but it will be much more pleasant to me. 'Tis legally yours, you know. But nobody need know that. You shall take it as if by choice. I'll talk to my lawyer – I don't know the law of it exactly; but will you do this – let me put a few lines into the newspaper that such is to be your name?'

'If it is my name I must have it, mustn't I?' she asked.

'Well, well; usage is everything in these matters.'

'I wonder why mother didn't wish it?'

'Oh, some whim of the poor soul's. Now get a bit of paper and draw up a paragraph as I shall tell you. But let's have a light.'

'I can see by the firelight,' she answered. 'Yes – I'd rather.'

'Very well.'

She got a piece of paper, and bending over the fender wrote at his dictation words which he had evidently got by heart from some advertisement or other – words to the effect that she, the writer, hitherto known as Elizabeth-Jane Newson, was going to call herself Elizabeth-Jane Henchard forthwith. It was done, and fastened up, and directed to the office of the *Casterbridge Chronicle*.

'Now,' said Henchard, with the blaze of satisfaction that he always emitted when he had carried his point – though tenderness softened it this time – 'I'll go upstairs and hunt for some documents that will prove it all to you. But I won't trouble you with them till tomorrow. Good-night, my Elizabeth-Jane!'

He was gone before the bewilderd girl could realize what it all meant, or adjust her filial sense to the new centre of gravity. She was thankful that he had left her to herself for the evening, and sat down over the fire. Here she remained in silence, and wept – not for her mother now, but for the genial sailor Richard Newson, to whom she seemed doing a wrong.

Henchard in the meantime had gone upstairs. Papers of a domestic nature he kept in a drawer in his bedroom, and this he unlocked. Before turning them over he leant back and indulged in reposeful thought. Elizabeth was his at last, and she was a girl of such good sense and kind heart that she would be sure to like him. He was the kind of man to whom some human object for pouring out his heat upon – were it emotive or were it choleric – was almost a necessity. The craving of his heart for the re-establishment of this tenderest human tie had been great during his wife's lifetime, and now he had submitted to its mastery without reluctance and without fear. He bent over the drawer again, and proceeded in his search.

Among the other papers had been placed the contents of his wife's little desk, the keys of which had been handed to him at her request. Here was the letter addressed to him with the restriction, '*Not to be opened till Elizabeth-Jane's wedding-day.*'

Mrs Henchard, though more patient than her husband, had been no practical hand at anything. In sealing up the sheet, which was folded and tucked in without an envelope, in the old-fashioned way, she had overlaid the junction with a large mass of wax without the requisite under-touch of the same. The seal had cracked, and the letter was open. Henchard had no reason to suppose the restriction one of serious weight, and his feeling for his late wife had not been of the nature of deep respect. 'Some trifling fancy or other of poor Susan's, I suppose,' he said: and without curiosity he allowed his eyes to scan the letter:

MY DEAR MICHAEL, – For the good of all three of us I have kept one thing a secret from you till now. I hope you will understand why; I think you will; though perhaps you may not forgive me. But, dear Michael, I have done it for the best. I shall be in my grave when you read this, and Elizabeth-Jane will have a home. Don't curse me, Mike – think of how I was situated. I can hardly write it, but here it is. Elizabeth-Jane is not your Elizabeth-Jane – the child who was in my arms when you sold me. No; she died three months after that, and this living one is my other husband's. I christened her by the same name we had given to the first, and she filled up the ache I felt at the other's loss. Michael, I am dying, and I might have held my tongue; but I could not. Tell her husband of this or not, as you may judge; and forgive, if you can, a woman you once deeply wronged, as she forgives you.

                                                    SUSAN HENCHARD

Her husband regarded the paper as if it were a window-pane through which he saw for miles. His lip twitched, and he seemed to compress his frame, as if to bear better. His usual habit was not to consider whether destiny were hard upon him or not – the shape of his ideas in cases of affliction being simply a moody 'I am to suffer, I perceive.' 'This much scourging, then, is it for me?' But now through his passionate head there stormed this thought – that the blasting disclosure was what he had deserved.

His wife's extreme reluctance to have the girl's name altered from Newson to Henchard was now accounted for fully. It furnished another illustration of that honesty in dishonesty which had characterized her in other things.

He remained unnerved and purposeless for near a couple of hours; till he suddenly said, 'Ah – I wonder if it is true?'

He jumped up in an impulse, kicked off his slippers, and went with a candle to the door of Elizabeth-Jane's room, where he put his ear to the keyhole and listened. She was breathing profoundly. Henchard softly turned the handle, entered, and shading the light, approached the bedside. Gradually bringing the light from behind a screening curtain he held it in such manner that it fell slantwise on her face without shining on her eyes. He steadfastly regarded her features.

They were fair: his were dark. But this was an unimportant preliminary. In sleep there comes to the surface buried genealogical facts, ancestral curves, dead men's traits, which the mobility of daytime animation screens and overwhelms. In the present statuesque repose of the young girl's countenance Richard Newson's was unmistakably reflected. He could not endure the sight of her, and hastened away.

Misery taught him nothing more than defiant endurance of it. His wife was dead, and the first impulse for revenge died with the thought that she was beyond him. He looked out at the night as at a fiend. Henchard, like all his kind, was superstitious, and he could not help thinking that the concatenation of events this evening had produced was the scheme of some sinister intelligence bent on punishing him. Yet they had developed naturally. If he had not revealed his past history to Elizabeth he would not have searched the drawer for papers, and so on. The mockery was, that he should have no sooner taught a girl to claim the shelter of his paternity than he discovered her to have no kinship with him.

This ironical sequence of things angered him like an impish trick from a fellow-creature. Like Prester John's,* his table had been spread, and infernal harpies had snatched up the food. He went out of the house, and moved sullenly onward down the pavement till he came to the bridge at the bottom of the High Street. Here he turned in upon a bypath on the river bank, skirting the north-eastern limits of the town.

These precincts embodied the mournful phases of Casterbridge life, as the south avenues embodied its cheerful moods. The whole way along here was sunless, even in summer time; in spring, white frosts lingered here when other places were steaming with warmth; while in winter it was the seed-field of all the aches, rheumatisms, and torturing cramps of the year. The Casterbridge doctors must have pined away for want of sufficient nourishment but for the configuration of the landscape on the north-eastern side.

The river – slow, noiseless, and dark – the Schwarzwasser* of Casterbridge – ran beneath a low cliff, the two together forming a defence which had rendered walls and artificial earthworks on this side unnecessary. Here were ruins of a Franciscan priory, and a mill attached to the same, the water of which roared down a back-hatch like the voice of desolation. Above the cliff, and behind the river, rose a pile of buildings, and in the front of the pile a square mass cut into the sky. It was like a pedestal lacking its statue. This missing feature, without which the design remained incomplete, was, in truth, the corpse of a man; for the square mass formed the base of the gallows, the extensive buildings at the back being the county gaol. In the meadow where Henchard now walked the mob were wont to gather whenever an execution took place, and there to the tune of the roaring weir they stood and watched the spectacle.

The exaggeration which darkness imparted to the glooms of this region impressed Henchard more than he had expected. The lugubrious harmony of the spot with his domestic situation was too perfect for him, impatient of effects, scenes, and adumbrations. It reduced his heartburning to melancholy, and he exclaimed, 'Why the deuce did I come here!' He went on past the cottage in which the old local hangman had lived and died, in times before that calling was monopolized over all England by a single gentleman; and climbed up by a steep back lane into the town.

For the sufferings of that night, engendered by his bitter disappointment, he might well have been pitied. He was like one who had half fainted, and could neither recover nor complete the swoon. In words he could blame his wife, but not in his heart; and had he obeyed the wise directions outside her letter this pain would have been spared him for long – possibly for ever, Elizabeth-Jane seeming to show no ambition to quit her safe and secluded maiden courses for the speculative path of matrimony.

The morning came after this night of unrest, and with it the necessity for a plan. He was far too self-willed to recede from a position, especially as it would involve humiliation. His daughter he had asserted her to be, and his daughter she should always think herself, no matter what hypocrisy it involved.

But he was ill-prepared for the first step in this new situation. The moment he came into the breakfast-room Elizabeth advanced with open confidence to him and took him by the arm.

'I have thought and thought all night of it,' she said frankly. 'And I see that everything must be as you say. And I am going to look upon you as the father that you are, and not to call you Mr Henchard any more. It is so plain to me now. Indeed, father, it is. For, of course, you would not have done half the things you have done for me, and let me have my own way so entirely, and bought me presents, if I had only been your step-daughter! He – Mr Newson – whom my poor mother married by such a strange mistake' (Henchard was glad that he had disguised matters here), 'was very kind – O so kind!' (she spoke with tears in her eyes); 'but that is not the same thing as being one's real father after all. Now, father, breakfast is ready!' said she cheerfully.

Henchard bent and kissed her cheek. The moment and the act he had prefigured for weeks with a thrill of pleasure; yet it was no less than a miserable insipidity to him now that it had come. His reinstation of her mother had been chiefly for the girl's sake, and the fruition of the whole scheme was such dust and ashes as this.

Chapter 20

Of all the enigmas which ever confronted a girl there can have been seldom one like that which followed Henchard's announcement of himself to Elizabeth as her father. He had done it in an ardour and an agitation which had half carried the point of affection with her; yet, behold, from the next morning onwards his manner was constrained as she had never seen it before.

The coldness soon broke out into open chiding. One grievous failing of Elizabeth's was her occasional pretty and picturesque use of dialect words – those terrible marks of the beast to the truly genteel.

It was dinner-time – they never met except at meals – and she happened to say when he was rising from table, wishing to show him something, 'If you'll bide where you be a minute, father, I'll get it.'

' "Bide where you be," ' he echoed sharply. 'Good God, are you only fit to carry wash to a pig-trough, that ye use such words as those?'

She reddened with shame and sadness.

'I meant "Stay where you are", father,' she said, in a low, humble voice. 'I ought to have been more careful.'

He made no reply, and went out of the room.

The sharp reprimand was not lost upon her, and in time it came to pass that for 'fay' she said 'succeed'; that she no longer spoke of 'dumbledores' but of 'humble bees'; no longer said of young men and women that they 'walked together', but that they were 'engaged'; that she grew to talk of 'greggles' as 'wild hyacinths'; that when she had not slept she did not quaintly tell the servants next morning that she had been 'hag-rid', but that she had 'suffered from indigestion'.

These improvements, however, are somewhat in advance of the story. Henchard, being uncultivated himself, was the bitterest critic the fair girl could possibly have had of her own lapses – really slight now, for she read omnivorously. A gratuitous ordeal was in store for her in the matter of her handwriting. She was passing the dining-room door one evening, and had occasion to go in for something. It was not till she had opened the door that she knew the Mayor was there in the company of a man with whom he transacted business.

'Here, Elizabeth-Jane,' he said, looking round at her, 'just write down what I tell you – a few words of an agreement for me and this gentleman to sign. I am a poor tool with a pen.'

'Be jowned,* and so be I,' said the gentleman.

She brought forward blotting-book, paper, and ink, and sat down.

'Now then – "An agreement entered into this sixteenth day of October" – write that first.'

She started the pen in an elephantine march across the sheet. It was a splendid round, bold hand of her own conception, a style that would have stamped a woman as Minerva's* own in more recent days. But other ideas reigned then: Henchard's creed was that proper young girls wrote ladies'-hand – nay, he believed that bristling characters were as innate and inseparate a part of refined womanhood as sex itself. Hence when, instead of scribbling, like the Princess Ida,* –

> In such a hand as when a field of corn
> Bows all its ears before the roaring East,

Elizabeth-Jane produced a line of chain-shot* and sand-bags, he reddened in angry shame for her, and, peremptorily saying, 'Never mind – I'll finish it,' dismissed her there and then.

Her considerate disposition became a pitfall to her now. She was, it must be admitted, sometimes provokingly and unnecessarily willing to saddle herself with manual labours. She would go to the kitchen instead of ringing, 'Not to make Phœbe come up twice.' She went down on her knees, shovel in hand, when the cat overturned the coal-scuttle; moreover, she would persistently thank the parlour-maid for everything, till one day, as soon as the girl was gone from the room, Henchard broke out with, 'Good God, why dostn't leave off thanking that girl as if she were a goddess-born! Don't I pay her a dozen pound a year to do things for 'ee?' Elizabeth shrank so visibly at the exclamation that he became sorry a few minutes after, and said that he did not mean to be rough.

These domestic exhibitions were the small protruding needle-rocks which suggested rather than revealed what was underneath. But his passion had less terror for her than his coldness. The increasing frequency of the latter mood told her the sad news that he disliked her with a growing dislike. The more interesting that her appearance and manners became under the softening influences which she could now command, and in her wisdom did command, the more she seemed to estrange him. Sometimes she caught him looking at her with a louring invidiousness that she could hardly bear. Not knowing his secret it was a cruel mockery that she should for the first time excite his animosity when she had taken his surname.

But the most terrible ordeal was to come. Elizabeth had latterly been accustomed of an afternoon to present a cup of cider or ale and bread-and-cheese to Nance Mockridge, who worked in the yard wimbling hay-bonds.* Nance accepted this offering thankfully at first; afterwards as a matter of course. On a day when Henchard was on the premises he saw his stepdaughter enter the hay-barn on this errand; and, as there was no clear spot on which to deposit the provisions, she at once set to work arranging two trusses of hay as a table, Mockridge meanwhile standing with her hands on her hips, easefully looking at the preparations on her behalf.

'Elizabeth, come here!' said Henchard; and she obeyed.

'Why do you lower yourself so confoundedly?' he said with suppressed passion. 'Haven't I told you o't fifty times? Hey? Making yourself a drudge for a common workwoman of such a character as hers! Why, ye'll disgrace me to the dust!'

Now these words were uttered loud enough to reach Nance inside the barn door, who fired up immediately at the slur upon her personal character. Coming to the door she cried, regardless of consequences, 'Come to that, Mr Michael Henchard, I can let 'ee know she've waited on worse!'

'Then she must have had more charity than sense,' said Henchard.

'O no, she hadn't. 'Twere not for charity but for hire; and at a public-house in this town!'

'It is not true!' cried Henchard indignantly.

'Just ask her,' said Nance, folding her naked arms in such a manner that she could comfortably scratch her elbows.

Henchard glanced at Elizabeth-Jane, whose complexion, now pink and white from confinement, lost nearly all of the former colour. 'What does this mean?' he said to her. 'Anything or nothing?'

'It is true,' said Elizabeth-Jane. 'But it was only –'

'Did you do it, or didn't you? Where was it?'

'At the Three Mariners; one evening for a little while, when we were staying there.'

Nance glanced triumphantly at Henchard, and sailed into the barn; for assuming that she was to be discharged on the instant she had resolved to make the most of her victory. Henchard, however, said nothing about discharging her. Unduly sensitive on such points by reason of his own past, he had the look of one completely ground down to the last indignity. Elizabeth followed him to the house like a culprit; but when she got inside she could not see him. Nor did she see him again that day.

Convinced of the scathing damage to his local repute and position that must have been caused by such a fact, though it had never before reached his own ears, Henchard showed a positive distaste for the presence of this girl not his own, whenever he encountered her. He mostly dined with the farmers at the market-room of one of the two chief hotels, leaving her in utter solitude. Could he have seen how she made use of those silent hours he might have found reason to reverse his judgment on her quality. She read and took notes incessantly, mastering facts with painful laboriousness, but never flinching from her self-imposed task. She began the study of Latin, incited by the Roman characteristics of the town she lived in. 'If I am not well-informed it shall be by no fault of my own,' she would say to herself through the tears that would occasionaly glide down her peachy cheeks when she was fairly baffled by the portentous obscurity of many of these educational works.

Thus she lived on, a dumb, deep-feeling, great-eyed creature, construed by not a single contiguous being; quenching with patient fortitude her incipient interest in Farfrae, because it seemed to be one-sided, unmaidenly, and unwise. True, that for reasons best known to herself, she had, since Farfrae's dismissal, shifted her quarters from the back room affording a view of the yard (which she had occupied with such zest) to a front chamber overlooking the street; but as for the young man, whenever he passed the house he seldom or never turned his head.

Winter had almost come, and unsettled weather made her still more dependent upon indoor resources. But there were certain early winter days in Casterbridge – days of firmamental exhaustion which followed angry south-westerly tempests – when, if the sun shone, the air was like velvet. She seized on these days for her periodical visits to the spot where her mother lay buried – the still-used burial-ground of the old Roman-British city, whose curious feature was this, its continuity as a place of sepulture. Mrs Henchard's dust mingled with the dust of women who lay ornamented with glass hair-pins and amber necklaces, and men who held in their mouths coins of Hadrian, Posthumus, and the Constantines.*

Half-past ten in the morning was about her hour for seeking this spot – a time when the town avenues were deserted as the avenues of Karnac.* Business had long since passed down them into its daily cells, and Lesiure had not arrived there. So Elizabeth-Jane walked and read, or looked over the edge of the book to think, and thus reached the churchyard.

There, approaching her mother's grave, she saw a solitary dark figure in the middle of the gravel-walk. This figure, too, was reading; but not from a book: the words which engrossed it being the inscription of Mrs Henchard's tombstone. The personage was in mourning like herself, was about her age and size, and might have been her wraith or double, but for the fact that it was a lady much more beautifully dressed than she. Indeed, comparatively indifferent as Elizabeth-Jane was to dress, unless for some temporary whim or purpose, her eyes were arrested by the artistic perfection of the lady's appearance. Her gait, too, had a flexuousness about it, which seemed to avoid angularity of movement less from choice than from predisposition. It was a revelation to Elizabeth that human beings could reach this stage of external development – she had never suspected it. She felt all the freshness and grace to be stolen from herself on the instant by the neighbourhood of such a stranger. And this was in face of the fact that Elizabeth could now have been writ handsome, while the young lady was simply pretty.

Had she been envious she might have hated the woman; but she did not do that – she allowed herself the pleasure of feeling fascinated. She wondered where the lady had come from. The stumpy and practical walk of honest homeliness which mostly prevailed there, the two styles of dress thereabout, the simple and the mistaken, equally avouched that this figure was no Caster-bridge woman's, even if a book in her hand resembling a guide book had not also suggested it.

The stranger presently moved from the tombstone of Mrs Henchard, and vanished behind the corner of the wall. Elizabeth went to the tomb herself; beside it were two footprints distinct in the soil, signifying that the lady had stood there a long time. She returned homeward, musing on what she had seen, as she might have mused on a rainbow or the Northern Lights,* a rare butterfly or a cameo.

Interesting as things had been out of doors, at home it turned out to be one of her bad days. Henchard, whose two years' mayoralty was ending, had been made aware that he was not to be chosen to fill a vacancy in the list of aldermen; and that Farfrae was likely to become one of the Council. This caused the unfortunate discovery that she had played the waiting-maid in the town of which he was Mayor to rankle in his mind yet more poisonously. He had learnt by personal inquiry at the time that it was to Donald Farfrae – that treacherous upstart – that she had thus humiliated herself. And though Mrs Stannidge seemed to attach no great importance to the incident – the cheerful souls at the Three Mariners having exhausted its aspects long ago – such was Henchard's haughty spirit that the simple thrifty deed was regarded as little less than a social catastrophe by him.

Ever since the evening of his wife's arrival with her daughter there had been something in the air which had changed his luck. That dinner at the King's Arms with his friends had been Henchard's Austerlitz:* he had had his successes since, but his course had not been upward. He was not to be numbered among the aldermen – that Peerage of burghers – as he had expected to be, and the consciousness of this soured him to-day.

'Well, where have you been?' he said to her with off-hand laconism.

'I've been strolling in the Walks and churchyard, father, till I feel quite leery.'* She clapped her hand to her mouth, but too late.

This was just enough to incense Henchard after the other crosses of the day. 'I *won't* have you talk like that!' he thundered. ' "Leery", indeed. One would think you worked upon a farm! One day I learn that you lend a hand in public-houses. Then I hear you talk like a clodhopper. I'm burned,* if it goes on, this house can't hold us two.'

The only way of getting a single pleasant thought to go to sleep upon after this was by recalling the lady she had seen that day, and hoping she might see her again.

Meanwhile Henchard was sitting up, thinking over his jealous folly in forbidding Farfrae to pay his addresses to this girl who did not belong to him, when if he had allowed them to go on he might not have been encumbered with her. At last he said to himself with satisfaction as he jumped up and went to the writing-table: 'Ah! he'll think it means peace, and a marriage portion – not that I don't want my house to be troubled with her, and no portion at all!' He wrote as follows:

> Sir, – On consideration, I don't wish to interfere with your courtship of Elizabeth-Jane, if you care for her. I therefore withdraw my objection; excepting in this – that the business be not carried on in my house. – Yours,
>
> M. HENCHARD

> Mr Farfrae

The morrow, being fairly fine, found Elizabeth-Jane again in the churchyard; but while looking for the lady she was startled by the apparition of Farfrae, who passed outside the gate. He glanced up for a moment from a pocket-book in which he appeared to be making figures as he went; whether or not he saw her he took no notice, and disappeared.

Unduly depressed by a sense of her own superfluity she thought he probably scorned her; and quite broken in spirit sat down on a bench. She fell into painful thought on her position, which ended with her saying quite loud, 'O, I wish I was dead with dear mother!'

Behind the bench was a little promenade under the wall where people sometimes walked instead of on the gravel. The bench seemed to be touched by something; she looked round, and a face was bending over her, veiled, but still distinct, the face of the young woman she had seen yesterday.

Elizabeth-Jane looked confounded for a moment, knowing she had been overheard, though there was pleasure in her confusion. 'Yes, I heard you,' said the lady, in a vivacious voice, answering her look. 'What can have happened?'

'I don't – I can't tell you,' said Elizabeth, putting her hand to her face to hide a quick flush that had come.

There was no movement or word for a few seconds; then the girl felt that the young lady was sitting down beside her. 'I guess how it is with you,' said the latter. 'That was your mother.' She waved her hand towards the tombstone. Elizabeth looked up at her as if inquiring of herself whether there should be confidence. The lady's manner was so desirous, so anxious, that the girl decided there should be confidence. 'It was my mother,' she said, 'my only friend.'

'But your father, Mr Henchard. He is living?'

'Yes, he is living,' said Elizabeth-Jane.

'Is he not kind to you?'

'I've no wish to complain of him.'

'There has been a disagreement?'

'A little.'

'Perhaps you were to blame,' suggested the stranger.

'I was – in many ways,' sighed the meek Elizabeth. 'I swept up the coals when the servant ought to have done it; and I said I was leery; – and he was angry with me.'

The lady seemed to warm towards her for that reply. 'Do you know the impression your words give me?' she said ingenuously. 'That he is a hot-tempered man – a little proud – perhaps ambitious; but not a bad man.' Her anxiety not to condemn Henchard while siding with Elizabeth was curious.

'O no; certainly not *bad*,' agreed the honest girl. 'And he has not even been unkind to me till lately – since mother died. But it has been very much to bear while it has lasted. All is owing to my defects, I daresay; and my defects are owing to my history.'

'What is your history?'

Elizabeth-Jane looked wistfully at her questioner. She found that her questioner was looking at her; turned her eyes down; and then seemed compelled to look back again. 'My history is not gay or attractive,' she said. 'And yet I can tell it, if you really want to know.'

The lady assured her that she did want to know; whereupon Elizabeth-Jane told the tale of her life as she understood it, which was in general the true one, except that the sale at the fair had no part therein.

Contrary to the girl's expectation her new friend was not shocked. This cheered her; and it was not till she thought of returning to that home in which she had been treated so roughly of late that her spirits fell.

'I don't know how to return,' she murmured. 'I think of going away. But what can I do? Where can I go?'

'Perhaps it will be better soon,' said her friend gently. 'So I would not go far. Now what do you think of this: I shall soon want somebody to live in my house, partly as housekeeper, partly as companion; would you mind coming to me? But perhaps –'

'O yes,' cried Elizabeth, with tears in her eyes. 'I would, indeed – I would do anything to be independent; for then perhaps my father might get to love me. But, ah!'

'What?'

'I am no accomplished person. And a companion to *you* must be that.'

'O, not necessarily.'

'Not? But I can't help using rural words sometimes, when I don't mean to.'

'Never mind, I shall like to know them.'

'And – O, I know I shan't do!' – she cried with a distressful laugh. 'I accidentally learned to write round hand* instead of ladies'-hand. And, of course, you want some one who can write that?'

'Well, no.'

'What, not necessary to write ladies'-hand?' cried the joyous Elizabeth.

'Not at all.'

'But where do you live?'

'In Casterbridge, or rather I shall be living here after twelve o'clock to-day.'

Elizabeth expressed her astonishment.

'I have been staying at Budmouth for a few days while my house was getting ready. The house I am going into is that one they call High-Place Hall* – the old stone one looking down the lane to the Market. Two or three rooms are fit for occupation, though not all: I sleep there to-night for the first time. Now will you think over my proposal, and meet me here the first fine day next week, and say if you are still in the same mind?'

Elizabeth, her eyes shining at this prospect of a change from an unbearable position, joyfully assented; and the two parted at the gate of the churchyard.

Chapter 21

As a maxim glibly repeated from childhood remains practically unmarked till some mature experience enforces it, so did this High-Place Hall now for the first time really show itself to Elizabeth-Jane, though her ears had heard its name on a hundred occasions.

Her mind dwelt upon nothing else but the stranger, and the house, and her own chance of living there, all the rest of the day. In the afternoon she had occasion to pay a few bills in the town and do a little shopping, when she learnt that what was a new discovery to herself had become a common topic about the streets. High-Place Hall was undergoing repair; a lady was coming there to live shortly; all the shop-people knew it, and had already discounted the chance of her being a customer.

Elizabeth-Jane could, however, add a capping touch to information so new to her in the bulk. The lady, she said, had arrived that day.

When the lamps were lighted, and it was yet not so dark as to render chimneys, attics, and roofs invisible, Elizabeth, almost with a lover's feeling, thought she would like to look at the outside of High-Place Hall. She went up the street in that direction.

The Hall, with its grey *façade* and parapet, was the only residence of its sort so near the centre of the town. It had, in the first place, the characteristics of a country mansion – birds' nests in its chimneys, damp nooks where fungi grew, and irregularities of surface direct from Nature's trowel. At night the forms of passengers were patterned by the lamps in black shadows upon the pale walls.

This evening motes of straw lay around, and other signs of the premises having been in that lawless condition which accompanies the entry of a new tenant. The house was entirely of stone, and formed an example of dignity without great size. It was not altogether aristocratic, still less consequential, yet the old-fashioned stranger instinctively said, 'Blood built it, and Wealth enjoys it,' however vague his opinions of those accessories might be.

Yet as regards the enjoying it the stranger would have been wrong, for until this very evening, when the new lady had arrived, the house had been empty for a year or two, while before that interval its occupancy had been irregular. The reason of its unpopularity was soon made manifest. Some of its rooms overlooked the market-place; and such a prospect from such a house was not considered desirable or seemly by its would-be occupiers.

Elizabeth's eyes sought the upper rooms, and saw lights there. The lady had obviously arrived. The impression that this woman of comparatively practised manner had made upon the studious girl's mind was so deep that she enjoyed standing under an opposite archway merely to think that the charming lady was inside the confronting walls, and to wonder what she was doing. Her admiration for the architecture of that front was entirely on account of the inmate it screened. Though for that matter the architecture deserved admiration, or at least study, on its own account. It was Palladian,* and like most architecture erected since the Gothic age was a compilation rather than a design. But its reasonableness made it impressive. It was not rich, but rich enough. A timely consciousness of the ultimate vanity of human architecture, no less than of other human things, had prevented artistic superfluity.

Men had till quite recently been going in and out with parcels and packing-cases, rendering the door and hall within like a public thoroughfare. Elizabeth trotted through the open door in the dusk, but becoming alarmed at her own temerity she went quickly out again by another which stood open in the lofty wall of the back court. To her surprise she found herself in one of the little-used alleys of the town. Looking round at the door which had given her egress, by the light of the solitary lamp fixed in the alley, she saw that it was arched and old – older even than the house itself. The door was studded, and the keystone of the arch was a mask. Originally the mask had exhibited a comic leer, as could still be discerned; but generations of Casterbridge boys had thrown stones at the mask, aiming at its open mouth; and the blows thereon had chipped off the lips and jaws as if they had been eaten away by disease. The appearance was so ghastly by the weakly lamp-glimmer that she could not bear to look at it – the first unpleasant feature of her visit.

The position of the queer old door and the odd presence of the leering mask suggested one thing above all others as appertaining to the mansion's past history – intrigue. By the alley it had been possible to come unseen from all sorts of quarters in the town –

the old play-house, the old bull-stake, the old cock-pit, the pool wherein nameless infants had been used to disappear. High-Place Hall could boast of its conveniences undoubtedly.

She turned to come away in the nearest direction homeward, which was down the alley, but hearing footsteps approaching in that quarter, and having no great wish to be found in such a place at such a time she quickly retreated. There being no other way out she stood behind a brick pier* till the intruder should have gone his ways.

Had she watched she would have been surprised. She would have seen that the pedestrian on coming up made straight for the arched doorway: that as he paused with his hand upon the latch the lamplight fell upon the face of Henchard.

But Elizabeth-Jane clung so closely to her nook that she discerned nothing of this. Henchard passed in, as ignorant of her presence as she was ignorant of his identity, and disappeared in the darkness. Elizabeth came out a second time into the alley, and made the best of her way home.

Henchard's chiding, by begetting in her a nervous fear of doing anything definable as unlady-like, had operated thus curiously in keeping them unknown to each other at a critical moment. Much might have resulted from recognition – at the least a query on either side in one and the self-same form: What could he or she possibly be doing there?

Henchard, whatever his business at the lady's house, reached his own home only a few minutes later than Elizabeth-Jane. Her plan was to broach the question of leaving his roof this evening; the events of the day had urged her to the course. But its execution depended upon his mood, and she anxiously awaited his manner towards her. She found that it had changed. He showed no further tendency to be angry; he showed something worse. Absolute indifference had taken the place of irritability; and his coldness was such that it encouraged her to departure, even more than hot temper could have done.

'Father, have you any objection to my going away?' she asked.

'Going away! No – none whatever. Where are you going?'

She thought it undesirable and unnecessary to say anything at present about her destination to one who took so little interest in her. He would know that soon enough. 'I have heard of an opportunity of getting more cultivated and finished, and being less idle,' she answered, with hesitation. 'A chance of a place in a household where I can have advantages of study, and seeing refined life.'

'Then make the best of it, in Heaven's name – if you can't get cultivated where you are.'

'You don't object?'

'Object – I? Ho – no! Not at all.' After a pause he said, 'But you won't have enough money for this lively scheme without help, you know? If you like I should be willing to make you an allowance, so that you be not bound to live upon the starvation wages refined folk are likely to pay 'ee.'

She thanked him for this offer.

'It had better be done properly,' he added after a pause. 'A small annuity is what I should like you to have – so as to be independent of me – and so that I may be independent of you. Would that please ye?'

'Certainly.'

'Then I'll see about it this very day.' He seemed relieved to get her off his hands by this arrangement, and as far as they were concerned the matter was settled. She now simply waited to see the lady again.

The day and the hour came; but a drizzling rain fell. Elizabeth-Jane, having now changed her orbit from one of gay independence to laborious self-help, thought the weather good enough for such declined glory as hers, if her friend would only face it – a matter of doubt. She went to the boot-room where her pattens* had hung ever since her apotheosis,* took them down, had their mildewed leathers blacked, and put them on as she had done in old times. Thus mounted,* and with cloak and umbrella, she went off to the place of appointment – intending, if the lady were not there, to call at the house.

One side of the churchyard – the side towards the weather – was sheltered by an ancient thatched mud wall whose eaves overhung as much as one or two feet. At the back of the wall was a corn-yard with its granary and barns – the place wherein she had met Farfrae many months earlier. Under the projection of the thatch she saw a figure. The young lady had come.

Her presence so exceptionally substantiated the girl's utmost hopes that she almost feared her good fortune. Fancies find room in the strongest minds. Here, in a churchyard old as civilization, in the worst of weathers, was a strange woman of curious fascinations never seen elsewhere: there might be some devilry about her presence. However, Elizabeth went on to the church tower, on whose summit the rope of a flag-staff rattled in the wind; and thus she came to the wall.

The lady had such a cheerful aspect in the drizzle that Elizabeth forgot her fancy. 'Well,' said the lady, a little of the whiteness of her teeth appearing with the word through the black fleece that protected her face, 'have you decided?'

'Yes, quite,' said the other eagerly.

'Your father is willing?'

'Yes.'

'Then come along.'

'When?'

'Now – as soon as you like. I had a good mind to send to you to come to my house, thinking you might not venture up here in the wind. But as I like getting out of doors, I thought I would come and see first.'

'It was my own thought.'

'That shows we shall agree. Then can you come to-day? My house is so hollow and dismal that I want some living thing there.'

'I think I might be able to,' said the girl, reflecting.

Voices were borne over to them at that instant on the wind and raindrops from the other side of the wall. There came such words as 'sacks', 'quarters', 'threshing', 'tailing', 'next Saturday's market', each sentence being disorganized by the gusts like a face in a cracked mirror. Both the women listened.

'Who are those?' said the lady.

'One is my father. He rents that yard and barn.'

The lady seemed to forget the immediate business in listening to the technicalities of the corn trade. At last she said suddenly, 'Did you tell him where you were going to?'

'No.'

'O – how was that?'

'I thought it safer to get away first – as he is so uncertain in his temper.'

'Perhaps you are right . . . Besides, I have never told you my name. It is Miss Templeman . . . Are they gone – on the other side?'

'No. They are only gone up into the granary.'

'Well, it is getting damp here. I shall expect you to-day – this evening, say, at six.'

'Which way shall I come, ma'am?'

'The front way – round by the gate. There is no other that I have noticed.'

Elizabeth-Jane had been thinking of the door in the alley.

'Perhaps, as you have not mentioned your destination, you may as well keep silent upon it till you are clear off. Who knows but that he may alter his mind?'

Elizabeth-Jane shook her head. 'On consideration I don't fear it,' she said sadly. 'He has grown quite cold to me.'

'Very well. Six o'clock then.'

When they had emerged upon the open road and parted they found enough to do in holding their bowed umbrellas to the wind. Nevertheless the lady looked in at the corn-yard gates as she passed them, and paused on one foot for a moment. But nothing was visible there save the ricks, and the humpbacked barn cushioned with moss, and the granary rising against the church-tower behind, where the smacking of the rope against the flag-staff still went on.

Now Henchard had not the slightest suspicion that Elizabeth-Jane's movement was to be so prompt. Hence when, just before six, he reached home and saw a fly* at the door from the King's Arms, and his stepdaughter, with all her little bags and boxes, getting into it, he was taken by surprise.

'But you said I might go, father?' she explained through the carriage window.

'Said! – yes. But I thought you meant next month, or next year. 'Od, seize it – you take time by the forelock!* This, then, is how you be going to treat me for all my trouble about ye?'

'O father! How can you speak like that? It is unjust of you!' she said with spirit.

'Well, well, have your own way,' he replied. He entered the house, and, seeing that all her things had not yet been brought down, went up to her room to look on. He had never been there since she had occupied it. Evidences of her care, of her endeavours for improvement, were visible all around, in the form of books, sketches, maps, and little arrangements for tasteful effects. Henchard had known nothing of these efforts. He gazed at them, turned suddenly about, and came down to the door.

'Look here,' he said, in an altered voice – he never called her by name now – 'don't 'ee go away from me. It may be I've spoke roughly to you – but I've been grieved beyond everything by you – there's something that caused it.'

'By me?' she said, with deep concern. 'What have I done?'

'I can't tell you now. But if you'll stop, and go on living as my daughter, I'll tell you all in time.'

But the proposal had come ten minutes too late. She was in the fly – was already, in imagination, at the house of the lady whose manner had such charms for her. 'Father,' she said, as considerately as she could, 'I think it best for us that I go on now. I need not stay long; I shall not be far away; and if you want me badly I can soon come back again.'

He nodded ever so slightly, as a receipt of her decision and no more. 'You are not going far, you say. What will be your address, in case I wish to write to you? Or am I not to know?'

'Oh yes – certainly. It is only in the town – High-Place Hall.'

'Where?' said Henchard, his face stilling.

She repeated the words. He neither moved nor spoke, and waving her hand to him in utmost friendliness she signified to the flyman to drive up the street.

Chapter 22

We go back for a moment to the preceding night, to account for Henchard's attitude.

At the hour when Elizabeth-Jane was contemplating her stealthy reconnoitring excursion to the abode of the lady of her fancy, he had been not a little amazed at receiving a letter by hand in Lucetta's well-known characters. The self-repression, the resignation of her previous communication had vanished from her mood; she wrote with some of the natural lightness which had marked her in their early acquaintance.

HIGH-PLACE HALL

MY DEAR MR HENCHARD, – Don't be surprised. It is for your good and mine, as I hope, that I have come to live at Casterbridge – for how long I cannot tell. That depends upon another; and he is a man, and a merchant, and a Mayor, and one who has the first right to my affections.

Seriously, *mon ami*, I am not so light-hearted as I may seem to be from this. I have come here in consequence of hearing of the death of your wife – whom you used to think of as dead so many years before! Poor woman, she seems to have been a sufferer, though un-complaining, and though weak in intellect not an imbecile. I am glad you acted fairly by her. As soon as I knew she was no more, it was brought home to me very forcibly by my conscience that I ought to endeavour to disperse the shade which my *étourderie** flung over my name, by asking you to carry out your promise to me. I hope you are of the same mind, and that you will take steps to this end. As, however, I did not know how you were situated, or what had happened since our separation, I decided to come and establish myself here before communicating with you.

You probably feel as I do about this. I shall be able to see you in a day or two. Till then, farewell. – Yours,

LUCETTA

P.S. – I was unable to keep my appointment to meet you for a moment or two in passing through Casterbridge the other day. My plans were altered by a family event, which it will surprise you to hear of.

Henchard had already heard that High-Place was being prepared for a tenant. He said with a puzzled air to the first person he encountered, 'Who is coming to live at the Hall?'

'A lady of the name of Templeman, I believe, sir,' said his informant.

Henchard thought it over. 'Lucetta is related to her, I suppose,' he said to himself. 'Yes, I must put her in her proper position, undoubtedly.'

It was by no means with the oppression that would once have accompanied the thought that he regarded the moral necessity now; it was, indeed, with interest, if not warmth. His bitter disappointment at finding Elizabeth-Jane to be none of his, and himself a childless man, had left an emotional void in Henchard that he unconsciously craved to fill. In this frame of mind, though without strong feeling, he had strolled up the alley and into High-Place Hall by the postern* at which Elizabeth had so nearly encountered him. He had gone on thence into the court, and inquired of a man whom he saw unpacking china from a crate if Miss Le Sueur was living there. Miss Le Sueur had been the name under which he had known Lucetta – or 'Lucette', as she had called herself at that time.

The man replied in the negative; that Miss Templeman only had come. Henchard went away, concluding that Lucetta had not as yet settled in.

He was in this interested stage of the inquiry when he witnessed Elizabeth-Jane's departure the next day. On hearing her announce the address there suddenly took possession of him the strange thought that Lucetta and Miss Templeman were one and the same person, for he could recall that in her season of intimacy with him the name of the rich relative whom he had deemed somewhat a mythical personage had been given as Templeman. Though he was not a fortune-hunter, the possibility that Lucetta had been sublimed into a lady of means by some munificent testament on the part of this relative lent a charm to her image which it might not otherwise have acquired. He was getting on towards the dead level of middle age, when material things increasingly possess the mind.

But Henchard was not left long in suspense. Lucetta was rather addicted to scribbling, as had been shown by the torrent of letters after the *fiasco* in their marriage arrangements, and hardly had Elizabeth gone away when another note came to the Mayor's house from High-Place Hall.

'I am in residence,' she said, 'and comfortable, though getting here has been a wearisome undertaking. You probably know what I am going to tell you, or do you not? My good Aunt Templeman, the banker's widow, whose very existence you used to doubt, much more her affluence, has lately died, and bequeathed some of her property to me. I will not enter into details except to say that I have taken her name – as a means of escape from mine, and its wrongs.

'I am now my own mistress, and have chosen to reside in Casterbridge – to be tenant of High-Place Hall, that at least you may be put to no trouble if you wish to see me. My first intention was to keep you in ignorance of the changes in my life till you should meet me in the street; but I have thought better of this.

'You probably are aware of my arrangement with your daughter, and have doubtless laughed at the – what shall I call it? – practical joke (in all affection) of my getting her to live with me. But my first meeting with her was purely an accident. Do you see, Michael, partly why I have done it? – why, to give you an excuse for coming here as if to visit *her*, and thus to form my aquaintance naturally. She is a dear, good girl, and she thinks you have treated her with undue severity. You may have done so in your haste, but not deliberately, I am sure. As the result has been to bring her to me I am not disposed to upbraid you. – In haste, yours always,

LUCETTA'

The excitement which these announcements produced in Henchard's gloomy soul was to him most pleasurable. He sat over his dining-table long and dreamily, and by an almost mechanical transfer the sentiments which had run to waste since his estrangement from Elizabeth-Jane and Donald Farfrae gathered around Lucetta before they had grown dry. She was plainly in a very coming-on disposition for marriage. But what else could a poor woman be who had given her time and heart to him so thoughtlessly, at that former time, as to lose her credit by it? Probably conscience no less than affection had brought her here. On the whole he did not blame her.

'The artful little woman!' he said, smiling (with reference to Lucetta's adroit and pleasant manœuvre with Elizabeth-Jane).

To feel that he would like to see Lucetta was with Henchard to start for her house. He put on his hat and went. It was between eight and nine o'clock when he reached her door. The answer brought him was that Miss Templeman was engaged for that evening; but that she would be happy to see him the next day.

'That's rather like giving herself airs!' he thought. 'And considering what we –' But after all, she plainly had not expected him, and he took the refusal quietly. Nevertheless he resolved not to go next day. 'These cursed women – there's not an inch of straight grain in 'em!' he said.

Let us follow the track of Mr Henchard's thought as if it were a clue line,* and view the interior of High-Place Hall on this particular evening.

On Elizabeth-Jane's arrival she had been phlegmatically asked by an elderly woman to go upstairs and take off her things. She had replied with great earnestness that she would not think of giving that trouble, and on the instant divested herself of her bonnet and cloak in the passage. She was then conducted to the first door on the landing, and left to find her way further alone.

The room disclosed was prettily furnished as a boudoir or small drawing-room, and on a sofa with two cylindrical pillows reclined a dark-haired, large-eyed, pretty woman, of unmistakably French extraction on one side or the other. She was probably some years older than Elizabeth, and had a sparkling light in her eye. In front of the sofa was a small table, with a pack of cards scattered upon it faces upward.

The attitude had been so full of abandonment that she bounded up like a spring on hearing the door open.

Perceiving that it was Elizabeth she lapsed into ease, and came across to her with a reckless skip that innate grace only prevented from being boisterous.

'Why, you are late,' she said, taking hold of Elizabeth-Jane's hands.

'There were so many little things to put up.'

'And you seem dead-alive and tired. Let me try to enliven you by some wonderful tricks I have learnt, to kill time. Sit there and don't move.' She gathered up the pack of cards, pulled the table in front of her, and began to deal them rapidly, telling Elizabeth to choose some.

'Well, have you chosen?' she asked, flinging down the last card.

'No,' stammered Elizabeth, arousing herself from a reverie. 'I quite forgot, I was thinking of – you, and me – and how strange it is that I am here.'

Miss Templeman looked at Elizabeth-Jane with interest, and laid down the cards. 'Ah! never mind,' she said. 'I'll lie here while you sit by me; and we'll talk.'

Elizabeth drew up silently to the head of the sofa, but with obvious pleasure. It could be seen that though in years she was younger than her entertainer in manner and general vision she seemed more of the sage. Miss Templeman deposited herself on the sofa in her former flexuous position, and throwing her arm above her brow – somewhat in the pose of a well-known conception of Titian's* – talked up at Elizabeth-Jane invertedly across her forehead and arm.

'I must tell you something,' she said. 'I wonder if you have suspected it. I have only been mistress of a large house and a fortune a little while.'

'Oh – only a little while?' murmured Elizabeth-Jane, her countenance slightly falling.

'As a girl I lived about in garrison towns and elsewhere with my father, till I was quite flighty and unsettled. He was an officer in the army. I should not have mentioned this had I not thought it best you should know the truth.'

'Yes, yes.' She looked thoughtfully round the room – at the little square piano with brass inlayings, at the window-curtains, at the lamp, at the fair and dark kings and queens on the card-table, and finally at the inverted face of Lucetta Templeman, whose large lustrous eyes had such an odd effect upside down.

Elizabeth's mind ran on acquirements to an almost morbid

degree. 'You speak French and Italian fluently, no doubt,' she said. 'I have not been able to get beyond a wretched bit of Latin yet.'

'Well, for that matter, in my native isle speaking French does not go for much. It is rather the other way.'

'Where is your native isle?'

It was with rather more reluctance that Miss Templeman said, 'Jersey. There they speak French on one side of the street and English on the other, and a mixed tongue in the middle of the road. But it is a long time since I was there. Bath is where my people really belong to, though my ancestors in Jersey were as good as anybody in England. They were the Le Sueurs, an old family who have done great things in their time. I went back and lived there after my father's death. But I don't value such past matters, and am quite an English person in my feelings and tastes.'

Lucetta's tongue had for a moment outrun her discretion. She had arrived at Casterbridge as a Bath lady, and there were obvious reasons why Jersey should drop out of her life. But Elizabeth had tempted her to make free, and a deliberately formed resolve had been broken.

It could not, however, have been broken in safer company. Lucetta's words went no further, and after this day she was so much upon her guard that there appeared no chance of her identification with the young Jersey woman who had been Henchard's dear comrade at a critical time. Not the least amusing of her safeguards was her resolute avoidance of a French word if one by accident came to her tongue more readily than its English equivalent. She shirked it with the suddenness of the weak Apostle at the accusation, 'Thy speech bewrayeth thee!'*

Expectancy sat visibly upon Lucetta the next morning. She dressed herself for Mr Henchard, and restlessly awaited his call before mid-day; as he did not come she waited on through the afternoon. But she did not tell Elizabeth that the person expected was the girl's stepfather.

They sat in adjoining windows of the same room in Lucetta's great stone mansion, netting,* and looking out upon the market, which formed an animated scene. Elizabeth could see the crown of her stepfather's hat among the rest beneath, and was not aware that Lucetta watched the same object with yet intenser interest. He moved about amid the throng, at this point lively as an ant-hill; elsewhere more reposeful, and broken up by stalls of fruit and vegetables. The farmers as a rule preferred the open *carrefour** for their transactions, despite its inconvenient jostlings and the danger from crossing vehicles, to the gloomy sheltered market-room provided for them. Here they surged on this one day of the week, forming a little world of leggings, switches, and sample-bags; men of extensive stomachs, sloping like mountain sides; men whose heads in walking swayed as the trees in November gales; who in conversing varied their attitudes much, lowering themselves by spreading their knees, and thrusting their hands into the pockets of remote inner jackets. Their faces radiated tropical warmth; for though when at home their countenances varied with the seasons, their market-faces all the year round were glowing little fires.

All over-clothes here were worn as if they were an inconvenience, a hampering necessity. Some men were well-dressed; but the majority were careless in that respect, appearing in suits which were historical records of their wearer's deeds, sun-scorchings, and daily struggles for many years past. Yet many carried ruffled cheque-books in their pockets which regulated at the bank hard by a balance of never less than four figures. In fact, what these gibbous* human shapes specially represented was ready money – money insistently ready – not ready next year like a nobleman's –often not merely ready at the bank like a professional man's, but ready in their large plump hands.

It happened that to-day there rose in the midst of them all two or three tall apple-trees standing as if they grew on the spot; till it was perceived that they were held by men from the cider-districts who came here to sell them, bringing the clay of their county on their boots. Elizabeth-Jane, who had often observed them, said, 'I wonder if the same trees come every week?'

'What trees?' said Lucetta, absorbed in watching for Henchard.

Elizabeth replied vaguely, for an incident checked her. Behind one of the trees stood Farfrae, briskly discussing a sample-bag with a farmer. Henchard had come up, accidentally encountering the young man, whose face seemed to inquire, 'Do we speak to each other?'

She saw her stepfather throw a shine into his eye which answered 'No!' Elizabeth-Jane sighed.

'Are you particularly interested in anybody out there?' said Lucetta.

'O no,' said her companion, a quick red shooting over her face.

Luckily Farfrae's figure was immediately covered by the apple-tree.

Lucetta looked hard at her. 'Quite sure?' she said.

'O yes,' said Elizabeth-Jane.

Again Lucetta looked out. 'They are all farmers, I suppose?' she said.

'No. There's Mr Bulge – he's a wine merchant; there's Benjamin Brownlet – a horse dealer; and Kitson, the pig breeder; and Yopper, the auctioneer; besides maltsters, and millers – and so on.' Farfrae stood out quite distinctly now; but she did not mention him.

The Saturday afternoon slipped on thus desultorily. The market changed from the sample-showing hour to the idle hour before starting homewards, when tales were told. Henchard had not called on Lucetta though he had stood so near. He must have been too busy, she thought. He would come on Sunday or Monday.

The days came but not the visitor, though Lucetta repeated her dressing with scrupulous care. She was disheartened. It may at once be declared that Lucetta no longer bore towards Henchard all that warm allegiance which had characterized her in their first acquaintance; the then unfortunate issue of things had chilled pure love considerably. But there remained a conscientious wish to bring about her union with him, now that there was nothing to hinder it – to right her position – which in itself was a happiness to sigh for. With strong social reasons on her side why their marriage should take place there had ceased to be any worldly reason on his why it should be postponed, since she had succeeded to fortune.

Tuesday was the great Candlemas* fair. At breakfast she said to Elizabeth-Jane quite coolly: 'I imagine your father may call to see you to-day. I suppose he stands close by in the market-place with the rest of the corn-dealers?'

She shook her head. 'He won't come.'

'Why?'

'He has taken against me,' she said in a husky voice.

'You have quarrelled more deeply than I know of.'

Elizabeth, wishing to shield the man she believed to be her father from any charge of unnatural dislike, said 'Yes.'

'Then where you are is, of all places, the one he will avoid?'

Elizabeth nodded sadly.

Lucetta looked blank, twitched up her lovely eyebrows and

lips, and burst into hysterical sobs. Here was a disaster – her ingenious scheme completely stultified.

'O, my dear Miss Templeman – what's the matter?' cried her companion.

'I like your company much!' said Lucetta, as soon as she could speak.

'Yes, yes – and so do I yours!' Elizabeth chimed in soothingly.

'But – but –' She could not finish the sentence, which was, naturally, that if Henchard had such a rooted dislike for the girl as now seemed to be the case, Elizabeth-Jane would have to be got rid of – a disagreeable necessity.

A provisional resource suggested itself. 'Miss Henchard – will you go on an errand for me as soon as breakfast is over? – Ah, that's very good of you. Will you go and order –' Here she enumerated several commissions at sundry shops, which would occupy Elizabeth's time for the next hour or two, at least.

'And have you ever seen the Museum?'

Elizabeth-Jane had not.

'Then you should do so at once. You can finish the morning by going there. It is an old house in a back street – I forget where – but you'll find out – and there are crowds of interesting things – skeletons, teeth, old pots and pans, ancient boots and shoes, birds' eggs – all charmingly instructive. You'll be sure to stay till you get quite hungry.'

Elizabeth hastily put on her things and departed. 'I wonder why she wants to get rid of me to-day!' she said sorrowfully as she went. That her absence, rather than her services or instruction, was in request, had been readily apparent to Elizabeth-Jane, simple as she seemed, and difficult as it was to attribute a motive for the desire.

She had not been gone ten minutes when one of Lucetta's servants was sent to Henchard's with a note. The contents were briefly:

DEAR MICHAEL, – You will be standing in view of my house to-day for two or three hours in the course of your business, so do please call and see me. I am sadly disappointed that you have not come before, for can I help anxiety about my own equivocal relation to you? – especially now my aunt's fortune has brought me more prominently before society? Your daughter's presence here may be the cause of your neglect; and I have therefore sent her away for the morning. Say you come on business – I shall be quite alone.

LUCETTA

When the messenger returned her mistress gave directions that if a gentleman called he was to be admitted at once, and sat down to await results.

Sentimentally she did not much care to see him – his delays had wearied her; but it was necessary; and with a sigh she arranged herself picturesquely in the chair; first this way, then that; next so that the light fell over her head. Next she flung herself on the couch in the cyma-recta* curve which so became her, and with her arm over her brow looked towards the door. This, she decided, was the best position after all; and thus she remained till a man's step was heard on the stairs. Whereupon Lucetta, forgetting her curve (for Nature was too strong for Art as yet), jumped up and ran and hid herself behind one of the window-curtains in a freak of timidity. In spite of the waning of passion the situation was an agitating one – she had not seen Henchard since his (supposed) temporary parting from her in Jersey.

She could hear the servant showing the visitor into the room, shutting the door upon him, and leaving as if to go and look for her mistress. Lucetta flung back the curtain with a nervous greeting. The man before her was not Henchard.

Chapter 23

A conjecture that her visitor might be some other person had, indeed, flashed through Lucetta's mind when she was on the point of bursting out; but it was just too late to recede.

He was years younger than the Mayor of Casterbridge; fair, fresh, and slenderly handsome. He wore genteel cloth leggings with white buttons, polished boots with infinite lace holes, light cord breeches under a black velveteen coat and waistcoat; and he had a silver-topped switch in his hand. Lucetta blushed, and said with a curious mixture of pout and laugh on her face – 'O, I've made a mistake!'

The visitor, on the contrary, did not laugh half a wrinkle.

'But I'm very sorry!' he said, in deprecating tones. 'I came and I inquired for Miss Henchard, and they showed me up heere, and in no case would I have caught ye so unmannerly if I had known!'

'I was the unmannerly one,' said she.

'But is it that I have come to the wrong house, madam?' said Mr Farfrae, blinking a little in his bewilderment and nervously tapping his leggings with his switch.

'O no, sir, – sit down. You must come and sit down now you are here,' replied Lucetta kindly, to relieve his embarrassmeent. 'Miss Henchard will be here directly.'

Now this was not strictly true; but that something about the young man – that hyperborean* crispness, stringency, and charm, as of a well-braced musical instrument, which had awakened the interest of Henchard, and of Elizabeth-Jane, and of the Three Mariners' jovial crew, at sight, made his unexpected presence here attractive to Lucetta. He hesitated, looked at the chair, thought there was no danger in it (though there was), and sat down.

Farfrae's sudden entry was simply the result of Henchard's permission to him to see Elizabeth if he were minded to woo her. At first he had taken no notice of Henchard's brusque letter; but an exceptionally fortunate business transaction put him on good terms with everybody, and revealed to him that he could undeniably marry if he chose. Then who so pleasing, thrifty, and satisfactory in every way as Elizabeth-Jane? Apart from her personal recommendations a reconciliation with his former friend Henchard would, in the natural course of things, flow from such a union. He therefore forgave the Mayor his curtness; and this morning on his way to the fair he had called at her house, where he learnt that she was staying at Miss Templeman's. A little stimulated at not finding her ready and waiting – so fanciful are men! – he hastened on to High-Place Hall to encounter no Elizabeth but its mistress herself.

'The fair to-day seems a large one,' she said when, by a natural deviation, their eyes sought the busy scene without. 'Your numerous fairs and markets keep me interested. How many things I think of while I watch from here!'

He seemed in doubt how to answer, and the babble without reached them as they sat – voices as of wavelets on a lopping* sea, one ever and anon rising above the rest. 'Do you look out often?' he asked.

'Yes – very often.'

'Do you look for any one you know?'

Why should she have answered as she did?

'I look as at a picture merely. But,' she went on, turning pleasantly to him, 'I may do so now – I may look for you. You are always there, are you not? Ah – I don't mean it seriously! But it is amusing to look for somebody one knows in a crowd, even if one does not want him. It takes off the terrible oppressiveness of being surrounded by a throng, and having no point of junction with it through a single individual.'

'Ay! Maybe you'll be very lonely, ma'am?'

'Nobody knows how lonely.'

'But you are rich, they say?'

'If so, I don't know how to enjoy my riches. I came to Casterbridge thinking I should like to live here. But I wonder if I shall.'

'Where did ye come from, ma'am?'

'The neighbourhood of Bath.'

'And I from near Edinboro',' he murmured. 'It's better to stay at home, and that's true; but a man must live where his money is made. It is a great pity, but it's always so! Yet I've done very well this year. O yes,' he went on with ingenuous enthusiasm. 'You see that man with the drab kerseymere* coat? I bought largely of him in the autumn when wheat was down, and then afterwards when it rose a little I sold off all I had! It brought only a small profit to me; while the farmers kept theirs, expecting higher figures – yes, though the rats were gnawing the ricks hollow. Just when I sold the markets went lower, and I bought up the corn of those who had been holding back at less price than my first purchases. And then,' cried Farfrae impetuously, his face alight, 'I sold it a few weeks after, when it happened to go up again! And so, by contenting mysel' with small profits frequently repeated, I soon made five hundred pounds – yes!' – (bringing down his hand upon the table, and quite forgetting where he was) – 'while the others by keeping theirs in hand made nothing at all!'

Lucetta regarded him with a critical interest. He was quite a new type of person to her. At last his eye fell upon the lady's and their glances met.

'Ay, now, I'm wearying you!' he exclaimed.

She said, 'No, indeed,' colouring a shade.

'What then?'

'Quite otherwise. You are most interesting.'

It was now Farfrae who showed the modest pink.

'I mean all you Scotchmen,' she added in hasty correction. 'So free from Southern extremes We common people are all one way or the other – warm or cold, passionate or frigid. You have both temperatures going on in you at the same time.'

'But how do you mean that? Ye were best to explain clearly, ma'am.'

'You are animated – then you are thinking of getting on. You are sad the next moment – then you are thinking of Scotland and friends.'

'Yes. I think of home sometimes!' he said simply.

'So do I – as far as I can. But it was an old house where I was born, and they pulled it down for improvements, so I seem hardly to have any home to think of now.'

Lucetta did not add, as she might have done, that the house was in St Helier, and not in Bath.

'But the mountains, and the mists and the rocks, they are there! And don't they seem like home?'

She shook her head.

'They do to me – they do to me,' he murmured. And his mind could be seen flying away northwards. Whether its origin were national or personal, it was quite true what Lucetta had said, that the curious double strands in Farfrae's thread of life – the commercial and the romantic – were very distinct at times. Like the colours in a variegated cord those contrasts could be seen inter-twisted, yet not mingling.

'You are wishing you were back again,' said she.

'Ah, no, ma'am,' said Farfrae, suddenly recalling himself.

The fair without the windows was now raging thick and loud. It was the chief hiring fair of the year, and differed quite from the market of a few days earlier. In substance it was a whitey-brown crowd flecked with white – this being the body of labourers waiting for places. The long bonnets of the women, like waggon-tilts,* their cotton gowns and checked shawls, mixed with the carters' smock-frocks;* for they, too, entered into the hiring. Among the rest, at the corner of the pavement, stood an old shepherd, who attracted the eyes of Lucetta and Farfrae by his stillness. He was evidently a chastened man. The battle of life had been a sharp one with him, for, to begin with, he was a man of small frame. He was now so bowed by hard work and years that, approaching from behind, a person could hardly see his head. He had planted the stem of his crook in the gutter and was resting upon the bow, which was polished to silver brightness by the long friction of his hands. He had quite forgotten where he was, and what he had come for, his eyes being bent on the ground. A little way off negotiations were proceeding which had reference to him;

but he did not hear them, and there seemed to be passing through his mind pleasant visions of the hiring successes of his prime, when his skill laid open to him any farm for the asking.

The negotiations were between a farmer from a distant county and the old man's son. In these there was a difficulty. The farmer would not take the crust without the crumb of the bargain, in other words, the old man without the younger; and the son had a sweetheart on his present farm, who stood by, waiting the issue with pale lips.

'I'm sorry to leave ye, Nelly,' said the young man with emotion. 'But, you see, I can't starve father, and he's out o' work at Lady-day.* 'Tis only thirty-five mile.'

The girl's lips quivered. 'Thirty-five mile!' she murmured. 'Ah! 'tis enough! I shall never see 'ee again!' It was, indeed, a hopeless length of traction for Dan Cupid's magnet;* for young men were young men at Casterbridge as elsewhere.

'O! no, no – I never shall,' she insisted, when he pressed her hand; and she turned her face to Lucetta's wall to hide her weeping. The farmer said he would give the young man half-an-hour for his answer, and went away, leaving the group sorrowing.

Lucetta's eyes, full of tears, met Farfrae's. His, too, to her surprise, were moist at the scene.

'It is very hard,' she said with strong feelings. 'Lovers ought not to be parted like that! O, if I had my wish, I'd let people live and love at their pleasure!'

'Maybe I can manage that they'll not be parted,' said Farfrae. 'I want a young carter; and perhaps I'll take the old man too – yes; he'll not be very expensive, and doubtless he will answer my pairrpose somehow.'

'O, you are so good!' she cried, delighted. 'Go and tell them, and let me know if you have succeeded!'

Farfrae went out, and she saw him speak to the group. The eyes of all brightened; the bargain was soon struck. Farfrae returned to her immediately it was concluded.

'It is kind-hearted of you, indeed,' said Lucetta. 'For my part, I have resolved that all my servants shall have lovers if they want them! Do make the same resolve!'

Farfrae looked serious, waving his head a half turn. 'I must be a little stricter than that,' he said.

'Why?'

'You are a – a thriving woman; and I am a struggling hay-and-corn merchant.'

'I am a very ambitious woman.'

'Ah, well, I cannet explain. I don't know how to talk to ladies, ambitious or no; and that's true,' said Donald with grave regret. 'I try to be civil to a' folk – no more!'

'I see you are as you say,' replied she, sensibly getting the upper hand in these exchanges of sentiment. Under this revelation of insight Farfrae again looked out of the window into the thick of the fair.

Two farmers met and shook hands, and being quite near the window their remarks could be heard as others' had been.

'Have you seen young Mr Farfrae this morning?' asked one. 'He promised to meet me here at the stroke of twelve; but I've gone athwart and about the fair half-a-dozen times, and never a sign of him: though he's mostly a man to his word.'

'I quite forgot the engagement,' murmured Farfrae.

'Now you must go,' said she; 'must you not?'

'Yes,' he replied. But he still remained.

'You had better go,' she urged. 'You will lose a customer.'

'Now, Miss Templeman, you will make me angry,' exclaimed Farfrae.

'Then suppose you don't go; but stay a little longer?'

He looked anxiously at the farmer who was seeking him, and who just then ominously walked across to where Henchard was standing, and he looked into the room and at her. 'I like staying; but I fear I must go!' he said. 'Business ought not to be neglected, ought it?'

'Not for a single minute.'

'It's true. I'll come another time – if I may, ma'am?'

'Certainly,' she said. 'What has happened to us to-day is very curious.'

'Something to think over when we are alone, it's like to be?'

'Oh, I don't know that. It is commonplace after all.'

'No, I'll not say that. O no!'

'Well, whatever it has been, it is now over; and the market calls you to be gone.'

'Yes, yes. Market – business! I wish there were no business in the warrld.'

Lucetta almost laughed – she would quite have laughed – but that there was a little emotion going in her at the time. 'How you change!' she said. 'You should not change like this.'

'I have never wished such things before,' said the Scotchman, with a simple, shamed, apologetic look for his weakness. 'It is only since coming heere and seeing you!'

'If that's the case, you had better not look at me any longer. Dear me, I feel I have quite demoralized you!'

'But look or look not, I will see you in my thoughts. Well, I'll go – thank you for the pleasure of this visit.'

'Thank you for staying.'

'Maybe I'll get into my market-mind when I've been out a few minutes,' he murmured. 'But I don't know – I don't know!'

As he went she said eagerly, 'You may hear them speak of me in Casterbridge as time goes on. If they tell you I'm a coquette, which some may, because of the incidents of my life, don't believe it, for I am not.'

'I swear I will not!' he said fervidly.

Thus the two. She had enkindled the young man's enthusiasm till he was quite brimming with sentiment; while he, from merely affording her a new form of idleness had gone on to wake her serious solicitude. Why was this? They could not have told.

Lucetta as a young girl would hardly have looked at a tradesman. But her ups and downs, capped by her indiscretions with Henchard, had made her uncritical as to station. In her poverty she had met with repulse from the society to which she had belonged, and she had no great zest for renewing an attempt upon it now. Her heart longed for some ark into which it could fly and be at rest. Rough or smooth she did not care so long as it was warm.

Farfrae was shown out, it having entirely escaped him that he had called to see Elizabeth. Lucetta at the window watched him threading the maze of farmers and farmers' men. She could see by his gait that he was conscious of her eyes, and her heart went out to him for his modesty – pleaded with her sense of his unfitness that he might be allowed to come again. He entered the market-house, and she could see him no more.

Three minutes later, when she had left the window, knocks, not of multitude but of strength, sounded through the house, and the waiting-maid tripped up.

'The Mayor,' she said.

Lucetta had reclined herself, and was looking dreamily through her fingers. She did not answer at once, and the maid repeated the information with the addition, 'And he's afraid he hasn't much time to spare, he says.'

'Oh! Then tell him that as I have a headache I won't detain him to-day.'

The message was taken down, and she heard the door close.

Lucetta had come to Casterbridge to quicken Henchard's feelings with regard to her. She had quickened them, and now she was indifferent to the achievement.

Her morning view of Elizabeth-Jane as a disturbing element changed, and she no longer felt strongly the necessity of getting rid of the girl for her stepfather's sake. When the young woman came in, sweetly unconscious of the turn in the tide, Lucetta went up to her, and said quite sincerely –

'I'm so glad you've come. You'll live with me a long time, won't you?'

Elizabeth as a watch-dog to keep her father off – what a new idea. Yet it was not unpleasing. Henchard had neglected her all these days, after compromising her indescribably in the past. The least he could have done when he found himself free, and herself affluent, would have been to respond heartily and promptly to her invitation.

Her emotions rose, fell, undulated, filled her with wild surmise at their suddenness; and so passed Lucetta's experiences of that day.

Chapter 24

Poor Elizabeth-Jane, little thinking what her malignant star had done to blast the budding attentions she had won from Donald Farfrae, was glad to hear Lucetta's words about remaining.

For in addition to Lucetta's house being a home, that raking view of the market-place which it afforded had as much attraction for her as Lucetta. The *carrefour* was like the regulation Open Place in spectacular dramas,* where the incidents that occur always happen to bear on the lives of the adjoining residents. Farmers, merchants, dairymen, quacks, hawkers, appeared there from week to week, and disappeared as the afternoon wasted away. It was the node of all orbits.

From Saturday to Saturday was as from day to day with the two young women now. In an emotional sense they did not live at all during the intervals. Wherever they might go wandering on other days, on market-day they were sure to be at home. Both stole sly glances out of the window at Farfrae's shoulders and poll.* His face they seldom saw, for, either through shyness, or not to disturb his mercantile mood, he avoided looking towards their quarters.

Thus things went on, till a certain market-morning brought a new sensation. Elizabeth and Lucetta were sitting at breakfast when a parcel containing two dresses arrived for the latter from London. She called Elizabeth from her breakfast, and entering her friend's bedroom Elizabeth saw the gowns spread out on the bed, one of a deep cherry colour, the other lighter – a glove lying at the end of each sleeve, a bonnet at the top of each neck, and parasols across the gloves, Lucetta standing beside the suggested human figure in an attitude of contemplation.

'I wouldn't think so hard about it,' said Elizabeth, marking the intensity with which Lucetta was alternating the questioin whether this or that would suit best.

'But setting upon new clothes is so trying,' said Lucetta. 'You are that person' (pointing to one of the arrangements), 'or you are *that* totally different person' (pointing to the other), 'for the whole of the coming spring: and one of the two, you don't know which, may turn out to be very objectionable.'

It was finally decided by Miss Templeman that she would be the cherry-coloured person at all hazards. The dress was pronounced to be a fit, and Lucetta walked with it into the front room, Elizabeth following her.

The morning was exceptionally bright for the time of year. The sun fell so flat on the houses and pavement opposite Lucetta's residence that they poured their brightness into her rooms. Suddenly, after a rumbling of wheels, there were added to this steady light a fantastic series of circling irradiations upon the ceiling, and the companions turned to the window. Immediately opposite a vehicle of strange description had come to a standstill, as if it had been placed there for exhibition.

It was the new-fashioned agricultural implement called a horse-drill,* till then unknown, in its modern shape, in this part of the country, where the venerable seed-lip* was still used for sowing as in the days of the Heptarchy.* Its arrival created about as much sensation in the corn-market as a flying machine would create at Charing Cross. The farmers crowded round it, women drew near it, children crept under and into it. The machine was painted in bright hues of green, yellow, and red, and it resembled as a whole a compound of hornet, grasshopper, and shrimp, magnified enormously. Or it might have been likened to an upright musical instrument with the front gone. That was how it struck Lucetta. 'Why, it is a sort of agricultural piano,' she said.

'It has something to do with corn,' said Elizabeth.

'I wonder who thought of introducing it here?'

Donald Farfrae was in the minds of both as the innovator, for though not a farmer he was closely leagued with farming operations. And as if in response to their thought he came up at that moment, looked at the machine, walked round it, and handled it as if he knew something about its make. The two watchers had inwardly started at his coming, and Elizabeth left the window, went to the back of the room, and stood as if absorbed in the panelling of the wall. She hardly knew that she had done this till Lucetta, animated by the conjunction of her new attire with the sight of Farfrae, spoke out: 'Let us go and look at the instrument, whatever it is.'

Elizabeth-Jane's bonnet and shawl were pitchforked on in a moment, and they went out. Among all the agriculturists gathering round the only appropriate possessor of the new machine seemed to be Lucetta, because she alone rivalled it in colour.

They examined it curiously; observing the rows of trumpet-shaped tubes one within the other, the little scoops, like revolving salt-spoons, which tossed the seed into the upper ends of the tubes that conducted it to the ground; till somebody said, 'Good morning, Elizabeth-Jane.' She looked up, and there was her stepfather.

His greeting had been somewhat dry and thunderous, and Elizabeth-Jane, embarrassed out of her equanimity, stammered at random, 'This is the lady I live with, father – Miss Templeman.'

Henchard put his hand to his hat, which he brought down with a great wave till it met his body at the knee. Miss Templeman bowed. 'I am happy to become acquainted with you, Mr Henchard,' she said. 'This is a curious machine.'

'Yes,' Henchard replied; and he proceeded to explain it, and still more forcibly to ridicule it.

'Who brought it here?' said Lucetta.

'Oh, don't ask me, ma'am!' said Henchard. 'The thing – why

'tis impossible it should act. 'Twas brought here by one of our machinists on the recommendation of a jumped-up jackanapes of a fellow who thinks –' His eye caught Elizabeth-Jane's imploring face, and he stopped, probably thinking that the suit might be progressing.

He turned to go away. Then something seemed to occur which his stepdaughter fancied must really be a hallucination of hers. A murmur apparently came from Henchard's lips in which she detected the words, 'You refused to see me!' reproachfully addressed to Lucetta. She could not believe that they had been uttered by her stepfather; unless, indeed, they might have been spoken to one of the yellow-gaitered farmers near them. Yet Lucetta seemed silent; and then all thought of the incident was dissipated by the humming of a song, which sounded as though from the interior of the machine. Henchard had by this time vanished into the market-house, and both the women glanced towards the corn-drill. They could see behind it the bent back of a man who was pushing his head into the internal works to master their simple secrets. The hummed song went on –

> 'Tw—s on a s—m—r aftern—n,
> A wee be—re the s—n w—nt d—n,
> When Kitty wi' a braw n—w g—wn
> C—me ow're the h—lls to Gowrie.

Elizabeth-Jane had apprehended the singer in a moment, and looked guilty of she did not know what. Lucetta next recognized him, and the more mistress of herself said archly, 'The "Lass of Gowrie"* from the inside of a seed-drill – what a phenomenon!'

Satisfied at last with his investigation the young man stood upright, and met their eyes across the summit.

'We are looking at the wonderful new drill,' Miss Templeman said. 'But practically it is a stupid thing – is it not?' she added, on the strength of Henchard's information.

'Stupid? O no!' said Farfrae gravely. 'It will revolutionize sowing heerabout! No more sowers flinging their seed about broadcast, so that some falls by the wayside and some among thorns,* and all that. Each grain will go straight to its intended place, and nowhere else whatever!'

'Then the romance of the sower is gone for good,' observed Elizabeth-Jane, who felt herself at one with Farfrae in Bible-reading at least. ' "He that observeth the wind shall not sow,"* so the Preacher said; but his words will not be to the point any more. How things change!'

'Ay; ay . . . It must be so!' Donald admitted, his gaze fixing itself on a blank point far away. 'But the machines are already very common in the East and North of England,' he added apologetically.

Lucetta seemed to be outside this train of sentiment, her acquaintance with the Scriptures being somewhat limited. 'Is the machine yours?' she asked of Farfrae.

'O no, madam,' said he, becoming embarrassed and deferential at the sound of her voice, though with Elizabeth-Jane he was quite at his ease. 'No, no – I merely recommended that it should be got.'

In the silence which followed Farfrae appeared only conscious of her; to have passed from perception of Elizabeth into a brighter sphere of existence than she appertained to. Lucetta, discerning that he was much mixed that day, partly in his mercantile mood and partly in his romantic one, said gaily to him –

'Well, don't forsake the machine for us,' and went indoors with her companion.

The latter felt that she had been in the way, though why was unaccountable to her. Lucetta explained the matter somewhat by saying when they were again in the sitting-room –

'I had occasion to speak to Mr Farfrae the other day, and so I knew him this morning.'

Lucetta was very kind towards Elizabeth that day. Together they saw the market thicken, and in course of time thin away with the slow decline of the sun towards the upper end of the town, its rays taking the street endways and enfilading* the long thoroughfare from top to bottom. The gigs and vans disappeared one by one till there was not a vehicle in the street. The time of the riding world was over; the pedestrian world held sway. Field labourers and their wives and children trooped in from the villages for their weekly shopping, and instead of a rattle of wheels and a tramp of horses ruling the sound as earlier, there was nothing but the shuffle of many feet. All the implements were gone; all the farmers; all the moneyed class. The character of the town's trading had changed from bulk to multiplicity, and pence were handled now as pounds had been handled earlier in the day.

Lucetta and Elizabeth looked out upon this, for though it was night and the street lamps were lighted, they had kept their shutters unclosed. In the faint blink of the fire they spoke more freely.

'Your father was distant with you,' said Lucetta.

'Yes.' And having forgotten the momentary mystery of Henchard's seeming speech to Lucetta she continued, 'It is because he does not think I am respectable. I have tried to be so more than you can imagine, but in vain! My mother's separation from my father was unfortunate for me. You don't know what it is to have shadows like that upon your life.'

Lucetta seemed to wince. 'I do not – of that kind precisely,' she said, 'but you may feel a – sense of disgrace – shame – in other ways.'

'Have you ever had any such feeling?' said the younger innocently.

'O no,' said Lucetta quickly. 'I was thinking of – what happens sometimes when women get themselves in strange positions in the eyes of the world from no fault of their own.'

'It must make them very unhappy afterwards.'

'It makes them anxious; for might not other women despise them?'

'Not altogether despise them. Yet not quite like or respect them.'

Lucetta winced again. Her past was by no means secure from investigation, even in Casterbridge. For one thing Henchard had never returned to her the cloud of letters she had written and sent him in her first excitement. Possibly they were destroyed; but she could have wished that they had never been written.

The rencounter with Farfrae and his bearing towards Lucetta had made the reflective Elizabeth more observant of her brilliant and amiable companion. A few days afterwards, when her eyes met Lucetta's as the latter was going out, she somehow knew that Miss Templeman was nourishing a hope of seeing the attractive Scotchman. The fact was printed large all over Lucetta's cheeks and eyes to any one who could read her as Elizabeth-Jane was beginning to do. Lucetta passed on and closed the street door.

A seer's spirit took possession of Elizabeth, impelling her to sit down by the fire and divine events so surely from data already her own that they could be held as witnessed. She followed Lucetta thus mentally – saw her encounter Donald somewhere as if by chance – saw him wear his special look when meeting women, with an added intensity because this one was Lucetta. She depicted his impassioned manner; beheld the indecision of both between their lothness to separate and their desire not to be observed; depicted their shaking of hands; how they probably parted with frigidity in their general contour and movements, only in the smaller features showing the spark of passion, thus invisible to all but themselves. This discerning silent witch had not done thinking of these things when Lucetta came noiselessly behind her and made her start.

It was all true as she had pictured – she could have sworn it. Lucetta had a heightened luminousness in her eye over and above the advanced colour of her cheeks.

'You've seen Mr Farfrae,' said Elizabeth demurely.

'Yes,' said Lucetta. 'How did you know?'

She knelt down on the hearth and took her friend's hands excitedly in her own. But after all she did not say when or how she had seen him or what he had said.

That night she became restless; in the morning she was feverish; and at breakfast-time she told her companion that she had something on her mind – something which concerned a person in whom she was interested much. Elizabeth was earnest to listen and sympathize.

'This person – a lady – once admired a man much – very much,' she said tentatively.

'Ah,' said Elizabeth-Jane.

'They were intimate – rather. He did not think so deeply of her as she did of him. But in an impulsive moment, purely out of reparation, he proposed to make her his wife. She agreed. But there was an unexpected hitch in the proceedings; though she had been so far compromised with him that she felt she could never belong to another man, as a pure matter of conscience, even if she should wish to. After that they were much apart, heard nothing of each other for a long time, and she felt her life quite closed up for her.'

'Ah – poor girl!'

'She suffered much on account of him; though I should add that he could not altogether be blamed for what had happened. At last the obstacle which separated them was providentially removed; and he came to marry her.'

'How delightful!'

'But in the interval she – my poor friend – had seen a man she liked better than him. Now comes the point: Could she in honour dismiss the first?'

'A new man she liked better – that's bad!'

'Yes,' said Lucetta, looking pained at a boy who was swinging the town pump-handle. 'It is bad! Though you must remember that she was forced into an equivocal position with the first man by an accident – that he was not so well educated or refined as the second, and that she had discovered some qualities in the first that rendered him less desirable as a husband than she had at first thought him to be.'

'I cannot answer,' said Elizabeth-Jane thoughtfully. 'It is so difficult. It wants a Pope to settle that!'

'You prefer not to, perhaps?' Lucetta showed in her appealing tone how much she leant on Elizabeth's judgment.

'Yes, Miss Templeman,' admitted Elizabeth. 'I would rather not say.'

Nevertheless, Lucetta seemed relieved by the simple fact of having opened out the situation a little, and was slowly convalescent of her headache. 'Bring me a looking-glass. How do I appear to people?' she said languidly.

'Well – a little worn,' answered Elizabeth, eyeing her as a critic eyes a doubtful painting; fetching the glass she enabled Lucetta to survey herself in it, which Lucetta anxiously did.

'I wonder if I wear well, as times go!' she observed after a while.

'Yes – fairly.'

'Where am I worst?'

'Under your eyes – I notice a little brownness there.'

'Yes. That is my worst place, I know. How many years more do you think I shall last before I get hopelessly plain?'

There was something curious in the way Elizabeth, though the younger, had come to play the part of experienced sage in these discussions. 'It may be five years,' she said judicially. 'Or, with a quiet life, as many as ten. With no love you might calculate on ten.'

Lucetta seemed to reflect on this as on an unalterable, impartial verdict. She told Elizabeth-Jane no more of the past attachment she had roughly adumbrated as the experiences of a third person; and Elizabeth, who in spite of her philosophy was very tender-hearted, sighed that night in bed at the thought that her pretty, rich Lucetta did not treat her to the full confidence of names and dates in her confessions. For by the 'she' of Lucetta's story Elizabeth had not been beguiled.

Chapter 25

The next phase of the supersession of Henchard in Lucetta's heart was an experiment in calling on her performed by Farfrae with some apparent trepidation. Conventionally speaking he conversed with both Miss Templeman and her companion; but in fact it was rather that Elizabeth sat invisible in the room. Donald appeared not to see her at all, and answered her wise little remarks with curtly indifferent monosyllables, his looks and faculties hanging on the woman who could boast of a more Protean* variety in her phases, moods, opinions, and also principles, than could Elizabeth. Lucetta had persisted in dragging her into the circle; but she had remained like an awkward third point which that circle would not touch.

Susan Henchard's daughter bore up against the frosty ache of the treatment, as she had borne up under worse things, and contrived as soon as possible to get out of the inharmonious room without being missed. The Scotchman seemed hardly the same Farfrae who had danced with her and walked with her in a delicate poise between love and friendship – that period in the history of a love when alone it can be said to be unalloyed with pain.

She stoically looked from her bedroom window, and contemplated her fate as if it were written on the top of the church-tower hard by. 'Yes,' she said at last, bringing down her palm upon the sill with a pat: '*He* is the second man of that story she told me!'

All this time Henchard's smouldering sentiments towards Lucetta had been fanned into higher and higher inflammation by the circumstances of the case. He was discovering that the young woman for whom he once felt a pitying warmth which had been almost chilled out of him by reflection, was, when now qualified with a slight inaccessibility and a more matured beauty, the very being to make him satisfied with life. Day after day proved to him, by her silence, that it was no use to think of bringing her round by holding aloof; so he gave in, and called upon her again, Elizabeth-Jane being absent.

He crossed the room to her with a heavy tread of some awkwardness, his strong, warm gaze upon her – like the sun beside the moon in comparison with Farfrae's modest look – and with something of a hail-fellow bearing, as, indeed, was not unnatural. But she seemed so transubstantiated by her change of position, and held out her hand to him in such cool friendship, that he became deferential, and sat down with a perceptible loss of power. He understood but little of fashion in dress, yet enough to feel himself inadequate in appearance beside her whom he had hitherto been dreaming of as almost his property. She said something very polite about his being good enough to call. This caused him to recover balance. He looked her oddly in the face, losing his awe.

'Why, of course I have called, Lucetta,' he said. 'What does that nonsense mean? You know I couldn't have helped myself if I had wished – that is, if I had any kindness at all. I've called to say that I am ready, as soon as custom will permit, to give you my name in return for your devotion, and what you lost by it in thinking too little of yourself and too much of me; to say that you can fix the day or month, with my full consent, whenever in your opinion it would be seemly: you know more of these things than I.'

'It is full early yet,' she said evasively.

'Yes, yes; I suppose it is. But you know, Lucetta, I felt directly my poor ill-used Susan died, and when I could not bear the idea of marrying again, that after what had happened between us it was my duty not to let any unnecessary delay occur before putting things to rights. Still, I wouldn't call in a hurry, because – well, you can guess how this money you've come into made me feel.' His voice slowly fell; he was conscious that in this room his accents and manner wore a roughness not observable in the street. He looked about the room at the novel hangings and ingenious furniture with which she had surrounded herself.

'Upon my life I didn't know such furniture as this could be bought in Casterbridge,' he said.

'Nor can it be,' said she. 'Nor will it till fifty years more of civilization have passed over the town. It took a waggon and four horses to get it here.'

'H'm. It looks as if you were living on capital.'

'O no, I am not.'

'So much the better. But the fact is, your setting up like this makes my bearing towards you rather awkward.'

'Why?'

An answer was not really needed, and he did not furnish one. 'Well,' he went on, 'there's nobody in the world I would have wished to see enter into this wealth before you, Lucetta, and nobody, I am sure, who will become it more.' He turned to her with congratulatory admiration so fervid that she shrank somewhat, notwithstanding that she knew him so well.

'I am greatly obliged to you for all that,' said she, rather with an air of speaking ritual. The stint of reciprocal feeling was perceived, and Henchard showed chagrin at once – nobody was more quick to show that than he.

'You may be obliged or not for't. Though the things I say may not have the polish of what you've lately learnt to expect for the first time in your life, they are real, my lady Lucetta.'

'That's rather a rude way of speaking to me,' pouted Lucetta, with stormy eyes.

'Not at all!' replied Henchard hotly. 'But there, there, I don't wish to quarrel with 'ee. I come with an honest proposal for silencing your Jersey enemies, and you ought to be thankful.'

'How can you speak so!' she answered, firing quickly. 'Knowing that my only crime was the indulging in a foolish girl's passion for you with too little regard for correctness, and that I was what I call innocent all the time they called me guilty, you ought not to be so cutting! I suffered enough at that worrying time, when you wrote to tell me of your wife's return and my consequent dismissal, and if I am a little independent now, surely the privilege is due to me!'

'Yes, it is,' he said. 'But it is not by what is, in this life, but by what appears, that you are judged; and I therefore think you ought to accept me – for your own good name's sake. What is known in your native Jersey may get known here.'

'How you keep on about Jersey! I am English!'

'Yes, yes. Well, what do you say to my proposal?'

For the first time in their acquaintance Lucetta had the move; and yet she was backward. 'For the present let things be,' she said with some embarrassment. 'Treat me as an acquaintance; and I'll treat you as one. Time will –' she stopped; and he said nothing to fill the gap for awhile, there being no pressure of half acquaintance to drive them into speech if they were not minded for it.

'That's the way the wind blows, is it?' he said at last grimly, nodding an affirmative to his own thoughts.

A yellow flood of reflected sunlight filled the room for a few instants. It was produced by the passing of a load of newly trussed hay from the country, in a waggon marked with Farfrae's name.

Beside it rode Farfrae himself on horseback. Lucetta's face became – as a woman's face becomes when the man she loves rises upon her gaze like an apparition.

A turn of the eye by Henchard, a glance from the window, and the secret of her inaccessibility would have been revealed. But Henchard in estimating her tone was looking down so plumb-straight that he did not note the warm consciousness upon Lucetta's face.

'I shouldn't have thought it – I shouldn't have thought it of women!' he said emphatically by-and-by, rising and shaking himself into activity; while Lucetta was so anxious to divert him from any suspicion of the truth she asked him to be in no hurry. Bringing him some apples she insisted upon paring one for him.

He would not take it. 'No, no; such is not for me,' he said drily, and moved to the door. At going out he turned his eye upon her.

'You came to live in Casterbridge entirely on my account,' he said. 'Yet now you are here you won't have anything to say to my offer!'

He had hardly gone down the staircase when she dropped upon the sofa and jumped up again in a fit of desperation. 'I *will* love him!' she cried passionately; 'as for *him* – he's hot-tempered and stern, and it would be madness to bind myself to him knowing that. I won't be a slave to the past – I'll love where I choose!'

Yet having decided to break away from Henchard one might have supposed her capable of aiming higher than Farfrae. But Lucetta reasoned nothing: she feared hard words from the people with whom she had been earlier associated; she had no relatives left; and with native lightness of heart took kindly to what fate offered.

Elizabeth-Jane, surveying the position of Lucetta between her two lovers from the crystalline sphere of a straightforward mind, did not fail to perceive that her father, as she called him, and Donald Farfrae became more desperately enamoured of her friend every day. On Farfrae's side it was the unforced passion of youth. On Henchard's the artificially stimulated coveting of maturer age.

The pain she experienced from the almost absolute oblivious-ness to her existence that was shown by the pair of them became at times half dissipated by her sense of its humorousness. When Lucetta had pricked her finger they were as deeply concerned as if she were dying; when she herself had been seriously sick or in danger they uttered a conventional word of sympathy at the news, and forgot all about it immediately. But, as regarded Henchard, this perception of hers also caused her some filial grief; she could not help asking what she had done to be neglected so, after the professions of solicitude he had made. As regarded Farfrae, she thought, after honest reflection, that it was quite natural. What was she beside Lucetta? – as one of the 'meaner beauties of the night',* when the moon had risen in the skies.

She had learnt the lesson of renunciation, and was as familiar with the wreck of each day's wishes as with the diurnal setting of the sun. If her earthly career had taught her few book philosophies it had at least well practised her in this. Yet her experience had consisted less in a series of pure disappointments than in a series of substitutions. Continually it had happened that what she had desired had not been granted her, and that what had been granted her she had not desired. So she viewed with an approach to equanimity the now cancelled days when Donald had been her undeclared lover, and wondered what unwished-for thing Heaven might send her in place of him.

Chapter 26

It chanced that on a fine spring morning Henchard and Farfrae met in the chestnut-walk which ran along the south wall of the town. Each had just come out from his early breakfast, and there was not another soul near. Henchard was reading a letter from Lucetta, sent in answer to a note from him, in which she made some excuse for not immediately granting him a second interview that he had desired.

Donald had no wish to enter into conversation with his former friend on their present constrained terms; neither would he pass him in scowling silence. He nodded, and Henchard did the same. They had receded from each other several paces when a voice cried 'Farfrae!' It was Henchard's, who stood regarding him.

'Do you remember,' said Henchard, as if it were the presence of the thought and not of the man which made him speak, 'do you remember my story of that second woman – who suffered for her thoughtless intimacy with me?'

'I do,' said Farfrae.

'Do you remember my telling 'ee how it all began and how it ended?'

'Yes.'

'Well, I have offered to marry her now that I can; but she won't marry me. Now what would you think of her – I put it to you?'

'Well, ye owe her nothing more now,' said Farfrae heartily.

'It is true,' said Henchard, and went on.

That he had looked up from a letter to ask his questions completely shut out from Farfrae's mind all vision of Lucetta as the culprit. Indeed, her present position was so different from that of the young woman of Henchard's story as of itself to be sufficient to blind him absolutely to her identity. As for Henchard, he was reassured by Farfrae's words and manner against a suspicion which had crossed his mind. They were not those of a conscious rival.

Yet that there was rivalry by some one he was firmly persuaded. He could feel it in the air around Lucetta, see it in the turn of her pen. There was an antagonistic force in exercise, so that when he had tried to hang near her he seemed standing in a refluent current. That it was not innate caprice he was more and more certain. Her windows gleamed as if they did not want him; her curtains seemed to hang slily, as if they screened an ousting presence. To discover whose presence that was – whether really Farfrae's after all, or another's – he exerted himself to the utmost to see her again; and at length succeeded.

At the interview, when she offered him tea, he made it a point to launch a cautious inquiry if she knew Mr Farfrae.

O yes, she knew him, she declared; she could not help knowing almost everybody in Casterbridge, living in such a gazebo* over the centre and arena of the town.

'Pleasant young fellow,' said Henchard.

'Yes,' said Lucetta.

'We both know him,' said kind Elizabeth-Jane, to relieve her companion's divined embarrassment.

There was a knock at the door; literally, three full knocks and a little one at the end.

'That kind of knock means half-and-half – somebody between gentle and simple,' said the corn-merchant to himself. 'I shouldn't wonder therefore if it is he.' In a few seconds surely enough Donald walked in.

Lucetta was full of little fidgets and flutters, which increased

Henchard's suspicions without affording any special proof of their correctness. He was well-nigh ferocious at the sense of the queer situation in which he stood towards this woman. One who had reproached him for deserting her when calumniated, who had urged claims upon his consideration on that account, who had lived waiting for him, who at the first decent moment had come to ask him to rectify, by making her his, the false position into which she had placed herself for his sake; such she had been. And now he sat at her tea-table eager to gain her attention, and in his amatory rage feeling the other man present to be a villain, just as any young fool of a lover might feel.

They sat stiffly side by side at the darkening table, like some Tuscan painting of the two disciples supping at Emmaus.* Lucetta, forming the third and haloed figure, was opposite them; Elizabeth-Jane, being out of the game, and out of the group, could observe from afar, like the evangelist who had to write it down:* that there were long spaces of taciturnity, when all exterior circumstance was subdued to the touch of spoons and china, the click of a heel on the pavement under the window, the passing of a wheelbarrow or cart, the whistling of the carter, the gush of water into householders' buckets at the town-pump opposite; the exchange of greetings among their neighbours, and the rattle of the yokes by which they carried off their evening supply.

'More bread-and-butter?' said Lucetta to Henchard and Farfrae, equally, holding out between them a plateful of long slices. Henchard took a slice by one end and Donald by the other; each feeling certain he was the man meant; neither let go, and the slice came in two.

'Oh – I am so sorry!' cried Lucetta, with a nervous titter. Farfrae tried to laugh; but he was too much in love to see the incident in any but a tragic light.

'How ridiculous of all three of them!' said Elizabeth to herself.

Henchard left the house with a ton of conjecture, though without a grain of proof, that the counter-attraction was Farfrae; and therefore he would not make up his mind. Yet to Elizabeth-Jane it was plain as the town-pump that Donald and Lucetta were incipient lovers. More than once, in spite of her care, Lucetta had been unable to restrain her glance from flitting across into Farfrae's eyes like a bird to its nest. But Henchard was constructed upon too large a scale to discern such minutiæ as these by any evening light, which to him were as the notes of an insect that lie above the compass of the human ear.

But he was disturbed. And the sense of occult rivalry in suitorship was so much superadded to the palpable rivalry of their business lives. To the coarse materiality of that rivalry it added an inflaming soul.

The thus vitalized antagonism took the form of action by Henchard sending for Jopp, the manager originally displaced by Farfrae's arrival. Henchard had frequently met this man about the streets, observed that his clothing spoke of neediness, heard that he lived in Mixen Lane – a back slum of the town, the *pis aller** of Casterbridge domiciliation – itself almost a proof that a man had reached a stage when he would not stick at trifles.

Jopp came after dark, by the gates of the store-yard, and felt his way through the hay and straw to the office where Henchard sat in solitude awaiting him.

'I am again out of a foreman,' said the corn-factor. 'Are you in a place?'

'Not so much as a beggar's, sir.'

'How much do you ask?'

Jopp named his price, which was very moderate.

'When can you come?'

'At this hour and moment, sir,' said Jopp, who, standing hands-pocketed at the street corner till the sun had faded the shoulders of his coat to scarecrow green, had regularly watched Henchard in the market-place, measured him, and learnt him, by virtue of the power which the still man has in his stillness of knowing the busy one better than he knows himself. Jopp, too, had had a convenient experience; he was the only one in Casterbridge besides Henchard and the close-lipped Elizabeth who knew that Lucetta came truly from Jersey, and but proximately from Bath. 'I know Jersey, too, sir,' he said. 'Was living there when you used to do business that way. O yes – have often seen ye there.'

'Indeed! Very good. Then the thing is settled. The testimonials you showed me when you first tried for't are sufficient.'

That characters deteriorate in time of need possibly did not occur to Henchard. Jopp said, 'Thank you,' and stood more firmly, in the consciousness that at last he officially belonged to that spot.

'Now,' said Henchard, digging his strong eyes into Jopp's face, 'one thing is necessary to me, as the biggest corn-and-hay-dealer in these parts. The Scotchman, who's taking the town trade so bold into his hands, must be cut out. D'ye hear? We two can't live side by side – that's clear and certain.'

'I've seen it all,' said Jopp.

'By fair competition I mean, of course,' Henchard continued. 'But as hard, keen, and unflinching as fair – rather more so. By such a desperate bid against him for the farmers' custom as will grind him into the ground – starve him out. I've capital, mind ye, and I can do it.'

'I'm all that way of thinking,' said the new foreman. Jopp's dislike of Farfrae as the man who had once usurped his place, while it made him a willing tool, made him, at the same time, commercially as unsafe a colleague as Henchard could have chosen.

'I sometimes think,' he added, 'that he must have some glass that he sees next year in. He has such a knack of making everything bring him fortune.'

'He's deep beyond all honest men's discerning; but we must make him shallower. We'll under-sell him, and over-buy him, and so snuff him out.'

They then entered into specific details of the process by which this would be accomplished, and parted at a late hour.

Elizabeth-Jane heard by accident that Jopp had been engaged by her stepfather. She was so fully convinced that he was not the right man for the place that, at the risk of making Henchard angry, she expressed her apprehension to him when they met. But it was done to no purpose. Henchard shut up her argument with a sharp rebuff.

The season's weather seemed to favour their scheme. The time was in the years immediately before foreign competition had revolutionized the trade in grain; when still, as from the earliest ages, the wheat quotations from month to month depended entirely upon the home harvest. A bad harvest, or the prospect of one, would double the price of corn in a few weeks; and the promise of a good yield would lower it as rapidly.* Prices were like the roads of the period, steep in gradient, reflecting in their phases the local conditions, without engineering, levellings, or averages.

The farmer's income was ruled by the wheat-crop within his own horizon, and the wheat-crop by the weather. Thus, in person, he became a sort of flesh-barometer, with feelers always directed to the sky and wind around him. The local atmosphere was everything to him; the atmospheres of other countries a matter of indifference. The people, too, who were not farmers, the rural multitude, saw in the god of the weather a more important personage than they do now. Indeed, the feeling of the peasantry in this matter was so intense as to be almost unrealizable in these equable days. Their impulse was well-nigh to prostrate themselves in lamentation before untimely rains and tempests, which came as the Alastor* of those households whose crime it was to be poor.

After midsummer they watched the weather-cocks as men waiting in antechambers watch the lackey. Sun elated them; quiet rain sobered them; weeks of watery tempest stupefied them. That aspect of the sky which they now regard as disagreeable they then beheld as maleficent.

It was June, and the weather was very unfavourable. Casterbridge, being as it were the bell-board on which all the adjacent hamlets and villages sounded their notes, was decidedly dull. Instead of new articles in the shop-windows those that had been rejected in the foregoing summer were brought out again; superseded reap-hooks,* badly-shaped rakes, shop-worn leggings, and time-stiffened water-tights reappeared, furbished up as near to new as possible.

Henchard, backed by Jopp, read a disastrous garnering, and resolved to base his strategy against Farfrae upon that reading. But before acting he wished – what so many have wished – that he could know for certain what was at present only strong probability. He was superstitious – as such headstrong natures often are – and he nourished in his mind an idea bearing on the matter; an idea he shrank from disclosing even to Jopp.

In a lonely hamlet a few miles from the town – so lonely that what are called lonely villages were teeming by comparison – there lived a man of curious repute as a forecaster or weather-prophet. The way to his house was crooked and miry – even difficult in the present unpropitious season. One evening when it was raining so heavily that ivy and laurel resounded like distant musketry, and an out-door man could be excused for shrouding himself to his ears and eyes, such a shrouded figure on foot might have been perceived travelling in the direction of the hazel-copse which dripped over the prophet's cot. The turnpike-road became a lane, the lane a cart-track, the cart-track a bridle-path, the bridle-path a foot-way, the foot-way overgrown. The solitary walker slipped here and there, and stumbled over the natural springes* formed by the brambles, till at length he reached the house, which, with its garden, was surrounded with a high, dense hedge. The cottage, comparatively a large one, had been built of mud by the occupier's own hands, and thatched also by himself. Here he had always lived, and here it was assumed he would die.

He existed on unseen supplies; for it was an anomalous thing that while there was hardly a soul in the neighbourhood but affected to laugh at this man's assertions, uttering the formula, 'There's nothing in 'em', with full assurance on the surface of their faces, very few of them were unbelievers in their secret hearts. Whenever they consulted him they did it 'for a fancy'. When they paid him they said, 'Just a trifle for Christmas', or 'Candlemas',* as the case might be.

He would have preferred more honesty in his clients, and less sham ridicule; but fundamental belief consoled him for superficial irony. As stated, he was enabled to live; people supported him with their backs turned. He was sometimes astonished that men could profess so little and believe so much at his house, when at church they professed so much and believed so little.

Behind his back he was called 'Wide-oh', on account of his reputation; to his face 'Mr' Fall.

The hedge of his garden formed an arch over the entrance, and a door was inserted as in a wall. Outside the door the tall traveller stopped, bandaged his face with a handkerchief as if he were suffering from toothache, and went up the path. The window shutters were not closed, and he could see the prophet within, preparing his supper.

In answer to the knock Fall came to the door, candle in hand. The visitor stepped back a little from the light, and said, 'Can I speak to 'ee?' in significant tones. The other's invitation to come in was responded to by the country formula, 'This will do, thank 'ee', after which the householder has no alternative but to come out. He placed the candle on the corner of the dresser, took his hat from a nail, and joined the stranger in the porch, shutting the door behind him.

'I've long heard that you can – do things of a sort?' began the other, repressing his individuality as much as he could.

'Maybe so, Mr Henchard,' said the weather-caster.

'Ah – why do you call me that?' asked the visitor with a start.

'Because it's your name. Feeling you'd come I've waited for 'ee; and thinking you might be leery* from your walk I laid two supper plates – look ye here.' He threw open the door and disclosed the supper-table, at which appeared a second chair, knife and fork, plate and mug, as he had declared.

Henchard felt like Saul at his reception by Samuel;* he remained in silence for a few moments, then throwing off the disguise of frigidity which he had hitherto preserved, he said, 'Then I have not come in vain . . . Now, for instance, can ye charm away warts?'

'Without trouble.'

'Cure the evil?'*

'That I've done – with consideration – if they will wear the toad-bag* by night as well as by day.'

'Forecast the weather?'

'With labour and time.'

'Then take this,' said Henchard. ' 'Tis a crown-piece. Now, what is the harvest fortnight to be? When can I know?'

'I've worked it out already, and you can know at once.' (The fact was that five farmers had already been there on the same errand from different parts of the country.) 'By the sun, moon, and stars, by the clouds, the winds, the trees, and grass, the candleflame and swallows, the smell of the herbs; likewise by the cats' eyes, the ravens, the leeches, the spiders, and the dung-mixen,* the last fortnight in August will be – rain and tempest.'

'You are not certain, of course?'

'As one can be in a world where all's unsure. 'Twill be more like living in Revelations* this autumn than in England. Shall I sketch it out for 'ee in a scheme?'

'O no, no,' said Henchard. 'I don't altogether believe in forecasts, come to second thoughts on such. But I –'

'You don't – you don't – 'tis quite understood,' said Wide-oh, without a sound of scorn. 'You have given me a crown because you've one too many. But won't you join me at supper, now 'tis waiting and all?'

Henchard would gladly have joined; for the savour of the stew had floated from the cottage into the porch with such appetizing distinctness that the meat, the onions, the pepper, and the herbs could be severally recognized by his nose. But as sitting down to hob-and-nob there would have seemed to mark him too implicitly as the weather-caster's apostle, he declined, and went his way.

The next Saturday Henchard bought grain to such an enormous extent that there was quite a talk about his purchases among his neighbours the lawyer, the wine merchant, and the doctor; also on the next, and on all available days. When his granaries were full to choking, all the weathercocks of Casterbridge creaked and set their faces in another direction, as if tired of the south-west. The weather changed; the sunlight, which had been like tin for weeks, assumed the hues of topaz. The temperature of the welkin* passed from the phlegmatic to the sanguine; an excellent harvest was almost a certainty; and as a consequence prices rushed down.

All these transformations, lovely to the outsider, to the wrong-headed corn-dealer were terrible. He was reminded of what he had well known before, that a man might gamble upon the square green areas of fields as readily as upon those of a card-room.

Henchard had backed bad weather, and apparently lost. He had mistaken the turn of the flood for the turn of the ebb. His dealings had been so extensive that settlement could not long be postponed, and to settle he was obliged to sell off corn that he had bought only a few weeks before at figures higher by many shillings a quarter. Much of the corn he had never seen; it had not even been moved from the ricks in which it lay stacked miles away. Thus he lost heavily.

In the blaze of an early August day he met Farfrae in the market-place. Farfrae knew of his dealings (though he did not guess their intended bearing on himself) and commiserated him; for since their exchange of words in the South Walk they had been on stiffly speaking terms. Henchard for the moment appeared to resent the sympathy; but he suddenly took a careless turn.

'Ho, no no! – nothing serious, man!' he cried with fierce gaiety. 'These things always happen, don't they? I know it has been said that figures have touched me tight lately; but is that anything rare? The case is not so bad as folk make out perhaps. And dammy, a man must be a fool to mind the common hazards of trade!'

But he had to enter the Casterbridge Bank that day for reasons which had never before sent him there – and to sit a long time in the partners' room with a constrained bearing. It was rumoured soon after that much real property as well as vast stores of produce, which had stood in Henchard's name in the town and neighbourhood, was actually the possession of his bankers.

Coming down the steps of the bank he encountered Jopp. The gloomy transactions just completed within had added fever to the original sting of Farfrae's sympathy that morning, which Henchard fancied might be satire disguised, so that Jopp met with anything but a bland reception. The latter was in the act of taking off his hat to wipe his forehead, and saying, 'A fine hot day,' to an acquaintance.

'You can wipe and wipe, and say, "A fine hot day," can ye!' cried Henchard in a savage undertone, imprisoning Jopp between himself and the bank wall. 'If it hadn't been for your blasted advice it might have been a fine day enough! Why did ye let me go on, hey? — when a word of doubt from you or anybody would have made me think twice! For you can never be sure of weather till 'tis past.'

'My advice, sir, was to do what you thought best.'

'A useful fellow! And the sooner you help somebody else in that way the better!' Henchard continued his address to Jopp in similar terms till it ended in Jopp's dismissal there and then, Henchard turning upon his heel and leaving him.

'You shall be sorry for this, sir; sorry as a man can be!' said Jopp, standing pale, and looking after the corn-merchant as he disappeared in the crowd of market-men hard by.

Chapter 27

It was the eve of harvest. Prices being low Farfrae was buying. As was usual, after reckoning too surely on famine weather the local farmers had flown to the other extreme, and (in Farfrae's opinion) were selling off too recklessly — calculating with just a trifle too much certainty upon an abundant yield. So he went on buying old corn at its comparatively ridiculous price: for the produce of the previous year, though not large, had been of excellent quality.

When Henchard had squared off his affairs in a disastrous way, and got rid of his burdensome purchases at a monstrous loss, the harvest began. There were three days of excellent weather, and then — 'What if that curst conjuror should be right after all!' said Henchard.

The fact was, that no sooner had the sickles begun to play than the atmosphere suddenly felt as if cress would grow in it without other nourishment. It rubbed people's cheeks like damp flannel when they walked abroad. There was a gusty, high, warm wind; isolated raindrops starred the window-panes at remote distances: the sunlight would flap out like a quickly opened fan, throw the pattern of the window upon the floor of the room in a milky, colourless shine, and withdraw as suddenly as it had appeared.

From that day and hour it was clear that there was not to be so successful an ingathering after all. If Henchard had only waited long enough he might at least have avoided loss though he had not made a profit. But the momentum of his character knew no patience. At this turn of the scales he remained silent. The movements of his mind seemed to tend to the thought that some power was working against him.

'I wonder,' he asked himself with eerie misgiving; 'I wonder if it can be that somebody has been roasting a waxen image of me, or stirring an unholy brew to confound me!* I don't believe in such power; and yet – what if they should ha' been doing it!' Even he could not admit that the perpetrator, if any, might be Farfrae. These isolated hours of superstition came to Henchard in time of moody depression, when all his practical largeness of view had oozed out of him.

Meanwhile Donald Farfrae prospered. He had purchased in so depressed a market that the present moderate stiffness of prices was sufficient to pile for him a large heap of gold where a little one had been.

'Why, he'll soon be Mayor!' said Henchard. It was indeed hard that the speaker should, of all others, have to follow the triumphal chariot of this man to the Capitol.*

The rivalry of the masters was taken up by the men.

September-night shades had fallen upon Casterbridge; the clocks had struck half-past eight, and the moon had risen. The streets of the town were curiously silent for such a comparatively early hour. A sound of jangling horse-bells and heavy wheels passed up the street. These were followed by angry voices outside Lucetta's house, which led her and Elizabeth-Jane to run to the windows, and pull up the blinds.

The neighbouring Market House and Town Hall abutted against its neighbour the Church except in the lower storey, where an arched thoroughfare gave admittance to a large square called

Bull Stake. A stone post rose in the midst, to which the oxen had formerly been tied for baiting with dogs to make them tender before they were killed in the adjoining shambles. In a corner stood the stocks.

The thoroughfare leading to this spot was now blocked by two four-horse waggons and horses, one laden with hay-trusses, the leaders having already passed each other, and become entangled head to tail. The passage of the vehicles might have been practicable if empty; but built up with hay to the bedroom windows as one was, it was impossible.

'You must have done it a' purpose!' said Farfrae's waggoner. 'You can here my horses' bells half-a-mile such a night as this!'

'If ye'd been minding your business instead of zwailing along in such a gawk-hammer way,* you would have zeed* me!' retorted the wroth representative of Henchard.

However, according to the strict rule of the road it appeared that Henchard's man was most in the wrong; he therefore attempted to back into the High Street. In doing this the near hind-wheel rose against the churchyard wall, and the whole mountainous load went over, two of the four wheels rising in the air, and the legs of the thill* horse.

Instead of considering how to gather up the load the two men closed in a fight with their fists. Before the first round was quite over Henchard came upon the spot, somebody having run for him.

Henchard sent the two men staggering in contrary directions by collaring one with each hand, turned to the horse that was down, and extricated him after some trouble. He then inquired into the circumstances; and seeing the state of his waggon and its load began hotly rating Farfrae's man.

Lucetta and Elizabeth-Jane had by this time run down to the street corner, whence they watched the bright heap of new hay lying in the moon's rays, and passed and re-passed by the forms of Henchard and the waggoners. The women had witnessed what nobody else had seen — the origin of the mishap; and Lucetta spoke.

'I saw it all, Mr Henchard,' she cried; 'and your man was most in the wrong!'

Henchard paused in his harangue and turned. 'Oh, I didn't notice you, Miss Templeman,' said he. 'My man in the wrong? Ah, to be sure; to be sure! But I beg your pardon notwithstanding.

The other's is the empty waggon, and he must have been most to blame for coming on.'

'No; I saw it, too,' said Elizabeth-Jane. 'And I can assure you he couldn't help it.'

'You can't trust *their* senses!' murmured Henchard's man.

'Why not?' asked Henchard sharply.

'Why, you see, sir, all the women side with Farfrae – being a damn young dand – of the sort that he is – one that creeps into a maid's heart like the giddying worm into a sheep's brain* – making crooked seem straight to their eyes!'

'But do you know who that lady is you talk about in such a fashion? Do you know that I pay my attentions to her, and have for some time? Just be careful!'

'Not I. I know nothing, sir, outside eight shillings a week.'*

'And that Mr Farfrae is well aware of it? He's sharp in trade, but he wouldn't do anything so underhand as what you hint at.'

Whether because Lucetta heard this low dialogue, or not, her white figure disappeared from her doorway inward, and the door was shut before Henchard could reach it to converse with her further. This disappointed him, for he had been sufficiently disturbed by what the man had said to wish to speak to her more closely. While pausing the old constable came up.

'Just see that nobody drives against that hay and waggon to-night, Stubberd,' said the corn-merchant. 'It must bide till the morning, for all hands are in the fields still. And if any coach or road-waggon wants to come along, tell 'em they must go round by the back street, and be hanged to 'em . . . Any case to-morrow up in Hall?'

'Yes, sir. One in number, sir.'

'Oh, what's that?'

'An old flagrant female, sir, swearing and committing a nuisance in a horrible profane manner against the church wall, sir, as if 'twere no more than a pot-house! That's all, sir.'

'Oh. The Mayor's out o' town, isn't he?'

'He is, sir.'

'Very well, then I'll be there. Don't forget to keep an eye on that hay. Good night t' 'ee.'

During those moments Henchard had determined to follow up Lucetta notwithstanding her elusiveness, and he knocked for admission.

The answer he received was an expression of Miss

Templeman's sorrow at being unable to see him again that evening because she had an engagement to go out.

Henchard walked away from the door to the opposite side of the street, and stood by his hay in a lonely reverie, the constable having strolled elsewhere, and the horses being removed. Though the moon was not bright as yet there were no lamps lighted, and he entered the shadow of one of the projecting jambs which formed the thoroughfare to Bull Stake; here he watched Lucetta's door.

Candle-lights were flitting in and out of her bedroom, and it was obvious that she was dressing for the appointment, whatever the nature of that might be at such an hour. The lights disappeared, the clock struck nine, and almost at the moment Farfrae came round the opposite corner and knocked. That she had been waiting just inside for him was certain, for she instantly opened the door herself. They went together by the way of a back lane westward, avoiding the front street; guessing where they were going he determined to follow.

The harvest had been so delayed by the capricious weather that whenever a fine day occurred all sinews were strained to save what could be saved of the damaged crops. On account of the rapid shortening of the days the harvesters worked by moonlight. Hence to-night the wheat-fields abutting on the two sides of the square formed by Casterbridge town were animated by the gathering hands. Their shouts and laughter had reached Henchard at the Market House, while he stood there waiting, and he had little doubt from the turn which Farfrae and Lucetta had taken that they were bound for the spot.

Nearly the whole town had gone into the fields. The Casterbridge populace still retained the primitive habit of helping one another in time of need; and thus, though the corn belonged to the farming section of the little community — that inhabiting the Durnover quarter — the remainder was no less interested in the labour of getting it home.

Reaching the top of the lane Henchard crossed the shaded avenue on the walls, slid down the green rampart, and stood amongst the stubble. The 'stitches' or shocks* rose like tents about the yellow expanse, those in the distance becoming lost in the moonlit hazes.

He had entered at a point removed from the scene of immediate operations; but two others had entered at that place, and he could see them winding among the shocks. They were paying no regard to the direction of their walk, whose vague serpentining soon began to bear down towards Henchard. A meeting promised to be awkward, and he therefore stepped into the hollow of the nearest shock, and sat down.

'You have my leave,' Lucetta was saying gaily. 'Speak what you like.'

'Well, then,' replied Farfrae, with the unmistakable inflection of the lover pure, which Henchard had never heard in full resonance on his lips before, 'you are sure to be much sought after for your position, wealth, talents, and beauty. But will ye resist the temptation to be one of those ladies with lots of admirers – ay – and be content to have only a homely one?'

'And he the speaker?' said she, laughing. 'Very well, sir, what next?'

'Ah! I'm afraid that what I feel will make me forget my manners!'

'Then I hope you'll never have any, if you lack them only for that cause.' After some broken words which Henchard lost she added, 'Are you sure you won't be jealous?'

Farfrae seemed to assure her that he would not, by taking her hand.

'You are convinced, Donald, that I love nobody else,' she presently said. 'But I should wish to have my own way in some things.'

'In everything! What special thing did you mean?'

'If I wished not to live always in Casterbridge, for instance, upon finding that I should not be happy here?'

Henchard did not hear the reply; he might have done so and much more, but he did not care to play the eavesdropper. They went on towards the scene of activity, where the sheaves were being handed, a dozen a minute, upon the carts and waggons which carried them away.

Lucetta insisted on parting from Farfrae when they drew near the workpeople. He had some business with them and, though he entreated her to wait a few minutes, she was inexorable, and tripped off homeward alone.

Henchard thereupon left the field and followed her. His state of mind was such that on reaching Lucetta's door he did not knock but opened it, and walked straight up to her sitting-room, expecting to find her there. But the room was empty, and he perceived that in his haste he had somehow passed her on the way hither. He had not to wait many minutes, however, for he soon heard her dress rustling in the hall, followed by a soft closing of the door. In a moment she appeared.

The light was so low that she did not notice Henchard at first. As soon as she saw him she uttered a little cry, almost of terror.

'How can you frighten me so?' she exclaimed, with a flushed face. 'It is past ten o'clock, and you have no right to surprise me here at such a time.'

'I don't know that I've not the right. At any rate I have the excuse. Is it so necessary that I should stop to think of manners and customs?'

'It is too late for propriety, and might injure me.'

'I called an hour ago, and you would not see me, and I thought you were in when I called now. It is you, Lucetta, who are doing wrong. It is not proper in 'ee to throw me over like this. I have a little matter to remind you of, which you seem to forget.'

She sank into a chair, and turned pale.

'I don't want to hear it – I don't want to hear it!' she said through her hands, as he, standing close to the edge of her gown, began to allude to the Jersey days.

'But you ought to hear it,' said he.

'It came to nothing; and through you. Then why not leave me the freedom that I gained with such sorrow! Had I found that you proposed to marry me for pure love I might have felt bound now. But I soon learnt that you had planned it out of mere charity – almost as an unpleasant duty – because I had nursed you, and compromised myself, and you thought you must repay me. After that I did not care for you so deeply as before.'

'Why did you come here to find me, then?'

'I thought I ought to marry you for conscience' sake, since you were free, even though I – did not like you so well.'

'And why then don't you think so now?'

She was silent. It was only too obvious that conscience had ruled well enough till new love had intervened and usurped that rule. In feeling this she herself forgot for the moment her partially justifying argument – that having discovered Henchard's infirmities of temper, she had some excuse for not risking her happiness in his hands after once escaping them. The only thing she could say was, 'I was a poor girl then; and now my circumstances have altered, so I am hardly the same person.'

'That's true. And it makes the case awkward for me. But I don't want to touch your money. I am quite willing that every penny of your property shall remain to your personal use. Besides, that argument has nothing in it. The man you are thinking of is no better than I.'

'If you were as good as he you would leave me!' she cried passionately.

This unluckily aroused Henchard. 'You cannot in honour refuse me,' he said. 'And unless you give me your promise this very night to be my wife, before a witness, I'll reveal our intimacy – in common fairness to other men!'

A look of resignation settled upon her. Henchard saw its bitterness; and had Lucetta's heart been given to any other man in the world than Farfrae he would probably have had pity upon her at that moment. But the supplanter was the upstart (as Henchard called him) who had mounted into prominence upon his shoulders, and he could bring himself to show no mercy.

Without another word she rang the bell, and directed that Elizabeth-Jane should be fetched from her room. The latter appeared, surprised in the midst of her lucubrations.* As soon as she saw Henchard she went across to him dutifully.

'Elizabeth-Jane,' he said, taking her hand, 'I want you to hear this.' And turning to Lucetta: 'Will you, or will you not, marry me?'

'If you – wish it, I must agree!'

'You say yes?'

'I do.'

No sooner had she given the promise than she fell back in a fainting state.

'What dreadful thing drives her to say this, father, when it is such a pain to her?' asked Elizabeth, kneeling down by Lucetta. 'Don't compel her to do anything against her will! I have lived with her, and know that she cannot bear much.'

'Don't be a no'thern* simpleton!' said Henchard drily. 'This promise will leave him free for you, if you want him, won't it?'

At this Lucetta seemed to wake from her swoon with a start.

'Him? Who are you talking about?' she said wildly.

'Nobody, as far as I am concerned,' said Elizabeth firmly.

'Oh – well. Then it is my mistake,' said Henchard. 'But the business is between me and Miss Templeman. She agrees to be my wife.'

'But don't dwell on it just now,' entreated Elizabeth, holding Lucetta's hand.

'I don't wish to, if she promises,' said Henchard.

'I have, I have,' groaned Lucetta, her limbs hanging like flails, from very misery and faintness. 'Michael, please don't argue it any more!'

'I will not,' he said. And taking up his hat he went away.

Elizabeth-Jane continued to kneel by Lucetta. 'What is this?' she said. 'You called my father "Michael" as if you knew him well? And how is it he has got this power over you, that you promise to marry him against your will? Ah – you have many secrets from me!'

'Perhaps you have some from me,' Lucetta murmured with closed eyes, little thinking, however, so unsuspicious was she, that the secret of Elizabeth's heart concerned the young man who had caused this damage to her own.

'I would not – do anything against you at all!' stammered Elizabeth, keeping in all signs of emotion till she was ready to burst. 'I cannot understand how my father can command you so; I don't sympathize with him in it at all. I'll go to him and ask him to release you.'

'No, no,' said Lucetta. 'Let it all be.'

Chapter 28

The next morning Henchard went to the Town Hall below Lucetta's house, to attend Petty Sessions,* being still a magistrate for the year by virtue of his late position as Mayor. In passing he looked up at her windows, but nothing of her was to be seen.

Henchard as a Justice of the Peace may at first seem to be an even greater incongruity than Shallow and Silence* themselves. But his rough and ready perceptions, his sledge-hammer direct-ness, had often served him better than nice legal knowledge in despatching such simple business as fell to his hands in this Court. To-day Dr Chalkfield, the Mayor for the year, being absent, the corn-merchant took the big chair, his eyes still abstractedly stretching out of the window to the ashlar* front of High-Place Hall.

There was one case only, and the offender stood before him. She was an old woman of mottled countenance, attired in a shawl of that nameless tertiary hue which comes, but cannot be made – a hue neither tawny, russet, hazel, nor ash; a sticky black bonnet that seemed to have been worn in the country of the Psalmist where the clouds drop fatness;* and an apron that had been white in times so comparatively recent as still to contrast visibly with the rest of her clothes. The steeped aspect of the woman as a whole showed her to be no native of the country-side or even of a country-town.

She looked cursorily at Henchard and the second magistrate, and Henchard looked at her, with a momentary pause, as if she had reminded him indistinctly of somebody or something which passed from his mind as quickly as it had come. 'Well, and what has she been doing?' he said, looking down at the charge-sheet.

'She is charged, sir, with the offence of disorderly female and nuisance,' whispered Stubberd.

'Where did she do that?' said the other magistrate.

'By the church, sir, of all the horrible places in the world! – I caught her in the act, your worship.'

'Stand back then,' said Henchard, 'and let's hear what you've got to say.'

Stubberd was sworn, the magistrate's clerk dipped his pen, Henchard being no note-taker himself, and the constable began –

'Hearing a' illegal noise I went down the street at twenty-five minutes past eleven p.m. on the night of the fifth instinct, Hannah Dominy. When I had –'

'Don't got on so fast, Stubberd,' said the clerk.

The constable waited, with his eyes on the clerk's pen, till the latter stopped scratching and said, 'yes.' Stubberd continued: 'When I had proceeded to the spot I saw the defendant at another spot, namely, the gutter.' He paused, watching the point of the clerk's pen again.

'Gutter, yes, Stubberd.'

'Spot measuring twelve feet nine inches or thereabouts, from where I –' Still careful not to outrun the clerk's penmanship Stubberd pulled up again; for having got his evidence by heart it was immaterial to him whereabouts he broke off.

'I object to that,' spoke up the old woman, ' "spot measuring twelve feet nine or thereabouts from where I," is not sound testimony!'

The magistrates consulted, and the second one said that the bench was of opinion that twelve feet nine inches from a man on his oath was admissible.

Stubberd, with a suppressed gaze of victorious rectitude at the old woman, continued: 'Was standing myself. She was wambling* about quite dangerous to the thoroughfare, and when I approached to draw near she committed the nuisance, and insulted me.'

' "Insulted me." . . . Yes, what did she say?'

'She said, "Put away that dee lantern," she says.'

'Yes.'

'Says she, "Dost hear, old turmit-head?* Put away that dee lantern. I have floored fellows a dee sight finer-looking than a dee fool like thee, you son of a bee, dee me if I haint," she says.'

'I object to that conversation!' interposed the old woman. 'I was not capable enough to hear what I said, and what is said out of my hearing is not evidence.'

There was another stoppage for consultation, a book was referred to, and finally Stubberd was allowed to go on again. The truth was that the old woman had appeared in court so many more times than the magistrates themselves, that they were obliged to keep a sharp look-out upon their procedure. However, when Stubberd had rambled on a little further Henchard broke out impatiently, 'Come – we don't want to hear any more of them cust dees and bees! Say the words out like a man, and don't be so modest, Stubberd; or else leave it alone!' Turning to the woman, 'Now then, have you any questions to ask him, or anything to say?'

'Yes,' she replied with a twinkle in her eye; and the clerk dipped his pen.

'Twenty years ago or thereabout I was selling of furmity in a tent at Weydon Fair –'

' "Twenty years ago" – well, that's beginning at the beginning; suppose you go back to the Creation!' said the clerk, not without satire.

But Henchard stared, and quite forgot what was evidence and what was not.

'A man and a woman with a little child came into my tent,' the woman continued. 'They sat down and had a basin apiece. Ah, Lord's my life! I was of a more respectable station in the world than I am now, being a land smuggler* in a large way of business;

and I used to season my furmity with rum for them who asked fo't. I did it for the man; and then he had more and more; till at last he quarrelled with his wife, and offered to sell her to the highest bidder. A sailor came in and bid five guineas, and paid the money, and led her away. And the man who sold his wife in that fashion is the man sitting there in the great big chair.' The speaker concluded by nodding her head at Henchard and folding her arms.

Everybody looked at Henchard. His face seemed strange, and in tint as if it had been powdered over with ashes. 'We don't want to hear your life and adventures,' said the second magistrate sharply, filling the pause which followed. 'You've been asked if you've anything to say bearing on the case.'

'That bears on the case. It proves that he's no better than I, and has no right to sit there in judgment upon me.'

' 'Tis a concocted story,' said the clerk. 'So hold your tongue!'

'No – 'tis true.' The words came from Henchard. ' 'Tis as true as the light,' he said slowly. 'And upon my soul it does prove that I'm no better than she! And to keep out of any temptation to treat her hard for her revenge, I'll leave her to you.'

The sensation in the court was indescribably great. Henchard left the chair, and came out, passing through a group of people on the steps and outside that was much larger than usual; for it seemed that the old furmity dealer had mysteriously hinted to the denizens of the lane in which she had been lodging since her arrival, that she knew a queer thing or two about their great local man Mr Henchard, if she chose to tell it. This had brought them hither.

'Why are there so many idlers round the Town Hall to-day?' said Lucetta to her servant when the case was over. She had risen late, and had just looked out of the window.

'Oh, please, ma'am, 'tis this larry* about Mr Henchard. A woman has proved that before he became a gentleman he sold his wife for five guineas in a booth at the fair.'

In all the accounts which Henchard had given her of the separation from his wife Susan for so many years, of his belief in her death, and so on, he had never clearly explained the actual and immediate cause of that separation. The story she now heard for the first time.

A gradual misery overspread Lucetta's face as she dwelt upon the promise wrung from her the night before. At bottom, then,

Henchard was this. How terrible a contingency for a woman who should commit herself to his care.

During the day she went out to the Ring and to other places, not coming in till nearly dusk. As soon as she saw Elizabeth-Jane after her return indoors she told her that she had resolved to go away from home to the seaside for a few days – to Port-Bredy;* Casterbridge was so gloomy.

Elizabeth, seeing that she looked wan and disturbed, encouraged her in the idea, thinking a change would afford her relief. She could not help suspecting that the gloom which seemed to have come over Casterbridge in Lucetta's eyes might be partially owing to the fact that Farfrae was away from home.

Elizabeth saw her friend depart for Port-Bredy, and took charge of High-Place Hall till her return. After two or three days of solitude and incessant rain Henchard called at the house. He seemed disappointed to hear of Lucetta's absence, and though he nodded with outward indifference he went away handling his beard with a nettled mien.

The next day he called again. 'Is she come now?' he asked.

'Yes. She returned this morning,' replied his stepdaughter. 'But she is not indoors. She has gone for a walk along the turnpike-road to Port-Bredy. She will be home by dusk.'

After a few words, which only served to reveal his restless impatience, he left the house again.

Chapter 29

At this hour Lucetta was bounding along the road to Port-Bredy just as Elizabeth had announced. That she had chosen for her afternoon walk the road along which she had returned to Casterbridge three hours earlier in a carriage was curious – if anything should be called curious in concatenations of phenomena wherein each is known to have its accounting cause. It was the day of the chief market – Saturday – and Farfrae for once had been missed from his corn-stand in the dealers' room. Nevertheless, it was known that he would be home that night – 'for Sunday', as Casterbridge expressed it.

Lucetta, in continuing her walk, had at length reached the end of the ranked trees which bordered the highway in this and other directions out of the town. This end marked a mile; and here she stopped.

The spot was a vale between two gentle acclivities, and the road, still adhering to its Roman foundation, stretched onward straight as a surveyor's line till lost to sight on the most distant ridge. There was neither hedge nor tree in the prospect now, the road clinging to the stubbly expanse of corn-land like a stripe to an undulating garment. Near her was a barn – the single building of any kind within her horizon.

She strained her eyes up the lessening road, but nothing appeared thereon – not so much as a speck. She sighed one word – 'Donald!' and turned her face to the town for retreat.

Here the case was different. A single figure was approaching her – Elizabeth-Jane's.

Lucetta, in spite of her loneliness, seemed a little vexed. Elizabeth's face, as soon as she recognized her friend, shaped itself into affectionate lines while yet beyond speaking distance. 'I suddenly thought I would come and meet you,' she said, smiling.

Lucetta's reply was taken from her lips by an unexpected diversion. A by-road on her right hand descended from the fields into the highway at the point where she stood, and down the track a bull was rambling uncertainly towards her and Elizabeth, who, facing the other way, did not observe him.

In the latter quarter of each year cattle were at once the mainstay and the terror of families about Casterbridge and its neighbourhood, where breeding was carried on with Abrahamic success.* The head of stock driven into and out of the town at this season to be sold by the local auctioneer was very large; and all these horned beasts, in travelling to and fro, sent women and children to shelter as nothing else could do. In the main the animals would have walked along quietly enough; but the Casterbridge tradition was that to drive stock it was indispensable that hideous cries, coupled with Yahoo* antics and gestures, should be used, large sticks flourished, stray dogs called in, and in general everything done that was likely to infuriate the viciously disposed and terrify the mild. Nothing was commoner than for a house-holder on going out of his parlour to find his hall or passage full of little children, nursemaids, aged women, or a ladies' school, who apologized for their presence by saying, 'A bull passing down street from the sale.'

Lucetta and Elizabeth regarded the animal in doubt, he meanwhile drawing vaguely towards them. It was a large specimen of the breed, in colour rich dun, though disfigured at present by splotches of mud about his seamy sides. His horns were thick and tipped with brass; his two nostrils like the Thames Tunnel as seen in the perspective toys of yore.* Between them, through the gristle of his nose, was a stout copper ring, welded on, and irremovable as Gurth's collar of brass.* To the ring was attached an ash staff about a yard long, which the bull with the motions of his head flung about like a flail.

It was not till they observed this dangling stick that the young women were really alarmed; for it revealed to them that the bull was an old one, too savage to be driven, which had in some way escaped, the staff being the means by which the drover controlled him and kept his horns at arms' length.

They looked round for some shelter or hiding-place, and thought of the barn hard by. As long as they had kept their eyes on the bull he had shown some deference in his manner of approach; but no sooner did they turn their backs to seek the barn than he tossed his head and decided to thoroughly terrify them. This caused the two helpless girls to run wildly, whereupon the bull advanced in a deliberate charge.

The barn stood behind a green slimy pond, and it was closed save as to one of the usual pair of doors facing them, which had been propped open by a hurdle-stake, and for this opening they made. The interior had been cleared by a recent bout of threshing except at one end, where there was a stack of dry clover. Elizabeth-Jane took in the situation. 'We must climb up there,' she said.

But before they had even approached it they heard the bull scampering through the pond without, and in a second he dashed into the barn, knocking down the hurdle-stake in passing; the heavy door slammed behind him; and all three were imprisoned in the barn together. The mistaken creature saw them, and stalked towards the end of the barn into which they had fled. The girls doubled so adroitly that their pursuer was against the wall when the fugitives were already half way to the other end. By the time that his length would allow him to turn and follow them thither they had crossed over; thus the pursuit went on, the hot air from his nostrils blowing over them like a sirocco,* and not a moment being attainable by Elizabeth or Lucetta in which to open the door. What might have happened had their situation continued cannot be said; but in a few moments a rattling of the door distracted their adversary's attention, and a man appeared. He ran forward towards the leading-staff, seized it, and wrenched the animal's head as if he would snap it off. The wrench was in reality so violent that the thick neck seemed to have lost its stiffness and to become half-paralysed, whilst the nose dropped blood. The premeditated human contrivance of the nose-ring was too cunning for impulsive brute force, and the creature flinched.

The man was seen in the partial gloom to be large-framed and unhesitating. He led the bull to the door, and the light revealed Henchard. He made the bull fast without, and re-entered to the succour of Lucetta; for he had not perceived Elizabeth, who had climbed on to the clover-heap. Lucetta was hysterical, and Henchard took her in his arms and carried her to the door.

'You – have saved me!' she cried, as soon as she could speak.

'I have returned your kindness,' he responded tenderly. 'You once saved me.'

'How – comes it to be you – you?' she asked, not heeding his reply.

'I came out here to look for you. I have been wanting to tell you something these two or three days; but you have been away, and I could not. Perhaps you cannot talk now?'

'O – no! Where is Elizabeth?'

'Here am I!' cried the missing one cheerfully; and without waiting for the ladder to be placed she slid down the face of the clover-stack to the floor.

Henchard supporting Lucetta on one side, and Elizabeth-Jane on the other, they went slowly along the rising road. They had reached the top and were descending again when Lucetta, now much recovered, recollected that she had dropped her muff in the barn.

'I'll run back,' said Elizabeth-Jane. 'I don't mind at all, as I am not tired as you are.' She thereupon hastened down again to the barn, the others pursuing their way.

Elizabeth soon found the muff, such an article being by no means small at that time. Coming out she paused to look for a moment at the bull, now rather to be pitied with his bleeding nose, having perhaps rather intended a practical joke than a murder. Henchard had secured him by jamming the staff into the hinge of the barn-door, and wedging it there with a stake. At length she turned to hasten onward after her contemplation, when she saw a green-and-black gig* approaching from the contrary direction, the vehicle being driven by Farfrae.

His presence here seemed to explain Lucetta's walk that way. Donald saw her, drew up, and was hastily made acquainted with what had occurred. At Elizabeth-Jane mentioning how greatly Lucetta had been jeopardized, he exhibited an agitation different in kind no less than in intensity from any she had seen in him before. He became so absorbed in the circumstance that he scarcely had sufficient knowledge of what he was doing to think of helping her up beside him.

'She has gone on with Mr Henchard, you say?' he inquired at last.

'Yes. He is taking her home. They are almost there by this time.'

'And you are sure she can get home?'

Elizabeth-Jane was quite sure.

'Your stepfather saved her?'

'Entirely.'

Farfrae checked his horse's pace; she guessed why. He was thinking that it would be best not to intrude on the other two just now. Henchard had saved Lucetta, and to provoke a possible exhibition of her deeper affection for himself was as ungenerous as it was unwise.

The immediate subject of their talk being exhausted she felt more embarrassed at sitting thus beside her past lover; but soon the two figures of the others were visible at the entrance to the town. The face of the woman was frequently turned back, but Farfrae did not whip on the horse. When these reached the town walls Henchard and his companion had disappeared down the street; Farfrae set down Elizabeth-Jane on her expressing a particular wish to alight there, and drove round to the stables at the back of his lodgings.

On this account he entered the house through his garden, and going up to his apartments found them in a particularly disturbed state, his boxes being hauled out upon the landing, and his bookcase standing in three pieces. These phenomena, however, seemed to cause him not the least surprise. 'When will everything be sent up?' he said to the mistress of the house, who was superintending.

'I am afraid not before eight, sir,' said she. 'You see we wasn't aware till this morning that you were going to move, or we could have been forwarder.'

'A – well, never mind, never mind!' said Farfrae cheerily. 'Eight o'clock will do well enough if it be not later. Now, don't ye be standing here talking, or it will be twelve, I doubt.' Thus speaking he went out by the front door and up the street.

During this interval Henchard and Lucetta had had experiences of a different kind. After Elizabeth's departure for the muff the corn-merchant opened himself frankly, holding her hand within his arm, though she would fain have withdrawn it. 'Dear Lucetta, I have been very, very anxious to see you these two or three days,' he said; 'ever since I saw you last! I have thought over the way I got your promise that night. You said to me, "If I were a man I should not insist." That cut me deep. I felt that there was some truth in it. I don't want to make you wretched; and to marry me just now would do that as nothing else could – it is but too plain. Therefore I agree to an indefinite engagement – to put off all thought of marriage for a year or two.'

'But – but – can I do nothing of a different kind?' said Lucetta. 'I am full of gratitude to you – you have saved my life. And your care of me is like coals of fire on my head!* I am a monied person now. Surely I can do something in return for your goodness – something practical?'

Henchard remained in thought. He had evidently not expected this. 'There is one thing you might do, Lucetta,' he said. 'But not exactly of that kind.'

'Then of what kind is it?' she asked with renewed misgiving.

'I must tell you a secret to ask it. – You may have heard that I have been unlucky this year? I did what I have never done before – speculated rashly; and I lost. That's just put me in a strait.'

'And you would wish me to advance some money?'

'No, no!' said Henchard, almost in anger. 'I'm not the man to sponge on a woman, even though she may be so nearly my own as you. No, Lucetta; what you can do is this; and it would save me. My great creditor is Grower, and it is at his hands I shall suffer if at anybody's; while a fortnight's forbearance on his part would be enough to allow me to pull through. This may be got out of him in one way – that you would let it be known to him that you are my intended – that we are to be quietly married in the next fortnight. – Now stop, you haven't heard all! Let him have this story, without, of course, any prejudice to the fact that the actual engagement between us is to be a long one. Nobody else need know: you could go with me to Mr Grower and just let me speak to 'ee before him as if we were on such terms. We'll ask him to keep it secret. He will willingly wait then. At the fortnight's end I shall be able to face him; and I can coolly tell him all is postponed between us for a year or two. Not a soul in the town need know how you've helped me. Since you wish to be of use, there's your way.'

It being now what the people called the 'pinking in' of the day, that is, the quarter-hour just before dusk, he did not at first observe the result of his own words upon her.

'If it were anything else,' she began, and the dryness of her lips was represented in her voice.

'But it is such a little thing!' he said, with a deep reproach. 'Less than you have offered – just the beginning of what you have so lately promised! I could have told him as much myself, but he would not have believed me.'

'It is not because I won't – it is because I absolutely can't,' she said, with rising distress.

'You are provoking!' he burst out. 'It is enough to make me force you to carry out at once what you have promised.'

'I cannot!' she insisted desperately.

'Why? When I have only within these few minutes released you from your promise to do the thing off-hand.'

'Because – he was a witness!'

'Witness? Of what?'

'If I must tell you –. Don't, don't upbraid me!'

'Well! Let's hear what you mean?'

'Witness of my marriage – Mr Grower was!'

'Marriage?'

'Yes. With Mr Farfrae. O Michael! I am already his wife. We were married this week at Port-Bredy. There were reasons against our doing it here. Mr Grower was a witness because he happened to be in Port-Bredy at the time.'

Henchard stood as if idiotized. She was so alarmed at his silence that she murmured something about lending him sufficient money to tide over the perilous fortnight.

'Married him?' said Henchard at length. 'My good – what, married him whilst – bound to marry me?'

'It was like this,' she explained, with tears in her eyes and quavers in her voice; 'don't – don't be cruel! I loved him so much, and I thought you might tell him of the past – and that grieved me! And then, when I had promised you, I learnt of the rumour that you had – sold your first wife at a fair like a horse or a cow! How could I keep my promise after hearing that? I could not risk myself in your hands; it would have been letting myself down to take your name after such a scandal. But I knew I should lose Donald if I did not secure him at once – for you would carry out your threat of telling him of our former acquaintance, as long as there was a chance of keeping me for yourself by doing so. But you will not do so now, will you, Michael? for it is too late to separate us.'

The notes of St Peter's bells in full peal had been wafted to them while she spoke; and now the genial thumping of the town band, renowned for its unstinted use of the drum-stick, throbbed down the street.

'Then this racket they are making is on account of it, I suppose?' said he.

'Yes – I think he has told them, or else Mr Grower has . . . May I leave you now? My – he was detained at Port-Bredy to-day, and sent me on a few hours before him.'

'Then it is *his wife's* life I have saved this afternoon.'

'Yes – and he will be for ever grateful to you.'

'I am much obliged to him . . . O you false woman!' burst from Henchard. 'You promised me!'

'Yes, yes! But it was under compulsion, and I did not know all your past –'

'And now I've a mind to punish you as you deserve! One word to this bran-new husband of how you courted me, and your precious happiness is blown to atoms!'

'Michael – pity me, and be generous!'

'You don't deserve pity! You did; but you don't now.'

'I'll help you to pay off your debt.'

'A pensioner of Farfrae's wife – not I! Don't stay with me longer – I shall say something worse. Go home!'

She disappeared under the trees of the south walk as the band came round the corner, awaking the echoes of every stock and stone in celebration of her happiness. Lucetta took no heed, but ran up the back street and reached her own home unperceived.

Chapter 30

Farfrae's words to his landlady had referred to the removal of his boxes and other effects from his late lodgings to Lucetta's house. The work was not heavy, but it had been much hindered on account of the frequent pauses necessitated by exclamations of surprise at the event, of which the good woman had been briefly informed by letter a few hours earlier.

At the late moment of leaving Port-Bredy, Farfrae, like John Gilpin,* had been detained by important customers, whom, even in the exceptional circumstances, he was not the man to neglect. Moreover, there was a convenience in Lucetta arriving first at her house. Nobody there as yet knew what had happened; and she was best in a position to break the news to the inmates, and give directions for her husband's accommodation. He had, therefore, sent on his two-days' bride in a hired brougham,* whilst he went across the country to a certain group of wheat and barley ricks a few miles off, telling her the hour at which he might be expected the same evening. This accounted for her trotting out to meet him after their separation of four hours.

By a strenuous effort, after leaving Henchard she calmed herself in readiness to receive Donald at High-Place Hall when he came on from his lodgings. One supreme fact empowered her to this, the sense that, come what would, she had secured him. Half-an-hour after her arrival he walked in, and she met him with a relieved gladness, which a month's perilous absence could not have intensified.

'There is one thing I have not done; and yet it is important,' she said earnestly, when she had finished talking about the adventure with the bull. 'That is, broken the news of our marriage to my dear Elizabeth-Jane.'

'Ah, and you have not?' he said thoughtfully. 'I gave her a lift from the barn homewards; but I did not tell her either; for I thought she might have heard of it in the town, and was keeping back her congratulations from shyness, and all that.'

'She can hardly have heard of it. But I'll find out; I'll go to her now. And, Donald, you don't mind her living on with me just the same as before? She is so quiet and unassuming.'

'O no, indeed I don't,' Farfrae answered with, perhaps, a faint awkwardness. 'But I wonder if she would care to?'

'O yes!' said Lucetta eagerly. 'I am sure she would like to. Besides, poor thing, she has no other home.'

Farfrae looked at her and saw that she did not suspect the secret of her more reserved friend. He liked her all the better for the blindness. 'Arrange as you like with her by all means,' he said. 'It is I who have come to your house, not you to mine.'

'I'll run and speak to her,' said Lucetta.

When she got upstairs to Elizabeth-Jane's room the latter had taken off her out-door things, and was resting over a book. Lucetta found in a moment that she had not yet learnt the news.

'I did not come down to you, Miss Templeman,' she said simply. 'I was coming to ask you if you had quite recovered from your fright, but I found you had a visitor. What are the bells ringing for, I wonder? And the band, too, is playing. Somebody must be married; or else they are practising for Christmas.'

Lucetta uttered a vague 'Yes', and seating herself by the other young woman looked musingly at her. 'What a lonely creature you are,' she presently said; 'never knowing what's going on, or what people are talking about everywhere with keen interest. You should get out, and gossip about as other women do, and then you wouldn't be obliged to ask me a question of that kind. Well, now, I have something to tell you.'

Elizabeth-Jane said she was so glad, and made herself receptive.

'I must go rather a long way back,' said Lucetta, the difficulty of explaining herself satisfactorily to the pondering one beside her growing more apparent at each syllable. 'You remember that trying case of conscience I told you of some time ago – about the first lover and the second lover?' She let out in jerky phrases a leading word or two of the story she had told.

'O yes – I remember; the story of *your friend*,' said Elizabeth drily, regarding the irises of Lucetta's eyes as though to catch their exact shade. 'The two lovers – the old and the new: how she wanted to marry the second, but felt she ought to marry the first; so that she neglected the better course to follow the evil, like the poet Ovid I've just been construing: "Video meliora proboque, deteriora sequor." '*

'Oh no; she didn't follow evil exactly!' said Lucetta hastily.

'But you said that she – or as I may say *you*' – answered Elizabeth, dropping the mask, 'were in honour and conscience bound to marry the first?'

Lucetta's blush at being seen through came and went again

before she replied anxiously, 'You will never breathe this, will you, Elizabeth-Jane?'

'Certainly not, if you say not.'

'Then I will tell you that the case is more complicated – worse, in fact – than it seemed in my story. I and the first man were thrown together in a strange way, and felt that we ought to be united, as the world had talked of us. He was a widower, as he supposed. He had not heard of his first wife for many years. But the wife returned, and we parted. She is now dead; and the husband comes paying me addresses again, saying, "Now we'll complete our purpose." But, Elizabeth-Jane, all this amounts to a new courtship of me by him; I was absolved from all vows by the return of the other woman.'

'Have you not lately renewed your promise?' said the younger with quiet surmise. She had divined Man Number One.

'That was wrung from me by a threat.'

'Yes, it was. But I think when any one gets coupled up with a man in the past so unfortunately as you have done, she ought to become his wife if she can, even if she were not the sinning party.'

Lucetta's countenance lost its sparkle. 'He turned out to be a man I should be afraid to marry,' she pleaded. 'Really afraid! And it was not till after my renewed promise that I knew it.'

'Then there is only one course left to honesty. You must remain a single woman.'

'But think again! Do consider –'

'I am certain,' interrupted her companion hardily. 'I have guessed very well who the man is. My father; and I say it is him or nobody for you.'

Any suspicion of impropriety was to Elizabeth-Jane like a red rag to a bull. Her craving for correctness of procedure was, indeed, almost vicious. Owing to her early troubles with regard to her mother a semblance of irregularity had terrors for her which those whose names are safeguarded from suspicion know nothing of. 'You ought to marry Mr Henchard or nobody – certainly not another man!' she went on with a quivering lip in whose movement two passions shared.

'I don't admit that!' said Lucetta passionately.

'Admit it or not, it is true!'

Lucetta covered her eyes with her right hand, as if she could plead no more, holding out her left to Elizabeth-Jane.

'Why, you *have* married him!' cried the latter, jumping up with pleasure after a glance at Lucetta's fingers. 'When did you do it? Why did you not tell me, instead of teasing me like this? How very honourable of you! He did treat my mother badly once, it seems, in a moment of intoxication. And it is true that he is stern sometimes. But you will rule him entirely, I am sure, with your beauty and wealth and accomplishments. You are the woman he will adore, and we shall be happy together now!'

'O, my Elizabeth-Jane!' cried Lucetta distressfully. ' 'Tis somebody else that I have married! I was so desperate – so afraid of being forced to anything else – so afraid of revelations that would quench his love for me, that I resolved to do it off-hand, come what might, and purchase a week of happiness at any cost!'

'You – have – married Mr Farfrae!' cried Elizabeth-Jane, in Nathan tones.*

Lucetta bowed. She had recovered herself.

'The bells are ringing on that account,' she said. 'My husband is downstairs. He will live here till a more suitable house is ready for us; and I have told him that I want you to stay with me just as before.'

'Let me think of it alone,' the girl quickly replied, corking up the turmoil of her feeling with grand control.

'You shall. I am sure we shall be happy together.'

Lucetta departed to join Donald below, a vague uneasiness floating over her joy at seeing him quite at home there. Not on account of her friend Elizabeth did she feel it: for of the bearings of Elizabeth-Jane's emotions she had not the least suspicion; but on Henchard's alone.

Now the instant decision of Susan Henchard's daughter was to dwell in that house no more. Apart from her estimate of the propriety of Lucetta's conduct, Farfrae had been so nearly her avowed lover that she felt she could not abide there.

It was still early in the evening when she hastily put on her things and went out. In a few minutes, knowing the ground, she had found a suitable lodging, and arranged to enter it that night. Returning and entering noiselessly she took off her pretty dress and arrayed herself in a plain one, packing up the other to keep as her best; for she would have to be very economical now. She wrote a note to leave for Lucetta, who was closely shut up in the drawing-room with Farfrae; and then Elizabeth-Jane called a man with a wheelbarrow; and seeing her boxes put into it she trotted off down the street to her rooms. They were in the street in which Henchard lived, and almost opposite his door.

Here she sat down and considered the means of subsistence. The little annual sum settled on her by her stepfather would keep body and soul together. A wonderful skill in netting* of all sorts – acquired in childhood by making seines* in Newson's home – might serve her in good stead; and her studies, which were pursued unremittingly, might serve her in still better.

By this time the marriage that had taken place was known throughout Casterbridge; had been discussed noisily on kerb-stones, confidentially behind counters, and jovially at the Three Mariners. Whether Farfrae would sell his business and set up for a gentleman on his wife's money, or whether he would show independence enough to stick to his trade in spite of his brilliant alliance, was a great point of interest.

Chapter 31

The retort of the furmity-woman before the magistrates had spread; and in four-and-twenty hours there was not a person in Casterbridge who remained unacquainted with the story of Henchard's mad freak at Weydon-Priors Fair, long years before. The amends he had made in after life were lost sight of in the dramatic glare of the original act. Had the incident been well known of old and always, it might by this time have grown to be lightly regarded as the rather tall wild oat, but well-nigh the single one, of a young man with whom the steady and mature (if somewhat headstrong) burgher of today had scarcely a point in common. But the act having lain as dead and buried ever since, the interspace of years was unperceived; and the black spot of his youth wore the aspect of a recent crime.

Small as the police-court incident had been in itself, it formed the edge or turn in the incline of Henchard's fortunes. On that day – almost at that minute – he passed the ridge of prosperity and honour, and began to descend rapidly on the other side. It was strange how soon he sank in esteem. Socially he had received a startling fillip* downwards; and, having already lost commercial bouyancy from rash transactions, the velocity of his descent in both aspects became accelerated every hour.

He now gazed more at the pavements and less at the house-fronts when he walked about; more at the feet and leggings of men, and less into the pupils of their eyes with the blazing regard which formerly had made them blink.

New events combined to undo him. It had been a bad year for others besides himself, and the heavy failure of a debtor whom he had trusted generously completed the overthrow of his tottering credit. And now, in his desperation, he failed to preserve that strict correspondence between bulk and sample which is the soul of commerce in grain. For this, one of his men was mainly to blame; that worthy, in his great unwisdom, having picked over the sample of an enormous quantity of second-rate corn which Henchard had in hand, and removed the pinched, blasted, and smutted grains* in great numbers. The produce if honestly offered would have created no scandal; but the blunder of misrepresenta-tion, coming at such a moment, dragged Henchard's name into the ditch.

The details of his failure were of the ordinary kind. One day Elizabeth-Jane was passing the King's Arms, when she saw people bustling in and out more than usual when there was no market. A bystander informed her, with some surprise at her ignorance, that it was a meeting of the Commissioners under Mr Henchard's bankruptcy. She felt quite tearful, and when she heard that he was present in the hotel she wished to go in and see him, but was advised not to intrude that day.

The room in which debtor and creditors had assembled was a front one, and Henchard looking out of the window, had caught sight of Elizabeth-Jane through the wire blind. His examination had closed, and the creditors were leaving. The appearance of Elizabeth threw him into a reverie; till, turning his face from the window, and towering above all the rest, he called their attention for a moment more. His countenance had somewhat changed from its flush of prosperity; the black hair and whiskers were the same as ever, but a film of ash was over the rest.

'Gentlemen,' he said, 'over and above the assets that we've been talking about, and that appear on the balance-sheet, there be these. It all belongs to ye, as much as everything else I've got, and I don't wish to keep it from you, not I.' Saying this, he took his gold watch from his pocket and laid it on the table; then his purse – the yellow canvas money-bag, such as was carried by all farmers and dealers – untying it, and shaking the money out upon the table beside the watch. The latter he drew back quickly for an instant, to remove the hair-guard made and given him by Lucetta. 'There, now you have all I've got in the world,' he said. 'And I wish for your sakes 'twas more.'

The creditors, farmers almost to a man, looked at the watch, and at the money, and into the street; when Farmer James Everdene of Weatherbury* spoke.

'No, no, Henchard,' he said warmly. 'We don't want that. 'Tis honourable in ye; but keep it. What do you say, neighbours – do ye agree?'

'Ay, sure: we don't wish it at all,' said Grower, another creditor.

'Let him keep it, of course,' murmured another in the background – a silent, reserved young man named Boldwood;* and the rest responded unanimously.

'Well,' said the senior Commissioner, addressing Henchard, 'though the case is a desperate one, I am bound to admit that I have never met a debtor who behaved more fairly. I've proved the balance-sheet to be as honestly made out as it could possibly be; we have had no trouble; there have been no evasions and no concealments. The rashness of dealing which led to this unhappy situation is obvious enough; but as far as I can see every attempt has been made to avoid wronging anybody.'

Henchard was more affected by this than he cared to let them perceive, and he turned aside to the window again. A general murmur of agreement followed the Commissioner's words; and the meeting dispersed.* When they were gone Henchard regarded the watch they had returned to him. ' 'Tisn't mine by rights,' he said to himself. 'Why the devil didn't they take it? – I don't want what don't belong to me!' Moved by a recollection he took the watch to the maker's just opposite, sold it there and then for what the tradesman offered, and went with the proceeds to one among the smaller of his creditors, a cottager of Durnover in straitened circumstances, to whom he handed the money.

When everything was ticketed that Henchard had owned, and the auctions were in progress, there was quite a sympathetic reaction in the town, which till then for some time past had done nothing but condemn him. Now that Henchard's whole career was pictured distinctly to his neighbours, and they could see how admirably he had used his one talent of energy to create a position of affluence out of absolutely nothing – which was really all he could show when he came to town as a journeyman hay-trusser, with his wimble* and knife in his basket – they wondered and regretted his fall.

Try as she might, Elizabeth could never meet with him. She believed in him still, though nobody else did; and she wanted to be allowed to forgive him for his roughness to her, and to help him in his trouble.

She wrote to him; he did not reply. She then went to his house – the great house she had lived in so happily for a time – with its front of dun brick, vitrified* here and there, and its heavy sash-bars – but Henchard was to be found there no more. The ex-Mayor had left the house of his prosperity, and gone into Jopp's cottage by the Priory Mill – the sad purlieu to which he had wandered on the night of his discovery that she was not his daughter. Thither she went.

Elizabeth thought it odd that he had fixed on this spot to retire to, but assumed that necessity had no choice. Trees which seemed old enough to have been planted by the friars still stood around, and the back hatch of the original mill yet formed a cascade which had raised its terrific roar for centuries. The cottage itself was built of old stones from the long dismantled Priory, scraps of tracery, moulded window-jambs, and arch-labels,* being mixed in with the rubble of the walls.

In this cottage he occupied a couple of rooms, Jopp, whom Henchard had employed, abused, cajoled, and dismissed by turns, being the householder. But even here her stepfather could not be seen.

'Not by his daughter?' pleaded Elizabeth.

'By nobody – at present: that's his order,' she was informed.

Afterwards she was passing by the corn-stores and hay-barns which had been the headquarters of his business. She knew that he ruled there no longer; but it was with amazement that she regarded the familiar gateway. A smear of decisive lead-coloured paint had been laid on to obliterate Henchard's name, though its letters dimly loomed through like ships in a fog. Over these, in fresh white, spread the name of Farfrae.

Abel Whittle was edging his skeleton in at the wicket, and she said, 'Mr Farfrae is master here?'

'Yaas, Miss Henchet,' he said, 'Mr Farfrae have bought the

concern and all of we work-folk with it; and 'tis better for us than
'twas – though I shouldn't say that to you as a daughter-law. We
work harder, but we bain't made afeard now. It was fear made my
few poor hairs so thin! No busting out, no slamming of doors, no
meddling with yer eternal soul and all that; and though 'tis a
shilling a week less I'm the richer man; for what's all the world if
yer mind is always in a larry,* Miss Henchet?'

The intelligence was in a general sense true; and Henchard's
stores, which had remained in a paralysed condition during the
settlement of his bankruptcy, were stirred into activity again
when the new tenant had possession. Thenceforward the full
sacks, looped with the shining chain, went scurrying up and down
under the cathead,* hairy arms were thrust out from the different
door-ways, and the grain was hauled in; trusses of hay were
tossed anew in and out of the barns, and the wimbles creaked;
while the scales and steelyards* began to be busy where guess-
work had formerly been the rule.

Chapter 32

Two bridges* stood near the lower part of Casterbridge town.
The first, of weather-stained brick, was immediately at the end of
High Street, where a diverging branch from that thoroughfare ran
round to the low-lying Durnover lanes; so that the precincts of the
bridge formed the merging point of respectability and indigence.
The second bridge, of stone, was further out on the highway – in
fact, fairly in the meadows, though still within the town
boundary.

These bridges had speaking countenances. Every projection in
each was worn down to obtuseness partly by weather, more by
friction from generations of loungers, whose toes and heels had from
year to year made restless movements against these parapets, as they
had stood there meditating on the aspect of affairs. In the case of the
more friable* bricks and stones even the flat faces were worn into
hollows by the same mixed mechanism. The masonry of the top was
clamped with iron at each joint; since it had been no uncommon
thing for desperate men to wrench the coping off and throw it down
the river, in reckless defiance of the magistrates.

For to this pair of bridges gravitated all the failures of the town; those who had failed in business, in love, in sobriety, in crime. Why the unhappy hereabout usually chose the bridges for their meditations in preference to a railing, a gate, or a stile, was not so clear.

There was a marked difference of quality between the personages who haunted the near bridge of brick and the personages who haunted the far one of stone. Those of lowest character preferred the former, adjoining the town; they did not mind the glare of the public eye. They had been of comparatively no account during their successes; and, though they might feel dispirited, they had no particular sense of shame in their ruin. Their hands were mostly kept in their pockets; they wore a leather strap round their hips or knees, and boots that required a great deal of lacing, but seemed never to get any. Instead of sighing at their adversities they spat, and instead of saying the iron had entered into their souls they said they were down on their luck. Jopp in his times of distress had often stood here; so had Mother Cuxsom, Christopher Coney, and poor Abel Whittle.

The *misérables** who would pause on the remoter bridge were of a politer stamp. They included bankrupts, hypochondriacs, persons who were what is called 'out of a situation' from fault or lucklessness, the inefficient of the professional class – shabby-genteel men, who did not know how to get rid of the weary time between breakfast and dinner, and the yet more weary time between dinner and dark. The eyes of this species were mostly directed over the parapet upon the running water below. A man seen there looking thus fixedly into the river was pretty sure to be one whom the world did not treat kindly for some reason or other. While one in straits on the townward bridge did not mind who saw him so, and kept his back to the parapet to survey the passers-by, one in straits on this never faced the road, never turned his head at coming footsteps, but, sensitive to his own condition, watched the current whenever a stranger approached, as if some strange fish interested him, though every finned thing had been poached out of the river years before.

There and thus they would muse; if their grief were the grief of oppression they would wish themselves kings; if their grief were poverty, wish themselves millionaires; if sin, they would wish they were saints or angels; if despised love, that they were some much-courted Adonis* of county fame. Some had been known to stand

and think so long with this fixed gaze downward that eventually they had allowed their poor carcases to follow that gaze; and they were discovered the next morning out of reach of their troubles, either here or in the deep pool called Blackwater, a little higher up the river.

To this bridge came Henchard, as other unfortunates had come before him, his way thither being by the riverside path on the chilly edge of the town. Here he was standing one windy afternoon when Durnover church clock struck five. While the gusts were bringing the notes to his ears across the damp intervening flat a man passed behind him and greeted Henchard by name. Henchard turned slightly and saw that the comer was Jopp, his old foreman, now employed elsewhere, to whom, though he hated him, he had gone for lodgings because Jopp was the one man in Casterbridge whose observation and opinion the fallen corn-merchant despised to the point of indifference.

Henchard returned him a scarcely perceptible nod, and Jopp stopped.

'He and she are gone into their new house to-day,' said Jopp.

'Oh,' said Henchard absently. 'Which house is that?'

'Your old one.'

'Gone into my house?' And starting up Henchard added, '*My* house of all others in the town!'

'Well, as somebody was sure to live there, and you couldn't, it can do 'ee no harm that he's the man.'

It was quite true: he felt that it was doing him no harm. Farfrae, who had already taken the yards and stores, had acquired possession of the house for the obvious convenience of its contiguity. And yet this act of his taking up residence within those roomy chambers while he, their former tenant, lived in a cottage, galled Henchard indescribably.

Jopp continued: 'And you heard of that fellow who bought all the best furniture at your sale? He was bidding for no other than Farfrae all the while! It has never been moved out of the house, as he'd already got the lease.'

'My furniture too! Surely he'll buy my body and soul likewise!'

'There's no saying he won't, if you be willing to sell.' And having planted these wounds in the heart of his once imperious master Jopp went on his way; while Henchard stared and stared into the racing river till the bridge seemed moving backward with him.

The low land grew blacker, and the sky a deeper grey. When the landscape looked like a picture blotted in with ink, another traveller approached the great stone bridge. He was driving a gig, his direction being also townwards. On the round of the middle of the arch the gig stopped. 'Mr Henchard?' came from it in the voice of Farfrae. Henchard turned his face.

Finding that he had guessed rightly Farfrae told the man who accompanied him to drive home, while he alighted and went up to his former friend.

'I have heard that you think of emigrating, Mr Henchard,' he said. 'Is it true? I have a real reason for asking.'

Henchard withheld his answer for several instants, and then said, 'Yes; it is true. I am going where you were going to a few years ago, when I prevented you and got you to bide here. 'Tis turn and turn about, isn't it! Do ye mind how we stood like this in the Chalk Walk when I persuaded 'ee to stay? You then stood without a chattel* to your name, and I was the master of the house in Corn Street. But now I stand without a stick or a rag, and the master of that house is you.'

'Yes, yes; that's so! It's the way o' the warrld,' said Farfrae.

'Ha, ha, true!' cried Henchard, throwing himself into a mood of jocularity. 'Up and down! I'm used to it. What's the odds after all!'

'Now listen to me, if it's no taking up your time,' said Farfrae, 'just as I listened to you. Don't go. Stay at home.'

'But I can do nothing else, man!' said Henchard scornfully. 'The little money I have will just keep body and soul together for a few weeks, and no more. I have not felt inclined to go back to journey-work* yet; but I can't stay doing nothing, and my best chance is elsewhere.'

'No; but what I propose is this – if ye will listen. Come and live in your old house. We can spare some rooms very well – I am sure my wife would not mind it at all – until there's an opening for ye.'

Henchard started. Probably the picture drawn by the un-suspecting Donald of himself under the same roof with Lucetta was too striking to be received with equanimity. 'No, no,' he said gruffly; 'we should quarrel.'

'You should hae a part to yourself,' said Farfrae; 'and nobody to interfere wi' you. It will be a deal healthier than down there by the river where you live now.'

Still Henchard refused. 'You don't know what you ask,' he said. 'However, I can do no less than thank 'ee.'

They walked into the town together side by side, as they had done when Henchard persuaded the young Scotchman to remain. 'Will you come in and have some supper?' said Farfrae when they reached the middle of the town, where their paths diverged right and left.

'No, no.'

'By-the-bye, I had nearly forgot. I bought a good deal of your furniture.'

'So I have heard.'

'Well, it was no that I wanted it so very much for myself; but I wish ye to pick out all that you care to have – such things as may be endeared to ye by associations, or particularly suited to your use. And take them to your own house – it will not be depriving me; we can do with less very well, and I will have plenty of opportunities of getting more.'

'What – give it to me for nothing?' said Henchard. 'But you paid the creditors for it!'

'Ah, yes; but maybe it's worth more to you than it is to me.'

Henchard was a little moved. 'I – sometimes think I've wronged 'ee!' he said, in tones which showed the disquietude that the night shades hid in his face. He shook Farfrae abruptly by the hand, and hastened away as if unwilling to betray himself further. Farfrae saw him turn through the thoroughfare into Bull Stake and vanish down towards the Priory Mill.

Meanwhile Elizabeth-Jane, in an upper room no larger than the Prophet's chamber,* and with the silk attire of her palmy days* packed away in a box, was netting with great industry between the hours which she devoted to studying such books as she could get hold of.

Her lodgings being nearly opposite her stepfather's former residence, now Farfrae's, she could see Donald and Lucetta speeding in and out of their door with all the bounding enthusiasm of their situation. She avoided looking that way as much as possible, but it was hardly in human nature to keep the eyes averted when the door slammed.

While living on thus quietly she heard the news that Henchard had caught cold and was confined to his room – possibly a result of standing about the meads in damp weather. She went off to his house at once. This time she was determined not to be denied admittance, and made her way upstairs. He was sitting up in the bed with a greatcoat round him, and at first resented her intrusion. 'Go away – go away,' he said. 'I don't like to see 'ee!'

'But, father –'

'I don't like to see 'ee,' he repeated.

However, the ice was broken, and she remained. She made the room more comfortable, gave directions to the people below, and by the time she went away had reconciled her stepfather to her visiting him.

The effect, either of her ministrations or of her mere presence, was a rapid recovery. He soon was well enough to go out; and now things seemed to wear a new colour in his eyes. He no longer thought of emigration, and thought more of Elizabeth. The having nothing to do made him more dreary than any other circumstance; and one day, with better views of Farfrae than he had held for some time, and a sense that honest work was not a thing to be ashamed of, he stoically went down to Farfrae's yard and asked to be taken on as a journeyman* hay-trusser. He was engaged at once. This hiring of Henchard was done through a foreman, Farfrae feeling that it was undesirable to come personally in contact with the ex-corn-factor more than was absolutely necessary. While anxious to help him he was well aware by this time of his uncertain temper, and thought reserved relations best. For the same reason his orders to Henchard to proceed to this and that country farm trussing in the usual way were always given through a third person.

For a time these arrangements worked well, it being the custom to truss in the respective stack-yards, before bringing it away, the hay bought at the different farms about the neighbourhood; so that Henchard was often absent at such places the whole week long. When this was all done, and Henchard had become in a measure broken in, he came to work daily on the home premises like the rest. And thus the once flourishing merchant and Mayor and what not stood as a day-labourer in the barns and granaries he formerly had owned.

'I have worked as a journeyman before now, ha'n't I?' he would say in his defiant way; 'and why shouldn't I do it again?' But he looked a far different journeyman from the one he had been in his earlier days. Then he had worn clean, suitable clothes, light and cheerful in hue; leggings yellow as marigolds, corduroys immaculate as new flax, and a neckerchief like a flower-garden. Now he wore the remains of an old blue cloth suit of his gentlemanly times, a rusty silk hat, and a once black satin stock,* soiled and shabby. Clad thus he went to and fro, still comparatively an active man – for he was not much over forty – and saw with the other men in the yard Donald Farfrae going in and out of the green door that led to the garden, and the big house, and Lucetta.

At the beginning of the winter it was rumoured about Casterbridge that Mr Farfrae, already in the Town Council, was to be proposed for Mayor in a year or two.

'Yes; she was wise, she was wise in her generation!'* said Henchard to himself when he heard of this one day on his way to Farfrae's hay-barn. He thought it over as he wimbled his bonds, and the piece of news acted as a reviviscent* breath to that old view of his – of Donald Farfrae as his triumphant rival who rode rough-shod over him.

'A fellow of his age going to be Mayor, indeed!' he murmured with a corner-drawn smile on his mouth. 'But 'tis her money that floats en upward. Ha-ha – how cust odd it is! Here be I, his former master, working for him as man, and he the man standing as master, with my house and my furniture and my what-you-may-call wife all his own.'

He repeated these things a hundred times a day. During the whole period of his acquaintance with Lucetta he had never wished to claim her as his own so desperately as he now regretted her loss. It was no mercenary hankering after her fortune that moved him; though that fortune had been the means of making her so much the more desired by giving her the air of independence and sauciness which attracts men of his composition. It had given her servants, house, and fine clothing – a setting that invested Lucetta with a startling novelty in the eyes of him who had known her in her narrow days.

He accordingly lapsed into moodiness, and at every allusion to the possibility of Farfrae's near election to the municipal chair his former hatred of the Scotchman returned. Concurrently with this he underwent a moral change. It resulted in his significantly saying every now and then, in tones of recklessness, 'Only a fortnight more!' – 'Only a dozen days!' and so forth, lessening his figures day by day.

'Why d'ye say only a dozen days?' asked Solomon Longways as he worked beside Henchard in the granary weighing oats.

'Because in twelve days I shall be released from my oath.'

'What oath?'

'The oath to drink no spirituous liquid. In twelve days it will be twenty-one years since I swore it, and then I mean to enjoy myself, please God!'

Elizabeth-Jane sat at her window one Sunday, and while there she heard in the street below a conversation which introduced Henchard's name. She was wondering what was the matter, when a third person who was passing by asked the question in her mind.

'Michael Henchard have busted out drinking after taking nothing for twenty-one years!'

Elizabeth-Jane jumped in, put on her things, and went out.

Chapter 33

At this date there prevailed in Casterbridge a convivial custom – scarcely recognized as such, yet none the less established. On the afternoon of every Sunday a large contingent of the Casterbridge journeymen – steady church-goers and sedate characters – having attended service, filed from the church doors across the way to the Three Mariners inn. The rear was usually brought up by the choir,* with their bass-viols, fiddles, and flutes under their arms.

The great point, the point of honour, on these sacred occasions was for each man to strictly limit himself to half-a-pint of liquor. This scrupulosity was so well understood by the landlord that the whole company was served in cups of that measure. They were all exactly alike – straight-sided, with two leafless lime-trees done in eel-brown on the sides – one towards the drinker's lips, the other confronting his comrade. To wonder how many of these cups the landlord possessed altogether was a favourite exercise of children in the marvellous. Forty at least might have been seen at these times in the large room, forming a ring round the margin of the great sixteen-legged oak table, like the monolithic circle at Stonehenge in its pristine days. Outside and above the forty cups came a circle of forty smoke-jets from forty clay pipes; outside the pipes the countenances of the forty church-goers, supported at the back by a circle of forty chairs.

The conversation was not the conversation of weekdays, but a thing altogether finer in point and higher in tone. They invariably discussed the sermon, dissecting it, weighing it, as above or below the average – the general tendency being to regard it as a scientific feat or performance which had no relation to their own lives, except as between critics and the thing criticized. The bass-viol player* and the clerk usually spoke with more authority than the rest on account of their official connection with the preacher.

Now the Three Mariners was the inn chosen by Henchard as the place for closing his long term of dramless years. He had so timed his entry as to be well established in the large room by the time the forty church-goers entered to their customary cups. The flush upon his face proclaimed at once that the vow of twenty-one years had lapsed, and the era of recklessness begun anew. He was seated on a small table, drawn up to the side of the massive oak board reserved for the churchmen, a few of whom nodded to him as they took their places and said, 'How be ye, Mr Henchard? Quite a stranger here.'

Henchard did not take the trouble to reply for a few moments, and his eyes rested on his stretched-out legs and boots. 'Yes,' he said at length; 'that's true. I've been down in spirit for weeks; some of ye know the cause. I am better now; but not quite serene. I want you fellows of the choir to strike up a tune; and what with that and this brew of Stannidge's, I am in hopes of getting altogether out of my minor key.'

'With all my heart,' said the first fiddle. 'We've let back our strings, that's true; but we can soon pull 'em up again. Sound A, neighbours, and give the man a stave.'

'I don't care a curse what the words be,' said Henchard. 'Hymns, ballets,* or rantipole* rubbish; the Rogue's March* or the cherubim's warble* – 'tis all the same to me if 'tis good harmony, and well put out.'

'Well – heh, heh – it may be we can do that, and not a man among us that have sat in the gallery less than twenty year,' said the leader of the band. 'As 'tis Sunday, neighbours, suppose we raise the Fourth Psa'am, to Samuel Wakely's tune, as improved by me?'

'Hang Samuel Wakely's tune, as improved by thee!' said Henchard. 'Chuck across one of your psalters – old Wiltshire* is the only tune worth singing – the psalm-tune that would make my blood ebb and flow like the sea when I was a steady chap. I'll find some words to fit en.' He took one of the psalters and began turning over the leaves.

Chancing to look out of the window at that moment he saw a flock of people passing by, and perceived them to be the congregation of the upper church, now just dismissed, their sermon having been a longer one than that the lower parish was favoured with. Among the rest of the leading inhabitants walked Mr Councillor Farfrae with Lucetta upon his arm, the observed and imitated of all the smaller tradesmen's womankind. Henchard's mouth changed a little, and he continued to turn over the leaves.

'Now then,' he said. 'Psalm the Hundred-and-Ninth, to the tune of Wiltshire: verses ten to fifteen. I gi'e ye the words:

> His seed shall orphans be, his wife
>   A widow plunged in grief;
> His vagrant children beg their bread
>   Where none can give relief.
>
> His ill-got riches shall be made
>   To usurers a prey;
> The fruit of all his toil shall be
>   By strangers borne away.
>
> None shall be found that to his wants
>   Their mercy will extend,
> Or to his helpless orphan seed
>   The least assistance lend.
>
> A swift destruction soon shall seize
>   On his unhappy race;
> And the next age his hated name
>   Shall utterly deface.

'I know the Psa'am – I know the psa'am!' said the leader hastily; 'but I would as lief not sing it. 'Twasn't made for singing. We chose it once when the gipsy stole the pa'son's mare, thinking to please him, but pa'son was quite upset. Whatever Servant David* were thinking about when he made a Psalm that nobody can sing without disgracing himself, I can't fathom! Now then, the Fourth Psalm, to Samuel Wakely's tune, as improved by me.'

' 'Od seize your sauce – I tell ye to sing the Hundred-and-Ninth to Wiltshire, and sing it you shall!' roared Henchard. 'Not a single one of all the droning crew of ye goes out of this room till that Psalm is sung!' He slipped off the table, seized the poker, and going to the door placed his back against it. 'Now then, go ahead, if you don't wish to have your cust pates broke!'

'Don't 'ee, don't 'ee take on so! — As 'tis the Sabbath-day, and 'tis Servant David's words and not ours, perhaps we don't mind for once, hey?' said one of the terrified choir, looking round upon the rest. So the instruments were tuned and the comminatory verses sung.

'Thank ye, thank ye,' said Henchard in a softened voice, his eyes growing downcast, and his manner that of a man much moved by the strains. 'Don't you blame David,' he went on in low tones, shaking his head without raising his eyes. 'He knew what he was about when he wrote that! ... If I could afford it, be hanged if I wouldn't keep a church choir at my own expense to play and sing to me at these low, dark times of my life. But the bitter thing is, that when I was rich I didn't need what I could have, and now I be poor I can't have what I need!'

While they paused, Lucetta and Farfrae passed again, this time homeward, it being their custom to take, like others, a short walk out on the highway and back, between church and tea-time. 'There's the man we've been singing about,' said Henchard.

The players and singers turned their heads and saw his meaning. 'Heaven forbid!' said the bass-player.

' 'Tis the man,' repeated Henchard doggedly.

'Then if I'd known,' said the performer on the clarionet solemnly, 'that 'twas meant for a living man, nothing should have drawn out of my wynd-pipe the breath for that Psalm, so help me!'

'Nor from mine,' said the first singer. 'But, thought I, as it was made so long ago perhaps there isn't much in it, so I'll oblige a neighbour; for there's nothing to be said against the tune.'

'Ah, my boys, you've sung it,' said Henchard triumphantly. 'As for him, it was partly by his songs that he got over me, and heaved me out ... I could double him up like that — and yet I don't. 'He laid the poker across his knee, bent it as if it were a twig, flung it down, and came away from the door.

It was at this time that Elizabeth-Jane, having heard where her stepfather was, entered the room with a pale and agonized countenance. The choir and the rest of the company moved off, in accordance with their half-pint regulation. Elizabeth-Jane went up to Henchard, and entreated him to accompany her home.

By this hour the volcanic fires of his nature had burnt down, and having drunk no great quantity as yet he was inclined to acquiesce. She took his arm, and together they went on. Henchard walked blankly, like a blind man, repeating to himself the last words of the singers –

> And the next age his hated name
> Shall utterly deface.

At length he said to her, 'I am a man to my word. I have kept my oath for twenty-one years; and now I can drink with a good conscience . . . If I don't do for him – well, I am a fearful practical joker when I choose! He has taken away everything from me, and by heavens, if I meet him I won't answer for my deeds!'

These half-uttered words alarmed Elizabeth – all the more by reason of the still determination of Henchard's mien.

'What will you do?' she asked cautiously, while trembling with disquietude, and guessing Henchard's allusion only too well.

Henchard did not answer, and they went on till they had reached his cottage. 'May I come in?' she said.

'No, no; not to-day,' said Henchard; and she went away; feeling that to caution Farfrae was almost her duty, as it was certainly her strong desire.

As on the Sunday, so on the week-days, Farfrae and Lucetta might have been seen flitting about the town like two butterflies – or rather like a bee and a butterfly in league for life. She seemed to take no pleasure in going anywhere except in her husband's company; and hence when business would not permit him to waste an afternoon she remained indoors waiting for the time to pass till his return, her face being visible to Elizabeth-Jane from her window aloft. The latter, however, did not say to herself that Farfrae should be thankful for such devotion, but, full of her reading, she cited Rosalind's exclamation:* 'Mistress, know yourself; down on your knees and thank Heaven fasting for a good man's love.'

She kept her eye upon Henchard also. One day he answered her inquiry for his health by saying that he could not endure Abel Whittle's pitying eyes upon him while they worked together in the yard. 'He is such a fool,' said Henchard, 'that he can never get out of his mind the time when I was master there.'

'I'll come and wimble for you instead of him, if you will allow me,' said she. Her motive on going to the yard was to get an opportunity of observing the general position of affairs on Farfrae's premises now that her stepfather was a workman there. Henchard's threats had alarmed her so much that she wished to see his behaviour when the two were face to face.

For two or three days after her arrival Donald did not make any appearance. Then one afternoon the green door opened, and through came, first Farfrae, and at his heels Lucetta. Donald brought his wife forward without hesitation, it being obvious that he had no suspicion whatever of any antecedents in common between her and the now journeyman hay-trusser.

Henchard did not turn his eyes toward either of the pair, keeping them fixed on the bond he twisted, as if that alone absorbed him. A feeling of delicacy, which ever prompted Farfrae to avoid anything that might seem like triumphing over a fallen rival, led him to keep away from the hay-barn where Henchard and his daughter were working, and to go on to the corn department. Meanwhile Lucetta, never having been informed that Henchard had entered her husband's service, rambled straight on to the barn, where she came suddenly upon Henchard, and gave vent to a little 'Oh!' which the happy and busy Donald was too far off to hear. Henchard, with withering humility of demeanour, touched the brim of his hat to her as Whittle and the rest had done, to which she breathed a dead-alive 'Good afternoon'.

'I beg your pardon, ma'am?' said Henchard, as if he had not heard.

'I said good afternoon,' she faltered.

'O yes, good afternoon, ma'am,' he replied, touching his hat again. 'I am glad to see you, ma'am.' Lucetta looked embarrassed, and Henchard continued: 'For we humble workmen here feel it a great honour that a lady should look in and take an interest in us.'

She glanced at him entreatingly; the sarcasm was too bitter, too unendurable.

'Can you tell me the time, ma'am?' he asked.

'Yes,' she said hastily; 'half-past four.'

'Thank 'ee. An hour and a half longer before we are released from work. Ah, ma'am, we of the lower classes know nothing of the gay leisure that such as you enjoy!'

As soon as she could do so Lucetta left him, nodded and smiled to Elizabeth-Jane, and joined her husband at the other end of the enclosure, where she could be seen leading him away by the outer gates, so as to avoid passing Henchard again. That she had been taken by surprise was obvious. The result of this casual ren-counter was that the next morning a note was put into Henchard's hand by the postman.

'Will you,' said Lucetta, with as much bitterness as she could put into a small communication, 'will you kindly undertake not to speak to me in the biting undertones you used to-day, if I walk through the yard at any time? I bear you no ill-will, and I am only too glad that you should have employment of my dear husband; but in common fairness treat me as his wife, and do not try to make me wretched by covert sneers. I have committed no crime, and done you no injury.'

'Poor fool!' said Henchard with fond savagery, holding out the note. 'To know no better than commit herself in writing like this! Why, if I were to show that to her dear husband – pooh!' He threw the letter into the fire.

Lucetta took care not to come again among the hay and corn. She would rather have died than run the risk of encountering Henchard at such close quarters a second time. The gulf between them was growing wider every day. Farfrae was always considerate to his fallen acquaintance; but it was impossible that he should not, by degrees, cease to regard the ex-corn-merchant as more than one of his other workmen. Henchard saw this, and concealed his feelings under a cover of stolidity, fortifying his heart by drinking more freely at the Three Mariners every evening.

Often did Elizabeth-Jane, in her endeavours to prevent his taking other liquor, carry tea to him in a little basket at five o'clock. Arriving one day on this errand she found her stepfather was measuring up clover-seed and rape-seed in the corn-stores on the top floor, and she ascended to him. Each floor had a door opening into the air under a cat-head, from which a chain dangled for hoisting the sacks.

When Elizabeth's head rose through the trap she perceived that the upper door was open, and that her stepfather and Farfrae stood just within it in conversation, Farfrae being nearest the dizzy edge, and Henchard a little way behind. Not to interrupt them she remained on the steps without raising her head any higher. While waiting thus she saw – or fancied she saw, for she had a terror of feeling certain – her stepfather slowly raise his hand to a level behind Farfrae's shoulders, a curious expression taking possession of his face. The young man was quite unconscious of the action, which was so indirect that, if Farfrae had observed it, he might almost have regarded it as an idle outstretching of the arm. But it would have been possible, by a comparatively light touch, to push Farfrae off his balance, and send him head over heels into the air.

Elizabeth felt quite sick at heart on thinking of what this *might* have meant. As soon as they turned she mechanically took the tea to Henchard, left it, and went away. Reflecting, she endeavoured to assure herself that the movement was an idle eccentricity, and no more. Yet, on the other hand, his subordinate position in an establishment where he once had been master might be acting on him like an irritant poison; and she finally resolved to caution Donald.

Chapter 34

Next morning, accordingly, she rose at five o'clock and went into the street. It was not yet light; a dense fog prevailed, and the town was as silent as it was dark, except that from the rectangular avenues which framed in the borough there came a chorus of tiny rappings, caused by the fall of water-drops condensed on the boughs; now it was wafted from the West Walk, now from the South Walk; and then from both quarters simultaneously. She moved on to the bottom of Corn Street, and, knowing his time well, waited only a few minutes before she heard the familiar bang of his door, and then his quick walk towards her. She met him at the point where the last tree of the engirding avenue flanked the last house in the street.

He could hardly discern her till, glancing inquiringly, he said, 'What – Miss Henchard – and are ye up so airly?'

She asked him to pardon her for waylaying him at such an unseemly time. 'But I am anxious to mention something,' she said. 'And I wished not to alarm Mrs Farfrae by calling.'

'Yes?' said he, with the cheeriness of a superior. 'And what may it be? It's very kind of ye, I'm sure.'

She now felt the difficulty of conveying to his mind the exact aspect of possibilities in her own. But she somehow began, and introduced Henchard's name. 'I sometimes fear,' she said with an effort, 'that he may be betrayed into some attempt to – insult you, sir.'

'But we are the best of friends?'

'Or to play some practical joke upon you, sir. Remember that he has been hardly used.'

'But we are quite friendly?'

'Or to do something – that would injure you – hurt you – wound you.' Every word cost her twice its length of pain. And she could see that Farfrae was still incredulous. Henchard, a poor man in his employ, was not to Farfrae's view the Henchard who had ruled him. Yet he was not only the same man, but that man with his sinister qualities, formerly latent, quickened into life by his buffetings.

Farfrae, happy, and thinking no evil, persisted in making light of her fears. Thus they parted, and she went homeward, journeymen now being in the street, waggoners going to the harness-makers for articles left to be repaired, farm-horses going to the shoeing-smiths, and the sons of labour showing themselves generally on the move. Elizabeth entered her lodging unhappily, thinking she had done no good, and only made herself appear foolish by her weak note of warning.

But Donald Farfrae was one of those men upon whom an incident is never absolutely lost. He revised impressions from a subsequent point of view, and the impulsive judgment of the moment was not always his permanent one. The vision of Elizabeth's earnest face in the rimy* dawn came back to him several times during the day. Knowing the solidity of her character he did not treat her hints altogether as idle sounds.

But he did not desist from a kindly scheme on Henchard's account that engaged him just then; and when he met Lawyer Joyce, the town-clerk, later in the day, he spoke of it as if nothing had occurred to damp it.

'About that little seedsman's shop,' he said; 'the shop overlooking the churchyard, which is to let. It is not for myself I want it, but for our unlucky fellow-townsman Henchard. It would be a new beginning for him, if a small one; and I have told the Council that I would head a private subscription among them to set him up in it – that I would be fifty pounds, if they would make up the other fifty among them.'

'Yes, yes; so I've heard; and there's nothing to say against it for that matter,' the town-clerk replied, in his plain, frank way. 'But, Farfrae, others see what you don't. Henchard hates 'ee – ay, hates 'ee; and 'tis right that you should know it. To my knowledge he was at the Three Mariners last night, saying in public that about you which a man ought not to say about another.'

'Is that so – ah, is that so?' said Farfrae, looking down. 'Why should he do it?' added the young man bitterly; 'what harm have I done him that he should try to wrong me?'

'God only knows,' said Joyce, lifting his eyebrows. 'It shows much long-suffering in you to put up with him, and keep him in your employ.'

'But I cannet discharge a man who was once a good friend to me? How can I forget that when I came here 'twas he enabled me to make a footing for mysel'? No, no. As long as I've a day's wark to offer he shall do it if he chooses. 'Tis not I who will deny him such a little as that. But I'll drop the idea of establishing him in a shop till I can think more about it.'

It grieved Farfrae much to give up this scheme. But a damp having been thrown over it by these and other voices in the air, he went and countermanded his orders. The then occupier of the shop was in it when Farfrae spoke to him, and feeling it necessary to give some explanation of his withdrawal from the negotiation Donald mentioned Henchard's name, and stated that the intentions of the Council had been changed.

The occupier was much disappointed, and straightway informed Henchard, as soon as he saw him, that a scheme of the Council for setting him up in a shop had been knocked on the head by Farfrae. And thus out of error enmity grew.

When Farfrae got indoors that evening the tea-kettle was singing on the high hob of the semi-egg-shaped grate. Lucetta, light as a sylph, ran forward and seized his hands, whereupon Farfrae duly kissed her.

'Oh!' she cried playfully, turning to the window. 'See – the blinds are not drawn down, and the people can look in – what a scandal!'

When the candles were lighted, the curtains drawn, and the twain sat at tea, she noticed that he looked serious. Without directly inquiring why she let her eyes linger solicitously on his face.

'Who has called?' he absently asked. 'Any folk for me?'

'No,' said Lucetta. 'What's the matter, Donald?'

'Well – nothing worth talking of,' he responded sadly.

'Then, never mind it. You will get through it. Scotchmen are always lucky.'

'No – not always!' he said, shaking his head gloomily as he contemplated a crumb on the table. 'I know many who have not been so! There was Sandy Macfarlane, who started to America to try his fortune, and he was drowned; and Archibald Leith, he was murdered! And poor Willie Dunbleeze and Maitland Macfreeze – they fell into bad courses, and went the way of all such!'

'Why – you old goosey – I was only speaking in a general sense, of course! You are always so literal. Now when we have finished tea, sing me that funny song about high-heeled shoon and siller tags, and the one-and-forty wooers.'

'No, no. I couldna sing to-night! It's Henchard – he hates me; so that I may not be his friend if I would. I would understand why there should be a wee bit envy; but I cannet see a reason for the whole intensity of what he feels. Now, can you, Lucetta? It is more like old-fashioned rivalry in love than just a bit of rivalry in trade.'

Lucetta had grown somewhat wan. 'No,' she replied.

'I give him employment – I cannet refuse it. But neither can I blind myself to the fact that with a man of passions such as his, there is no safeguard for conduct!'

'What have you heard – O Donald, dearest?' said Lucetta in alarm. The words on her lips were 'anything about me?' – but she did not utter them. She could not, however, suppress her agitation, and her eyes filled with tears.

'No, no – it is not so serious as ye fancy,' declared Farfrae soothingly; though he did not know its seriousness so well as she.

'I wish you would do what we have talked of,' mournfully remarked Lucetta. 'Give up business, and go away from here. We have plenty of money, and why should we stay?'

Farfrae seemed seriously disposed to discuss this move, and they talked thereon till a visitor was announced. Their neighbour Alderman Vatt came in.

'You've heard, I suppose, of poor Doctor Chalkfield's death? Yes – died this afternoon at five,' said Mr Vatt. Chalkfield was the Councilman who had succeeded to the Mayoralty in the preceding November.

Farfrae was sorry at the intelligence, and Mr Vatt continued: 'Well, we know he's been going some days, and as his family is well provided for we must take it all as it is. Now I have called to ask 'ee this – quite privately. If I should nominate 'ee to succeed him, and there should be no particular opposition, will 'ee accept the chair?'

'But there are folk whose turn is before mine; and I'm over young, and may be thought pushing!' said Farfrae after a pause.

'Not at all. I don't speak for myself only, several have named it. You won't refuse?'

'We thought of going away,' interposed Lucetta, looking at Farfrae anxiously.

'It was only a fancy,' Farfrae murmured. 'I wouldna refuse if it is the wish of a respectable majority in the Council.'

'Very well, then, look upon yourself as elected. We have had older men long enough.'

When he was gone Farfrae said musingly, 'See now how it's ourselves that are ruled by the Powers above us! We plan this, but we do that. If they want to make me Mayor I will stay, and Henchard must rave as he will.'

From this evening onward Lucetta was very uneasy. If she had not been imprudence incarnate she would not have acted as she did when she met Henchard by accident a day or two later. It was in the bustle of the market, when no one could readily notice their discourse.

'Michael,' said she, 'I must again ask you what I asked you months ago – to return me any letters or papers of mine that you may have – unless you have destroyed them? You must see how desirable it is that the times at Jersey should be blotted out, for the good of all parties.'

'Why, bless the woman! – I packed up every scrap of your handwriting to give you in the coach – but you never appeared.'

She explained how the death of her aunt had prevented her taking the journey on that day. 'And what became of the parcel then?' she asked.

He could not say – he would consider. When she was gone he recollected that he had left a heap of useless papers in his former dining-room safe – built up in the wall of his old house – now occupied by Farfrae. The letters might have been amongst them.

A grotesque grin shaped itself on Henchard's face. Had that safe been opened?

On the very evening which followed this there was a great ringing of bells in Casterbridge, and the combined brass, wood, catgut, and leather bands played round the town with more prodigality of percussion-notes than ever. Farfrae was Mayor – the two-hundredth odd of a series forming an elective dynasty dating back to the days of Charles I – and the fair Lucetta was the courted of the town . . . But, ah! that worm i' the bud* – Henchard; what he could tell!

He, in the meantime, festering with indignation at some erroneous intelligence of Farfrae's opposition to the scheme for installing him in the little seed-shop, was greeted with the news of the municipal election (which, by reason of Farfrae's comparative youth and his Scottish nativity – a thing unprecedented in the case – had an interest far beyond the ordinary). The bell-ringing and the band-playing, loud as Tamerlane's trumpet,* goaded the downfallen Henchard indescribably: the ousting now seemed to him to be complete.

The next morning he went to the corn-yard as usual, and about eleven o'clock Donald entered through the green door, with no trace of the worshipful about him. The yet more emphatic change of places between him and Henchard which this election had established renewed a slight embarrassment in the manner of the modest younger man; but Henchard showed the front of one who had overlooked all this; and Farfrae met his amenities half-way at once.

'I was going to ask you,' said Henchard, 'about a packet that I may possibly have left in my old safe in the dining-room.' He added particulars.

'If so, it is there now,' said Farfrae. 'I have never opened the safe at all as yet; for I keep ma papers at the bank, to sleep easy o' nights.'

'It was not of much consequence – to me,' said Henchard. 'But I'll call for it this evening, if you don't mind?'

It was quite late when he fulfilled his promise. He had primed himself with grog, as he did very frequently now, and a curl of sardonic humour hung on his lip as he approached the house, as though he were contemplating some terrible form of amusement.

Whatever it was, the incident of his entry did not diminish its force, this being his first visit to the house since he had lived there as owner. The ring of the bell spoke to him like the voice of a familiar drudge who had been bribed to forsake him; the movements of the doors were revivals of dead days.

Farfrae invited him into the dining-room, where he at once unlocked the iron safe built into the wall, *his*, Henchard's safe, made by an ingenious locksmith under his direction. Farfrae drew thence the parcel, and other papers, with apologies for not having returned them.

'Never mind,' said Henchard drily. 'The fact is they are letters mostly. . . Yes,' he went on, sitting down and unfolding Lucetta's passionate bundle, 'here they be. That ever I should see 'em again! I hope Mrs Farfrae is well after her exertions of yesterday?'

'She has felt a bit weary; and has gone to bed airly on that account.'

Henchard returned to the letters, sorting them over with interest, Farfrae being seated at the other end of the dining-table. 'You don't forget, of course,' he resumed, 'that curious chapter in the history of my past which I told you of, and that you gave me some assistance in? These letters are, in fact, related to that unhappy business. Though, thank God, it is all over now.'

'What became of the poor woman?' asked Farfrae.

'Luckily she married, and married well,' said Henchard. 'So that these reproaches she poured out on me do not now cause me any twinges, as they might otherwise have done . . . Just listen to what an angry woman will say!'

Farfrae, willing to humour Henchard, though quite unin- terested, and bursting with yawns, gave well mannered attention.

' "For me," ' Henchard read, ' "there is practically no future. A creature too unconventionally devoted to you – who feels it impossible that she can be wife of any other man; and who is yet no more to you than the first woman you meet in the street – such am I. I quite acquit you of any intention to wrong me, yet you are the door through which wrong has come to me. That in the event of your present wife's death you will place me in her position is a consolation so far as it goes – but how far does it go? Thus I sit here, forsaken by my few acquaintance, and forsaken by you!" '

'That's how she went on to me,' said Henchard, 'acres of words like that, when what had happened was what I could not cure.'

'Yes,' said Farfrae absently, 'it is the way wi' women.' But the fact was that he knew very little of the sex; yet detecting a sort of resemblance in style between the effusions of the woman he worshipped and those of the supposed stranger, he concluded that Aphrodite* ever spoke thus, whosesoever the personality she assumed.

Henchard unfolded another letter, and read it through likewise, stopping at the subscription as before. 'Her name I don't give,' he said blandly. 'As I didn't marry her, and another man did, I can scarcely do that in fairness to her.'

'Tr-rue, tr-rue,' said Farfrae. 'But why didn't you marry her when your wife Susan died?' Farfrae asked this and the other questions in the comfortably indifferent tone of one whom the matter very remotely concerned.

'Ah – well you may ask that!' said Henchard, the new-moon-shaped grin adumbrating itself again upon his mouth. 'In spite of all her protestations, when I came forward to do so, as in generosity bound, she was not the woman for me.'

'She had already married another – maybe?'

Henchard seemed to think it would be sailing too near the wind to descend further into particulars, and he answered 'Yes.'

'The young lady must have had a heart that bore transplanting very readily!'

'She had, she had,' said Henchard emphatically.

He opened a third and fourth letter, and read. This time he approached the conclusion as if the signature were indeed coming with the rest. But again he stopped short. The truth was that, as may be divined, he had quite intended to effect a grand catastrophe at the end of this drama by reading out the name; he had come to the house with no other thought. But sitting there in cold blood he could not do it. Such a wrecking of hearts appalled even him. His quality was such that he could have annihilated them both in the heat of action; but to accomplish the deed by oral poison was beyond the nerve of his enmity.

Chapter 35

As Donald stated, Lucetta had returned early to her room because of fatigue. She had, however, not gone to rest, but sat in the bedside chair reading and thinking over the events of the day. At the ringing of the door-bell by Henchard she wondered who it should be that would call at that comparatively late hour. The dining-room was almost under her bedroom; she could hear that somebody was admitted there, and presently the indistinct murmur of a person reading became audible.

The usual time for Donald's arrival upstairs came and passed, yet still the reading and conversation went on. This was very singular. She could think of nothing but that some extraordinary crime had been committed, and that the visitor, whoever he might be, was reading an account of it from a special edition of the *Casterbridge Chronicle*. At last she left the room, and descended the stairs. The dining-room door was ajar, and in the silence of the resting household the voice and the words were recognizable before she reached the lower flight. She stood transfixed. Her own words greeted her in Henchard's voice, like spirits from the grave.

Lucetta leant upon the banister with her cheek against the smooth hand-rail, as if she would make a friend of it in her misery. Rigid in this position, more and more words fell successively upon her ear. But what amazed her most was the tone of her husband. He spoke merely in the accents of a man who made a present of his time.

'One word,' he was saying, as the crackling of paper denoted that Henchard was unfolding yet another sheet. 'Is it quite fair to this young woman's memory to read at such length to a stranger what was intended for your eye alone?'

'Well, yes,' said Henchard, 'By not giving her name I make it an example of all womankind, and not a scandal to one.'

'If I were you I would destroy them,' said Farfrae, giving more thought to the letters than he had hitherto done. 'As another man's wife it would injure the woman if it were known.'

'No, I shall not destroy them,' murmured Henchard, putting the letters away. Then he arose, and Lucetta heard no more.

She went back to her bedroom in a semi-paralysed state. For very fear she could not undress, but sat on the edge of the bed, waiting. Would Henchard let out the secret in his parting words? Her suspense was terrible. Had she confessed all to Donald in their early acquaintance he might possibly have got over it, and married her just the same – unlikely as it had once seemed; but for her or any one else to tell him now would be fatal.

The door slammed; she could her her husband bolting it. After looking round in his customary way he came leisurely up the stairs. The spark in her eyes well-nigh went out when he appeared round the bedroom door. Her gaze hung doubtful for a moment, then to her joyous amazement she saw that he looked at her with the rallying smile of one who had just been relieved of a scene that was irksome. She could hold out no longer, and sobbed hysterically.

When he had restored her Farfrae naturally enough spoke of Henchard. 'Of all men he was the least desirable as a visitor,' he said, 'but it is my belief that he's just a bit crazed. He has been reading to me a long lot of letters relating to his past life, and I could do no less than indulge him by listening.'

This was sufficient. Henchard, then, had not hold. Henchard's last words to Farfrae, in short, as he stood on the door-step, had been these: 'Well – I'm much obliged to 'ee for listening. I may tell more about her some day.'

Finding this, she was much perplexed as to Henchard's motives in opening the matter at all; for in such cases we attribute to an enemy a power of consistent action which we never find in ourselves or in our friends; and forget that abortive efforts from want of heart are as possible to revenge as to generosity.

Next morning Lucetta remained in bed, meditating how to parry this incipient attack. The bold stroke of telling Donald the truth, dimly conceived, was yet too bold; for she dreaded lest in doing so he, like the rest of the world, should believe that the episode was rather her fault than her misfortune. She decided to employ persuasion – not with Donald, but with the enemy himself. It seemed the only practicable weapon left her as a woman. Having laid her plan she rose, and wrote to him who kept her on these tenterhooks:

'I overheard your interview with my husband last night, and saw the drift of your revenge. The very thought of it crushes me! Have pity on a distressed woman! If you could see me you would relent. You do not know how anxiety has told upon me lately. I will be at the Ring at the time you leave work – just before the sun goes down. Please come that way. I cannot rest till I have seen you face to face, and heard from your mouth that you will carry this horse-play no further.'

To herself she said, on closing up this appeal: 'If ever tears and pleadings have served the weak to fight the strong, let them do so now!'

With this view she made a toilette which differed from all she had ever attempted before. To heighten her natural attractions had hitherto been the unvarying endeavour of her adult life, and one in which she was no novice. But now she neglected this, and even proceeded to impair the natural presentation. Beyond a natural reason for her slightly drawn look, she had not slept all the previous night, and this had produced upon her pretty though slightly worn features the aspect of a countenance ageing prematurely from extreme sorrow. She selected – as much from want of spirit as design – her poorest, plainest, and longest discarded attire.

To avoid the contingency of being recognized she veiled herself, and slipped out of the house quickly. The sun was resting on the hill like a drop of blood on an eyelid by the time she had got up the road opposite the amphitheatre, which she speedily entered. The interior was shadowy, and emphatic of the absence of every living thing.

She was not disappointed in the fearful hope with which she awaited him. Henchard came over the top, descended, and Lucetta waited breathlessly. But having reached the arena she saw a change in his bearing; he stood still at a little distance from her; she could not think why.

Nor could any one else have known. The truth was that in appointing this spot, and this hour, for the rendezvous, Lucetta had unwittingly backed up her entreaty by the strongest argument she could have used outside words, with this man of moods, glooms, and superstitions. Her figure in the midst of the huge enclosure, the unusual plainness of her dress, her attitude of hope and appeal, so strongly revived in his soul the memory of another ill-used woman who had stood there and thus in bygone days, and had now passed away into her rest, that he was unmanned, and his heart smote him for having attempted reprisals on one of a sex so weak. When he approached her, and before she had spoken a word, her point was half gained.

His manner as he had come down had been one of cynical carelessness; but he now put away his grim half-smile, and said in a kindly subdued tone, 'Good-night t'ye. Of course I'm glad to come if you want me.'

'O, thank you,' she said apprehensively.

'I am sorry to see 'ee looking so ill,' he stammered with unconcealed compunction.

She shook her head. 'How can you be sorry,' she asked, 'when you deliberately cause it?'

'What!' said Henchard uneasily. 'Is it anything I have done that has pulled you down like that?'

'It is all your doing,' said she. 'I have no other grief. My happiness would be secure enough but for your threats. O Michael! don't wreck me like this! You might think that you have done enough! When I came here I was a young woman; now I am rapidly becoming an old one. Neither my husband nor any other man will regard me with interest long.'

Henchard was disarmed. His old feeling of supercilious pity for womankind in general was intensified by this suppliant appearing here as the double of the first. Moreover, that thoughtless want of foresight which had led to all her trouble remained with poor

Lucetta still; she had come to meet him here in this compromising way without perceiving the risk. Such a woman was very small deer to hunt; he felt ashamed, lost all zest and desire to humiliate Lucetta there and then, and no longer envied Farfrae his bargain. He had married money, but nothing more. Henchard was anxious to wash his hands of the game.

'Well, what do you want me to do?' he said gently. 'I am sure I shall be very willing. My reading of those letters was only a sort of practical joke, and I revealed nothing.'

'To give me back the letters and any papers you may have that breathe of matrimony or worse.'

'So be it. Every scrap shall be yours . . . But, between you and me, Lucetta, he is sure to find out something of the matter, sooner or later.'

'Ah!' she said with eager tremulousness; 'but not till I have proved myself a faithful and deserving wife to him, and then he may forgive me everything!'

Henchard silently looked at her: he almost envied Farfrae such love as that, even now. 'H'm – I hope so,' he said. 'But you shall have the letters without fail. And your secret shall be kept. I swear it.'

'How good you are! – how shall I get them?'

He reflected, and said he would send them the next morning. 'Now don't doubt me,' he added. 'I can keep my word.'

Chapter 36

Returning from her appointment Lucetta saw a man waiting by the lamp nearest to her own door. When she stopped to go in he came and spoke to her. It was Jopp.

He begged her pardon for addressing her. But he had heard that Mr Farfrae had been applied to by a neighbouring corn-merchant to recommend a working partner; if so, he wished to offer himself. He could give good security, and had stated as much to Mr Farfrae in a letter; but he would feel much obliged if Lucetta would say a word in his favour to her husband.

'It is a thing I know nothing about,' said Lucetta coldly.

'But you can testify to my trustworthiness better than anybody, ma'am,' said Jopp. 'I was in Jersey several years, and knew you there by sight.'

'Indeed,' she replied. 'But I knew nothing of you.'

'I think, ma'am, that a word or two from you would secure for me what I covet very much,' he persisted.

She steadily refused to have anything to do with the affair, and cutting him short, because of her anxiety to get indoors before her husband should miss her, left him on the pavement.

He watched her till she had vanished, and then went home. When he got there he sat down in the fireless chimney corner looking at the iron dogs,* and the wood laid across them for heating the morning kettle. A movement upstairs disturbed him, and Henchard came down from his bedroom, where he seemed to have been rummaging boxes.

'I wish,' said Henchard, 'you would do me a service, Jopp, now – to-night, I mean, if you can. Leave this at Mrs Farfrae's for her. I should take it myself, of course, but I don't wish to be seen there.'

He handed a package in brown paper, sealed. Henchard had been as good as his word. Immediately on coming indoors he had searched over his few belongings; and every scrap of Lucetta's writing that he possessed was here. Jopp indifferently expressed his willingness.

'Well, how have ye got on to-day?' his lodger asked. 'Any prospect of an opening?'

'I am afraid not,' said Jopp, who had not told the other of his application to Farfrae.

'There never will be in Casterbridge,' declared Henchard decisively. 'You must roam further afield.' He said good-night to Jopp, and returned to his own part of the house.

Jopp sat on till his eyes were attracted by the shadow of the candle-snuff on the wall, and looking at the original he found that it had formed itself into a head like a red-hot cauliflower. Henchard's packet next met his gaze. He knew there had been something of the nature of wooing between Henchard and the now Mrs Farfrae; and his vague ideas on the subject narrowed themselves down to these: Henchard had a parcel belonging to Mrs Farfrae, and he had reasons for not returning that parcel to her in person. What could be inside it? So he went on and on till, animated by resentment at Lucetta's haughtiness, as he thought it, and curiosity to learn if there were any weak sides to this transaction with Henchard, he examined the package. The pen and all its relations being awkward tools in Henchard's hands he had affixed the seals without an impression, it never occurring to him that the efficacy of such a fastening depended on this. Jopp was far less of a tyro; he lifted one of the seals with his penknife, peeped in at the end thus opened, saw that the bundle consisted of letters; and, having satisfied himself thus far, sealed up the end again by simply softening the wax with the candle, and went off with the parcel as requested.

His path was by the river-side at the foot of the town. Coming into the light at the bridge which stood at the end of High Street he beheld lounging thereon Mother Cuxsom and Nance Mockridge.

'We be just going down Mixen Lane way, to look into Peter's Finger* afore creeping to bed,' said Mrs Cuxsom. 'There's a fiddle and tambourine going on there. Lord, what's all the world – do ye come along too, Jopp – 'twon't hinder ye five minutes.'

Jopp had mostly kept himself out of this company, but present circumstance made him somewhat more reckless than usual, and without many words he decided to go to his destination that way.

Though the upper part of Durnover was mainly composed of a curious congeries* of barns and farmsteads, there was a less picturesque side to the parish. This was Mixen Lane, now in great part pulled down.

Mixen Lane was the Adullam* of all the surrounding villages. It was the hiding-place of those who were in distress, and in debt, and trouble of every kind. Farm-labourers and other peasants, who combined a little poaching with their farming, and a little brawling and bibbing* with their poaching, found themselves sooner or later in Mixen Lane. Rural mechanics too idle to mechanize, rural servants too rebellious to serve, drifted or were forced into Mixen Lane.

The lane and its surrounding thicket of thatched cottages stretched out like a spit into the moist and misty lowland. Much that was sad, much that was low, some things that were baneful, could be seen in Mixen Lane. Vice ran freely in and out certain of the doors of the neighbourhood; recklessness dwelt under the roof with the crooked chimney; shame in some bow-windows; theft (in times of privation) in the thatched and mud-walled houses by the sallows. Even slaughter had not been altogether unknown here. In a block of cottages up an alley there might have been erected an altar to disease in years gone by. Such was

Mixen Lane in the times when Henchard and Farfrae were Mayors.

Yet this mildewed leaf in the sturdy and flourishing Casterbridge plant lay close to the open country; not a hundred yards from a row of noble elms, and commanding a view across the moor of airy uplands and corn-fields, and mansions of the great. A brook divided the moor from the tenements, and to outward view there was no way across it – no way to the houses but round about by the road. But under every householder's stairs there was kept a mysterious plank nine inches wide; which plank was a secret bridge.

If you, as one of those refugee householders, came in from business after dark – and this was the business time here – you stealthily crossed the moor, approached the border of the aforesaid brook, and whistled opposite the house to which you belonged. A shape thereupon made its appearance on the other side bearing the bridge on end against the sky; it was lowered; you crossed, and a hand helped you to land yourself, together with the pheasants and hares gathered from neighbouring manors. You sold them slily the next morning, and the day after you stood before the magistrates with the eyes of all your sympathizing neighbours concentrated on your back. You disappeared for a time; then you were again found quietly living in Mixen Lane.

Walking along the lane at dusk the stranger was struck by two or three peculiar features therein. One was an intermittent rumbling from the back premises of the inn half-way up; this meant a skittle alley. Another was the extensive prevalence of whistling in the various domiciles – a piped note of some kind coming from nearly every open door. Another was the frequency of white aprons over dingy gowns among the women around the doorways. A white apron is a suspicious vesture in situations where spotlessness is difficult; moreover, the industry and cleanliness which the white apron expressed were belied by the postures and gaits of the women who wore it – their knuckles being mostly on their hips (an attitude which lent them the aspect of two-handled mugs), and their shoulders against door-posts; while there was a curious alacrity in the turn of each honest woman's head upon her neck and in the twirl of her honest eyes, at any noise resembling a masculine footfall along the lane.

Yet amid so much that was bad needy respectability also found a home. Under some of the roofs abode pure and virtuous souls whose presence there was due to the iron hand of necessity, and to that alone. Families from decayed villages – families of that once bulky, but now nearly extinct, section of village society called 'liviers', or lifeholders* – copyholders* and others, whose roof-trees* had fallen for some reason or other, compelling them to quit the rural spot that had been their home for generations – came here, unless they chose to lie under a hedge by the wayside.

The inn called Peter's Finger was the church of Mixen Lane.

It was centrally situate, as such places should be, and bore about the same social relation to the Three Mariners as the latter bore to the King's Arms. At first sight the inn was so respectable as to be puzzling. The front door was kept shut, and the step was so clean that evidently but few persons entered over its sanded surface. But at the corner of the public-house was an alley, a mere slit, dividing it from the next building. Half-way up the alley was a narrow door, shiny and paintless from the rub of infinite hands and shoulders. This was the actual entrance to the inn.

A pedestrian would be seen, abstractedly passing along Mixen Lane; and then, in a moment, he would vanish, causing the gazer to blink like Ashton at the disappearance of Ravenswood.* That abstracted pedestrian had edged into the slit by the adroit fillip* of his person sideways; from the slit he edged into the tavern by a similar exercise of skill.

The company at the Three Mariners were persons of quality in comparison with the company which gathered here; though it must be admitted that the lowest fringe of the Mariners' party touched the crest of Peter's at points. Waifs and strays of all sorts loitered about here. The landlady was a virtuous woman who years ago had been unjustly sent to gaol as an accessory to something or other after the fact. She underwent her twelve-month, and had worn a martyr's countenance ever since, except at times of meeting the constable who apprehended her, when she winked her eye.

To this house Jopp and his acquaintances had arrived. The settles on which they sat down were thin and tall, their tops being guyed by pieces of twine to hooks in the ceiling; for when the guests grew boisterous the settles would rock and overturn without some such security. The thunder of bowls echoed from the backyard; swingels* hung behind the blower of the chimney; and ex-poachers and ex-gamekeepers, whom squires had perse-cuted without a cause, sat elbowing each other – men who in past times had met in fights under the moon, till lapse of sentences on the one part, and loss of favour and expulsion from service on the other, brought them here together to a common level, where they sat calmly discussing old times.

'Dos't mind how you could jerk a trout ashore with a bramble, and not ruffle the stream, Charl?' a deposed keeper was saying. ' 'Twas at that I caught 'ee once, if you can mind?'

'That can I. But the worst larry* for me was that pheasant business at Yalbury Wood. Your wife swore false that time, Joe – O, by Gad, she did – there's no denying it.'

'How was that?' asked Jopp.

'Why – Joe closed wi' me, and we rolled down together, close to his garden hedge. Hearing the noise, out ran his wife with the oven pyle,* and it being dark under the trees she couldn't see which was uppermost. "Where beest thee, Joe, under or top?" she screeched. "O – under, by Gad!" says he. She then began to rap down upon my skull, back, and ribs with the pyle till we'd roll over again. "Where beest now, dear Joe, under or top?" she'd scream again. By George, 'twas through her I was took! And then when we got up in hall she sware that the cock pheasant was one of her rearing, when 'twas not your bird at all, Joe; 'twas Squire Brown's bird – that whose 'twas – one that we'd picked off as we passed his wood, an hour afore. It did hurt my feelings to be so wronged! . . . Ah well – 'tis over now.'

'I might have had 'ee days afore that,' said the keeper. 'I was within a few yards of 'ee dozens of times, with a sight more of birds than that poor one.'

'Yes – 'tis not our greatest doings that the world gets wind of,' said the furmity-woman, who, lately settled in this purlieu, sat among the rest. Having travelled a great deal in her time she spoke with cosmopolitan largeness of idea. It was she who presently asked Jopp what was the parcel he kept so snugly under his arm.

'Ah, therein lies a grand secret,' said Jopp. 'It is the passion of love. To think that a woman should love one man so well, and hate another so unmercifully.'

'Who's the object of your meditation, sir?'

'One that stands high in this town. I'd like to shame her! Upon my life, 'twould be as good as a play to read her love-letters, the proud piece of silk and wax-work! For 'tis her love-letters that I've got here.'

'Love-letters? then let's hear 'em, good soul,' said Mother

Cuxsom. 'Lord, do ye mind, Richard, what fools we use to be when we were younger? Getting a schoolboy to write ours for us; and giving him a penny, do ye mind, not to tell other folks what he'd put inside, do ye mind?'

By this time Jopp had pushed his finger under the seals, and unfastened the letters, tumbling them over and picking up one here and there at random, which he read aloud. These passages soon began to uncover the secret which Lucetta had so earnestly hoped to keep buried, though the epistles, being allusive only, did not make it altogether plain.

'Mrs Farfrae wrote that!' said Nance Mockridge. ' 'Tis a humbling thing for us, as respectable women, that one of the same sex could do it. And now she's vowed herself to another man!'

'So much the better for her,' said the aged furmity-woman. 'Ah, I saved her from a real bad marriage, and she's never been the one to thank me.'

'I say, what a good foundation for a skimmity-ride,'* said Nance.

'True,' said Mrs Cuxsom, reflecting. ' 'Tis as good a ground for a skimmity-ride as ever I knowed; and it ought not to be wasted. The last one seen in Casterbridge must have been ten years ago, if a day.'

At this moment there was a shrill whistle, and the landlady said to the man who had been called Charl, ' 'Tis Jim coming in. Would ye go and let down the bridge for me?'

Without replying Charl and his comrade Joe rose, and receiving a lantern from her went out at the back door and down the garden-path, which ended abruptly at the edge of the stream already mentioned. Beyond the stream was the open moor, from which a clammy breeze smote upon their faces as they advanced. Taking up the board that had lain in readiness one of them lowered it across the water, and the instant its further end touched the ground footsteps entered upon it, and there appeared from the shade a stalwart man with straps round his knees, a double-barrelled gun under his arm and some birds slung up behind him. They asked him if he had had much luck.

'Not much,' he said indifferently. 'All safe inside?'

Receiving a reply in the affirmative he went on inwards, the others withdrawing the bridge and beginning to retreat in his rear. Before, however, they had entered the house a cry of 'Ahoy' from the moor led them to pause.

The cry was repeated. They pushed the lantern into an out-house, and went back to the brink of the stream.

'Ahoy — is this the way to Casterbridge?' said some one from the other side.

'Not in particular,' said Charl. 'There's a river afore 'ee.'

'I don't care — here's for through it!' said the man in the moor. 'I've had travelling enough for to-day.'

'Stop a minute, then,' said Charl, finding that the man was no enemy, 'Joe, bring the plank and lantern; here's somebody that's lost his way. You should have kept along the turnpike road, friend, and not have strook across here.'

'I should — as I see now. But I saw a light here, and says I to myself, that's an outlying house, depend on't.'

The plank was now lowered; and the stranger's form shaped itself from the darkness. He was a middle-aged man, with hair and whiskers prematurely grey, and a broad and genial face. He had crossed on the plank without hesitation, and seemed to see nothing odd in the transit. He thanked them, and walked between them up the garden. 'What place is this?' he asked, when they reached the door.

'A public-house.'

'Ah. Perhaps it will suit me to put up at. Now then, come in and wet your whistle at my expense for the lift over you have given me.'

They followed him into the inn, where the increased light exhibited him as one who would stand higher in an estimate by the eye than in one by the ear. He was dressed with a certain clumsy richness — his coat being furred, and his head covered by a cap of seal-skin, which, though the nights were chilly, must have been warm for the daytime, spring being somewhat advanced. In his hand he carried a small mahogany case, strapped, and clamped with brass.

Apparently surprised at the kind of company which confronted him through the kitchen door, he at once abandoned his idea of putting up at the house; but taking the situation lightly, he called for glasses of the best, paid for them as he stood in the passage, and turned to proceed on his way by the front door. This was barred, and while the landlady was unfastening it the conversation about the skimmington was continued in the sitting-room, and reached his ears.

'What do they mean by a "skimmity-ride"?' he asked.

'O, sir!' said the landlady, swinging her long earrings with deprecating modesty; ' 'tis a' old foolish thing they do in these parts when a man's wife is – well, not too particularly his own. But as a respectable householder I don't encourage it.'

'Still, are they going to do it shortly? It is a good sight to see, I suppose?'

'Well, sir!' she simpered. And then, bursting into naturalness, and glancing from the corner of her eye, ''Tis the funniest thing under the sun! And it costs money.'

'Ah! I remember hearing of some such thing. Now I shall be in Casterbridge for two or three weeks to come, and should not mind seeing the performance. Wait a moment.' He turned back, entered the sitting-room, and said, 'Here, good folks; I should like to see the old custom you are talking of, and I don't mind being something towards it – take that.' He threw a sovereign on the table and returned to the landlady at the door, of whom, having inquired the way into the town, he took his leave.

'There were more where that one came from,' said Charl, when the sovereign had been taken up and handed to the landlady for safe keeping. 'By George! we ought to have got a few more while we had him here.'

'No, no,' answered the landlady. 'This is a respectable house, thank God! And I'll have nothing done but what's honourable.'

'Well,' said Jopp; 'now we'll consider the business begun, and will soon get it in train.'

'We will!' said Nance. 'A good laugh warms my heart more than a cordial, and that's the truth on't.'

Jopp gathered up the letters, and it being now somewhat late he did not attempt to call at Farfrae's with them that night. He reached home, sealed them up as before, and delivered the parcel at its address next morning. Within an hour its contents were reduced to ashes by Lucetta, who, poor soul! was inclined to fall down on her knees in thankfulness that at last no evidence remained of the unlucky episode with Henchard in her past. For though hers had been rather the laxity of inadvertence than of intention, that episode, if known, was not the less likely to operate fatally between herself and her husband.

Chapter 37

Such was the state of things when the current affairs of Casterbridge were interrupted by an event of such magnitude that its influence reached to the lowest social stratum there, stirring the depths of its society simultaneously with the preparations for the skimmington. It was one of those excitements which, when they move a country town, leave a permanent mark upon its chronicles, as a warm summer permanently marks the ring in the tree-trunk corresponding to its date.

A Royal Personage was about to pass through the borough on his course further west, to inaugurate an immense engineering work out that way.* He had consented to halt half-an-hour or so in the town, and to receive an address from the corporation of Casterbridge, which, as a representative centre of husbandry, wished thus to express its sense of the great services he had rendered to agricultural science and economics, by his zealous promotion of designs for placing the art of farming on a more scientific footing.

Royalty had not been seen in Casterbridge since the days of the third King George, and then only by candlelight for a few minutes, when that monarch, on a night-journey, had stopped to change horses at the King's Arms. The inhabitants therefore decided to make a thorough *fête carillonnée** of the unwonted occasion. Half-an-hour's pause was not long, it is true; but much might be done in it by a judicious grouping of incidents, above all, if the weather were fine.

The address was prepared on parchment by an artist who was handy at ornamental lettering, and was laid on with the best gold-leaf and colours that the sign-painter had in his shop. The Council met on the Tuesdy before the appointed day, to arrange the details of the procedure. While they were sitting, the door of the Council Chamber standing open, they heard a heavy footstep coming up the stairs. It advanced along the passage, and Henchard entered the room, in clothes of frayed and threadbare shabbiness, the very clothes which he had used to wear in the primal days when he had sat among them.

'I have a feeling,' he said, advancing to the table and laying his hand upon the green cloth, 'that I should like to join ye in this reception of our illustrious visitor. I suppose I could walk with the rest?'

Embarrassed glances were exchanged by the Council, and Grower nearly ate the end of his quill-pen off, so gnawed he it during the silence. Farfrae the young Mayor, who by virtue of his office sat in the large chair, intuitively caught the sense of the meeting, and as spokesman was obliged to utter it, glad as he would have been that the duty should have fallen to another tongue.

'I hardly see that it would be proper, Mr Henchard,' said he. 'The Council are the Council, and as ye are no longer one of the body, there would be an irregularity in the proceeding. If ye were included, why not others?'

'I have a particular reason for wishing to assist at the ceremony.'

Farfrae looked round. 'I think I have expressed the feeling of the Council,' he said.

'Yes, yes,' from Dr Bath, Lawyer Long, Alderman Tubber, and several more.

'Then I am not to be allowed to have anything to do with it officially?'

'I am afraid so; it is out of the question indeed. But of course you can see the doings full well, such as they are to be, like the rest of the spectators.'

Henchard did not reply to that very obvious suggestion, and turning on his heel, went away.

It had been only a passing fancy of his, but opposition crystallized it into a determination. 'I'll welcome his Royal Highness, or nobody shall!' he went about saying. 'I am not going to be sat upon by Farfrae, or any of the rest of the paltry crew! You shall see.'

The eventful morning was bright, a full-faced sun confronting early window-gazers eastward, and all perceived (for they were practised in weather-lore) that there was permanence in the glow. Visitors soon began to flock in from county houses, villages, remote copses, and lonely uplands, the latter in oiled boots and tilt bonnets,* to see the reception, or if not to see it, at any rate to be near it. There was hardly a workman in the town who did not put a clean shirt on. Solomon Longways, Christopher Coney, Buzzford, and the rest of that fraternity, showed their sense of the occasion by advancing their customary eleven o'clock pint to half-past ten; from which they found a difficulty in getting back to the proper hour for several days.

Henchard had determined to do no work that day. He primed himself in the morning with a glass of rum, and walking down the street met Elizabeth-Jane, whom he had not seen for a week. 'It was lucky,' he said to her, 'my twenty-one years had expired before this came on, or I should never have had the nerve to carry it out.'

'Carry out what?' said she, alarmed.

'This welcome I am going to give our Royal visitor.'

She was perplexed. 'Shall we go and see it together?' she said.

'See it! I have other fish to fry. You see it. It will be worth seeing!'

She could do nothing to elucidate this, and decked herself out with a heavy heart. As the appointed time drew near she got sight again of her stepfather. She thought he was going to the Three Mariners; but no, he elbowed his way through the gay throng to the shop of Woolfrey, the draper. She waited in the crowd without.

In a few minutes he emerged, wearing, to her surprise, a brilliant rosette, while more surprising still, in his hand he carried a flag of somewhat homely construction, formed by tacking one of the small Union Jacks, which abounded in the town to-day, to the end of a deal wand – probably the roller from a piece of calico. Henchard rolled up his flag on the doorstep, put it under his arm, and went down the street.

Suddenly the taller members of the crowd turned their heads, and the shorter stood on tiptoe. It was said that the Royal *cortège** approached. The railway had stretched out an arm towards Casterbridge at this time, but had not reached it by several miles as yet;* so that the intervening distance, as well as the remainder of the journey, was to be traversed by road in the old fashion. People thus waited – the county families in their carriages, the masses on foot – and watched the far-stretching London highway to the ringing of bells and chatter of tongues.

From the background Elizabeth-Jane watched the scene. Some seats had been arranged from which ladies could witness the spectacle, and the front seat was occupied by Lucetta, the Mayor's wife, just at present. In the road under her eyes stood Henchard. She appeared so bright and pretty that, as it seemed, he was experiencing the momentary weakness of wishing for her notice. But she was far from attractive to a woman's eye, ruled as that is so largely by the superficies of things. He was not only a journeyman, unable to appear as he formerly had appeared, but he disdained to appear as well as he might. Everybody else, from the Mayor to the washerwoman, shone in new vesture according to means; but Henchard had doggedly retained the fretted and weather-beaten garments of bygone years.

Hence, alas, this occurred: Lucetta's eyes slid over him to this side and to that without anchoring on his features – as gaily dressed women's eyes will too often do on such occasions. Her manner signified quite plainly that she meant to know him in public no more.

But she was never tired of watching Donald, as he stood in animated converse with his friends a few yards off, wearing round his young neck the official gold chain with great square links, like that round the Royal unicorn.* Every trifling emotion that her husband showed as he talked had its reflex on her face and lips, which moved in little duplicates to his. She was living his part rather than her own, and cared for no one's situation but Farfrae's that day.

At length a man stationed at the furthest turn of the high road, namely, on the second bridge of which mention has been made, gave a signal; and the Corporation in their robes proceeded from the front of the Town Hall to the archway erected at the entrance to the town. The carriages containing the Royal visitor and his suite arrived at the spot in a cloud of dust, a procession was formed, and the whole came on to the Town Hall at a walking pace.

This spot was the centre of interest. There were a few clear yards in front of the Royal carriage, sanded; and into this space a man stepped before any one could prevent him. It was Henchard. He had unrolled his private flag, and removing his hat he staggered to the side of the slowing vehicle, waving the Union Jack to and fro with his left hand, while he blandly held out his right to the Illustrious Personage.

All the ladies said with bated breath, 'O, look there!' and Lucetta was ready to faint. Elizabeth-Jane peeped through the shoulders of those in front, saw what it was, and was terrified; and then her interest in the spectacle as a strange phenomenon got the better of her fear.

Farfrae, with Mayoral authority, immediately rose to the occasion. He seized Henchard by the shoulder, dragged him back, and told him roughly to be off. Henchard's eyes met his, and

Farfrae observed the fierce light in them despite his excitement and irritation. For a moment Henchard stood his ground rigidly; then by an unaccountable impulse gave way and retired. Farfrae glanced to the ladies' gallery, and saw that his Calphurnia's cheek was pale.*

'Why – it is your husband's old patron!' said Mrs Blowbody, a lady of the neighbourhood who sat beside Lucetta.

'Patron!' said Donald's wife with quick indignation.

'Do you say the man is an acquaintance of Mr Farfrae's?' observed Mrs Bath, the physician's wife, a new-comer to the town through her recent marriage with the doctor.

'He works for my husband,' said Lucetta.

'Oh – is that all? They have been saying to me that it was through him your husband first got a footing in Casterbridge. What stories people will tell!'

'They will indeed. It was not so at all. Donald's genius would have enabled him to get a footing anywhere, without anybody's help! He would have been just the same if there had been no Henchard in the world!'

It was partly Lucetta's ignorance of the circumstances of Donald's arrival which led her to speak thus; partly the sensation that everybody seemed bent on snubbing her at this triumphant time. The incident had occupied but a few moments, but it was necessarily witnessed by the Royal Personage, who, however, with practised tact, affected not to have noticed anything unusual. He alighted, the Mayor advanced, the address was read; the Illustrious Personage replied, then said a few words to Farfrae, and shook hands with Lucetta as the Mayor's wife. The ceremony occupied but a few minutes, and the carriages rattled heavily as Pharaoh's chariots* down Corn Street and out upon the Budmouth Road, in continuation of the journey coastward.

In the crowd stood Coney, Buzzford, and Longways. 'Some difference between him now and when he zung at the Dree Mariners,' said the first. ' 'Tis wonderful how he could get a lady of her quality to go snacks wi' en* in such quick time.'

'True. Yet how folk do worship fine clothes! Now there's a better-looking woman than she that nobody notices at all, because she's akin to that hontish* fellow Henchard.'

'I could worship ye, Buzz, for saying that,' remarked Nance Mockridge. 'I do like to see the trimming pulled off such Christmas candles. I am quite unequal to the part of villain myself, or I'd gi'e all my small silver to see that lady toppered* . . . And perhaps I shall soon,' she added significantly.

'That's not a noble passiont for a 'oman to keep up,' said Longways.

Nance did not reply, but every one knew what she meant. The ideas diffused by the reading of Lucetta's letters at Peter's Finger had condensed into a scandal, which was spreading like a miasmatic fog through Mixen Lane, and thence up the back streets of Casterbridge.

This mixed assemblage of idlers known to each other presently fell apart into two bands by a process of natural selection, the frequenters of Peter's Finger going off Mixen Lane-wards, where most of them lived, while Coney, Buzzford, Longways, and that connection remained in the street.

'You know what's brewing down there, I suppose?' said Buzzford mysteriously to the others.

Coney looked at him. 'Not the skimmity-ride?'

Buzzford nodded.

'I have my doubts if it will be carried out,' said Longways. 'If they are getting it up they are keeping it mighty close.'

'I heard they were thinking of it a fortnight ago, at all events.'

'If I were sure o't I'd lay information,' said Longways emphatically. ' 'Tis too rough a joke, and apt to wake riots in towns. We know that the Scotchman is a right enough man, and that his lady has been a right enough 'oman since she came here, and if there was anything wrong about her afore, that's their business, not ours.'

Coney reflected. Farfrae was still liked in the community; but it must be owned that, as the Mayor and man of money, engrossed with affairs and ambitions, he had lost in the eyes of the poorer inhabitants something of that wondrous charm which he had had for them as a light-hearted penniless young man, who sang ditties as readily as the birds in the trees. Hence the anxiety to keep him from annoyance showed not quite the ardour that would have animated it in former days.

'Suppose we make inquiration into it, Christopher,' continued Longways; 'and if we find there's really anything in it, drop a letter to them most concerned, and advise 'em to keep out of the way?'

This course was decided on, and the group separated, Buzzford saying to Coney, 'Come, my ancient friend; let's move on. There's nothing more to see here.'

These well-intentioned ones would have been surprised had they known how ripe the great jocular plot really was. 'Yes, to-night,' Jopp had said to the Peter's party at the corner of Mixen Lane. 'As a wind-up to the Royal visit the hit will be all the more pat by reason of their great elevation to-day.'

To him, at least, it was not a joke, but a retaliation.

Chapter 38

The proceedings had been brief – too brief – to Lucetta, whom an intoxicating *Weltlust** had fairly mastered; but they had brought her a great triumph nevertheless. The shake of the Royal hand still lingered in her fingers; and the chit-chat she had overheard, that her husband might possibly receive the honour of knighthood, though idle to a degree, seemed not the wildest vision; stranger things had occurred to men so good and captivating as her Scotchman was.

After the collision with the Mayor, Henchard had withdrawn behind the ladies' stand; and there he stood, regarding with a stare of abstraction the spot on the lappel of his coat where Farfrae's hand had seized it. He put his own hand there, as if he could hardly realize such an outrage from one whom it had once been his wont to treat with ardent generosity. While pausing in this half-stupefied state the conversation of Lucetta with the other ladies reached his ears; and he distinctly heard her deny him – deny that he had assisted Donald, that he was anything more than a common journeyman.

He moved on homeward, and met Jopp in the archway to the Bull Stake. 'So you've had a snub,' said Jopp.

'And what if I have?' answered Henchard sternly.

'Why, I've had one too, so we are both under the same cold shade.' He briefly related his attempt to win Lucetta's intercession.

Henchard merely heard this story, without taking it deeply in. His own relation to Farfrae and Lucetta overshadowed all kindred ones. He went on saying brokenly to himself, 'She has supplicated to me in her time; and now her tongue won't own me nor her eyes see me! . . . And he – how angry he looked. He drove me back as if I were a bull breaking fence . . . I took it like a lamb, for I saw it could not be settled there. He can rub brine on a green wound!* . . . But he shall pay for it, and she shall be sorry. It must come to a tussle – face to face; and then we'll see how a coxcomb can front a man!'

Without further reflection the fallen merchant, bent on some wild purpose, ate a hasty dinner and went forth to find Farfrae. After being injured by him as a rival, and snubbed by him as a journeyman, the crowning degradation had been reserved for this day – that he should be shaken at the collar by him as a vagabond in the face of the whole town.

The crowds had dispersed. But for the green arches which still stood as they were erected Casterbridge life had resumed its ordinary shape. Henchard went down Corn Street till he came to Farfrae's house, where he knocked, and left a message that he would be glad to see his employer at the granaries as soon as he conveniently could come there. Having done this he proceeded round to the back and entered the yard.

Nobody was present, for, as he had been aware, the labourers and carters were enjoying a half-holiday on account of the events of the morning – though the carters would have to return for a short time later on, to feed and litter down the horses. He had reached the granary steps and was about to ascend, when he said to himself aloud, 'I'm stronger than he.'

Henchard returned to a shed, where he selected a short piece of rope from several pieces that were lying about; hitching one end of this to a nail, he took the other in his right hand and turned himself bodily round, while keeping his arm against his side; by this contrivance he pinioned the arm effectively. He now went up the ladders to the top floor of the corn-stores.

It was empty except of a few sacks, and at the further end was the door often mentioned, opening under the cathead and chain that hoisted the sacks. He fixed the door open and looked over the sill. There was a depth of thirty or forty feet to the ground; here was the spot on which he had been standing with Farfrae when Elizabeth-Jane had seen him lift his arm, with many misgivings as to what the movement portended.

He retired a few steps into the loft and waited. From this elevated perch his eye could sweep the roofs round about, the upper parts of the luxurious chestnut trees, now delicate in leaves of a week's age, and the drooping boughs of the limes; Farfrae's

garden and the green door leading therefrom. In course of time –
he could not say how long – that green door opened and Farfrae
came through. He was dressed as if for a journey. The low light of
the nearing evening caught his head and face when he emerged
from the shadow of the wall, warming them to a complexion of
flame-colour. Henchard watched him with his mouth firmly set,
the squareness of his jaw and the verticality of his profile being
unduly marked.

Farfrae came on with one hand in his pocket, and humming a
tune in a way which told that the words were most in his mind.
They were those of the song he had sung when he arrived years
before at the Three Mariners, a poor young man, adventuring for
life and fortune, and scarcely knowing whitherward:

> And here's a hand, my trusty fiere,
> And gie's a hand o' thine.*

Nothing moved Henchard like an old melody. He sank back. 'No;
I can't do it!' he gasped. 'Why does the infernal fool begin that
now!'

At length Farfrae was silent, and Henchard looked out of the
loft door. 'Will ye come up here?' he said.

'Ay, man,' said Farfrae. 'I couldn't see ye. What's wrang?'

A minute later Henchard heard his feet on the lowest ladder. He
heard him land on the first floor, ascend and land on the second,
begin the ascent to the third. And then his head rose through the
trap behind.

'What are you doing up here at this time?' he asked, coming
forward. 'Why didn't ye take your holiday like the rest of the
men?' He spoke in a tone which had just severity enough in it to
show that he remembered the untoward event of the forenoon,
and his conviction that Henchard had been drinking.

Henchard said nothing; but going back he closed the stair
hatchway, and stamped upon it so that it went tight into its frame;
he next turned to the wondering young man, who by this time
observed that one of Henchard's arms was bound to his side.

'Now,' said Henchard quietly, 'we stand face to face – man and
man. Your money and your fine wife no longer lift 'ee above me as
they did but now, and my poverty does not press me down.'

'What does it all mean?' asked Farfrae simply.

'Wait a bit, my lad. You should ha' thought twice before you
affronted to extremes a man who had nothing to lose. I've stood

your rivalry, which ruined me, and your snubbing, which humbled me; but your hustling, that disgraced me, I won't stand!'

Farfrae warmed a little at this. 'Ye'd no business there,' he said.

'As much as any one among ye! What, you forward stripling, tell a man of my age he'd no business there!' The anger-vein swelled in his forehead as he spoke.

'You insulted Royalty, Henchard; and 'twas my duty, as the chief magistrate, to stop you.'

'Royalty be damned,' said Henchard. 'I am as loyal as you, come to that!'

'I am not here to argue. Wait till you cool doon, wait till you cool; and you will see things the same way as I do.'

'You may be the one to cool first,' said Henchard grimly. 'Now this is the case. Here we be, in this four-square loft, to finish out that little wrestle you began this morning. There's the door, forty foot above ground. One of us two puts the other out by that door – the master stays inside. If he likes he may go down afterwards and give the alarm that the other has fallen out by accident – or he may tell the truth – that's his business. As the strongest man I've tied one arm to take no advantage of 'ee. D'ye understand? Then here's at 'ee!'

There was no time for Farfrae to do aught but one thing, to close with Henchard, for the latter had come on at once. It was a wrestling match, the object of each being to give his antagonist a back fall; and on Henchard's part, unquestionably, that it should be through the door.

At the outset Henchard's hold by his only free hand, the right, was on the left side of Farfrae's collar, which he firmly grappled, the latter holding Henchard by his collar with the contrary hand. With his right he endeavoured to get hold of his antagonist's left arm, which, however, he could not do, so adroitly did Henchard keep it in the rear as he gazed upon the lowered eyes of his fair and slim antagonist.

Henchard planted the first toe forward, Farfrae crossing him with his; and thus far the struggle had very much the appearance of the ordinary wrestling of those parts. Several minutes were passed by them in this attitude, the pair rocking and writhing like trees in a gale, both preserving an absolute silence. By this time their breathing could be heard. Then Farfrae tried to get hold of the other side of Henchard's collar, which was resisted by the larger man exerting all his force in a wrenching movement, and this part of the struggle ended by his forcing Farfrae down on his knees by sheer pressure of one of his muscular arms. Hampered as he was, however, he could not keep him there, and Farfrae finding his feet again the struggle proceeded as before.

By a whirl Henchard brought Donald dangerously near the precipice; seeing his position the Scotchman for the first time locked himself to his adversary, and all the efforts of that infuriated Prince of Darkness* – as he might have been called from his appearance just now – were inadequate to lift or loosen Farfrae for a time. By an extraordinary effort he succeeded at last, though not until they had got far back again from the fatal door. In doing so Henchard contrived to turn Farfrae a complete somersault. Had Henchard's other arm been free it would have been all over with Farfrae then. But again he regained his feet, wrenching Henchard's arm considerably, and causing him sharp pain, as could be seen from the twitching of his face. He instantly delivered the younger man an annihilating turn by the left fore-hip, as it used to be expressed, and following up his advantage thrust him towards the door, never loosening his hold till Farfrae's fair head was hanging over the window-sill, and his arm dangling down outside the wall.

'Now,' said Henchard between his gasps, 'this is the end of what you began this morning. Your life is in my hands.'

'Then take it, take it!' said Farfrae. 'Ye've wished to long enough!'

Henchard looked down upon him in silence, and their eyes met. 'O Farfrae! – that's not true!' he said bitterly. 'God is my witness that no man ever loved another as I did thee at one time . . . And now – though I came here to kill 'ee, I cannot hurt thee! Go and give me in charge – do what you will – I care nothing for what comes of me!'

He withdrew to the back part of the loft, loosened his arm, and flung himself into a corner upon some sacks, in the abandonment of remorse. Farfrae regarded him in silence; then went to the hatch and descended through it. Henchard would fain have recalled him; but his tongue failed in its task, and the young man's steps died on his ear.

Henchard took his full measure of shame and self-reproach. The scenes of his first acquaintance with Farfrae rushed back upon him – that time when the curious mixture of romance and thrift in the young man's composition so commanded his heart that Farfrae could play upon him as on an instrument. So thoroughly subdued was he that he remained on the sacks in a crouching attitude, unusual for a man, and for such a man. Its womanliness sat tragically on the figure of so stern a piece of virility. He heard a conversation below, the opening of the coach-house door, and the putting in of a horse, but took no notice.

Here he stayed till the thin shades thickened to opaque obscurity, and the loft-door became an oblong of gray light – the only visible shape around. At length he arose, shook the dust from his clothes wearily, felt his way to the hatch, and gropingly descended the steps till he stood in the yard.

'He thought highly of me once,' he murmured. 'Now he'll hate me and despise me for ever!'

He became possessed by an overpowering wish to see Farfrae again that night, and by some desperate pleading to attempt the well-nigh impossible task of winning pardon for his late mad attack. But as he walked towards Farfrae's door he recalled the unheeded doings in the yard while he had lain above in a sort of stupor. Farfrae he remembered had gone to the stable and put the horse into the gig; while doing so Whittle had brought him a letter; Farfrae had then said that he would not go towards Budmouth as he had intended – that he was unexpectedly summoned to Weatherbury, and meant to call at Mellstock on his way thither, that place lying but one or two miles out of his course.

He must have come prepared for a journey when he first arrived in the yard, unsuspecting enmity; and he must have driven off (though in a changed direction) without saying a word to any one on what had occurred between themselves.

It would therefore be useless to call at Farfrae's house till very late.

There was no help for it but to wait till his return, though waiting was almost torture to his restless and self-accusing soul. He walked about the streets and outskirts of the town, lingering here and there till he reached the stone bridge of which mention has been made, an accustomed halting-place with him now. Here he spent a long time, the purl* of waters through the weirs meeting his ear, and the Casterbridge lights glimmering at no great distance off.

While leaning thus upon the parapet his listless attention was awakened by sounds of an unaccustomed kind from the town quarter. They were a confusion of rhythmical noises, to which the streets added yet more confusion by encumbering them with echoes. His first incurious thought that the clangour arose from the town band, engaged in an attempt to round off a memorable day by a burst of evening harmony, was contradicted by certain peculiarities of reverberation. But inexplicability did not rouse him to more than a cursory heed; his sense of degradation was too strong for the admission of foreign ideas; and he leant against the parapet as before.

Chapter 39

When Farfrae descended out of the loft breathless from his encounter with Henchard, he paused at the bottom to recover himself. He arrived at the yard with the intention of putting the horse into the gig himself (all the men having a holiday), and driving to a village on the Budmouth Road. Despite the fearful struggle he decided still to persevere in his journey, so as to recover himself before going indoors and meeting the eyes of Lucetta. He wished to consider his course in a case so serious.

When he was just on the point of driving off Whittle arrived with a note badly addressed, and bearing the word 'immediate' upon the outside. On opening it he was surprised to see that it was unsigned. It contained a brief request that he would go to Weatherbury that evening about some business which he was conducting there. Farfrae knew nothing that could make it pressing; but as he was bent upon going out he yielded to the anonymous request, particularly as he had a call to make at Mellstock which could be included in the same tour. Thereupon he told Whittle of his change of direction, in words which Henchard had overheard; and set out on his way. Farfrae had not directed his man to take the message indoors, and Whittle had not been supposed to do so on his own responsibility.

Now the anonymous letter was a well-intentioned but clumsy contrivance of Longways and other of Farfrae's men to get him out of the way for the evening, in order that the satirical mummery* should fall flat, if it were attempted. By giving open information they would have brought down upon their heads the vengeance of those among their comrades who enjoyed these boisterous old games; and therefore the plan of sending a letter recommended itself by its indirectness.

For poor Lucetta they took no protective measure, believing with the majority there was some truth in the scandal, which she would have to bear as she best might.

It was about eight o'clock, and Lucetta was sitting in the drawing-room alone. Night had set in for more than half an hour, but she had not had the candles lighted, for when Farfrae was away she preferred waiting for him by the firelight, and, if it were not too cold, keeping one of the window-sashes a little way open that the sound of his wheels might reach her ears early. She was leaning back in her chair, in a more hopeful mood than she had enjoyed since her marriage. The day had been such a success; and the temporary uneasiness which Henchard's show of effrontery had wrought in her disappeared with the quiet disappearance of Henchard himself under her husband's reproof. The floating evidences of her absurd passion for him, and its consequences, had been destroyed, and she really seemed to have no cause for fear.

The reverie in which these and other subjects mingled was disturbed by a hubbub in the distance, that increased moment by moment. It did not greatly surprise her, the afternoon having been given up to recreation by a majority of the populace since the passage of the Royal equipages. But her attention was at once riveted to the matter by the voice of a maid-servant next door, who spoke from an upper window across the street to some other maid even more elevated than she.

'Which way be they going now?' inquired the first with interest.

'I can't be sure for a moment,' said the second, 'because of the malter's chimbley.* O yes – I can see 'em. Well, I declare, I declare!'

'What, what?' from the first, more enthusiastically.

'They are coming up Corn Street after all! They sit back to back!'

'What – two of 'em – are there two figures?'

'Yes. Two images on a donkey, back to back, their elbows tied to one another's! She's facing the head, and he's facing the tail.'

'Is it meant for anybody particular?'

'Well – it mid be. The man has got on a blue coat and kerseymere* leggings; he has black whiskers, and a reddish face. 'Tis a stuffed figure, with a falseface.'

The din was increasing now – then it lessened a little.

'There – I shan't see, after all!' cried the disappointed first maid.

'They have gone into a back street – that's all,' said the one who occupied the enviable position in the attic. 'There – now I have got 'em all endways nicely!'

'What's the woman like? Just say, and I can tell in a moment if 'tis meant for one I've in mind.'

'My – why – 'tis dressed just as *she* was dressed when she sat in the front seat at the time the play-actors came to the Town Hall!'

Lucetta started to her feet; and almost at the instant the door of the room was quickly and softly opened. Elizabeth-Jane advanced into the firelight.

'I have come to see you,' she said breathlessly. 'I did not stop to knock – forgive me! I see you have not shut your shutters, and the window is open.'

Without waiting for Lucetta's reply she crossed quickly to the window and pulled out one of the shutters. Lucetta glided to her side. 'Let it be – hush!' she said peremptorily, in a dry voice, while she seized Elizabeth-Jane by the hand, and held up her finger. Their intercourse had been so low and hurried that not a word had been lost of the conversation without; which had thus proceeded:

'Her neck is uncovered, and her hair in bands, and her backcomb in place; she's got on a puce silk, and white stockings, and coloured shoes.'

Again Elizabeth-Jane attempted to close the window, but Lucetta held her by main force.

' 'Tis me!' she said, with a face pale as death. 'A procession – a scandal – an effigy of me, and him!'

The look of Elizabeth betrayed that the latter knew it already.

'Let us shut it out,' coaxed Elizabeth-Jane, noting that the rigid wildness of Lucetta's features was growing yet more rigid and wild with the nearing of the noise and laughter. 'Let us shut it out!'

'It is no use!' she shrieked out. 'He will see it, won't he? Donald will see it! He is just coming home – and it will break his heart – he will never love me any more – and O, it will kill me – kill me!'

Elizabeth-Jane was frantic now. 'O, can't something be done to stop it?' she cried. 'Is there nobody to do it – not one?'

She relinquished Lucetta's hands, and ran to the door. Lucetta herself, saying recklessly 'I will see it!' turned to the window, threw up the sash, and went out upon the balcony. Elizabeth immediately followed her, and put her arm round her to pull her in. Lucetta's eyes were straight upon the spectacle of the uncanny revel, now advancing rapidly. The numerous lights around the two effigies threw them up into lurid distinctness; it was impossible to mistake the pair for other than the intended victims. 'Come in, come in,' implored Elizabeth; 'and let me shut the window!'

'She's me – she's me – even to the parasol – my green parasol!' cried Lucetta with a wild laugh as she stepped in. She stood motionless for one second – then fell heavily to the floor.

Almost at the instant of her fall the rude music of the skimmington ceased. The roars of sarcastic laughter went off in ripples, and the trampling died out like the rustle of a spent wind. Elizabeth was only indirectly conscious of this; she had rung the bell, and was bending over Lucetta, who remained convulsed on the carpet in the paroxysms of an epileptic seizure. She rang again and again, in vain; the probability being that the servants had all run out of the house to see more of the Dæmonic Sabbath than they could see within.

At last Farfrae's man, who had been agape on the door-step, came up; then the cook. The shutters, hastily pushed to by Elizabeth, were quite closed, a light was obtained, Lucetta carried to her room, and the man sent off for a doctor. While Elizabeth was undressing her she recovered consciousness; but as soon as she rememberd what had passed the fit returned.

The doctor arrived with unhoped-for promptitude; he had been standing at his door, like others, wondering what the uproar meant. As soon as he saw the unhappy sufferer he said, in answer to Elizabeth's mute appeal, 'This is serious.'

'It is a fit,' Elizabeth said.

'Yes. But a fit in the present state of her health means mischief. You must send at once for Mr Farfrae. Where is he?'

'He has driven into the country, sir,' said the parlour-maid; 'to some place on the Budmouth Road. He's likely to be back soon.'

'Never mind; he must be sent for, in case he should not hurry.' The doctor returned to the bedside again. The man was despatched, and they soon heard him clattering out of the yard at the back.

Meanwhile Mr Benjamin Grower, that prominent burgess of whom mention has been already made, hearing the din of cleavers, tongs, tambourines, kits, crouds, humstrums, serpents, rams'-horns,* and other historical kinds of music as he sat indoors in the High Street, had put on his hat and gone out to learn the cause. He came to the corner above Farfrae's, and soon guessed the nature of the proceedings; for being a native of the town he had witnessed such rough jests before. His first move was to search hither and thither for the constables; there were two in the town, shrivelled men whom he ultimately found in hiding up an alley yet more shrivelled than usual, having some not ungrounded fears that they might be roughly handled if seen.

'What can we two poor lammigers* do against such a multitude!' expostulated Stubberd, in answer to Mr Grower's chiding. ' 'Tis tempting 'em to commit *felo de se** upon us, and that would be the death of the perpetrator; and we wouldn't be the cause of a fellow-creature's death on no account, not we!'

'Get some help, then! Here, I'll come with you. We'll see what a few words of authority can do. Quick now; have you got your staves?'

'We didn't want the folk to notice us as law officers, being so short-handed, sir; so we pushed our Gover'ment staves up this water-pipe.'

'Out with 'em, and come along, for Heaven's sake! Ah, here's Mr Blowbody; that's lucky.' (Blowbody was the third of the three borough magistrates.)

'Well, what's the row?' said Blowbody. 'Got their names – hey?'

'No. Now,' said Grower to one of the constables, 'you go with Mr Blowbody round by the Old Walk and come up the street; and I'll go with Stubberd straight forward. By this plan we shall have 'em between us. Get their names only: no attack or interruption.'

Thus they started. But as Stubberd with Mr Grower advanced into Corn Street, whence the sounds had proceeded, they were surprised that no procession could be seen. They passed Farfrae's, and looked to the end of the street. The lamp flames waved, the Walk trees soughed, a few loungers stood about with their hands in their pockets. Everything was as usual.

'Have you seen a motley crowd making a disturbance?' Grower said magisterially to one of these in a fustian* jacket, who smoked a short pipe and wore straps round his knees.

'Beg yer pardon, sir?' blandly said the person addressed, who was no other than Charl, of Peter's Finger. Mr Grower repeated the words.

Charl shook his head to the zero of childlike ignorance. 'No;

we haven't seen anything; have we, Joe? And you was here afore
I.'

Joseph was quite as blank as the other in his reply.

'H'm – that's odd,' said Mr Grower. 'Ah – here's a respectable
man coming that I know by sight. Have you,' he inquired,
addressing the nearing shape of Jopp, 'have you seen any gang of
fellows making a devil of a noise – skimmington riding, or
something of the sort?'

'O no – nothing, sir,' Jopp replied, as if receiving the most
singular news. 'But I've not been far to-night, so perhaps –'

'Oh, 'twas here – just here,' said the magistrate.

'Now I've noticed, come to think o't, that the wind in the Walk
trees makes a peculiar poetical-like murmur to-night, sir; more
than common; so perhaps 'twas that?' Jopp suggested, as he
rearranged his hand in his greatcoat pocket (where it ingeniously
supported a pair of kitchen tongs and a cow's horn, thrust up
under his waistcoat).

'No, no, no, – d'ye think I'm a fool? Constable, come this way.
They must have gone into the back street.'

Neither in back street nor in front street, however, could the
disturbers be perceived; and Blowbody and the second constable,
who came up at this time, brought similar intelligence. Effigies,
donkey, lanterns, band, all had disappeared like the crew of
Comus.*

'Now,' said Mr Grower, 'there's only one thing more we can
do. Get ye half-a-dozen helpers, and go in a body to Mixen Lane,
and into Peter's Finger. I'm much mistaken if you don't find a clue
to the perpetrators there.'

The rusty-jointed executors of the law mustered assistance as
soon as they could, and the whole party marched off to the lane of
notoriety. It was no rapid matter to get there at night, not a lamp
or glimmer of any sort offering itself to light the way, except an
occasional pale radiance through some window-curtain, or
through the chink of some door which could not be closed
because of the smoky chimney within. At last they entered the inn
boldly, by the till then bolted front-door, after a prolonged
knocking of loudness commensurate with the importance of their
standing.

In the settles of the large room, guyed to the ceiling by cords as
usual for stability, an ordinary group sat drinking and smoking
with statuesque quiet of demeanour. The landlady looked mildly

at the invaders, saying in honest accents, 'Good evening, gentle-men; there's plenty of room. I hope there's nothing amiss?'

They looked round the room. 'Surely,' said Stubberd to one of the men, 'I saw you by now in Corn Street — Mr Grower spoke to 'ee?'

The man, who was Charl, shook his head absently. 'I've been here this last hour, hain't I, Nance?' he said to the woman who meditatively sipped her ale near him.

'Faith, that you have. I came in for my quiet supper-time half-pint, and you was here then, as was all the rest.'

The other constable was facing the clock-case, where he saw reflected in the glass a quick motion by the landlady. Turning sharply, he caught her closing the oven-door.

'Something curious about that oven, ma'am!' he observed advancing, opening it, and drawing out a tambourine.

'Ah,' she said apologetically, 'that's what we keep here to use when there's a little quiet dancing. You see damp weather spoils it, so I put it there to keep it dry.'

The constable nodded knowingly; but what he knew was nothing. Nohow could anything be elicited from this mute and inoffensive assembly. In a few minutes the investigators went out, and joining those of their auxiliaries who had been left at the door they pursued their way elsewhither.

Chapter 40

Long before this time Henchard, weary of his ruminations on the bridge, had repaired towards the town. When he stood at the bottom of the street a procession burst upon his view, in the act of turning out of an alley just above him. The lanterns, horns, and multitude startled him; he saw the mounted images, and knew what it all meant.

They crossed the way, entered another street, and disappeared. He turned back a few steps and was lost in grave reflection, finally wending his way homeward by the obscure river-side path. Unable to rest there he went to his stepdaughter's lodging, and was told that Elizabeth-Jane had gone to Mrs Farfrae's. Like one acting in obedience to a charm, and with a nameless apprehension, he followed in the same direction in the hope of meeting her, the roysterers having vanished. Disappointed in this he gave the gentlest of pulls to the door-bell, and then learnt particulars of what had occurred, together with the doctor's imperative orders that Farfrae should be brought home, and how they had set out to meet him on the Budmouth Road.

'But he has gone to Mellstock and Weatherbury!' exclaimed Henchard, now unspeakably grieved. 'Not Budmouth way at all.'

But, alas! for Henchard; he had lost his good name. They would not believe him, taking his words but as the frothy utterances of recklessness. Though Lucetta's life seemed at that moment to depend upon her husband's return (she being in great mental agony lest he should never know the unexaggerated truth of her past relations with Henchard), no messenger was despatched towards Weatherbury. Henchard, in a state of bitter anxiety and contrition, determined to seek Farfrae himself.

To this end he hastened down the town, ran along the eastern road over Durnover moor, up the hill beyond, and thus onward in the moderate darkness of this spring night till he had reached a second and almost a third hill about three miles distant. In Yalbury Bottom, or Plain, at the foot of the hill, he listened. At first nothing, beyond his own heart-throbs, was to be heard but the slow wind making its moan among the masses of spruce and larch of Yalbury Wood which clothed the heights on either hand; but presently there came the sound of light wheels whetting their felloes against the newly stoned patches of road, accompanied by the distant glimmer of lights.

He knew it was Farfrae's gig descending the hill from an indescribable personality in its noise, the vehicle having been his own till bought by the Scotchman at the sale of his effects. Henchard thereupon retraced his steps along Yalbury Plain, the gig coming up with him as its driver slackened speed between two plantations.

It was a point in the highway near which the road to Mellstock branched off from the homeward direction. By diverging to that village, as he had intended to do, Farfrae might probably delay his return by a couple of hours. It soon appeared that his intention was to do so still, the light swerving towards Cuckoo Lane, the by-road aforesaid. Farfrae's off gig-lamp flashed in Henchard's face. At the same time, Farfrae discerned his late antagonist.

'Farfrae – Mr Farfrae!' cried the breathless Henchard, holding up his hand.

Farfrae allowed the horse to turn several steps into the branch lane before he pulled up. He then drew rein, and said 'Yes?' over his shoulder, as one would towards a pronounced enemy.

'Come back to Casterbridge at once!' Henchard said. 'There's something wrong at your house – requiring your return. I've run all the way here on purpose to tell ye.'

Farfrae was silent, and at his silence Henchard's soul sank within him. Why had he not, before this, thought of what was only too obvious? He who, four hours earlier, had enticed Farfrae into a deadly wrestle stood now in the darkness of late night-time on a lonely road, inviting him to come a particular way, where an assailant might have confederates, instead of going his purposed way, where there might be a better opportunity of guarding himself from attack. Henchard could almost feel this view of things in course of passage through Farfrae's mind.

'I have to go to Mellstock,' said Farfrae coldly, as he loosened his rein to move on.

'But,' implored Henchard, 'the matter is more serious than your business at Mellstock. It is – your wife! She is ill. I can tell you particulars as we go along.'

The very agitation and abruptness of Henchard increased Farfrae's suspicion that this was a *ruse* to decoy him on to the next wood, where might be effectually compassed what, from policy or want of nerve, Henchard had failed to do earlier in the day. He started the horse.

'I know what you think,' deprecated Henchard running after, almost bowed down with despair as he perceived the image of unscrupulous villainy that he assumed in his former friend's eyes. 'But I am not what you think!' he cried hoarsely. 'Believe me, Farfrae; I have come entirely on your own and your wife's account. She is in danger. I know no more; and they want you to come. Your man has gone the other way in a mistake. O Farfrae! don't mistrust me – I am a wretched man; but my heart is true to you still!'

Farfrae, however, did distrust him utterly. He knew his wife was with child, but he had left her not long ago in perfect health; and Henchard's treachery was more credible than his story. He had in his time heard bitter ironies from Henchard's lips, and there might be ironies now. He quickened the horse's pace, and had soon risen into the high country lying between there and Mellstock, Henchard's spasmodic run after him lending yet more substance to his thought of evil purposes.

The gig and its driver lessened against the sky in Henchard's eyes; his exertions for Farfrae's good had been in vain. Over this repentant sinner, at least, there was to be no joy in heaven.* He cursed himself like a less scrupulous Job,* as a vehement man will do when he loses self-respect, the last mental prop under poverty. To this he had come after a time of emotional darkness of which the adjoining woodland shade afforded inadequate illustration. Presently he began to walk back again along the way by which he had arrived. Farfrae should at all events have no reason for delay upon the road by seeing him there when he took his journey homeward later on.

Arriving at Casterbridge Henchard went again to Farfrae's house to make inquiries. As soon as the door opened anxious faces confronted his from the staircase, hall, and landing; and they all said in grievous disappointment, 'O – it is not he!' The manservant, finding his mistake, had long since returned, and all hopes had been centred upon Henchard.

'But haven't you found him?' said the doctor.

'Yes . . . I cannot tell 'ee!' Henchard replied as he sank down on a chair within the entrance. 'He can't be home for two hours.'

'H'm,' said the surgeon, returning upstairs.

'How is she?' asked Henchard of Elizabeth, who formed one of the group.

'In great danger, father. Her anxiety to see her husband makes her fearfully restless. Poor woman – I fear they have killed her!'

Henchard regarded the sympathetic speaker for a few instants as if she struck him in a new light; then, without further remark, went out of the door and onward to his lonely cottage. So much for man's rivalry, he thought. Death was to have the oyster, and Farfrae and himself the shells. But about Elizabeth-Jane; in the midst of his gloom she seemed to him as a pin-point of light. He had liked the look of her face as she answered him from the stairs. There had been affection in it, and above all things what he desired now was affection from anything that was good and pure. She was not his own; yet, for the first time, he had a faint dream that he might get to like her as his own, – if she would only continue to love him.

Jopp was just going to bed when Henchard got home. As the latter entered the door Jopp said, 'This is rather bad about Mrs Farfrae's illness.'

'Yes,' said Henchard shortly, though little dreaming of Jopp's complicity in the night's harlequinade, and raising his eyes just sufficiently to observe that Jopp's face was lined with anxiety.

'Somebody has called for you,' continued Jopp, when Henchard was shutting himself into his own apartment. 'A kind of traveller, or sea-captain of some sort.'

'Oh? – who could he be?'

'He seemed a well-be-doing man – had grey hair and a broadish face; but he gave no name, and no message.'

'Nor do I gi'e him any attention.' And, saying this, Henchard closed his door.

The divergence to Mellstock delayed Farfrae's return very nearly the two hours of Henchard's estimate. Among the other urgent reasons for his presence had been the need of his authority to send to Budmouth for a second physician; and when at length Farfrae did come back he was in a state bordering on distraction at his misconception of Henchard's motives.

A messenger was despatched to Budmouth, late as it had grown; the night wore on, and the other doctor came in the small hours. Lucetta had been much soothed by Donald's arrival; he seldom or never left her side; and when, immediately after his entry, she had tried to lisp out to him the secret which so oppressed her, he checked her feeble words, lest talking should be dangerous, assuring her there was plenty of time to tell him everything.

Up to this time he knew nothing of the skimmington-ride. The dangerous illness and miscarriage of Mrs Farfrae was soon rumoured through the town, and an apprehensive guess having been given as to its cause by the leaders in the exploit, compunction and fear threw a dead silence over all particulars of their orgie; while those immediately around Lucetta would not venture to add to her husband's distress by alluding to the subject.

What, and how much, Farfrae's wife ultimately explained to him of her past entanglement with Henchard, when they were alone in the solitude of that sad night, cannot be told. That she informed him of the bare facts of her peculiar intimacy with the corn-merchant became plain from Farfrae's own statements. But in respect of her subsequent conduct – her motive in coming to Casterbridge to unite herself with Henchard – her assumed justification in abandoning him when she discovered reasons for fearing him (though in truth her inconsequent passion for another man at first sight had most to do with that abandonment) – her method of reconciling to her conscience a marriage with the second when she was in a measure committed to the first: to what extent she spoke of these things remained Farfrae's secret alone.

Besides the watchman who called the hours and weather in Casterbridge that night there walked a figure up and down Corn Street hardly less frequently. It was Henchard's, whose retiring to rest had proved itself a futility as soon as attempted; and he gave it up to go hither and thither, and make inquiries about the patient every now and then. He called as much on Farfrae's account as on Lucetta's, and on Elizabeth-Jane's even more than on either's. Shorn one by one of all other interests, his life seemed centring on the personality of the stepdaughter whose presence but recently he could not endure. To see her on each occasion of his inquiry at Lucetta's was a comfort to him.

The last of his calls was made about four o'clock in the morning, in the steely light of dawn. Lucifer* was fading into day across Durnover Moor, the sparrows were just alighting into the street, and the hens had begun to cackle from the outhouses. When within a few yards of Farfrae's he saw the door gently opened, and a servant raise her hand to the knocker, to untie the piece of cloth which had muffled it. He went across, the sparrows in his way scarcely flying up from the road-litter, so little did they believe in human aggression at so early a time.

'Why do you take off that?' said Henchard.

She turned in some surprise at his presence, and did not answer for an instant or two. Recognizing him, she said, 'Because they may knock as loud as they will; she will never hear it any more.'

Chapter 41

Henchard went home. The morning having now fully broke he lit his fire, and sat abstractedly beside it. He had not sat there long when a gentle footstep approached the house and entered the passage, a finger tapping lightly at the door. Henchard's face brightened, for he knew the motions to be Elizabeth's. She came into his room, looking wan and sad.

'Have you heard?' she asked. 'Mrs Farfrae! She is – dead! Yes, indeed – about an hour ago!'

'I know it,' said Henchard. 'I have but lately come in from there. It is so very good of 'ee, Elizabeth, to come and tell me. You must be so tired out, too, with sitting up. Now do you bide here with me this morning. You can go and rest in the other room; and I will call 'ee when breakfast is ready.'

To please him, and herself – for his recent kindliness was winning a surprised gratitude from the lonely girl – she did as he bade her, and lay down on a sort of couch which Henchard had rigged up out of a settle in the adjoining room. She could hear him moving about in his preparations; but her mind ran most strongly on Lucetta, whose death in such fulness of life and amid such cheerful hopes of maternity was appallingly unexpected. Presently she fell asleep.

Meanwhile her stepfather in the outer room had set the breakfast in readiness; but finding that she dozed he would not call her; he waited on, looking into the fire and keeping the kettle boiling with housewifely care, as if it were an honour to have her in his house. In truth, a great change had come over him with regard to her, and he was developing the dream of a future lit by her filial presence, as though that way alone could happiness lie.

He was disturbed by another knock at the door, and rose to open it, rather deprecating a call from anybody just then. A stoutly built man stood on the doorstep, with an alien, unfamiliar air about his figure and bearing – an air which might have been called colonial by people of cosmopolitan experience. It was the man who had asked the way at Peter's Finger. Henchard nodded, and looked inquiry.

'Good morning, good morning,' said the stranger with profuse heartiness. 'Is it Mr Henchard I am talking to?'

'My name is Henchard.'

'Then I've caught 'ee at home – that's right. Morning's the time for business, says I. Can I have a few words with you?'

'By all means,' Henchard answered, showing the way in.

'You may remember me?' said his visitor, seating himself.

Henchard observed him indifferently, and shook his head.

'Well – perhaps you may not. My name is Newson.'

Henchard's face and eyes seemed to die. The other did not notice it. 'I know the name well,' Henchard said at last, looking on the floor.

'I make no doubt of that. Well, the fact is, I've been looking for 'ee this fortnight past. I landed at Havenpool and went through Casterbridge on my way to Falmouth, and when I got there, they told me you had some years before been living at Casterbridge. Back came I again, and by long and by late I got here by coach, ten minutes ago. "He lives down by the mill," says they. So here I am. Now – that transaction between us some twenty years agone – 'tis that I've called about. 'Twas a curious business. I was younger then than I am now, and perhaps the less said about it, in one sense, the better.'

'Curious business! 'Twas worse than curious. I cannot even allow that I'm the man you met then. I was not in my senses, and a man's senses are himself.'

'We were young and thoughtless,' said Newson. 'However, I've come to mend matters rather than open arguments. Poor Susan – hers was a strange experience.'

'It was.'

'She was a warm-hearted, home-spun woman. She was not what they call shrewd or sharp at all – better she had been.'

'She was not.'

'As you in all likelihood know, she was simple-minded enough to think that the sale was in a way binding. She was as guiltless o' wrong-doing in that particular as a saint in the clouds.'

'I know it, I know it. I found it out directly,' said Henchard, still with averted eyes. 'There lay the sting o't to me. If she had seen it as what it was she would never have left me. Never! But how should she be expected to know? What advantages had she? None. She could write her own name, and no more.'*

'Well, it was not in my heart to undeceive her when the deed was done,' said the sailor of former days. 'I thought, and there was not much vanity in thinking it, that she would be happier with me. She was fairly happy, and I never would have undeceived her till the day of her death. Your child died; she had another, and all went well. But a time came – mind me, a time always does come. A time came – it was some while after she and I and the child returned from America – when somebody she had confided her history to, told her my claim to her was a mockery, and made a jest of her belief in my right. After that she was never happy with me. She pined and pined, and socked* and sighed. She said she must leave me, and then came the question of our child. Then a man advised me how to act, and I did it, for I thought it was best. I left her at Falmouth, and went off to sea. When I got to the other side of the Atlantic there was a storm, and it was supposed that a lot of us, including myself, had been washed overboard. I got ashore at Newfoundland, and then I asked myself what I should do. "Since I'm here, here I'll bide," I thought to myself; " 'twill be most kindness to her, now she's taken against me, to let her believe me lost; for," I thought, "while she supposes us both alive she'll be miserable; but if she thinks me dead she'll go back to him, and the child will have a home." I've never returned to this country till a month ago, and I found that, as I had supposed, she went to you, and my daughter with her. They told me in Falmouth that Susan was dead. But my Elizabeth-Jane – where is she?'

'Dead likewise,' said Henchard doggedly. 'Surely you learnt that too?'

The sailor started up, and took an enervated pace or two down the room. 'Dead!' he said, in a low voice. 'Then what's the use of my money to me?'

Henchard, without answering, shook his head as if that were rather a question for Newson himself than for him.

'Where is she buried?' the traveller inquired.

'Beside her mother,' said Henchard, in the same stolid tones.

'When did she die?'

'A year ago and more,' replied the other without hesitation.

The sailor continued standing. Henchard never looked up from the floor. At last Newson said: 'My journey hither has been for nothing! I may as well go as I came! It has served me right. I'll trouble you no longer.'

Henchard heard the retreating footsteps of Newson upon the sanded floor, the mechanical lifting of the latch, the slow opening and closing of the door that was natural to a baulked or dejected man; but he did not turn his head. Newson's shadow passed the window. He was gone.

Then Henchard, scarcely believing the evidence of his senses, rose from his seat amazed at what he had done. It had been the impulse of a moment. The regard he had lately acquired for Elizabeth, the new-sprung hope of his loneliness that she would be to him a daughter of whom he could feel as proud as of the actual daughter she still believed herself to be, had been stimulated by the unexpected coming of Newson to a greedy exclusiveness in relation to her; so that the sudden prospect of her loss had caused him to speak mad lies like a child, in pure mockery of consequences. He had expected questions to close in round him, and unmask his fabrication in five minutes; yet such questioning had not come. But surely they would come; Newson's departure could be but momentary; he would learn all by inquiries in the town; and return to curse him, and carry his last treasure away!

He hastily put on his hat, and went out in the direction that Newson had taken. Newson's back was soon visible up the road, crossing Bull-stake. Henchard followed; and saw his visitor stop at the King's Arms, where the morning coach which had brought him waited half-an-hour for another coach which crossed there. The coach Newson had come by was now about to move again. Newson mounted; his luggage was put in, and in a few minutes the vehicle disappeared with him.

He had not so much as turned his head. It was an act of simple faith in Henchard's words — faith so simple as to be almost sublime. The young sailor who had taken Susan Henchard on the spur of the moment and on the faith of a glance at her face, more than twenty years before, was still living and acting under the form of the grizzled traveller who had taken Henchard's words on trust so absolute as to shame him as he stood.

Was Elizabeth-Jane to remain his by virtue of this hardy invention of a moment? 'Perhaps not for long,' said he. Newson might converse with his fellow-travellers, some of whom might be Casterbridge people; and the trick would be discovered.

This probability threw Henchard into a defensive attitude, and instead of considering how best to right the wrong, and acquaint Elizabeth's father with the truth at once, he bethought himself of ways to keep the position he had accidentally won. Towards the young woman herself his affection grew more jealously strong with each new hazard to which his claim to her was exposed.

He watched the distant highway expecting to see Newson return on foot, enlightened and indignant, to claim his child. But no figure appeared. Possibly he had spoken to nobody on the coach, but buried his grief in his own heart.

His grief! — what was it, after all, to that which he, Henchard, would feel at the loss of her? Newson's affection, cooled by years, could not equal his who had been constantly in her presence. And thus his jealous soul speciously argued to excuse the separation of father and child.

He returned to the house half expecting that she would have vanished. No; there she was — just coming out from the inner room, the marks of sleep upon her eyelids, and exhibiting a generally refreshed air.

'O father!' she said, smiling. 'I had no sooner lain down that I napped, though I did not mean to. I wonder I did not dream about poor Mrs Farfrae, after thinking of her so; but I did not. How strange it is that we do not often dream of latest events, absorbing as they may be.'

'I am glad you have been able to sleep,' he said, taking her hand with anxious proprietorship – an act which gave her a pleasant surprise.

They sat down to breakfast, and Elizabeth-Jane's thoughts reverted to Lucetta. Their sadness added charm to a countenance whose beauty had ever lain in its meditative soberness.

'Father,' she said, as soon as she recalled herself to the out-spread meal, 'it is so kind of you to get this nice breakfast with your own hands, and I idly asleep the while.'

'I do it every day,' he replied. 'You have left me; everybody has left me; how should I live but by my own hands.'

'You are very lonely, are you not?'

'Ay, child – to a degree that you know nothing of! It is my own fault. You are the only one who has been near me for weeks. And you will come no more.'

'Why do you say that? Indeed I will, if you would like to see me.'

Henchard signified dubiousness. Though he had so lately hoped that Elizabeth-Jane might again live in his house as daughter, he would not ask her to do so now. Newson might return at any moment, and what Elizabeth would think of him for his deception it were best to bear apart from her.

When they had breakfasted his stepdaughter still lingered, till the moment arrived at which Henchard was accustomed to go to his daily work. Then she arose, and with assurances of coming again soon went up the hill in the morning sunlight.

'At this moment her heart is as warm towards me as mine is towards her; she would live with me here in this humble cottage for the asking! Yet before the evening probably he will have come; and then she will scorn me!'

This reflection, constantly repeated by Henchard to himself, accompanied him everywhere through the day. His mood was no longer that of the rebellious, ironical, reckless misadventurer; but the leaden gloom of one who has lost all that can make life interesting, or even tolerable. There would remain nobody for him to be proud of, nobody to fortify him; for Elizabeth-Jane would soon be but as a stranger, and worse. Susan, Farfrae, Lucetta, Elizabeth – all had gone from him, one after one, either by his fault or by his misfortune.

In place of them he had no interest, hobby, or desire. If he could have summoned music to his aid his existence might even now have been borne; for with Henchard music was of regal power. The merest trumpet or organ tone was enough to move him, and high harmonies transubstantiated him. But hard fate had ordained that he should be unable to call up this Divine spirit in his need.

The whole land ahead of him was as darkness itself; there was nothing to come, nothing to wait for. Yet in the natural course of life he might possibly have to linger on earth another thirty or forty years – scoffed at; at best pitied.

The thought of it was unendurable.

To the east of Casterbridge lay moors and meadows through which much water flowed. The wanderer in this direction who should stand still for a few moments on a quiet night, might hear singular symphonies from these waters, as from a lampless orchestra, all playing in their sundry tones from near and far parts of the moor. At a hole in a rotten weir they executed a recitative; where a tributary brook fell over a stone breastwork they trilled cheerily; under an arch they performed a metallic cymballing; and at Durnover Hole they hissed. The spot at which their instrumentation rose loudest was a place called Ten Hatches, whence during high springs there proceeded a very fugue of sounds.

The river here was deep and strong at all times, and the hatches on this account were raised and lowered by cogs and a winch. A path led from the second bridge over the highway (so often mentioned) to these Hatches, crossing the stream at their head by a narrow plank-bridge. But after night-fall human beings were seldom found going that way, the path leading only to a deep reach of the stream called Blackwater, and the passage being dangerous.

Henchard, however, leaving the town by the east road, proceeded to the second, or stone bridge, and thence struck into this path of solitude, following its course beside the stream till the dark shapes of the Ten Hatches cut the sheen thrown upon the river by the weak lustre that still lingered in the west. In a second or two he stood beside the weir-hole where the water was at its deepest. He looked backwards and forwards, and no creature appeared in view. He then took off his coat and hat, and stood on the brink of the stream with his hands clasped in front of him.

While his eyes were bent on the water beneath there slowly became visible a something floating in the circular pool formed by the wash of centuries; the pool he was intending to make his death-bed. At first it was indistinct by reason of the shadow from the bank; but it emerged thence and took shape, which was that of a human body, lying stiff and stark upon the surface of the stream.

In the circular current imparted by the central flow the form was brought forward, till it passed under his eyes; and then he perceived with a sense of horror that it was *himself*. Not a man somewhat resembling him, but one in all respects his counterpart, his actual double, was floating as if dead in Ten Hatches Hole.

The sense of the supernatural was strong in this unhappy man, and he turned away as one might have done in the actual presence of an appalling miracle. He covered his eyes and bowed his head. Without looking again into the stream he took his coat and hat, and went slowly away.

Presently he found himself by the door of his own dwelling. To his surprise Elizabeth-Jane was standing there. She came forward, spoke, called him 'father' just as before. Newson, then, had not even yet returned.

'I thought you seemed very sad this morning,' she said, 'so I have come again to see you. Not that I am anything but sad myself. But everybody and everything seem against you so; and I know you must be suffering.'

How this woman divined things! Yet she had not divined their whole extremity.

He said to her, 'Are miracles still worked, do ye think, Elizabeth? I am not a read man. I don't know so much as I could wish. I have tried to peruse and learn all my life; but the more I try to know the more ignorant I seem.'

'I don't quite think there are any miracles nowadays,' she said.

'No interference in the case of desperate intentions, for instance? Well, perhaps not, in a direct way. Perhaps not. But will you come and walk with me, and I will show 'ee what I mean?'

She agreed willingly, and he took her over the highway, and by the lonely path to Ten Hatches. He walked restlessly, as if some haunting shade, unseen of her, hovered round him and troubled his glance. She would gladly have talked of Lucetta, but feared to disturb him. When they got near the weir he stood still, and asked her to go forward and look into the pool, and tell him what she saw.

She went, and soon returned to him. 'Nothing,' she said.

'Go again,' said Henchard, 'and look narrowly.'

She proceeded to the river brink a second time. On her return, after some delay, she told him that she saw something floating round and round there; but what it was she could not discern. It seemed to be a bundle of old clothes.

'Are they like mine?' asked Henchard.

'Well – they are. Dear me – I wonder if – Father, let us go away!'

'Go and look once more; and then we will get home.'

She went back, and he could see her stoop till her head was close to the margin of the pool. She started up, and hastened back to his side.

'Well,' said Henchard; 'what do you say now?'

'Let us go home.'

'But tell me – do – what is floating there?'

'The effigy,' she answered hastily. 'They must have thrown it into the river higher up amongst the willows at Blackwater, to get rid of it in their alarm at discovery by the magistrates; and it must have floated down here.'

'Ah – to be sure – the image o' me! But where is the other? Why that one only? . . . That performance of theirs killed her, but kept me alive!'

Elizabeth-Jane thought and thought of these words 'kept me alive', as they slowly retraced their way to the town, and at length guessed their meaning. 'Father! – I will not leave you alone like this!' she cried. 'May I live with you, and tend upon you as I used to do? I do not mind your being poor. I would have agreed to come this morning, but you did not ask me.'

'May you come to me?' he cried bitterly. 'Elizabeth, don't mock me! If you only would come!'

'I will,' said she.

'How will you forgive all my roughness in former days? You cannot!'

'I have forgotten it. Talk of that no more.'

Thus she assured him, and arranged their plans for reunion; and at length each went home. Then Henchard shaved for the first time during many days, and put on clean linen, and combed his hair; and was as a man resuscitated thenceforward.

The next morning the fact turned out to be as Elizabeth-Jane had stated; the effigy was discovered by a cowherd, and that of Lucetta a little higher up in the same stream. But as little as possible was said of the matter, and the figures were privately destroyed.

Despite this natural solution of the mystery Henchard no less regarded it as an intervention that the figure should have been floating there. Elizabeth-Jane heard him say, 'Who is such a reprobate as I! And yet it seems that even I be in Somebody's hand!'

Chapter 42

But the emotional conviction that he was in Somebody's hand began to die out of Henchard's breast as time slowly removed into distance the event which had given that feeling birth. The apparition of Newson haunted him. He would surely return.

Yet Newson did not arrive. Lucetta had been borne along the churchyard path; Casterbridge had for the last time turned its regard upon her, before proceeding to its work as if she had never lived. But Elizabeth remained undisturbed in the belief of her relationship to Henchard, and now shared his home. Perhaps, after all, Newson was gone for ever.

In due time the bereaved Farfrae had learnt the, at least, proximate cause of Lucetta's illness and death; and his first impulse was naturally enough to wreak vengeance in the name of the law upon the perpetrators of the mischief. He resolved to wait till the funeral was over ere he moved in the matter. The time having come he reflected. Disastrous as the result had been, it was obviously in no way foreseen or intended by the thoughtless crew who arranged the motley procession. The tempting prospect of putting to the blush people who stand at the head of affairs – that supreme and piquant enjoyment of those who writhe under the heel of the same – had alone animated them, so far as he could see; for he knew nothing of Jopp's incitements. Other considerations were also involved. Lucetta had confessed everything to him before her death, and it was not altogether desirable to make much ado about her history, alike for her sake, for Henchard's, and for his own. To regard the event as an untoward accident seemed, to Farfrae, truest consideration for the dead one's memory, as well as best philosophy.

Henchard and himself mutually forbore to meet. For Elizabeth's sake the former had fettered his pride sufficiently to accept the small seed and root business* which some of the Town Council, headed by Farfrae, had purchased to afford him a new opening. Had he been only personally concerned Henchard, without doubt, would have declined assistance even remotely brought about by the man whom he had so fiercely assailed. But the sympathy of the girl seemed necessary to his very existence; and on her account pride itself wore the garments of humility.

Here they settled themselves; and on each day of their lives Henchard anticipated her every wish with a watchfulness in which paternal regard was heightened by a burning jealous dread of rivalry. Yet that Newson would ever now return to Caster-bridge to claim her as a daughter there was little reason to suppose. He was a wanderer and a stranger, almost an alien; he had not seen his daughter for several years; his affection for her could not in the nature of things be keen; other interests would probably soon obscure his recollections of her, and prevent any such renewal of inquiry into the past as would lead to a discovery that she was still a creature of the present. To satisfy his conscience somewhat Henchard repeated to himself that the lie which had retained for him the coveted treasure had not been deliberately told to that end, but had come from him as the last defiant word of a despair which took no thought of consequences. Furthermore he pleaded within himself that no Newson could love her as he loved her, or would tend her to his life's extremity as he was prepared to do cheerfully.

Thus they lived on in the shop overlooking the churchyard, and nothing occurred to mark their days during the remainder of the year. Going out but seldom, and never on a market-day, they saw Donald Farfrae only at rarest intervals, and then mostly as a transitory object in the distance of the street. Yet he was pursuing his ordinary avocations, smiling mechanically to fellow-tradesmen, and arguing with bargainers – as bereaved men do after a while.

Time, 'in his own grey style',* taught Farfrae how to estimate his experience of Lucetta – all that it was, and all that it was not. There are men whose hearts insist upon a dogged fidelity to some image or cause thrown by chance into their keeping, long after their judgment has pronounced it no rarity – even the reverse, indeed; and without them the band of the worthy is incomplete. But Farfrae was not of those. It was inevitable that the insight, briskness, and rapidity of his nature should take him out of the dead blank which his loss threw about him. He could not but perceive that by the death of Lucetta he had exchanged a looming misery for a simple sorrow. After that revelation of her history, which must have come sooner or later in any circumstances, it was hard to believe that life with her would have been productive of further happiness.

But as a memory, notwithstanding such conditions, Lucetta's image still lived on with him, her weaknesses provoking only the gentlest criticism, and her sufferings attenuating wrath at her concealments to momentary spark now and then.

By the end of a year Henchard's little retail seed and grain shop, not much larger than a cupboard, had developed its trade considerably, and the stepfather and daughter enjoyed much serenity in the pleasant, sunny corner in which it stood. The quiet bearing of one who brimmed with an inner activity characterized Elizabeth-Jane at this period. She took long walks into the country two or three times a week, mostly in the direction of Budmouth. Sometimes it occurred to him that when she sat with him in the evening after these invigorating walks she was civil rather than affectionate; and he was troubled; one more bitter regret being added to those he had already experienced at having, by his severe censorship, frozen up her precious affection when originally offered.

She had her own way in everything now. In going and coming, in buying and selling, her word was law.

'You have got a new muff, Elizabeth,' he said to her one day quite humbly.

'Yes; I bought it,' she said.

He looked at it again as it lay on an adjoining table. The fur was of a glossy brown, and, though he was no judge of such articles, he thought it seemed an unusually good one for her to possess.

'Rather costly, I suppose, my dear, was it not?' he hazarded.

'It was rather above my figure,' she said quietly. 'But it is not showy.'

'O no,' said the netted lion,* anxious not to pique her in the least.

Some little time after, when the year had advanced into another spring, he paused opposite her empty bedroom in passing it. He thought of the time when she had cleared out of his then large and handsome house in Corn Street, in consequence of his dislike and harshness, and he had looked into her chamber in just the same way. The present room was much humbler, but what struck him about it was the abundance of books lying everywhere. Their number and quality made the meagre furniture that supported them seem absurdly disproportionate. Some, indeed many, must have been recently purchased; and though he encouraged her to buy in reason, he had no notion that she indulged her innate passion so extensively in proportion to the narrowness of their income. For the first time he felt a little hurt by what he thought her extravagance, and resolved to say a word to her about it. But, before he had found the courage to speak, an event happened which set his thoughts flying in quite another direction.

The busy time of the seed trade was over; and the quiet weeks that preceded the hay-season had come – setting their special stamp upon Casterbridge by thronging the market with wood rakes, new waggons in yellow, green, and red, formidable scythes, and pitch-forks of prong sufficient to skewer up a small family. Henchard, contrary to his wont, went out one Saturday afternoon towards the market-place, from a curious feeling that he would like to pass a few minutes on the spot of his former triumphs. Farfrae, to whom he was still a comparative stranger, stood a few steps below the Corn Exchange door – a usual position with him at this hour – and he appeared lost in thought about something he was looking at a little way off.

Henchard's eyes followed Farfrae's, and he saw that the object of his gaze was no sample-showing farmer, but his own step-daughter, who had just come out of a shop over the way. She, on her part, was quite unconscious of his attention, and in this was less fortunate than those young women whose very plumes, like those of Juno's bird, are set with Argus eyes* whenever possible admirers are within ken.*

Henchard went away, thinking that perhaps there was nothing significant after all in Farfrae's look at Elizabeth-Jane at that juncture. Yet he could not forget that the Scotchman had once shown a tender interest in her, of a fleeting kind. Thereupon promptly came to the surface that idiosyncrasy of Henchard's which had ruled his courses from the beginning and had mainly made him what he was. Instead of thinking that a union between his cherished stepdaughter and the energetic thriving Donald was a thing to be desired for her good and his own, he hated the very possibility.

Time had been when such instinctive opposition would have taken shape in action. But he was not now the Henchard of former days. He schooled himself to accept her will, in this as in other matters, as absolute and unquestionable. He dreaded lest an antagonistic word should lose for him such regard as he had regained from her by his devotion, feeling that to retain this under separation was better than to incur her dislike by keeping her near.

But the mere thought of such separation fevered his spirit much, and in the evening he said, with the stillness of suspense: 'Have you seen Mr Farfrae to-day, Elizabeth?'

Elizabeth-Jane started at the question; and it was with some confusion that she replied 'No'.

'Oh – that's right – that's right . . . It was only that I saw him in the street when we both were there.' He was wondering if her embarrassment justified him in a new suspicion – that the long walks which she had latterly been taking, that the new books which had so surprised him, had anything to do with the young man. She did not enlighten him, and lest silence should allow her to shape thoughts unfavourable to their present friendly relations, he diverted the discourse into another channel.

Henchard was, by original make, the last man to act stealthily, for good or for evil. But the *solicitus timor** of his love – the dependence upon Elizabeth's regard into which he had declined (or, in another sense, to which he had advanced) – denaturalized him. He would often weigh and consider for hours together the meaning of such and such a deed or phrase of hers, when a blunt settling question would formerly have been his first instinct. And now, uneasy at the thought of a passion for Farfrae which should entirely displace her mild filial sympathy with himself, he observed her going and coming more narrowly.

There was nothing secret in Elizabeth-Jane's movements beyong what habitual reserve induced; and it may at once be owned on her account that she was guilty of occasional conversations with Donald when they chanced to meet. Whatever the origin of her walks on the Budmouth Road, her return from those walks was often coincident with Farfrae's emergence from Corn

Street for a twenty minutes' blow on that rather windy highway – just to winnow the seeds and chaff out of him before sitting down to tea, as he said. Henchard became aware of this by going to the Ring, and, screened by its enclosure, keeping his eye upon the road till he saw them meet. His face assumed an expression of extreme anguish.

'Of her, too, he means to rob me!' he whispered. 'But he has the right. I do not wish to interfere.'

The meeting, in truth, was of a very innocent kind, and matters were by no means so far advanced between the young people as Henchard's jealous grief inferred. Could he have heard such conversation as passed he would have been enlightened thus much:

He. – 'You like walking this way, Miss Henchard – and is it not so?' (uttered in his undulatory accents, and with an appraising, pondering gaze at her).

She. – 'O yes. I have chosen this road latterly. I have no great reason for it.'

He. – 'But that may make a reason for others.'

She (reddening). – 'I don't know that. My reason, however, such as it is, is that I wish to get a glimpse of the sea every day.'

He. – 'Is it a secret why?'

She (reluctantly). – 'Yes.'

He (with the pathos of one of his native ballads). – 'Ah, I doubt there will be any good in secrets! A secret cast a deep shadow over my life. And well you know what it was.'

Elizabeth admitted that she did, but she refrained from confessing why the sea attracted her. She could not herself account for it fully, not knowing the secret possibly to be that, in addition to early marine associations, her blood was a sailor's.

'Thank you for those new books, Mr Farfrae,' she added shyly. 'I wonder if I ought to accept so many!'

'Ay! why not? It gives me more pleasure to get them for you, than you to have them!'

'It cannot!'

They proceeded along the road together till they reached the town, and their paths diverged.

Henchard vowed that he would leave them to their own devices, put nothing in the way of their courses, whatever they might mean. If he were doomed to be bereft of her, so it must be. In the situation which their marriage would create he could see no *locus standi** for himself at all. Farfrae would never recognize him more than superciliously; his poverty ensured that, no less than his past conduct. And so Elizabeth would grow to be a stranger to him, and the end of his life would be friendless solitude.

With such a possibility impending he could not help watchfulness. Indeed, within certain lines, he had the right to keep an eye upon her as his charge. The meetings seemed to become matters of course with them on special days of the week.

At last full proof was given him. He was standing behind a wall close to the place at which Farfrae encountered her. He heard the young man address her as 'Dearest Elizabeth-Jane', and then kiss her, the girl looking quickly round to assure herself that nobody was near.

When they were gone their way Henchard came out from the wall, and mournfully followed them to Casterbridge. The chief looming trouble in this engagement had not decreased. Both Farfrae and Elizabeth-Jane, unlike the rest of the people, must suppose Elizabeth to be his actual daughter, from his own assertion while he himself had the same belief; and though Farfrae must have so far forgiven him as to have no objection to own him as a father-in-law, intimate they could never be. Thus would the girl, who was his only friend, be withdrawn from him by degrees through her husband's influence, and learn to despise him.

Had she lost her heart to any other man in the world than the one he had rivalled, cursed, wrestled with for life in days before his spirit was broken, Henchard would have said, 'I am content.' But content with the prospect as now depicted was hard to acquire.

There is an outer chamber of the brain in which thoughts unowned, unsolicited, and of noxious kind, are sometimes allowed to wander for a moment prior to being sent off whence they came. One of these thoughts sailed into Henchard's ken now.

Suppose he were to communicate to Farfrae the fact that his betrothed was not the child of Michael Henchard at all – legally, nobody's child; how would the correct and leading townsman receive the information? He might possibly forsake Elizabeth-Jane, and then she would be her stepsire's own again.

Henchard shuddered, and exclaimed, 'God forbid such a thing! Why should I still be subject to these visitations of the devil, when I try so hard to keep him away?'

Chapter 43

What Henchard saw thus early was, naturally enough, seen at a little later date by other people. That Mr Farfrae 'walked with that bankrupt Henchard's stepdaughter, of all women,' became a common topic in the town, the simple perambulating term being used hereabout to signify a wooing; and the nineteen superior young ladies of Casterbridge, who had each looked upon herself as the only woman capable of making the merchant Councilman happy, indignantly left off going to the church Farfrae attended, left off conscious mannerisms, left off putting him in their prayers at night amongst their blood relations; in short, reverted to their natural courses.

Perhaps the only inhabitants of the town to whom this looming choice of the Scotchman's gave unmixed satisfaction were the members of the philosophic party, which included Longways, Christopher Coney, Billy Wills, Mr Buzzford, and the like. The Three Mariners having been, years before, the house in which they had witnessed the young man and woman's first and humble appearance on the Casterbridge stage, they took a kindly interest in their career, not unconnected, perhaps, with visions of festive treatment at their hands hereafter. Mrs Stannidge, having rolled into the large parlour one evening and said that it was a wonder such a man as Mr Farfrae, 'a pillow of the town', who might have chosen one of the daughters of the professional men or private residents, should stoop so low, Coney ventured to disagree with her.

'No, ma'am, no wonder at all. 'Tis she that's a stooping to he – that's my opinion. A widow man – whose first wife was no credit to him – what is it for a young perusing woman that's her own mistress and well liked? But as a neat patching up of things I see much good in it. When a man have put up a tomb of best marble-stone to the other one, as he've done, and weeped his fill, and thought it all over and said to hisself, "T'other took me in; I knowed this one first; she's a sensible piece for a partner, and there's no faithful woman in high life now", – well, he may do worse than not to take her, if she's tender-inclined.'

Thus they talked at the Mariners. But we must guard against a too liberal use of the conventional declaration that a great sensation was caused by the prospective event, that all the gossips' tongues were set wagging thereby, and so on, even though such a declaration might lend some *éclat** to the career of our poor only heroine. When all has been said about busy rumourers, a superficial and temporary thing is the interest of anybody in affairs which do not directly touch them. It would be a truer representation to say that Casterbridge (ever excepting the nineteen young ladies) looked up for a moment at the news, and withdrawing its attention, went on labouring and victualling, bringing up its children, and burying its dead, without caring a tittle for Farfrae's domestic plans.

Not a hint of the matter was thrown out to her stepfather by Elizabeth herself or by Farfrae either. Reasoning on the cause of their reticence he concluded that, estimating him by his past, the throbbing pair were afraid to broach the subject, and looked upon him as an irksome obstacle whom they would be heartily glad to get out of the way. Embittered as he was against society, this moody view of himself took deeper and deeper hold of Henchard, till the daily necessity of facing mankind, and of them particularly Elizabeth-Jane, became well-nigh more than he could endure. His health declined; he became morbidly sensitive. He wished he could escape those who did not want him, and hide his head for ever.

But what if he were mistaken in his views, and there were no necessity that his own absolute separation from her should be involved in the incident of her marriage?

He proceeded to draw a picture of the alternative – himself living like a fangless lion* about the back rooms of a house in which his stepdaughter was mistress; an inoffensive old man, tenderly smiled on by Elizabeth, and good-naturedly tolerated by her husband. It was terrible to his pride to think of descending so low; and yet, for the girl's sake he might put up with anything; even from Farfrae; even snubbings and masterful tongue-scourings. The privilege of being in the house she occupied would almost outweigh the personal humiliation.

Whether this were a dim possibility or the reverse, the courtship – which it evidently now was – had an absorbing interest for him. Elizabeth, as has been said, often took her walks on the Budmouth Road, and Farfrae as often made it convenient to create an accidental meeting with her there. Two miles out, a quarter of a mile from the highway, was the prehistoric fort called Mai Dun,* of huge dimensions and many ramparts, within or upon whose enclosures a human being, as seen from the road, was but an insignificant speck. Hitherward Henchard often resorted, glass in hand, and scanned the hedgeless *Via** – for it was the original track laid out by the legions of the Empire – to a distance of two or three miles, his object being to read the progress of affairs between Farfrae and his charmer.

One day Henchard was at this spot when a masculine figure came along the road from Budmouth, and lingered. Applying his telescope to his eye Henchard expected that Farfrae's features would be disclosed as usual. But the lenses revealed that to-day the man was not Elizabeth-Jane's lover.

It was one clothed as a merchant captain; and as he turned in his scrutiny of the road he revealed his face. Henchard lived a lifetime the moment he saw it. The face was Newson's.

Henchard dropped the glass, and for some seconds made no other movement. Newson waited, and Henchard waited – if that could be called a waiting which was a transfixture.* But Elizabeth-Jane did not come. Something or other had caused her to neglect her customary walk that day. Perhaps Farfrae and she had chosen another road for variety's sake. But what did that amount to? She might be here to-morrow, and in any case Newson, if bent on a private meeting and a revelation of the truth to her, would soon make his opportunity.

Then he would tell her not only of his paternity, but of the ruse by which he had been once sent away. Elizabeth's strict nature would cause her for the first time to despise her stepfather, would root out his image as that of an arch-deceiver, and Newson would reign in her heart in his stead.

But Newson did not see anything of her that morning. Having stood still awhile he at last retraced his steps, and Henchard felt like a condemned man who has a few hours' respite. When he reached his own house he found her there.

'O father!' she said innocently. 'I have had a letter – a strange one – not signed. Somebody has asked me to meet him, either on the Budmouth Road at noon to-day, or in the evening at Mr Farfrae's. He says he came to see me some time ago, but a trick was played him, so that he did not see me. I don't understand it; but between you and me I think Donald is at the bottom of the mystery, and that it is a relation of his who wants to pass an opinion on his choice. But I did not like to go till I had seen you. Shall I go?'

Henchard replied heavily, 'Yes; go.'

The question of his remaining in Casterbridge was for ever disposed of by this closing in of Newson on the scene. Henchard was not the man to stand the certainty of condemnation on a matter so near his heart. And being an old hand at bearing anguish in silence, and haughty withal, he resolved to make as light as he could of his intention, while immediately taking his measures.

He surprised the young woman whom he had looked upon as his all in this world by saying to her, as if he did not care about her more: 'I am going to leave Casterbridge, Elizabeth-Jane.'

'Leave Casterbridge!' she cried, 'and leave – me?'

'Yes, this little shop can be managed by you alone as well as by us both; I don't care about shops and streets and folks – I would rather get into the country by myself, out of sight, and follow my own ways, and leave you to yours.'

She looked down and her tears fell silently. It seemed to her that this resolve of his had come on account of her attachment and its probable result. She showed her devotion to Farfrae, however, by mastering her emotion and speaking out.

'I am sorry you have decided on this,' she said with difficult firmness. 'For I thought it probable – possible – that I might marry Mr Farfrae some little time hence, and I did not know that you disapproved of the step!'

'I approve of anything you desire to do, Izzy,' said Henchard huskily. 'If I did not approve it would be no matter! I wish to go away. My presence might make things awkward in the future; and, in short, it is best that I go.'

Nothing that her affection could urge would induce him to reconsider his determination; for she could not urge what she did not know – that when she should learn he was not related to her other than as a step-parent she would refrain from despising him, and that when she knew what he had done to keep her in ignorance she would refrain from hating him. It was his conviction that she would not so refrain; and there existed as yet neither word nor event which could argue it away.

'Then,' she said at last, 'you will not be able to come to my wedding; and that is not as it ought to be.'

'I don't want to see it – I don't want to see it!' he exclaimed; adding more softly, 'but think of me sometimes in your future life – you'll do that, Izzy? – think of me when you are living as the wife of the richest, the foremost man in the town, and don't let my sins, *when you know them all*, cause 'ee to quite forget that though I loved 'ee late I loved 'ee well.'

'It is because of Donald!' she sobbed.

'I don't forbid you to marry him,' said Henchard. 'Promise not to quite forget me when –' He meant when Newson should come.

She promised mechanically, in her agitation; and the same evening at dusk Henchard left the town, to whose development he had been one of the chief stimulants for many years. During the day he had bought a new tool-basket, cleaned up his old hay-knife and wimble, set himself up in fresh leggings, knee-naps* and corduroys, and in other ways gone back to the working clothes of his young manhood, discarding for ever the shabby-genteel suit of cloth and rusty silk hat that since his decline had characterized him in the Casterbridge street as a man who had seen better days.

He went secretly and alone, not a soul of the many who had known him being aware of his departure. Elizabeth-Jane accompanied him as far as the second bridge on the highway – for the hour of her appointment with the unguessed visitor at Farfrae's had not yet arrived – and parted from him with unfeigned wonder and sorrow, keeping him back a minute or two before finally letting him go. She watched his form diminish across the moor, the yellow rush-basket at his back moving up and down with each tread, and the creases behind his knees coming and going alternately till she could no longer see them. Though she did not know it Henchard formed at this moment much the same picture as he had presented when entering Casterbridge for the first time nearly a quarter of a century before; except, to be sure, that the serious addition to his years had considerably lessened the spring of his stride, that his state of hopelessness had weakened him, and imparted to his shoulders, as weighted by the basket, a perceptible bend.

He went on till he came to the first milestone, which stood in the bank, half way up a steep hill. He rested his basket on the top of the stone, placed his elbows on it, and gave way to a convulsive twitch, which was worse than a sob, because it was so hard and so dry.

'If I had only got her with me – if I only had!' he said. 'Hard work would be nothing to me then! But that was not to be. I – Cain – go alone as I deserve – an outcast and a vagabond. But my punishment is *not* greater than I can bear!'*

He sternly subdued his anguish, shouldered his basket, and went on.

Elizabeth, in the meantime, had breathed him a sigh, recovered her equanimity, and turned her face to Casterbridge. Before she had reached the first house she was met in her walk by Donald Farfrae. This was evidently not their first meeting that day; they joined hands without ceremony, and Farfrae anxiously asked, 'And is he gone – and did you tell him? – I mean of the other matter – not of ours.'

'He is gone; and I told him all I knew of your friend. Donald, who is he?'

'Well, well, dearie; you will know soon about that. And Mr Henchard will hear of it if he does not go far.'

'He will go far – he's bent upon getting out of sight and sound!'

She walked beside her lover, and when they reached the Crossways, or Bow, turned with him into Corn Street instead of going straight on to her own door. At Farfrae's house they stopped and went in.

Farfrae flung open the door of the ground-floor sitting-room, saying, 'There he is waiting for you,' and Elizabeth entered. In the arm-chair sat the broad-faced genial man who had called on Henchard on a memorable morning between one and two years before this time, and whom the latter had seen mount the coach and depart within half-an-hour of his arrival. It was Richard Newson. The meeting with the light-hearted father from whom she had been separated half-a-dozen years, as if by death, need hardly be detailed. It was an affecting one, apart from the question of paternity. Henchard's departure was in a moment explained. When the true facts came to be handled the difficulty of restoring her to her old belief in Newson was not so great as might have seemed likely, for Henchard's conduct itself was a proof that those facts were true. Moreover, she had grown up under Newson's paternal care; and even had Henchard been her father in nature, this father in early domiciliation might almost have carried the point against him, when the incidents of her parting with Henchard had a little worn off.

Newson's pride in what she had grown up to be was more than he could express. He kissed her again and again.

'I've saved you the trouble to come and meet me – ha-ha!' said Newson. 'The fact is that Mr Farfrae here, he said, "Come up and stop with me for a day or two, Captain Newson, and I'll bring her round." "Faith," says I, "so I will"; and here I am.'

'Well, Henchard is gone,' said Farfrae, shutting the door. 'He has done it all voluntarily, and, as I gather from Elizabeth, he has been very nice with her. I was got rather uneasy; but all is as it should be, and we will have no more deefficulties at all.'

'Now, that's very much as I thought,' said Newson, looking into the face of each by turns. 'I said to myself, ay, a hundred times, when I tried to get a peep at her unknown to herself – "Depend upon it, 'tis best that I should live on quiet for a few days like this till something turns up for the better." I now know you are all right, and what can I wish for more?'

'Well, Captain Newson, I will be glad to see ye here every day now, since it can do no harm,' said Farfrae. 'And what I've been thinking is that the wedding may as well be kept under my own roof, the house being large, and you being in lodgings by yourself – so that a great deal of trouble and expense would be saved ye? – and 'tis a convenience when a couple's married not to hae far to go to get home!'

'With all my heart,' said Captain Newson; 'since, as ye say, it can do no harm, now poor Henchard's gone; though I wouldn't have done it otherwise, or put myself in his way at all; for I've already in my lifetime been an intruder into his family quite as far as politeness can be expected to put up with. But what do the young woman say herself about it? Elizabeth, my child, come and hearken to what we be talking about, and not bide staring out o' the window as if ye didn't hear.'

'Donald and you must settle it,' murmured Elizabeth, still keeping up a scrutinizing gaze at some small object in the street.

'Well then,' continued Newson, turning anew to Farfrae with a face expressing thorough entry into the subject, 'that's how we'll have it. And, Mr Farfrae, as you provide so much, and house-room, and all that, I'll do my part in the drinkables, and see to the rum and schiedam* – maybe a dozen jars will be sufficient? – as many of the folk will be ladies, and perhaps they won't drink hard enough to make a high average in the reckoning? But you know best. I've provided for men and shipmates times enough, but I'm as ignorant as a child how many glasses of grog a woman, that's not a drinking woman, is expected to consume at these cere-monies?'

'Oh, none – we'll no want much of that – O no!' said Farfrae, shaking his head with appalled gravity. 'Do you leave all to me.'

When they had gone a little further in these particulars Newson, leaning back in his chair and smiling reflectively at the ceiling, said, 'I've never told ye, or have I, Mr Farfrae, how Henchard put me off the scent that time?'

He expressed ignorance of what the Captain alluded to.

'Ah, I thought I hadn't. I resolved that I would not, I remember, not to hurt the man's name. But now he's gone I can tell ye. Why, I came to Casterbridge nine or ten months* before that day last week that I found ye out. I had been here twice before then. The first time I passed through the town on my way westward, not knowing Elizabeth lived here. Then hearing at some place – I forget where – that a man of the name of Henchard had been mayor here, I came back, and called at his house one morning. The old rascal! – he said Elizabeth-Jane had died years ago.'

Elizabeth now gave earnest heed to his story.

'Now, it never crossed my mind that the man was selling me a packet,' continued Newson. 'And, if you'll believe me, I was that upset, that I went back to the coach that had brought me, and took passage onward without lying in the town half-an-hour. Ha-ha! – 'twas a good joke, and well carried out, and I give the man credit for't!'

Elizabeth-Jane was amazed at the intelligence. 'A joke? – O no!' she cried. 'Then he kept you from me, father, all those months, when you might have been here?'

The father admitted that such was the case.

'He ought not to have done it!' said Farfrae.

Elizabeth sighed. 'I said I would never forget him. But O! I think I ought to forget him now!'

Newson, like a good many rovers and sojourners among strange men and strange moralities, failed to perceive the enormity of Henchard's crime, notwithstanding that he himself had been the chief sufferer therefrom. Indeed, the attack upon the absent culprit waxing serious, he began to take Henchard's part.

'Well, 'twas not ten words that he said, after all,' Newson pleaded. 'And how could he know that I should be such a simpleton as to believe him? 'Twas as much my fault as his, poor fellow!'

'No,' said Elizabeth-Jane firmly, in her revulsion of feeling. 'He knew your disposition – you always were so trusting, father; I've heard my mother say so hundreds of times – and he did it to wrong you. After weaning me from you these five years by saying he was my father, he should not have done this.'

Thus they conversed; and there was nobody to set before

Elizabeth any extenuation of the absent one's deceit. Even had he been present Henchard might scarce have pleaded it, so little did he value himself or his good name.

'Well, well – never mind – it is all over and past,' said Newson good-naturedly. 'Now, about this wedding again.'

Chapter 44

Meanwhile, the man of their talk had pursued his solitary way eastward till weariness overtook him, and he looked about for a place of rest. His heart was so exacerbated at parting from the girl that he could not face an inn, or even a household of the most humble kind; and entering a field he lay down under a wheatrick, feeling no want of food. The very heaviness of his soul caused him to sleep profoundly.

The bright autumn sun shining into his eyes across the stubble awoke him the next morning early. He opened his basket and ate for his breakfast what he had packed for his supper; and in doing so overhauled the remainder of his kit. Although everything he brought necessitated carriage at his own back, he had secreted among his tools a few of Elizabeth-Jane's cast-off belongings, in the shape of gloves, shoes, a scrap of her handwriting, and the like; and in his pocket he carried a curl of her hair. Having looked at these things he closed them up again, and went onward.

During five consecutive days Henchard's rush basket rode along upon his shoulder between the highway hedges, the new yellow of the rushes catching the eye of an occasional field-labourer as he glanced through the quickset,* together with the wayfarer's hat and head, and down-turned face, over which the twig shadows moved in endless procession. It now became apparent that the direction of his journey was Weydon-Priors, which he reached on the afternoon of the sixth day.

The renowned hill whereon the annual fair had been held for so many generations was now bare of human beings, and almost of aught besides. A few sheep grazed thereabout, but these ran off when Henchard halted upon the summit. He deposited his basket upon the turf, and looked about with sad curiosity; till he discovered the road by which his wife and himself had entered on the upland so memorable to both, five-and-twenty years before.

'Yes, we came up that way,' he said, after ascertaining his bearings. 'She was carrying the baby, and I was reading a ballet-sheet. Then we crossed about here – she so sad and weary, and I speaking to her hardly at all, because of my cursed pride and mortification at being poor. Then we saw the tent – that must have stood more this way.' He walked to another spot; it was not really where the tent had stood, but it seemed so to him. 'Here we went in, and here we sat down. I faced this way. Then I drank, and committed my crime. It must have been just on that very pixy-ring* that she was standing when she said her last words to me before going off with him; I can hear their sound now, and the sound of her sobs: "O Mike! I've lived with thee all this while, and had nothing but temper. Now I'm no more to 'ee – I'll try my luck elsewhere." '

He experienced not only the bitterness of a man who finds, in looking back upon an ambitious course, that what he has sacrificed in sentiment was worth as much as what he has gained in substance; but the superadded bitterness of seeing his very recantation nullified. He had been sorry for all this long ago; but his attempts to replace ambition by love had been as fully foiled as his ambition itself. His wronged wife had foiled them by a fraud so grandly simple as to be almost a virtue. It was an odd sequence that out of all this tampering with social law came that flower of Nature, Elizabeth. Part of his wish to wash his hands of life arose from his perception of its contrarious inconsistencies – of Nature's jaunty readiness to support unorthodox social principles.

He intended to go on from this place – visited as an act of penance – into another part of the country altogether. But he could not help thinking of Elizabeth, and the quarter of the horizon in which she lived. Out of this it happened that the centrifugal tendency imparted by weariness of the world was counteracted by the centripetal influence of his love for his step-daughter. As a consequence, instead of following a straight course yet further away from Casterbridge, Henchard gradually, almost unconsciously, deflected from that right line of his first intention; till, by degrees, his wandering, like that of the Canadian woodsman, became part of a circle of which Casterbridge formed the centre. In ascending any particular hill he ascertained the bearings as nearly as he could by means of the sun, moon, or stars, and settled in his mind the exact direction in which Casterbridge and Elizabeth-Jane lay. Sneering at himself for his weakness he yet every hour – nay, every few minutes – conjectured her actions for the time being – her sitting down and rising up, her goings and comings, till thought of Newson's and Farfrae's counter-influence would pass like a cold blast over a pool, and efface her image. And then he would say to himself, 'O you fool! All this about a daughter who is no daughter of thine!'

At length he obtained employment at his own occupation of hay-trusser, work of that sort being in demand at this autumn time. The scene of his hiring was a pastoral farm near the old western highway, whose course was the channel of all such communications as passed between the busy centres of novelty and the remote Wessex boroughs. He had chosen the neighbour-hood of this artery from a sense that, situated here, though at a distance of fifty miles, he was virtually nearer to her whose welfare was so dear than he would be at a roadless spot only half as remote.

And thus Henchard found himself again on the precise standing which he had occupied a quarter of a century before. Externally there was nothing to hinder his making another start on the upward slope, and by his new lights achieving higher things than his soul in its half-formed state had been able to accomplish. But the ingenious machinery contrived by the Gods for reducing human possibilities of amelioration to a minimum – which arranges that wisdom to do shall come *pari passu** with the departure of zest for doing – stood in the way of all that. He had no wish to make an arena a second time of a world that had become a mere painted scene to him.

Very often, as his hay-knife crunched down among the sweet-smelling grassy stems, he would survey mankind and say to himself: 'Here and everywhere be folk dying before their time like frosted leaves, though wanted by their families, the country, and the world; while I, an outcast, an encumberer of the ground, wanted by nobody, and despised by all, live on against my will!'

He often kept an eager ear upon the conversation of those who passed along the road – not from a general curiosity by any means – but in the hope that among these travellers between Caster-bridge and London some would, sooner or later, speak of the former place. The distance, however, was too great to lend much probability to his desire; and the highest result of his attention to wayside words was that he did indeed hear the name 'Caster-bridge' uttered one day by the driver of a road-waggon. Henchard ran to the gate of the field he worked in, and hailed the speaker, who was a stranger.

'Yes – I've come from there, maister,' he said, in answer to Henchard's inquiry. 'I trade up and down, ye know; though, what with this travelling without horses that's getting so common, my work will soon be done.'

'Anything moving in the old place, mid* I ask?'

'All the same as usual.'

'I've heard that Mr Farfrae, the late mayor, is thinking of getting married. Now is that true or not?'

'I couldn't say for the life o' me. O no, I should think not.'

'But yes, John – you forget,' said a woman inside the waggon-tilt. 'What were them packages we carr'd there at the beginning o' the week? Surely they said a wedding was coming off soon – on Martin's Day?'*

The man declared he remembered nothing about it; and the waggon went on jangling over the hill.

Henchard was convinced that the woman's memory served her well. The date was an extremely probable one, there being no reason for delay on either side. He might, for that matter, write and inquire of Elizabeth; but his instinct for sequestration had made the course difficult. Yet before he left her she had said that for him to be absent from her wedding was not as she wished it to be.

The remembrance would continually revive in him now that it was not Elizabeth and Farfrae who had driven him away from them, but his own haughty sense that his presence was no longer desired. He had assumed the return of Newson without absolute proof that the Captain meant to return; still less that Elizabeth-Jane would welcome him; and with no proof whatever that if he did return he would stay. What if he had been mistaken in his views; if there had been no necessity that his own absolute separation from her he loved should be involved in these untoward incidents? To make one more attempt to be near her: to go back; to see her, to plead his cause before her, to ask forgiveness for his fraud, to endeavour strenuously to hold his own in her love; it was worth the risk of repulse, ay, of life itself.

But how to initiate this reversal of all his former resolves without causing husband and wife to despise him for his inconsistency was a question which made him tremble and brood.

He cut and cut his trusses two days more, and then he concluded his hesitancies by a sudden reckless determination to go to the wedding festivity. Neither writing nor message would be expected of him. She had regretted his decision to be absent – his unanticipated presence would fill the little unsatisfied corner that would probably have place in her just heart without him.

To intrude as little of his personality as possible upon a gay event with which that personality could show nothing in keeping, he decided not to make his appearance till evening – when stiffness would have worn off, and a gentle wish to let bygones by bygones would exercise its sway in all hearts.

He started on foot, two mornings before St Martin's-tide, allowing himself about sixteen miles to perform for each of the three days' journey, reckoning the wedding-day as one. There were only two towns, Melchester and Shottsford, of any importance along his course, and at the latter he stopped on the second night, not only to rest, but to prepare himself for the next evening.

Possessing no clothes but the working suit he stood in – now stained and distorted by their two months of hard usage, he entered a shop to make some purchases which should put him, externally at any rate, a little in harmony with the prevailing tone of the morrow. A rough yet respectable coat and hat, a new shirt and neck-cloth, were the chief of these; and having satisfied himself that in appearance at least he would not now offend her, he proceeded to the more interesting particular of buying her some present.

What should that present be? He walked up and down the street, regarding dubiously the display in the shop windows, from a gloomy sense that what he might most like to give her would be beyond his miserable pocket. At length a caged goldfinch met his eye. The cage was a plain and small one, the shop humble, and on inquiry he concluded he could afford the modest sum asked. A sheet of newspaper was tied round the little creature's wire prison, and with the wrapped up cage in his hand Henchard sought a lodging for the night.

Next day he set out upon the last stage, and was soon within the district which had been his dealing ground in bygone years. Part of the distance he travelled by carrier, seating himself in the darkest corner at the back of that trader's van; and as the other passengers, mainly women going short journeys, mounted and alighted in front of Henchard, they talked over much local news, not the least portion of this being the wedding then in course of celebration at the town they were nearing. It appeared from their accounts that the town band had been hired for the evening party, and, lest the convivial instincts of that body should get the better of their skill, the further step had been taken of engaging the string band from Budmouth, so that there would be a reserve of harmony to fall back upon in case of need.

He heard, however, but few particulars beyond those known to him already, the incident of the deepest interest on the journey being the soft pealing of the Casterbridge bells, which reached the travellers' ears while the van paused on the top of Yalbury Hill to have the drag* lowered. The time was just after twelve o'clock.

Those notes were a signal that all had gone well; that there had been no slip 'twixt cup and lip in this case; that Elizabeth-Jane and Donald Farfrae were man and wife.

Henchard did not care to ride any further with his chattering companions after hearing this sound. Indeed, it quite unmanned him; and in pursuance of his plan of not showing himself in Casterbridge street till evening, lest he should mortify Farfrae and his bride, he alighted here, with his bundle and bird-cage, and was soon left as a lonely figure on the broad white highway.

It was the hill near which he had waited to meet Farfrae, almost two years earlier, to tell him of the serious illness of his wife Lucetta. The place was unchanged; the same larches sighed the same notes; but Farfrae had another wife – and, as Henchard knew, a better one. He only hoped that Elizabeth-Jane had obtained a better home than had been hers at the former time.

He passed the remainder of the afternoon in a curious high-strung condition, unable to do much but think of the approaching meeting with her, and sadly satirize himself for his emotions thereon, as a Samson shorn.* Such an innovation on Casterbridge customs as a flitting of bridegroom and bride from the town immediately after the ceremony, was not likely, but if it should have taken place he would wait till their return. To assure himself on this point he asked a market-man when near the borough if the newly-married couple had gone away, and was promptly informed that they had not; they were at that hour, according to all accounts, entertaining a houseful of guests at their home in Corn Street.

Henchard dusted his boots, washed his hands at the river-side, and proceeded up the town under the feeble lamps. He need have made no inquiries beforehand, for on drawing near Farfrae's residence it was plain to the least observant that festivity prevailed within, and that Donald himself shared it, his voice being distinctly audible in the street, giving strong expression to a song of his dear native country that he loved so well as never to have revisited it. Idlers were standing on the pavement in front; and wishing to escape the notice of these Henchard passed quickly on to the door.

It was wide open; the hall was lighted extravagantly, and people were going up and down the stairs. His courage failed him; to enter footsore, laden, and poorly dressed in to the midst of such resplendency was to bring needless humiliation upon her he loved, if not to court repulse from her husband. Accordingly he went round into the street at the back that he knew so well, entered the garden, and came quietly into the house through the kitchen, temporarily depositing the bird and cage under a bush outside, to lessen the awkwardness of his arrival.

Solitude and sadness had so emolliated Henchard that he now feared circumstances he would formerly have scorned, and he began to wish that he had not taken upon himself to arrive at such a juncture. However, his progress was made unexpectedly easy by his discovering alone in the kitchen an elderly woman who seemed to be acting as provisional housekeeper during the convulsions from which Farfrae's establishment was just then suffering. She was one of those people whom nothing surprises, and though to her, a total stranger, his request must have seemed odd, she willingly volunteered to go up and inform the master and mistress of the house that 'a humble old friend' had come.

On second thoughts she said that he had better not wait in the kitchen, but come up into the little back-parlour, which was empty. He thereupon followed her thither, and she left him. Just as she had got across the landing to the door of the best parlour a dance was struck up, and she returned to say that she would wait till that was over before announcing him – Mr and Mrs Farfrae having both joined in the figure.

The door of the front room had been taken off its hinges to give more space, and that of the room Henchard sat in being ajar, he could see fractional parts of the dancers whenever their gyrations brought them near the doorway, chiefly in the shape of the skirts of dresses and streaming curls of hair; together with about three-fifths of the band in profile, including the restless shadow of a fiddler's elbow, and the tip of the bass-viol bow.

The gaiety jarred upon Henchard's spirits; and he could not quite understand why Farfrae, a much-sobered man, and a widower, who had had his trials, should have cared for it all, notwithstanding the fact that he was quite a young man still, and quickly kindled to enthusiasm by dance and song. That the quiet Elizabeth, who had long ago appraised life at a moderate value, and who knew in spite of her maidenhood that marriage was as a rule no dancing matter, should have had zest for this revelry surprised him still more. However, young people could not be quite old people, he concluded, a custom was omnipotent.

With the progress of the dance the performers spread out somewhat, and then for the first time he caught a glimpse of the once despised daughter who had mastered him, and made his heart ache. She was in a dress of white silk or satin, he was not near enough to say which — snowy white, without a tinge of milk or cream; and the expression of her face was one of nervous pleasure rather than of gaiety. Presently Farfrae came round, his exuberant Scotch movement making him conspicuous in a moment. The pair were not dancing together, but Henchard could discern that whenever the changes of the figure made them the partners of a moment their emotions breathed a much subtler essence than at other times.

By degrees Henchard became aware that the measure was trod by some one who out-Farfraed Farfrae* in saltatory* intenseness. This was strange, and it was stranger to find that the eclipsing personage was Elizabeth-Jane's partner. The first time that Henchard saw him was sweeping grandly round, his head quivering and low down, his legs in the form of an X and his back towards the door. The next time he came round in the other direction, his white waistcoat preceding his face, and his toes preceding his white waistcoat. That happy face — Henchard's complete discomfiture lay in it. It was Newson's, who had indeed come and supplanted him.

Henchard pushed to the door, and for some seconds made no other movement. He rose to his feet, and stood like a dark ruin, obscured by 'the shade from his own soul upthrown'.*

But he was no longer the man to stand these reverses unmoved. His agitation was great, and he would fain have been gone, but before he could leave the dance had ended, the housekeeper had informed Elizabeth-Jane of the stranger who awaited her, and she entered the room immediately.

'O – it is – Mr Henchard!' she said, starting back.

'What; Elizabeth?' he cried, as he seized her hand. 'What do you say? – Mr Henchard? Don't, don't scourge me like that! Call me worthless old Henchard – anything – but don't 'ee be so cold as this! O my maid – I see you have another – a real father in my place. Then you know all; but don't give all your thought to him! Do ye save a little room for me!'

She flushed up, and gently drew her hand away. 'I could have loved you always – I would have, gladly,' said she. 'But how can I when I know you have deceived me so – so bitterly deceived me! You persuaded me that my father was not my father – allowed me to live on in ignorance of the truth for years; and then when he, my warm-hearted real father, came to find me, cruelly sent him away with a wicked invention of my death, which nearly broke his heart. O how can I love as I once did a man who has served us like this!'

Henchard's lips half parted to begin an explanation. But he shut them up like a vice, and uttered not a sound. How should he, there and then, set before her with any effect the palliatives of his great faults – that he had himself been deceived in her identity at first, till informed by her mother's letter that his own child had died; that, in the second accusation, his lie had been the last desperate throw of a gamester who loved her affection better than his own honour? Among the many hindrances to such a pleading not the least was this, that he did not sufficiently value himself to lessen his sufferings by strenuous appeal or elaborate argument.

Waiving, therefore, his privilege of self-defence, he regarded only her discomposure. 'Don't ye distress yourself on my account,' he said, with proud superiority. 'I would not wish it – at such a time, too, as this. I have done wrong in coming to 'ee – I see my error. But it is only for once, so forgive it. I'll never trouble 'ee again, Elizabeth-Jane – no, not to my dying day! Good-night. Good-bye!'

Then, before she could collect her thoughts, Henchard went out from her rooms, and departed from the house by the back way as he had come; and she saw him no more.

Chapter 45

It was about a month after the day which closed as in the last chapter. Elizabeth-Jane had grown accustomed to the novelty of her situation, and the only difference between Donald's movements now and formerly was that he hastened indoors rather more quickly after business hours than he had been in the habit of doing for some time.

Newson had stayed in Casterbridge three days after the wedding party (whose gaiety, as might have been surmised, was of his making rather than of the married couple's), and was stared at and honoured as became the returned Crusoe* of the hour. But whether or not because Casterbridge was difficult to excite by dramatic returns and disappearances, through having been for centuries an assize town, in which sensational exits from the world, antipodean absences,* and such like, were half-yearly occurrences, the inhabitants did not altogether lose their equanimity on his account. On the fourth morning he was discoverd disconsolately climbing a hill, in his craving to get a glimpse of the sea from somewhere or other. The contiguity of salt water proved to be such a necessity of his existence that he preferred Budmouth as a place of residence, notwithstanding the society of his daughter in the other town. Thither he went, and settled in lodgings in a green-shuttered cottage which had a bow-window, jutting out sufficiently to afford glimpses of a vertical strip of blue sea to any one opening the sash, and leaning forward far enough to look through a narrow lane of tall intervening houses.

Elizabeth-Jane was standing in the middle of her upstairs parlour, critically surveying some re-arrangement of articles with her head to one side, when the housemaid came in with the announcement, 'Oh, please ma'am, we know now how that bird-cage came there.'

In exploring her new domain during the first week of residence, gazing with critical satisfaction on this cheerful room and that, penetrating cautiously into dark cellars, sallying forth with gingerly tread to the garden, now leaf-strewn by autumn winds, and thus, like a wise field-marshal, estimating the capabilities of the site whereon she was about to open her house-keeping campaign – Mrs Donald Farfrae had discovered in a screened corner a new bird-cage, shrouded in newspaper, and at the bottom of the cage a little ball of feathers – the dead body of a goldfinch. Nobody could tell her how the bird and cage had come there; though that the poor little songster had been starved to death was evident. The sadness of the incident had made an impression on her. She had not been able to forget it for days, despite Farfrae's tender banter; and now when the matter had been nearly forgotten it was again revived.

'Oh, please ma'am, we know how that bird-cage came there. That farmer's man who called on the evening of the wedding – he was seen wi' it in his hand as he came up the street; and 'tis thoughted that he put it down while he came in with his message, and then went away forgetting where he had left it.'

This was enough to set Elizabeth thinking, and in thinking she seized hold of the idea, at one feminine bound, that the caged bird had been brought by Henchard for her as a wedding gift and token of repentance. He had not expressed to her any regrets or excuses for what he had done in the past; but it was a part of his nature to extenuate nothing,* and live on as one of his own worst accusers.* She went out, looked at the cage, buried the starved little singer, and from that hour her heart softened towards the self-alienated man.

When her husband came in she told him her solution of the bird-cage mystery; and begged Donald to help her in finding out, as soon as possible, whither Henchard had banished himself, that she might make her peace with him; try to do something to render his life less that of an outcast, and more tolerable to him. Although Farfrae had never so passionately like Henchard as Henchard had liked him, he had, on the other hand, never so passionately hated in the same direction as his former friend had done; and he was therefore not the least indisposed to assist Elizabeth-Jane in her laudable plan.

But it was by no means easy to set about discovering Henchard. He had apparently sunk into the earth on leaving Mr and Mrs Farfrae's door. Elizabeth-Jane remembered what he had once attempted; and trembled.

But though she did not know it Henchard had become a changed man since then – as far, that is, as change of emotional basis can justify such a radical phrase; and she needed not to fear. In a few days Farfrae's inquiries elicited that Henchard had been seen by one who knew him walking steadily along the Melchester highway eastward, at twelve o'clock at night – in other words, retracing his steps on the road by which he had come.

This was enough; and the next morning Farfrae might have been discovered driving his gig out of Casterbridge in that direction, Elizabeth-Jane sitting beside him, wrapped in a thick flat fur – the victorine of the period* – her complexion somewhat richer than formerly, and an incipient matronly dignity, which the serene Minerva-eyes* of one 'whose gestures beamed with mind'* made becoming, settling on her face. Having herself arrived at a promising haven from at least the grosser troubles of her life, her object was to place Henchard in some similar quietude before he should sink into that lower stage of existence which was only too possible to him now.

After driving along the highway for a few miles they made further inquiries, and learnt of a road-mender, who had been working thereabouts for weeks, that he had observed such a man at the time mentioned; he had left the Melchester coach-road at Weatherbury by a forking highway which skirted the north of Egdon Heath. Into this road they directed the horse's head, and soon were bowling across that ancient country whose surface never had been stirred to a finger's depth, save by the scratchings of rabbits, since brushed by the feet of the earliest tribes. The tumuli these had left behind, dun and shagged with heather, jutted roundly into the sky from the uplands, as though they were the full breasts of Diana Multimammia* supinely extended there.

They searched Egdon, but found no Henchard. Farfrae drove onward, and by the afternoon reached the neighbourhood of some extension of the heath to the north of Anglebury, a prominent feature of which, in the form of a blasted clump of firs on the summit of a hill, they soon passed under. That the road they were following had, up to this point, been Henchard's track on foot they were pretty certain; but the ramifications which now began to reveal themselves in the route made further progress in the right direction a matter of pure guess-work, and Donald strongly advised his wife to give up the search in person, and trust to other means for obtaining news of her stepfather. They were now a score of miles at least from home, but, by resting the horse for a couple of hours at a village they had just traversed, it would be possible to get back to Casterbridge that same day; while to go much further afield would reduce them to the necessity of camping out for the night; 'and that will make a hole in a sovereign,' said Farfrae. She pondered the position, and agreed with him.

He accordingly drew rein, but before reversing their direction paused a moment and looked vaguely round upon the wide country which the elevated position disclosed. While they looked a solitary human form came from under the clump of trees, and crossed ahead of them. The person was some labourer; his gait was shambling, his regard fixed in front of him as absolutely as if he wore blinkers; and in his hand he carried a few sticks. Having crossed the road he descended into a ravine, where a cottage revealed itself, which he entered.

'If it were not so far away from Casterbridge I should say that must be poor Whittle. 'Tis just like him,' observed Elizabeth-Jane.

'And it may be Whittle, for he's never been to the yard these three weeks, going away without saying any word at all; and I owing him for two days' work, without knowing who to pay it to.'

The possibility led them to alight, and at least make an inquiry at the cottage. Farfrae hitched the reins to the gate-post, and they approached what was of humble dwellings surely the humblest. The walls, built of kneaded clay originally faced with a trowel, had been worn by years of rain-washings to a lumpy crumbling surface, channelled and sunken from its plane, its gray rents held together here and there by a leafy strap of ivy which could scarcely find substance enough for the purpose. The rafters were sunken, and the thatch of the roof in ragged holes. Leaves from the fence had been blown into the corners of the doorway, and lay there undisturbed. The door was ajar; Farfrae knocked; and he who stood before them was Whittle, as they had conjectured.

His face showed marks of deep sadness, his eyes lighting on them with an unfocused gaze; and he still held in his hand the few sticks he had been out to gather. As soon as he recognized them he started.

'What, Abel Whittle; is it that ye are heere?' said Farfrae.

'Ay, yes, sir!' You see he was kind-like to mother when she wer here below, though 'a was rough to me.'

'Who are you talking of?'

'O sir – Mr Henchet! Didn't ye know it? He's just gone – about half-an-hour ago, by the sun; for I've got no watch to my name.'

'Not – dead?' faltered Elizabeth-Jane.

'Yes, ma'am, he's gone! He was kind-like to mother when she

wer here below, sending her the best ship-coal,* and hardly any ashes from it at all; and taties, and such-like that were very needful to her. I seed en go down street on the night of your worshipful's wedding to the lady at yer side, and I thought he looked low and faltering. And I followed en over Grey's Bridge, and he turned and zeed me, and said, "You go back!" But I followed, and he turned again, and said, "Do you hear, sir? Go back!" But I zeed that he was low, and I followed on still. Then 'a said, "Whittle, what do ye fellow me for when I've told ye to go back all these times?" And I said, "Because, sir, I see things be bad with 'ee, and ye wer kind-like to mother if ye were rough to me, and I would fain be kind-like to you." Then he walked on, and I followed; and he never complained at me no more. We walked on like that all night; and in the blue o' the morning, when 'twas hardly day, I looked ahead o' me, and I zeed that he wambled, and could hardly drag along. By that time we had got past here, but I had seen that this house was empty as I went by, and I got him to come back; and I took down the boards from the windows, and helped him inside. "What, Whittle," he said, "and can ye really be such a poor fond fool as to care for such a wretch as I!" Then I went on further, and some neighbourly woodmen lent me a bed, and a chair, and a few other traps, and we brought 'em here, and made him as comfortable as we could. But he didn't gain strength, for you see, ma'am, he couldn't eat – no, no appetite at all – and he got weaker; and to-day he died. One of the neighbous have gone to get a man to measure him.'

'Dear me – is that so!' said Farfrae.

As for Elizabeth, she said nothing.

'Upon the head of his bed he pinned a piece of paper, with some writing upon it,' continued Abel Whittle. 'But not being a man o' letters, I can't read writing; so I don't know what it is. I can get it and show ye.'

They stood in silence while he ran into the cottage; returning in a moment with a crumpled scrap of paper. On it there was pencilled as follows:

MICHAEL HENCHARD'S WILL

That Elizabeth-Jane Farfrae be not told of my death, or made to grieve on account of me.

& that I be not bury'd in consecrated ground.
& that no sexton be asked to toll the bell.
& that nobody is wished to see my dead body.
& that no murners walk behind me at my funeral.
& that no flours be planted on my grave.
& that no man remember me.
To this I put my name.

MICHAEL HENCHARD

'What are we to do?' said Donald, when he had handed the paper to her.

She could not answer distinctly. 'O Donald!' she said at last through her tears, 'what bitterness lies there! O I would not have minded so much if it had not been for my unkindness at that last parting! . . . But there's no altering – so it must be.'

What Henchard had written in the anguish of his dying was respected as far as practicable by Elizabeth-Jane, though less from a sense of the sacredness of last words, as such, than from her independent knowledge that the man who wrote them meant what he said. She knew the directions to be a piece of the same stuff that his whole life was made of, and hence were not to be tampered with to give herself a mournful pleasure, or her husband credit for large-heartedness.

All was over at last, even her regrets for having misunderstood him on his last visit, for not having searched him out sooner, though these were deep and sharp for a good while. From this time forward Elizabeth-Jane found herself in a latitude of calm weather, kindly and grateful in itself, and doubly so after the Capharnaum* in which some of her preceding years had been spent. As the lively and sparkling emotions of her early married life cohered into an equable serenity, the finer movements of her nature found scope in discovering to the narrow-lived ones around her the secret (as she had once learnt it) of making limited opportunities endurable; which she deemed to consist in the cunning enlargement, by a species of microscopic treatment, of those minute forms of satisfaction that offer themselves to everybody not in positive pain; which, thus handled, have much of the same inspiriting effect upon life as wider interests cursorily embraced.

Her teaching had a reflex action upon herself, insomuch that she thought she could perceive no great personal difference between being respected in the nether parts of Casterbridge and glorified at the uppermost end of the social world. Her position was, indeed, to a marked degree one that, in the common phrase, afforded much to be thankful for. That she was not demonstratively thankful was no fault of hers. Her experience had been of a kind to teach her, rightly or wrongly, that the doubtful honour of a brief transit through a sorry world hardly called for effusiveness, even when the path was suddenly irradiated at some half-way point by daybeams rich as hers. But her strong sense that neither she nor any human being deserved less than was given, did not blind her to the fact that there were others receiving less who had deserved much more. And in being forced to class herself among the fortunate she did not cease to wonder at the persistence of the unforeseen, when the one to whom such unbroken tranquillity had been accorded in the adult stage was she whose youth had seemed to teach that happiness was but the occasional episode in a general drama of pain.

GENERAL PREFACE TO THE
WESSEX EDITION OF 1912

In accepting a proposal for a definite edition of these productions in prose and verse I have found an opportunity of classifying the novels under heads that show approximately the author's aim, if not his achievement, in each book of the series at the date of its composition. Sometimes the aim was lower than at other times; sometimes, where the intention was primarily high, force of circumstances (among which the chief were the necessities of magazine publication) compelled a modification, great or slight, of the original plan. Of a few, however, of the longer novels, and of many of the shorter tales, it may be assumed that they stand to-day as much as they would have stood if no accidents had obstructed the channel between the writer and the public. That many of them, if any, stand as they would stand if written *now* is not to be supposed.

In the classification of these fictitious chronicles – for which the name of 'The Wessex Novels' was adopted, and is still retained – the first group is called 'Novels of Character and Environment', and contains those which approach most nearly to uninfluenced works; also one or two which, whatever their quality in some few of their episodes, may claim a verisimilitude in general treatment and detail.

The second group is distinguished as 'Romances and Fantasies', a sufficiently descriptive definition. The third class – 'Novels of Ingenuity' – show a not infrequent disregard of the probable in the chain of events, and depend for their interest mainly on the incidents themselves. They might also be characterized as 'Experiments', and were written for the nonce simply; though despite the artificiality of their fable some of their scenes are not without fidelity to life.

It will not be supposed that these differences are distinctly perceptible in every page of every volume. It was inevitable that blendings and alternations should occur in all. Moreover, as it was not thought desirable in every instance to change the arrangement of the shorter stories to which readers have grown accustomed, certain of these may be found under headings to which an acute judgment might deny appropriateness.

It has sometimes been conceived of novels that evolve their action on a circumscribed scene – as do many (though not all) of these – that they cannot be so inclusive in their exhibition of human nature as novels wherein the scenes cover large extents of country, in which events figure amid towns and cities, even wander over the four quarters of the globe. I am not concerned to argue this point further than to suggest that the conception is an untrue one in respect of the elementary passions. But I would state that the geographical limits of the stage here trodden were not absolutely forced upon the writer by circumstances; he forced them upon himself from judgment. I considered that our magnificent heritage from the Greeks in dramatic literature found sufficient room for a large proportion of its action in an extent of their country not much larger than the half-dozen counties here reunited under the old name of Wessex, that the domestic emotions have throbbed in Wessex nooks with as much intensity as in the palaces of Europe, and that, anyhow, there was quite enough human nature in Wessex for one man's literary purpose. So far was I possessed by this idea that I kept within the frontiers when it would have been easier to overleap them and give more cosmopolitan features to the narrative.

Thus, though the people in most of the novels (and in much of the shorter verse) are dwellers in a province bounded on the north by the Thames, on the south by the English Channel, on the east by a line running from Hayling Island to Windsor Forest, and on the west by the Cornish coast, they were meant to be typically and essentially those of any and every place where

> Thought's the slave of life, and the life time's fool

– beings in whose hearts and minds that which is apparently local should be really universal.

But whatever the success of this intention, and the value of these novels as delineations of humanity, they have at least a humble supplementary quality of which I may be justified in reminding the reader, though it is one that was quite unintentional and unforeseen. At the dates represented in the various narrations things were like that in Wessex: the inhabitants lived in certain ways, engaged in certain occupations, kept alive certain customs, just as they are shown doing in these pages. And in particularizing such I have often been reminded of Boswell's remarks on the trouble to which he was put and the pilgrimages he was obliged to make to authenticate some detail, though the labour was one which would bring him no praise. Unlike his achievement, however, on which an error would as he says have brought discredit, if these country customs and vocations, obsolete and obsolescent, had been detailed wrongly, nobody would have discovered such errors to the end of Time. Yet I have instituted inquiries to correct tricks of memory, and striven against temptations to exaggerate, in order to preserve for my own satisfaction a fairly true record of a vanishing life.

It is advisable also to state here, in response to inquiries from readers interested in landscape, prehistoric antiquities, and especially old English architecture, that the description of these backgrounds has been done from the real – that is to say, has something real for its basis, however illusively treated. Many features of the first two kinds have been given under their existing names; for instance, the Vale of Blackmoor or Blakemore, Hambledon Hill, Bulbarrow, Nettlecombe Tout, Dogbury Hill, High-Stoy, Bubb-Down Hill, The Devil's Kitchen, Cross-in-Hand, Long-Ash Lane, Benvill Lane, Giant's Hill, Crimmercrock Lane, and Stonehenge. The rivers Froom, or Frome, and Stour, are, of course, well known as such. And the further idea was that large towns and points tending to mark the outline of Wessex – such as Bath, Plymouth, The Start, Portland Bill, Southampton, etc. – should be named clearly. The scheme was not greatly elaborated, but, whatever its value, the names remain still.

In respect of places described under fictitious or ancient names in the novels – for reasons that seemed good at the time of writing them – and kept up in the poems – discerning people have affirmed in print that they clearly recognize the originals: such as Shaftesbury in 'Shaston', Sturminster Newton in 'Stourcastle', Dorchester in 'Casterbridge', Salisbury Plain in 'The Great Plain', Cranborne Chase in 'The Chase', Beaminster in 'Emminster', Bere Regis in 'Kingsbere', Woodbury Hill in 'Greenhill', Wool Bridge in 'Wellbridge', Harfoot or Harput Lane in 'Stagfoot Lane', Hazlebury in 'Nuttlebury', Bridport in 'Port Bredy', Maiden Newton in 'Chalk Newton', a farm near Nettlecombe Tout in 'Flintcomb Ash', Sherborne in 'Sherton Abbas', Milton Abbey in

'Middleton Abbey', Cerne Abbas in 'Abbot's Cernel', Evershot in 'Evershed', Taunton in 'Toneborough', Bournemouth in 'Sandbourne', Winchester in 'Wintoncester', Oxford in 'Christminster', Reading in 'Aldbrickham', Newbury in 'Kennetbridge', Wantage in 'Alfredston', Basingstoke in 'Stoke Barehills', and so on. Subject to the qualifications above given, that no detail is guaranteed – that the portraiture of fictitiously named towns and villages was only suggested by certain real places, and wantonly wanders from inventorial descriptions of them – I do not contradict these keen hunters for the real; I am satified with their statements as at least an indication of their interest in the scenes.

Thus much for the novels. Turning now to the verse – to myself the more individual part of my literary fruitage – I would say that, unlike some of the fiction, nothing interfered with the writer's freedom in respect of its form or content. Several of the poems – indeed many – were produced before novel-writing had been thought of as a pursuit; but few saw the light till all the novels had been published. The limited stage to which the majority of the latter confine their exhibitions has not been adhered to here in the same proportion, the dramatic part especially having a very broad theatre of action. It may thus relieve the circumscribed areas treated in the prose, if such relief be needed. To be sure, one might argue that by surveying Europe from a celestial point of vision – as in *The Dynasts* – that continent becomes virtually a province – a Wessex, an Attica, even a mere garden – and hence is made to conform to the principle of the novels, however far it outmeasures their region. But that may be as it will.

The few volumes filled by the verse cover a producing period of some eighteen years first and last, while the seventeen or more volumes of novels represent correspondingly about four-and-twenty years. One is reminded by this disproportion in time and result how much more concise and quintessential expression becomes when given in rhythmic form than when shaped in the language of prose.

One word on what has been called the present writer's philosophy of life, as exhibited more particularly in this metrical section of his compositions. Positive views on the Whence and the Wherefore of things have never been advanced by this pen as a consistent philosophy. Nor is it likely, indeed, that imaginative writings extending over more than forty years would exhibit a coherent scientific theory of the universe even if it had been attempted – of that universe concerning which Spencer owns to the 'paralyzing thought' that possibly there exists no comprehension of it anywhere. But such objectless consistency never has been attempted, and the sentiments in the following pages have been stated truly to be mere impressions of the moment, and not convictions or arguments.

That these impressions have been condemned as 'pessimistic' – as if that were a very wicked adjective – shows a curious muddle-mindedness. It must be obvious that there is a higher characteristic of philosophy than pessimism, or than meliorism, or even than the optimism of these critics – which is truth. Existence is either ordered in a certain way, or it is not so ordered, and conjectures which harmonize best with experience are removed above all comparison with other conjectures which do not so harmonize. So that to say one view is worse than other views without proving it erroneous implies the possibility of a false view being better or more expedient than a true view; and no pragmatic proppings can make that *idolum specus* stand on its feet, for it postulates a prescience denied to humanity.

And there is another consideration. Differing natures find their tongue in the presence of differing spectacles. Some natures become vocal at tragedy, some are made vocal by comedy, and it seems to me that to whichever of these aspects of life a writer's instinct for expression the more readily responds, to that he should allow it to respond. That before a contrasting side of things he remains undemonstrative need not be assumed to mean that he remains unperceiving.

It was my hope to add to these volumes of verse as many more as would make a fairly comprehensive cycle of the whole. I had wished that those in dramatic, ballad, and narrative form should include most of the cardinal situations which occur in social and public life, and those in lyric form a round of emotional experiences of some completeness. But

The petty done, the undone vast!

The more written the more seems to remain to be written; and the night cometh. I realize that these hopes and plans, except possibly to the extent of a volume or two, must remain unfulfilled.

October 1911   T. H.

NOTES

---

p. xxix the days recalled by the tale The period of the novel cannot be
defined exactly, but the action takes place before the repeal of the Corn
Laws in 1846, and prior to the coming of the railway to Dorchester in
1847 (see note below). It can probably be estimated that the main
events of the story end no later than the mid-1840s.

the home Corn Trade ... harvest weather The Corn Law of 1815
prohibited the import of corn until the price on the home market had
reached eighty shillings a quarter, a huge price at that period. The aim
of the law was to protect landowners and farmers in the period of
falling prices after the Napoleonic Wars, but the effect was disastrous
fluctuations in the price of bread when adverse weather and poor
harvests led to spiralling prices and a subsequent flooding of the
market with imported corn. A series of bad harvests before 1842 and
the trade depression of the early 1840s brought matters to a head, and
in 1846, following the failure of the potato crop in Ireland and another
bad corn harvest in England in 1845, Sir Robert Peel repealed the Corn
Laws, substantially reducing import duties and thereby helping to
stabilise the price of bread.

Casterbridge Dorchester, the county town of Dorset. For a map and
account of locations in Casterbridge/Dorchester, see F. B. Pinion, *A
Hardy Companion* (London, 1968), and Denys Kay-Robinson,
Hardy's Wessex Reappraised (Newton Abbot, 1972).

the sale of a wife by her husband This was not a common occurrence,
but a number of instances are recorded for the period. In his
Commonplace Book (III) Hardy noted reports of wife-selling in 1826
and 1827 from the *Dorset County Chronicle*.

the uncertain harvests ... Corn Laws See note above.

the visit of a Royal personage ... part of England Prince Albert passed
through Dorchester by train in 1849 on his way to lay the foundation
stone of the Portland Breakwater. The railway had reached Dorchester
in 1847, but Hardy's account of the royal visit (see p. 226) places it
before the coming of the railway.

The present edition ... the omission This refers to the final section of

Chapter 44 (Henchard's visit to Elizabeth-Jane with the goldfinch) which was reinstated on the advice of Rebekah and Catherine Owen, two ardent admirers of Hardy from New York.

Wessex life   In his preface to the 1895 edition of *Far from the Madding Crowd*, Hardy gave the following explanation of the genesis of the term 'Wessex' to describe the fictitious territory of his novels:

> In reprinting this story for a new edition I am reminded that it was in the chapters of *Far from the Madding Crowd*, as they appeared month by month in a popular magazine, that I first ventured to adopt the word 'Wessex' from the pages of early English history, and give it a fictitious significance as the existing name of the district once included in that extinct kingdom. The series of novels I projected being mainly of the kind called local, they seemed to require a territorial definition of some sort to lend unity to their scene. Finding that the area of a single county did not afford a canvas large enough for this purpose, and that there were objections to an invented name, I disinterred the old one. The region designated was known but vaguely, and I was often asked even by educated people where it lay. However, the press and the public were kind enough to welcome the fanciful plan, and willingly joined me in the anachronism of imagining a Wessex population living under Queen Victoria; – a modern Wessex of railways, the penny post, mowing and reaping machines, union workhouses, lucifer matches, labourers who could read and write, and National school children. But I believe I am correct in stating that, until the existence of this contemporaneous Wessex in place of the usual counties was announced in the present story, in 1874, it had never been heard of in fiction and current speech, if at all, and that the expression, 'a Wessex peasant', or 'a Wessex custom', would theretofore have been taken to refer to nothing later in date than the Norman Conquest . . .

Southron   Southern

p. xxx professor of the tongue in question   This refers to Hardy's friend Sir George Douglas, a Scottish landowner and author.

February 1895 – May 1912   The Preface originally appeared in the Osgood, McIlvaine edition of 1895. For the 1912 Wessex Edition, Hardy made a few minor revisions to the Preface and added the last sentence.

p. 3 Weydon-Priors   Refers to the village of Weyhill, near Andover in Hampshire, once famous for its annual sheep-selling fair.

fustian   A thick, twilled, cotton cloth with a short pile or nap, usually dark in colour.

a wimble for hay-bonds   This was an instrument for twisting together strands of hay to tie up trusses or bundles of hay.

a ballad sheet   A broadsheet, i.e. a large sheet of paper printed on one side, possibly containing the text of a song, or information about a topic of current interest.

p. 4 the hard . . . fair play   The young woman has already learned the random and unbenign nature of human destiny.

a nimbus   Deities were imagined appearing on earth surrounded by a bright cloud or nimbus; also used to refer to a saint's halo. Its usage here suggests irony.

breve   A musical note, of the value of two semibreves.

p. 5 nater   nature

volk   folk

a thatched hurdle   This was a portable shelter made of wood interwoven with straw, used to protect lambing ewes from the wind.

journeymen   Men who had completed their apprenticeship to a particular trade, but were still employees rather than principals: an important social distinction.

p. 6 thimble-riggers   Tricksters who 'rigged' the popular game of guessing the location of a pea under several thimbles.

Furmity   Also known as frumenty, this was a nourishing dish made of de-husked wheat boiled in milk and flavoured with the ingredients Hardy lists below.

bell-metal   An alloy of about four parts of copper to one of tin, used for making bells.

p. 7 the rocks . . . maelstrom depths   This probably refers to Scylla, the rock on the Italian side of the Straits of Messina that faced the whirlpool of Charybdis on the coast of Sicily, a horrible choice for sailors.

smugglers   Rum was smuggled to avoid the high import duty on wines and spirits during and after the Napoleonic Wars. Hardy's grandfather was involved in the active smuggling trade along the Dorset coast.

p. 8 if I were a free man again   Henchard blames his family for his lack of success; ironic, given his current 'thraldom' to alcohol.

holler   hollow

p. 9 chiel   child

staylace   The lace or laces that fastened a woman's corset.

p. 10 'pon my 'vation   i.e. upon my salvation

p. 12 clane   clean, entirely. The word may suggest the honest nature of the transaction, from Susan's point of view.

He rose . . . raging loud This paragraph is characteristic of Hardy's interest in the relationship between human beings and the natural world, although it is rarely stated so specifically as here. Throughout the Wessex novels, descriptions of nature illuminate the activities of the protagonists.

p. 13 keacorn throat

the great trumpet The trumpet announcing Judgment Day.

p. 14 unencumbered This reflects Henchard's feeling (p. 8) that marriage has robbed him of the opportunities for success that he would have had as 'a free man'.

felloe The rim of a spoked wheel.

p. 15 the Seven Sleepers had a dog The Seven Sleepers of Ephesus were noble Christian youths who fled from the persecution of Decius (AD 250) and slept hidden in a cave for two centuries, when they awoke, bore witness to the resurrection of the body, and died again. The version in Chapter 18 of the Koran says that they had a dog who lay at the entrance of the cave with legs outstretched.

p. 16 fetichistic I.e. believing in the magical powers of inanimate objects.

sacrarium The area around the altar or Communion-table.

foot-pace The raised platform on which the altar stands.

strook struck

p. 18 withy basket A basket made of flexible willow branches.

black stuff gown A dress made of woven material, probably wool.

coopers Makers of barrels, casks and other wooden containers.

November 184– Cf. p. 58, where Elizabeth-Jane says, 'Father was lost last spring.' An anomaly that Hardy failed to iron out when preparing the definitive editions of the text.

p. 20 *soi-disant* (French) self-styled; the term suggests the ambiguity of Susan's position.

p. 22 the liege subjects of Labour The vassals of Labour; those forced to work.

needle she was filling i.e. threading with twine

p. 23 carking harassing; wearing her down

p. 25 coomb a deep hollow; valley

burgh and champaign town and countryside

dimity A strong cotton fabric, given the effect of stripes or patterns by weaving several threads together.

p. 26 barge-boards A term for boards used to conceal jutting beams around a gable, often highly decorated.

brick-nogging The brick in-fill in timber-framed walls.

Scythes . . . pattens and clogs Agricultural tools and accoutrements: **reap-hook** instrument similar to a sickle, used for reaping; **bill-hook** a thick knife with a hooked end, used for pruning, etc; **mattock** tool used to loosen hard soil, dig up trees, etc; **butter-firkin** small cask, originally the size of a quarter-barrel; **field-flagon** beer-container, used when working in the fields; **seed-lip** basket in which to carry seed while sowing by hand; **pattens and clogs** wooden-soled overshoes to protect the feet from mud and wet.

The curfew This was the practice of ringing an evening bell, originally a signal that fires were to be extinguished for the night.

the Sicilian Mariners' Hymn A tune popular with hymn-writers of the period, possibly Sicilian in origin.

p. 27 manna-food Manna miraculously appeared to sustain the Israelites in the Wilderness (see Exodus 16); i.e. food that is divinely rather than humanly supplied.

swipes weak, poor quality beer

corn-factor dealer in corn or grain

growed wheat This was 'grown' wheat that had sprouted before being harvested, usually as a result of bad weather delaying the harvest.

pudden pudding

plim like blowed bladders swell up like inflated animal bladders (used as balls)

p. 28 'The Roast Beef of Old England' A song composed by the bass singer Richard Leveridge (c. 1670–1758).

fall A veil attached to the front of a woman's hat or bonnet.

p. 30 akin to a coach I.e. related to a man of sufficient standing to ride in an official coach, here the mayoral coach.

rummers These were large drinking glasses. The spoon would draw the heat and prevent the rummer from cracking as the hot grog was poured in.

p. 31 a banded teetotaller Someone pledged to abstain from alcohol. Possibly a reference to the teetotal Band of Hope, founded in the

1840s, although 'banded' is more likely to be used in its sense of 'bonded', i.e. restrained by a binding agreement, in this case Henchard's oath.

the Lord upon the jovial Jews While Moses was receiving the Ten Commandments on Mount Sinai, the Jews who had been safely evacuated from Egypt made a golden calf which they worshipped, and they drank and played. Moses persuaded the Lord not to wreak his anger on the profligates, but he himself used the sons of Levi to slaughter his disloyal followers (see Exodus 32).

Durnover Moor A flat meadowland near Dorchester.

Durnover The village of Fordington, to the east of Dorchester.

p.32 a list A thick layer of stodgy unrisen bread.

p.33 ruddy and of a fair countenance See the similar descriptions of the young shepherd David in 1 Samuel 16:12, 1 Samuel 17:42. The reference recalls David's troubled relationship with the moody King Saul.

p. 34 the Three Mariners Based on a real pub, The King of Prussia.

p. 35 flexuous bending and curving

p. 36 thin holland overcoat An overcoat made of linen, whose function would have been style rather than warmth. It suggests Henchard's superior status in the town.

mullioned Divided by vertical uprights; a feature of Gothic architecture.

polls heads

yard of clay long clay pipe

four-centred Tudor arch A pointed arch with four arcs, of the late-mediaeval period.

p. 39 settle A long wooden bench, usually with two arms and a high back.

twelve-bushel strength A strong beer, measured by the quantity of malt used in the brewing.

p. 41 quarters A quarter was eight bushels.

quag quagmire, i.e. problem

seconds second-class quality

p. 43 the dog days This refers to the hottest period of the year, when the rising of the Dog Star Sirius coincides with that of the sun; variously calculated, but usually from early July to around 11 August.

drink a quarter-barrel to the pitching   I.e. drink the entire contents of a quarter-barrel (nine gallons), so that the joints of the barrel, which were waterproofed with pitch, would be exposed.

p. 44 It's hame, etc   A Jacobite song.

p. 45 lammigers   cripples

we rebelled against the King   Buzzford is referring to Monmouth's unsuccessful rebellion of 1685 to claim the crown; it was followed by Judge Jeffreys' 'Bloody Assize' which led to public hangings on Gallows Hill just outside Dorchester and the quartering of victims as a warning to future rebels: 'our different jints [joints] sent about the country like butcher's meat'.

p. 46 wownded   concerned, struck to the heart

bruckle   rough

chaps   Cheeks, used for food: a humorous contrast to 'fair faces'.

claning   cleaning

'O Nannie'   This was an English ballad that was taken over by the Scots and collected by Bishop Percy in *Reliques of Ancient English Poetry* (1765). The song wonders whether Nannie can give up her glamorous city life for the quieter enchantments of 'silent glens'.

p. 47 chine   The projecting rim at the bottom of a cask by which the drayman was able to roll it from place to place.

'gaberlunzie'   (Scots) a wandering beggar

p. 48 As I came in, etc   Adapted from Robert Burns' 'Bonnie Peg'.

p. 52 'bloody warriors'   wallflowers

chassez-déchassez   (French) a dance movement to right and left, returning to the same central line of movement.

Terpsichorean   Terpsichore was the Greek muse of dance.

Mellstock . . . Overcombe   See Glossary of Place Names.

two feeble old constables   Men appointed by magistrates to carry out local law and order duties.

p. 53 Cranstoun's Goblin Page   A reference to Lord Cranstoun's dwarf in Sir Walter Scott's *Lay of the Last Minstrel*. He played practical jokes during his master's wedding.

p. 54 fish-seines   large fishing nets

stone staddles   These raised the floor of the granaries above ground level to protect their contents from damp, etc.

Flemish ladders   possibly short ladders

p. 57 the quicker cripple at Bethesda   See John 5: 2–9. The pool of Bethesda had magical healing properties for the person who was the first to enter it at a particular moment. Jesus healed a cripple who had not been able in many years to reach the pool in time.

rouge-et-noir   (French) literally, red and black, Henchard's florid skin and dark hair, his characteristic colouring (see the description of his red-sparked eyes above, and his appearance pp. 29, 71), which may hint of something demonic, certainly choleric in his personality.

p. 58 Pembroke tables   drop-leaf tables

'Josephus'   Flavius Josephus (AD 37–c. 98) was a Jewish soldier and scholar whose *History of the Jewish War* and *Jewish Antiquities*, a history of the Jews to AD 66, was popular in translation at this period.

'Whole Duty of Man'   Originally published in 1658, this was a devotional work discussing an individual's responsibility to God and to his or her fellow beings.

Chippendale and Sheraton   Famous eighteenth-century English furniture-designers

Father was lost last spring   See note on p. 18.

p. 60 The Ring at Casterbridge   A reference to Maumbury Ring which was neolithic in origin, and used by the Romans for entertainments of the kind suggested in the text. Hardy wrote an article on the Ring, see Harold Orel, ed. *Thomas Hardy's Personal Writings* (London, 1967), pp. 225–32.

fibula   clasp or buckle

p. 61 the Jötuns   Giants in Nordic mythology.

a woman who had murdered her husband   In his article on Maumbury Ring (see note on p. 60 above), Hardy discussed the story of Mary Channing, who poisoned her husband in controversial circumstances.

p. 62 Hadrian   Emperor of Rome AD 117–138, he attempted to consolidate Roman rule in Britain, constructing Hadrian's Wall in the north as a defence against invaders.

bents   stiff grass stalks

Æolian   Æolus was the Greek god of winds. An Æolian harp is an instrument that makes musical sounds when the wind blows across its strings. See Shelley, *Prometheus Unbound*, IV, i, 186–8:

> 'Tis the deep music of the rolling world
> Kindling within the strings of the waved air
> Æolian modulations.

p. 65 the education of Achilles Achilles was trained by the centaur Chion in physical or responsive arts such as athletics, fighting and music; writing was not considered a priority.

p. 66 espaliers A framework of stakes on which fruit-trees are trained. See too p. 54 where the garden wall is studded with rusty nails from training fruit-trees.

leafy Laocoöns Virgil's *Aeneid*, Book 2 describes how the Trojan priest Laocoön and his two sons were crushed and strangled by serpents, an incident graphically portrayed in the famous marble sculpture in the Vatican.

p. 67 like Job . . . birth See Job 3:3: 'Let the day perish wherein I was born, and the night in which it was said, There is a man child conceived.'

sequestrated legally seized for payment of debts

p. 70 tumuli The plural of tumulus (Latin), an ancient burial mound.

the flesh is weak See Mark 14:38: '. . . The spirit truly is ready, but the flesh is weak.'

p. 71 red and black visage See note on p. 57.

brougham A one-horse closed carriage with two or four wheels, named after Lord Brougham.

p. 72 leather breeches These were notoriously hard-wearing; i.e. even the toughest materials wear out in the end.

p. 73 Agricultural Society This was founded in the 1830s and -40s to promote better farming methods.

the wash pig-swill

zilver-snuffers silver candle-snuffers

cow-barton cow-yard

She'll wish her cake dough She'll wish she had not changed to her more elevated position.

bluebeardy Refers to the legendary Bluebeard, who murdered his wives.

twanking peevish, mournful

jumps An old-fashioned under-bodice, often used instead of stays.

night-rail   nightdress

p. 74 small table ninepenny   Weak beer, at ninepence a gallon.

clammy as a cockle-snail   Cold and damp as the snail in a cockle-shell.

A Martinmas summer   St Martin's Day was on 11 November, by tradition the last warm day of the year. Here the phrase is used to refer to an unusually late period of warmth; an 'Indian summer' in Susan's life.

p. 75 to paraphrase a recent poet   This seems to refer to Matthew Arnold's essay on Wordsworth in which Arnold corroborates the latter's view of Goethe: 'no line in Goethe, as Goethe said himself, but its maker knew well how it came there'.

fieldmouse fear of the coulter   A reference to Robert Burns' poem 'To a Mouse'. A coulter is the iron blade fixed in front of the share on a plough, cutting vertically into the ground.

spencer   A close-fitting jacket or bodice.

p. 76 leonine   See also p. 78 where Henchard's affection for Farfrae is described as 'tigerish'. These terms suggest his power and menace, but also the lack of subtlety in his character. He deals in giant paw-strokes – and wonders why confident affection eludes him.

p. 77 *vivâ voce*   (Latin) by word of mouth

p. 78 tigerish   See note to p. 76.

barley-mow   stack of barley

p. 79 as high as the gates of Solomon's temple   The dimensions of the gates are not actually specified, see 1 Kings 6, but the temple itself was thirty cubits high (v. 2). A cubit was about eighteen to twenty-two inches (the length of a forearm).

stone staddles   See note to p. 54.

p. 80 victorine   A fur scarf or cape fastened at the front, with two ends hanging down.

p. 81 'As I came down through Cannobie'   Possibly a variation on Burns' 'Bonnie Peg', see p. 48 and note.

p. 82 the prophet Baruch's sly definition   In fact, the words are the prophet Jeremiah's, recorded in the Apocryphal book of his companion and secretary Baruch, Ch. 6, v. 9: 'And taking gold, as it were for a virgin that loveth to go gay, they make crowns for the heads of their gods.'

the 'delicate imposition' of Rochefoucauld   See the *Maximes* of La

Rochefoucauld (1613–80), No. 289: '*La simplicité affectée est une imposture délicate.*'

p. 84 scrags scraps, fragments

fretted my gizzard green worried myself sick

scantling morsel

moment-hand The minute-hand of a clock that is in more or less perpetual motion.

Blackmoor Vale Hardy extended the real Blackmore Vale in his fiction; see F. B. Pinion, *A Hardy Companion* (London, 1976 edition), p. 241: Hardy's vale 'covers all the undulating pastoral and wooded country running north from the chalk hills which include Bubb Down, High Stoy, Nettlecombe-Tout, and Bulbarrow. The vale proper is mainly to the north of Sturminster Newton'.

p. 86 fairing A gift given at or brought away from a fair.

diment diamond

chap o' wax an up-and-coming man

p. 87 *sotto voce* (Italian) in an undertone

p. 88 a national event This would probably be related to the royal family: the birth of a royal child or special birthday.

rick-cloths These were heavy waterproof coverings to protect ricks of grain from rain, etc.

p. 90 Æolian See note to p. 62.

p. 91 Correggio An early sixteenth-century Italian painter, noted for his subtle use of light and shade.

stunpoll fool

p. 92 by a chaw by chewing it

honeycombed This could mean simply 'sweet-talked', or Henchard may be thinking of himself as 'hollowed out' like the cells of a honeycomb.

'Miss M'Leod of Ayr' This was one of Hardy's favourite dance tunes as a child, one of several that moved him to tears. See Florence Emily Hardy, *The Early Life of Thomas Hardy* (London, 1928), p. 18.

randy party, merrymaking

p. 96 voot foot

p. 97 wo'th a varden worth a farthing

sniff and snaff   Answering 'snaff' to someone else's 'sniff' meant easy agreement.

modus vivendi   (Latin) way of living harmoniously together.

p. 98 Jacob in Padan-Aram   This refers to Genesis 30: 25–43, in which Jacob outmanoeuvres his cheating uncle Laban so that he eventually owns a herd of superior cattle. Hardy may be suggesting that Farfrae is equally capable of clever dealing despite his apparent straight-forwardness; or the comparison may simply be with a successful venture. There is no doubt that, however shady Laban's behaviour, Jacob was more than his match.

Character is Fate, said Novalis   Novalis was the pseudonym of Baron Friedrich Leopold von Hardenberg (1772–1801), a poet and novelist who was influential in the German Romantic movement. It is unlikely that Hardy read Novalis in the original; he probably saw the quotation in Book 6, Chapter 6 of George Eliot's *The Mill on the Floss*: ' "Character" – says Novalis, in one of his questionable aphorisms – "character is destiny." '

Faust   This description of Faust is from Carlyle's essay on 'Goethe's Helena'.

p. 99 Bellerophon   A Greek hero who killed the Chimæra, a fire-breathing monster, with a lion's head, a goat's body, and a serpent's tail. Bellerophon antagonised the gods, and ended up wandering alone and bitter in the Aleian plain, 'eating his heart out' and shunning mankind. See Homer's *Iliad*, Book 6.

the box passenger   The passenger who sits next to the driver outside the coach, above the box. 'Box' was often used for the driver's seat itself.

p. 100 packet-boat   Mail-boat; also carried goods and passengers.

p. 103 ounce pennies   These were coined for private use and therefore heavier than standard pennies. It was believed that if the eyes of the dead were not closed in this way, the dead person would become a ghost, or her open eyes would be looking for the next corpse.

doxology   A brief formulaic hymn of praise to God. Longways probably means 'theology'.

varnished for 'natomies   This refers to the practice of 'body-snatching', in which fresh graves were dug up and bodies sold to medical practitioners or establishments for anatomical research.

And ... nothing!   For the reader, there is irony in Mother Cuxsom's reflections: Susan's life was not obviously marked by particular attention to her wishes. Death robs her of the fragile status she finally attained as Henchard's wife, and in particular her power to control her own secrets, but the notion that individuals can control what others find out about them is also open to question, as is revealed later in the novel.

p. 104 pier-glass A tall mirror, originally one designed to fill in the pier or solid masonry between two windows or over a chimney-piece.

entablature The ornamentation at the top of the side columns of the mirror.

p. 105 the avowal of Joseph See Genesis 45:3, where Joseph reveals his identity to the brothers who had sold him into slavery years earlier: 'And Joseph said unto his brethren, I am Joseph; doth my father yet live? And his brethren could not answer him; for they were troubled at his presence.' The brothers' anxiety is the result of guilt combined with unexpectedly finding Joseph in a position of power and authority over them. Elizabeth-Jane has no reason to feel guilt, but Henchard's new status as her father is of similar concern to her.

p. 108 Like Prester John's This is a reference to Ariosto's depiction in *Orlando Furioso* (1532) of the legendary Christian priest and king. He searches for Adam and Eve's Paradise and is punished by God with blindness and starvation: as food is placed on his table, harpies (creatures with the head of a woman and a vulture's body and claws) snatch it away. Henchard's emotional yearning and deprivation are made clear by the analogy.

Schwarzwasser (German) black water. Hardy uses the name Blackwater on p. 192 for a deep pool further up the river from the bridges on the lower side of the town; on p. 253, the term is used to describe the stretch of water again up-river from the second bridge and beyond Ten Hatches. The use of the German term here is probably intended to indicate that the stretch of river beneath the prison is 'black water', either from its proximity to the gallows or literally because of its dark appearance as it runs under the low cliff.

p. 111 Be jowned be damned

Minerva The Roman goddess of wisdom and handicrafts. She became identified with the Greek Pallas Athene, and hence with war and masculinity.

Princess Ida The reference is to Tennyson's *The Princess*. Princess Ida has set up a university for women; an aspiring suitor masquerades as a female student and writes to her in what he considers a 'lady's hand'. The quotation describes his handwriting not the Princess's.

chain-shot   This comprised two balls or half-balls connected by a chain and used primarily in naval warfare to destroy rigging, etc. Presumably refers to Elizabeth-Jane's large round letters.

p. 112 wimbling hay-bonds   See note to p. 3.

p. 114 Hadrian, Posthumus, and the Constantines   Roman emperors and rulers of Britain. The coins were to pay the boatman Charon who ferried the shades of the departed across the River Styx to the underworld.

Karnac   A village in ancient Thebes, on the upper Nile, the deserted site of a civilization in ruins.

p. 115 Northern Lights   The Aurora Borealis, a luminous atmospheric phenomenon radiating from the north pole and visible at night from the northern hemisphere.

Austerlitz   Napoleon's success in defeating the combined Russian and Austrian forces at the battle of Austerlitz in 1805 marked the high point of his career.

leery   hungry, faint for want of food

p. 116 burned   Probably means damned; but it may also suggest that she is seriously damaging his reputation, branding him or singeing his wings.

p. 118 round hand   A style of handwriting characterised by bold round letters.

High-Place Hall   Based on Colliton House in Dorchester. For discussion, see Denys Kay-Robinson, *Hardy's Wessex Reappraised* (Newton Abbot, 1972).

p. 120 Palladian   In the style of Andrea Palladio (1508–80), who revived classical forms in architecture, particularly those of early Roman buildings. His ideas were influential in English design well into the eighteenth century.

p. 121 pier   pillar

p. 122 pattens   See note to p. 26.

her apotheosis   Her deification, exaltation: Elizabeth-Jane has risen in social status since her mother's marriage to Henchard.

mounted   I.e. perched on the pattens above the mud.

p. 124 fly   A one-horse covered carriage, such as a cab or hansom, available for hire.

take time by the forelock   I.e. to take advantage of the means available; here Henchard seems to be implying that she is acting precipitately.

p. 126 *étourderie* (French) carelessness, blunder

postern back door, private door

p. 128 a clue line A guiding thread out of a maze or labyrinth.

p. 129 a well-known conception of Titian's The Venetian artist Titian (*c.* 1485–1576) painted a number of gracefully reclining women. Hardy perhaps refers here to the famous 'Venus of Urbino', now in the Uffizzi Gallery in Florence, although the 'Venus' supports herself on one arm, rather than holding it across her forehead. The study of Renaissance artists formed part of Hardy's self-education programme as a young man; see Michael Millgate, *Thomas Hardy: A Biography* (Oxford, 1982; Clarendon edition, 1992), p. 81.

p. 130 the weak Apostle . . . 'Thy speech bewrayeth thee!' See Matthew 26:73. After Jesus was arrested in the Garden of Gethsemane, Peter three times denied being one of his followers. The third accuser insists that his accent gives him away.

netting Fancywork made with needles.

p. 131 *carrefour* (French) where four ways meet, a square or crossroads.

gibbous Rounded or protuberant; it could suggest the effect on their contours of good living, or the bulges caused by substantial purses and cheque-books.

p. 132 Candlemas 2 February, the feast of thanksgiving for the Purification of the Virgin Mary. Hardy may have had in mind Old Candlemas Day, 14 February, when the Dorchester Fair was traditionally held. See Michael Millgate, *Thomas Hardy: His Career as a Novelist* (London, 1971), p. 245.

p. 134 cyma-recta An architectural term describing the meeting of two curves: the upper concave and the lower convex.

p. 135 hyperborean far northern

lopping Sea that breaks in short choppy waves.

p. 136 kerseymere Fine woollen cloth with a twill.

p. 137 waggon-tilts Canvas coverings over waggons.

smock-frocks Linen over-garments worn instead of a coat by farm labourers, etc.

p. 138 Lady-day People hired at the fair would take up their new appointments on Lady-day, 6 April, which was when the previous year's contracts would cease.

Dan Cupid's magnet The 'pulling' power of love; i.e. the 'magnet' would not operate at that distance.

p. 141 Open Place in spectacular dramas This refers to the customary staging of Greek drama in a public area.

p. 142 poll head

horse-drill This was a horse-drawn machine for planting seed: an example of the technical innovation that was changing the traditional pattern of English agricultural life (although the horse-drill had been invented by Jethro Tull as early as 1701, suggesting the slowness with which change penetrated rural communities).

seed-lip See note to p. 26.

the Heptarchy The seven Kingdoms that made up Anglo-Saxon England, and which included Wessex.

p. 144 'Lass of Gowrie' A Scots song by Lady Nairne (1766–1845).

No more sowers . . . thorns See the parable of the sower in Matthew 13:3–8; Mark 4:3–20.

'He that observeth . . . shall not sow' See Ecclesiastes 11:4: 'He that observeth the wind shall not sow; and he that regardeth the clouds shall not reap.' Elizabeth-Jane seems to be thinking of the physical act of sowing rather than the context of the quotation, which concerns getting on with one's work without undue questioning.

p. 145 enfilading traversing from end to end

p. 149 Protean I.e. like the Greek sea-god Proteus who was capable of changing shape as he wished.

p. 153 'meaner beauties of the night' From the poem 'On his Mistress, the Queen of Bohemia' by Sir Henry Wotton (1568–1639):

> You meaner beauties of the night,
>   That poorly satisfy our eyes
> More by your number than your light,
>   You common people of the skies;
>   What are you when the moon shall rise?

p. 154 gazebo Literally, a structure in a house or garden commanding an extensive view; here, several of Lucetta's rooms overlook the market-place (see p. 120).

p. 155 some Tuscan painting . . . Emmaus This refers to the account in Luke 24:13–35 of Jesus appearing after his resurrection to two disciples on the road from Jerusalem to the village of Emmaus. One of the most famous Renaissance renderings of the meal that followed is the painting in the National Gallery in London by the Lombardy artist

Caravaggio (1573–1610), which includes a fourth man (perhaps 'the evangelist who had to write it down' mentioned by Hardy below). However, the latter could not be described as observing 'from afar', and Christ does not have a halo, so Hardy may have had an earlier painting in mind (see note on p. 129 re. Hardy and Renaissance painters). The identification of the flawed Lucetta with the resurrected Christ may be ironic, but it also suggests Hardy's sympathetic recognition of her sacrificial potential.

the evangelist who had to write it down See note above. This was presumably Luke, who records the story in his gospel.

p. 156 *pis aller*   (French) a last resource

p. 157 The time . . . as rapidly See note to p. xxix re. the Corn Laws and the effects of weather on the corn trade.

p. 158 the Alastor avenging spirit, Nemesis

reap-hooks See note to p. 26.

p. 159 springe A snare or trap, often used in poaching.

Candlemas See note to p. 132.

p. 160 leery See note to p. 115.

Saul . . . Samuel See 1 Samuel 9:1–24, which tells of Saul's search for his father's asses, and unexpected welcome and entertainment by the holy man Samuel, who has been warned by the Lord that Saul is the future ruler of Israel. Samuel offers Saul food that he has set aside for him and promises to tell him 'all that is in thine heart'. Later in Saul's story (see 1 Samuel 28), after Samuel is dead and Saul, abandoned by God, is harassed by the Philistine forces, he goes secretly to visit the witch of Endor to ask her to invoke Samuel's spirit so that he can ask his advice. Samuel prophesies defeat and Saul's own death the following day. Saul collapses with shock and weakness from lack of food and is fed by the witch. Hardy's reference combines elements of the two stories.

the evil A term for scrofula, a disease in which the lymphatic glands become enlarged and degenerate; known as 'the King's evil' as the English King was believed able to heal it by a touch.

toad-bag An entry in Hardy's diary in 1876, when he was living with his first wife Emma Gifford in Sturminster Newton, reads: 'An old man, a wizard, used to bring toads' legs in little bags to Bagber Bridge [close to where Hardy was living], where he was met by crowds of people who came in vehicles and on foot, and bought them as charms to cure scrofula by wearing them round the neck. These legs were supposed to twitch occasionally in the bag, and probably did, when it gave the wearer's blood a "turn", and changed the course of the disease.' See Florence Emily Hardy, *The Early Life of Thomas Hardy* (London, 1928), p. 148.

dungmixen dunghill

Revelations A reference to the general sense of turbulent weather in the *Revelation of St John the Divine*.

p. 161 welkin sky

p. 163 somebody has been roasting . . . to confound me Henchard's claim that he doesn't believe in these superstitious practices (designed to cause harm to their object) is contradicted by his own recent recourse to the weather-prophet.

the Capitol A reference to the temple of Jupiter on the Capitoline Hill in Rome, where successful generals went in triumphal procession, followed by their defeated enemies.

p. 164 zwailing along in such a gawk-hammer way Wandering along in such an idiotic fashion

zeed seen

thill Horse fastened between the shafts of the waggon; here, the last in the team of four.

p. 165 the giddying worm into a sheep's brain This refers to a sheep disease known as 'Gid' or 'Sturdy', in which a worm causes the sheep to grow giddy and then die.

eight shillings a week i.e. his wages

p. 166 shocks Sheaves of corn balanced upright against one another to dry and ripen.

p. 169 lucubrations nocturnal studies

no'thern northern, i.e. stupid or deranged

p. 170 Petty Sessions A meeting of magistrates without a jury for the summary trying of minor offences.

Shallow and Silence The silly country justices in Shakespeare's *Henry IV*, Part 2.

ashlar Faced with masonry of thin slabs of hewn stone.

p. 171 the country . . . drop fatness See Psalm 65:11, where the Lord's bounty is celebrated: 'Thou crownest the year with thy goodness; and thy paths drop fatness.' Hardy is humorously referring to the greasy appearance of the old woman's bonnet.

p. 172 wambling walking unsteadily

turmit-head   turnip-head, idiot (like a scarecrow)

a land smuggler   She received smuggled goods on shore for distribution; see note to p. 7 re. smugglers.

p. 173 larry   commotion, disturbance

p. 174 Port-Bredy   Bridport

p. 175 Abrahamic success   There are various references in Genesis to Abraham's success as breeder of cattle and of men: he was the forefather of the race of Israel. See Genesis 12:2, 13:2, 13:16, 15:5, 17:2–6, 22:17.

Yahoo   See Book 4 of Swift's *Gulliver's Travels*, where humans are satirised as Yahoos: uncouth, hideous and cruel beings.

p. 176 the perspective toys of yore   These refer to peep-show toys which gave a three-dimensional view of scenes or buildings; popular in the early nineteenth century. The Thames Tunnel was designed by Marc Brunel (father of the famous Isambard Kingdom Brunel) and opened in 1843.

Gurth's collar of brass   In Sir Walter Scott's *Ivanhoe*, Gurth was a serf who wore a brass collar engraved with his owner's name welded round his neck.

sirocco   A dry hot wind from North Africa that blows across the Mediterranean, affecting Southern Europe, where it can become oppressively moist.

p. 178 gig   A light two-wheeled carriage, drawn by one horse.

p. 179 coals of fire on my head   See Proverbs 25:21–2, which advises kind treatment of an enemy: '. . . For thou shalt heap coals of fire upon his head, and the Lord shall reward thee.'

p. 182 like John Gilpin   See William Cowper's ballad, 'The Diverting History of John Gilpin', where Gilpin thriftily delays joining his wife to celebrate their wedding anniversary in order to attend to three customers.

brougham   See note to p. 71.

p. 183 'Video . . . sequor.'   See Ovid's *Metamorphoses*, 7:20–1, where Medea tries to explain her irrational passion for Jason by saying that a god has influenced her. Literally, 'I see and approve the better course, but I follow the worse.' Editions previous to 1912 had Elizabeth-Jane following St Paul, Romans 7:19: 'so that the good she would have done she did not, and the evil that she would not, that she did – exactly like the Apostle Paul'. The change to Ovid is obviously more appropriate to Lucetta's case, and indicates Elizabeth-Jane's progress in self-education.

p. 185 Nathan tones   I.e. very stern and condemnatory. See 2 Samuel 11 and 12:1–14. David commits adultery with Bathsheba who becomes pregnant. In order to prevent her husband, Uriah the Hittite, discovering the adultery, David sends him to certain death in battle and then marries Bathsheba. The prophet Nathan tells David the parable of the rich man who steals a poor man's one ewe lamb, which excites David into pronouncing sentence of death on the hypothetical criminal. Nathan then tells him, 'Thou art the man.' (12:7). The house of David is henceforth cursed and the child will die.

p. 186 netting   See note to p. 130.

seines   large fishing nets

fillip   A stimulus; the term refers to the action of flicking the top joint of a finger off the ball of the thumb.

p. 187 pinched, blasted, and smutted grains   i.e. withered, blighted or infected with the fungus disease known as 'smut'.

p. 188 Farmer James Everdene of Weatherbury   He is the uncle of Bathsheba Everdene in *Far from the Madding Crowd*. His unexpected death leaves her mistress of the tenancy of Weatherbury Upper Farm.

Boldwood   In *Far from the Madding Crowd* Boldwood's obsessive love for Bathsheba Everdene leads to disaster.

the meeting dispersed   Hardy based the foregoing account of Henchard's bankruptcy proceedings (p. 187–8) on an actual case recorded in the *Dorset County Chronicle* in 1826, when a Mr Harvey of Launceston similarly offered his gold watch and 'pocket-money', and was praised for his honourable behaviour and the honesty of his balance-sheet.

p. 189 wimble   See note to p. 3.

vitrified   i.e. resembling glass, glazed

arch-labels   Mouldings over window-frames, lintels.

p. 190 larry   state of confusion

cathead   This was a strong beam that projected from the roof of the storehouse bearing a pulley and tackle, so that the heavy bags of grain could be hoisted to the different floors and pulled in through the doorways for storage.

steelyard   A two-armed weighing machine on a fulcrum; the short arm holds the object to be weighed, the long notched or graduated arm carries a sliding weight which moves along until the machine is in equipoise.

Two bridges These were Swan Bridge (brick) and Grey's Bridge (stone) in Dorchester.

friable crumbly

p. 191 *misérables* (French) destitutes

Adonis The handsome youth beloved of Aphrodite, the Greek goddess of love.

p. 193 chattel possession

journey-work Hired labour, work done for daily wages; Henchard has come full circle.

p. 194 the Prophet's chamber See 2 Kings 4:10, where the woman of Shunem provides a 'little chamber' for Elisha to use at need, with 'a bed, and a table, and a stool, and a candlestick'.

palmy days triumphant, or flourishing period of her life

p. 195 journeyman See note to p. 5.

p. 196 stock stiff cloth that fitted closely round the neck

she was wise in her generation See Luke 16: 1–13, where Jesus rather puzzlingly appears to condone corrupt behaviour in the interests of self-preservation: 'for the children of this world are in their generation wiser than the children of light' (v. 8). The implication is that Lucetta has cleverly protected her own interests.

reviviscent reviving

p. 197 the choir church musicians, playing a variety of instruments

p. 198 The bass-viol player The leader of the church musicians, who would discuss the music to be played with the preacher.

ballet ballad, light simple song

rantipole rakish or wild

the Rogue's March This refers to a march tune played for the ceremony of expelling a disgraced soldier.

warble singing without words

Wiltshire The name of a psalm tune composed by G. Smart, and a favourite with Hardy. Usually used with Psalm 34.

p. 199 Servant David David was believed to have been the author of many of the Psalms, and appears as the Lord's servant in the Bible and in the *Benedictus* used for Morning Prayer (Book of Common Prayer).

p. 201 Rosalind's exclamation   See Shakespeare's *As You Like It*, Act 3, scene 5.

p. 205 rimy   Rime is hoar-frost or frozen dew, i.e. frosty.

p. 208 worm i' the bud   i.e. concealment. See Shakespeare's *Twelfth Night*, Act 2, scene 4:

> She never told her love,
> But let concealment, like a worm i' the bud,
> Feed on her damask cheek;

p. 209 Tamerlane's trumpet   The warrior Tamerlane (Timur the Lame, 1336–1405) conquered the territory from Mongolia to the Mediterranean. His army carried huge seven-foot trumpets.

p. 210 Aphrodite   The Greek goddess of love; i.e. a woman in love.

p. 216 iron dogs   I.e. andirons; a pair of horizontal iron bars supported on feet, placed at each end of the hearth to hold burning wood.

p. 217 Peter's Finger   The King's Head in Dorchester, which no longer exists. There is an inn called Peter's Finger at Lytchett Minster, near Poole: a corruption of the name of a church, St Peter-ad-Vincula (St Peter in Chains).

congeries   collection

Adullam   The cave where David hid from the angry Saul; 'every one that was in distress, and every one that was in debt, and every one that was discontented, gathered themselves unto him'. See 1 Samuel 22:1–2.

bibbing   drinking

p. 219 lifeholders   Refers to instances where the lease to a property was held for the duration of the lives of specific persons, often three generations of a family. The potentially tragic effects of the lapse of lifehold agreements is dealt with in *Tess of the d'Urbervilles* and *The Woodlanders*.

copyholders   Those whose tenure was held according to a copy of the court-roll, the record of rents and holdings on a manor. Although the tenancy was technically at the will of the lord of the manor, it was controlled by the custom of that manor, with which the lord could not arbitrarily interfere. It was therefore relatively secure.

roof-tree   Literally, the main beam or ridge-pole supporting the roof.

to blink like Ashton at the disappearance of Ravenswood   In Sir Walter Scott's *The Bride of Lammermoor*, Chapter 35, Ashton sees Ravenswood suddenly disappear into a quicksand, and rubs his eyes in astonishment.

fillip See note to p. 186; here, it seems to mean a quick flick of the body.

swingel flail or cudgel

p. 220 larry commotion, disturbance; cf. p. 173

oven pyle A long-handed wooden shovel for placing loaves, pies, etc. in the oven or withdrawing them from it.

p. 221 skimmity-ride or skimmington ride. The rural practice of expressing disapproval of adultery or ill-treatment by a husband or wife of their partner. In the case of adultery, effigies of the offending couple would be publicly paraded to the accompaniment of a terrible din.

p. 224 A Royal Personage ... that way See note to p. xxix re. Prince Albert passing through Dorchester. He actually arrived by train, but in Hardy's account the railway has not yet reached Casterbridge (see p. 226).

fête carillonnée (French) festival celebrated by special bell-ringing.

p. 225 tilt bonnet A bonnet shaped like the covering of a waggon to protect the face from the sun and wind.

p. 226 *cortège* (French) train of attendants

The railway ... as yet See notes to p. xxix and p. 224.

p. 227 the Royal unicorn In the royal coat-of-arms, the unicorn wears a chain.

p. 228 his Calphurnia's cheek was pale See Shakespeare's *Julius Caesar*, Act 1, scene 2. So Brutus describes Calphurnia, the wife of Julius Caesar, as she returns from the games at which Caesar has refused the crown three times. Hardy seems to be suggesting a comparison between Farfrae and Caesar, with the hint that elevation to high office is not always beneficial to the recipient.

rattled heavily as Pharaoh's chariots See Exodus 14: 23–5, where the Israelites are fleeing from the Egyptians through the Red Sea which the Lord has divided to make a dry passage for them. To disadvantage the Egyptians, the Lord 'took off', i.e. hobbled or clogged, their chariot wheels so that they did not function properly.

go snacks wi' en share; here, specifically, get married

hontish haughty

p. 229 toppered overcome, cut down to size

p. 230 *Weltlust* (German) pleasure in worldly things, desire for advancement.

p. 231 rub brine on a green wound A fresh wound was customarily bathed with brine to reduce infection and promote healing: the salt made this a painful cure.

p. 232 And here's a hand . . . o' thine From Robert Burns' 'Auld Lang Syne'.

p. 234 Prince of Darkness Here, Henchard resembles Satan; cf. note to p. 57.

p. 235 purl murmur caused by the agitation of the water

p. 236 mummery pantomime

p. 237 chimbley chimney

kerseymere See note to p. 136.

p. 240 cleavers . . . rams'-horns The various means by which the crowd created a din:
  cleaver: butcher's chopper; **tongs**: kitchen tongs; **kit**: small fiddle; **croud**: homemade, crude fiddle; **humstrum**: improvised stringed instrument, possibly a kind of Jew's harp; **serpent**: bass wind instrument, made of leather-covered wood, with huge coils like a snake; **rams'-horns**: crude wind instruments made of the horn of a ram.

lammigers cripples

felo de se (Latin) suicide, but Stubberd means 'murder'

fustian See note to p. 3

p. 241 the crew of *Comus* See Milton's masque *Comus*, ll.145–8, where Comus orders the unruly rabble who are his followers to hide when the Lady, a virtuous maiden, approaches.

p. 245 joy in heaven See Luke 15:7: 'I say unto you, that likewise joy shall be in heaven over one sinner that repenteth, more than over ninety and nine just persons, which need no repentance.'

a less scrupulous Job See Job 1–3; despite the misfortunes that suddenly fall upon him, Job at first refuses to complain, but then curses the hour of his birth. Henchard does not pause to attempt a balanced view, but plunges straight into self-reproach.

p. 247 Lucifer The planet Venus, as the morning star.

p. 249 She could write her own name, and no more. Susan may well have learnt to write in the intervening years (she left the letter for Henchard re. Elizabeth-Jane's parentage); or this may be a slip on Hardy's part, or even a deliberate attempt by Henchard to exaggerate

Susan's simplicity and hence exonerate himself. The latter, however, is unlikely as Newson would have known whether or not Susan could write.

socked   sighed heavily

p. 257 the small seed and root business   This seems to contradict p. 205–6 where Farfrae abandons the idea of setting Henchard up in the seed shop, unintentionally causing further enmity. However, Lucetta's confession may have helped explain Henchard's extreme behaviour and encouraged Farfrae once again to attempt to help his former benefactor.

Time, 'in his own grey style'   See Shelley's *Epipsychidion*, 55–7:

> Young love should teach Time, in his own grey style,
> All that thou art. Art thou not void of guile,
> A lovely soul formed to be blessed and bless?

p. 258 the netted lion   See note to p. 76. The lion has finally been caught in a net; this suggests Henchard's pent-up power, and his entrapment to his desire for Elizabeth-Jane's good will.

p. 259 Juno's bird ... Argus eyes   In classical myth, Argus had one hundred eyes of which only two ever slept simultaneously. Juno, the wife of Jupiter, set Argus to watch Io, with whom Jupiter was in love and whom he had changed into a heifer to conceal the infidelity from Juno. Mercury, at Jupiter's instigation, lulled all Argus' eyes to sleep and killed him; whereupon Juno put Argus' eyes on the tail of the peacock, her sacred bird.

ken   sight, knowledge

p. 260 *solicitus timor*   (Latin) anxious fear

p. 262 *locus standi*   (Latin) recognised position

p. 264 *éclat*   (French) brilliance

a fangless lion   See notes to p. 76 and p. 258.

Mai Dun   Maiden Castle, a prehistoric earthwork about two miles south-west of Dorchester.

p. 265 *Via*   (Latin) road

transfixture   Fixed to the spot by strong feeling.

p. 267 knee-naps   Leather patches or covers to protect the knees.

I – Cain – ... than I can bear!   See Genesis 4:12–13, where Cain, having been condemned for the murder of Abel to be 'a fugitive and a vagabond', says the punishment 'is greater than I can bear'. Here Hardy again stresses Henchard's gloomy willingness to blame himself for his impulsive actions and their negative consequences.

p. 269 schiedam Dutch gin (named after the town where it was made).

p. 270 nine or ten months Cf. 'between one and two years before this time' on p. 268. The discrepancy may be due to changes made by Hardy to the plot before the definitive edition of the text (see Note on Text); but Newson may simply have forgotten the exact time that has elapsed since his visit to Henchard.

p. 271 quickset hedge

p. 272 pixy-ring A circle of grass of a different colour from the surrounding grass; caused by fungi but popularly believed to be the result of fairies dancing.

p. 273 *pari passu* (Latin) at an equal pace, rate of progress

p. 274 mid might

Martin's Day See note to p. 74.

p. 276 drag i.e. the iron brake that 'dragged' on the wheels when descending a hill.

a Samson shorn See Judges 16:15–21. When Samson finally admits to Delilah that the secret of his great strength lies in his untrimmed hair, she has it shaven off while he is asleep. In his weakened state, the Philistines are able to put out his eyes and bind him in brass fetters, and 'he did grind in the prison house' in Gaza.

p. 278 out-Farfraed Farfrae See Shakespeare's *Hamlet*, Act 3, scene 2, where Hamlet complains about ranting actors who out-Herod Herod.

saltatory dancing in leaps and bounds

'the shade from his own soul upthrown' See Shelley, *The Revolt of Islam*, Canto 8, stanza 6:

What is that Power? Some moon-struck sophist stood
Watching the shade from his own soul upthrown
Fill Heaven and darken Earth, and in such mood
The Form he saw and worshipped was his own,

p. 280 Crusoe The shipwrecked sailor of Daniel Defoe's novel, *Robinson Crusoe*, who is rescued and returned home after years living on an island.

sensational exits ... antipodean absences Hangings and transportation of criminals to the penal colonies in Australia.

p. 281 extenuate nothing Possibly a reference to Shakespeare's *Othello*, Act 5, scene 2. Before he stabs himself, Othello begs that his story should be told plainly:

> I pray you, in your letters,
> When you shall these unlucky deeds relate,
> Speak of me as I am. Nothing extenuate,
> Nor set down aught in malice. Then must you speak
> Of one that loved not wisely, but too well;

live ... worst accusers See previous note and p. 279 where Henchard values himself too little to plead in his own defence.

p. 282 victorine of the period See note to p. 80.

Minerva-eyes See note to p. 111; here Minerva is invoked in her aspect as goddess of wisdom.

'whose gestures beamed with mind' See Shelley, *The Revolt of Islam*, Canto 1, stanza 54: 'Some, female forms, whose gestures beamed with mind'.

Diana Multimammia (Latin) Diana the Many-breasted, as in her temple at Ephesus where she is represented as a many-breasted fertility goddess.

p. 284 ship-coal I.e. imported by sea, perhaps from Newcastle, and therefore a luxury for Whittle's mother.

p. 285 Capharnaum I.e. Capernaum, a Galilean town where Jesus preached. See Matthew 4: 13–16, where 'The people which sat in darkness saw great light'. Similarly Elizabeth-Jane has moved from a shadowed or dark period to one of happiness.

A GLOSSARY OF PLACE NAMES
IN HARDY'S WESSEX

Anglebury   Wareham
Blackmoor Vale   Blackmore Vale; see note to p.84.
Budmouth   Weymouth
Casterbridge   Dorchester, the county town of Dorset.
Durnover   The village of Fordington, to the east of Dorchester.
Durnover Moor   A flat meadowland east of Dorchester.
Egdon Heath   Hardy's collective name for a string of at least a dozen heaths between Dorchester and Bournemouth.
Havenpool   Poole
The Hintocks   Based on the woodland villages of Melbury Osmond, Melbury Sampford and Minterne Magna to the north-west of Dorchester.
Kingsbere   The village of Bere Regis.
Mai Dun   Maiden Castle, a prehistoric earthwork about two miles south-west of Dorchester.
Melchester   Salisbury in Wiltshire.
Mellstock   Mellstock's three hamlets comprise the village of Stinsford, north-east of Dorchester, where Hardy's heart is buried, and Lower and Higher Bockhampton.
Overcombe   Probably mainly the village of Sutton Poyntz.
Port-Bredy   Bridport
Sherton-Abbas   Sherborne
Shottsford   Blandford Forum
Weatherbury   The village of Puddletown.
Weydon-Priors   The village of Weyhill, near Andover in Hampshire, once famous for its annual sheep-selling fair.
Yalbury Hill   Yellowham Hill, north-east of Dorchester towards Puddletown.

HARDY AND HIS CRITICS

Hardy's novels were published between 1871 and 1897, and were reviewed in British and North American periodicals both individually and in general assessments as his published work expanded. They attracted a variety of critical response but little serious controversy until the publication of *Tess of the d'Urbervilles* (1891) and *Jude the Obscure* (1895), both of which implied a critique of conventional sexual behaviour and religious values that caused serious alarm and polarised critical opinion. For a substantial selection of contemporary reviews up to 1914, see R. G. Cox, ed. *Thomas Hardy: The Critical Heritage* (London, 1970). In evaluating contemporary responses, Cox points out that it is important to remember that Victorian novels, whether serialised in 'family' magazines or published in volume form, were frequently read aloud *en famille*:

> It seems safe to assume that many of the readers of Hardy's earlier books were looking for conventional and undisturbing entertainment, melodramatic in its turns of plot and liberally seasoned with the pathetic, but uplifting in tone and observing a strict moral propriety.

Hardy's characterisation and plotting in the early novels frequently came under fire from the critics as improbable, but the overworked and melodramatic elements were influenced by the requirements of serial publication and popular taste as defined by his publishers.

Attempting to position Hardy in relation to other British novelists, reviewers compared his early novels with the work of the highly esteemed George Eliot, particularly in his treatment of rural scenes. But they criticised what they regarded as the unrealistically sophisticated language of the country people. Reviewing *Far from the Madding Crowd* in November 1874, the *Athenaeum* critic wrote of Hardy:

> He is evidently a shrewd observer of the talk and habits of the Somersetshire rustics; and yet he puts such expressions into their

mouths as 'Passably well put', 'Every looker-on's inside shook with the blows of the great drum to his deepest vitals, and there was not a dry eye throughout the town', and so on – expressions which we simply cannot believe possible from the illiterate clods whom he describes.

Hardy defended the dialect (but not the language) of his Shakespearean 'rustics' in a letter to the *Athenaeum* of 30 November 1878:

> An author may be said to fairly convey the spirit of intelligent peasant talk if he retains the idiom, compass and characteristic expressions . . . In the printing of standard speech hardly any phonetic principle at all is observed: and if a writer attempts to exhibit on paper the precise accents of a rustic speaker he disturbs the proper balance of a true representation by unduly insisting upon the grotesque element; thus directing attention to a point of inferior interest, and diverting it from the speaker's meaning, which is by far the chief concern where the aim is to depict the men and their natures rather than their dialect forms.

Henry James, reviewing *Far from the Madding Crowd* in the New York *Nation*, acknowledges a similarity between George Eliot and Hardy, but sees the latter's rural scenes as being the product of mere cleverness, 'the difference between original and imitative talent':

> Mr Hardy puts his figures through a variety of comical movements; he fills their mouths with quaint turns of speech; . . . he pulls the wires, in short, and produces a vast deal of sound and commotion; and his novel, at a cursory glance, has a rather promising air of life and warmth. But . . . it has a fatal lack of magic.

As with other critics, James praises Hardy's perception and description of nature:

> Mr Hardy describes nature with a great deal of felicity, and is evidently very much at home among rural phenomena. The most genuine thing in his book, to our sense, is a certain aroma of the meadows and lanes – a natural relish for harvesting and sheep-washings.

From the fastidious Mr James, this is something of a backhander.

An important general survey of Hardy's work before the publication of *The Mayor of Casterbridge* was Havelock Ellis's accomplished essay 'Thomas Hardy's Novels' published in the *Westminster Review* in April 1883. Ellis begins by addressing the relationship between George Eliot and Thomas Hardy, saying that *Far from the Madding Crowd* could not have been written by Eliot:

> Not only was this new novel without the massive quality, and the serious sustained power of George Eliot's work, but it possessed a vivid freshness, a quaint, unconventional simplicity equally without correspondence in George Eliot.

However, reviewers were justified in doubting the sex of Thomas Hardy:

> The minute observation, the delicate insight, the conception of love as the one business of life, and a singularly charming reticence in its delineation [a feature that later critics were to find lamentably lacking in *Tess* and *Jude*], are qualities which, if not universally characteristic of woman's work in fiction, are such as might with propriety be attributed to it[.]

Ellis continues, 'it seems now to stand beyond question that the most serious work in modern English fiction . . . has been done by women', and he defines what places Hardy in the ranks of such superior English novelists as Jane Austen, Charlotte Brontë and George Eliot:

> He has created a group of peasants, for the like of whom, in strong and living individuality, in wealth of quaint humour, we must go back to Shakspere [*sic*]; he has given us a gallery of women – 'Undines of the earth', they have been felicitously called – whose charm is unique; they have no like anywhere; he has added a fresh delight to certain aspects of Nature.

Ellis perceives Hardy's principal concerns as character and psychology, which he endeavours to indicate by 'the exercise of a fine and suggestive observation'. Himself an advanced thinker on sexual matters, the reviewer comments on Hardy's innovative approach to his female characters, whom Ellis sees as motivated by an instinct for love and admiration:

> Mr Hardy's way of regarding women is peculiar and difficult to define, not because it is not a perfectly defensible way, but because it is in a great degree new. It is, as we have already noted, far removed from a method, adopted by many distinguished novelists, in which women are considered as moral forces, centripetal tendencies providentially adapted to balance the centrifugal tendencies of men; being, indeed, almost the polar opposite to that view. . . Mr Hardy's women are creatures, always fascinating, made up of more or less untamed instincts for both love and admiration, who can never help some

degree of response when the satisfaction of those instincts lies open to them. They are all ultimately that; but with what intelligence, what an innate grace, at once delicate and frank, these instincts are manifested . . .

Hardy's limitations are seen by Ellis as his frequently 'random and inaccurate' style in the narrative sections, which lack 'strength and precision in the use of language'. He is also criticised for repetition of plot: ' a woman more or less in love with two men at the same time'. Of particular interest in relation to *The Mayor of Casterbridge* (published three years after this article), Ellis criticises Hardy for the lack of development in his characters and the way in which they are seen as isolated individuals rather than as part of the community.

The Mayor of Casterbridge was published in 1886 and widely reviewed. The *Athenaeum* reviewer (May 1886) praises characterisation and plotting in the novel, but predictably, Hardy's style and the language of his labourers come under fire:

> At the same time it must be said that his old faults, chiefly of style, are as prominent as ever. The worst of these is a tendency to far-fetched and unpleasant similes and epithets, e.g., 'the sun was resting on the hill *like a drop of blood on an eyelid*', or 'the espaliers . . . had pulled their stakes out of the ground, and stood distorted and writhing *in vegetable agony, like leafy Laocoons*'. The language of the peasants again is a point on which we have an old quarrel with Mr Hardy. It is neither one thing nor the other – neither dialect exactly reproduced nor a thorough rendering into educated English.

The *Saturday Review* (May 1886) also found the novel disappointing, criticising the improbable plot, the auction and Henchard's unlikely reformation: 'is it possible that Michael Henchard, thoroughly selfish and unprincipled when young, could have been refined by a temperance vow, and a hard-handed money-getting life, into a man of considerable delicacy, honour, and generosity?' Mrs Henchard 'is so colourless as to be almost imperceptible', and the 'excellent' Elizabeth-Jane 'rather more than a trifle dull'. But the reviewer praises Hardy's descriptive powers: 'Nothing can be better than his sketches of Casterbridge, the old Roman garrison town, overgrown rather than obliterated by an English *urbs in rure*.' Hardy's depiction of 'the average peasant' is particularly praised, including, perhaps surprisingly for this period, the latter's speech: 'The dialect of the agricultural labourer, his ways of thought, and his mode of speech are alike admirably given. The rustic dialogue, indeed, forms the most, if not the only, amusing portion of the book.'

The *Spectator* reviewer (June 1886) raises a question that was to interest a number of later commentators: what exactly did Hardy mean by calling Henchard a 'man of character'? For him, the word 'character' implies stability and consistency of behaviour:

> In one very good sense, the great deficiency of Michael Henchard might be said to be in 'character'. It might well be said that with a little *more* character, with a little more fixity of mind, with a little more power of recovering *himself* when he was losing his balance, his would have been a nature of gigantic mould; whereas, as Mr Hardy's novel is meant to show, it was a nature which ran mostly to waste.

By the time of Hardy's death in 1928, he had become well-established as a grand old man of English letters, but the enormous social and political change caused by World War I led to a re-evaluation of his work that placed it more firmly within a Victorian tradition. Compared with the innovative and sexually explicit work of James Joyce and D. H. Lawrence (already being published during Hardy's lifetime), the linguistic and formal experimentation of many writers in both fiction and poetry, and the pessimism of such works as T. S. Eliot's *The Waste Land*, Hardy's novels ceased to seem so innovative, and his weaknesses as well as his strengths began to be re-assessed. Of particular interest for the modern reader are the comments of fellow writers published in the decade after Hardy's death. In an essay on Hardy in *The Common Reader*, Second Series (London, 1932), Virginia Woolf, a writer who took a particular interest in the relationship between author and reader and who struggled in her own work to find appropriate ways of muting the authorial voice, criticises as a weakness in Hardy those places where he attempts to impose a point of view. The writer receives impressions, but 'It is for the reader, steeped in the impression, to supply the comment' and to interpret the writer's deeper, perhaps subconscious, intention. Woolf continues:

> Hardy himself was aware of this. A novel 'is an impression, not an argument', he has warned us, and, again

> Unadjusted impressions have their value, and the road to a true
> philosophy of life seems to lie in humbly recording diverse readings
> of its phenomena as they are forced upon us by chance and change.

Certainly it is true to say of him that, at his greatest, he gives us
impressions; at his weakest, arguments. In *The Woodlanders, The
Return of the Native, Far from the Madding Crowd*, and, above all, in
The Mayor of Casterbridge, we have Hardy's impression of life as it
came to him without conscious ordering. Let him once begin to
tamper with his direct intuitions and his power is gone. 'Did you say
the stars were worlds, Tess?' asks little Abraham as they drive to
market with their beehives. Tess replies that they are like 'the apples
on our stubbard-tree, most of them splendid and sound – a few
blighted'. 'Which do we live on – a splendid or a blighted one?' 'A
blighted one', she replies, or rather the mournful thinker who has
assumed her mask speaks for her. The words protrude, cold and raw,
like the springs of a machine where we had seen only flesh and blood.
We are crudely jolted out of that mood of sympathy which is renewed
a moment later when the little cart is run down and we have a concrete
instance of the ironical methods which rule our planet.

D. H. Lawrence, in his discursive 'Study of Thomas Hardy'
(published posthumously in *Phoenix* in 1936), sees the typical
Hardy hero or heroine as caught between individual identity and
his or her social identity as a member of a community. Charac-
teristically, the movement to free the trapped self from the strait-
jacket of convention is sudden and explosive (Lawrence comments, 'It would be amusing to count the number of special
marriage licenses [*sic*] taken out in Hardy's books'), but:

> In the long run, the State, the Community, the established form of life
> remained, remained intact and impregnable, the individual, trying to
> break forth from it, died of fear, of exhaustion, or of exposure to
> attacks from all sides, like men who have left the walled city to live
> outside in the precarious open.
>
>   This is the tragedy of Hardy, always the same: the tragedy of those
> who, more or less pioneers, have died in the wilderness, whither they
> had escaped for free action, after having left the walled security, and
> the comparative imprisonment, of the established convention. This is
> the theme of novel after novel: remain quite within the convention,
> and you are good, safe, and happy in the long run, though you never
> have the vivid pang of sympathy on your side: or, on the other hand,
> be passionate, individual, wilful, you will find the security of the
> convention a walled prison, you will escape, and you will die, either of
> your own lack of strength to bear the isolation and the exposure, or by
> direct revenge from the community, or from both.

Later in the same essay, Lawrence contrasts man's 'little, pathetic' moral life with the 'vast, incomprehensible pattern of some primal morality', the morality of the natural world, which forms a 'great background, vital and vivid, which matters more than the people who move upon it.' The struggle for Hardy's pioneering characters is between the walled city of human law and order, and the 'waste enormity of nature' beyond.

The relationship of Hardy with tradition, and in the case of *The Mayor of Casterbridge* specifically with dramatic tragedy, has been of key interest to critics. Lord David Cecil in *Hardy the Novelist: An Essay in Criticism*, first published in 1943, sees a direct link between Hardy and Fielding, and hence with Shakespeare, both in his interest in telling a good story and in the aspects of the narrative that he selected for emphasis, a literary tradition that allowed 'full scope for the expression of the spiritual and imaginative aspects of experience'. He concludes:

> So far from disliking the dramatic intensity and regularity which the first novelists had taken on from the playwrights, [Hardy] found it necessary for the expression of his vision . . . If he had masters, they are Shakespeare and that British novelist who learnt most from Shakespeare, Sir Walter Scott.

In an important essay, '*The Mayor of Casterbridge* as Tragedy', published in 1959 (*Victorian Studies*, 3, December, pp. 151–172), John Paterson argues that Hardy escapes from the romantic and scientific humanism of the late Victorian period to return in the novel to tragedy in the traditional sense of Sophocles or Shakespeare, where an individual's behaviour is measured against an external ethical force to which he or she is accountable:

> Temporarily freed from the disabling humanistic biases of his age, exploiting a level of the mind to which his romantic sympathies and naturalistic assumptions could not penetrate, Hardy here assumes what the literature of tragedy after Shakespeare has not found it easy or possible to assume: the existence of a moral order, an ethical substance, a standard of justice and rectitude, in terms of which man's experience can be rendered as the drama of his salvation as well as the drama of his damnation. Reviving a body of beliefs about man and fate, nature and society, that were once the ordinary possession of the Western imagination, he exploits a wisdom that makes possible the achievement of tragedy in the heroical sense of a Sophocles or a Shakespeare.

Thus Henchard's sale of his wife in Chapter 1 fulfils the same function in the plot as Lear's betrayal of Cordelia and Oedipus' murder of Laius, '[a]rousing such forces of retribution as will not be satisfied with less than the total humiliation of the offender and the ultimate restoration of the order offended'.

Similarly, Henchard's self-destructiveness is defined in terms of an 'ancient psychology'. The novel 'celebrates, first of all, the subordination of the passions that link man with nature to the reason that unites him with God. It is Henchard's tragedy that, like Lear and Othello, he reverses and destroys this order.' He sells his wife under the influence of drink and repeatedly explodes in bursts of rage and irritation that alienate both the people closest to him and his professional associates. Furthermore, like Faustus with whom he is explicitly compared by Hardy, Henchard subverts 'the order that has placed man in the middleground between God and nature'; by selling his wife, attempting to make damaged wheat whole, and consulting the weather-prophet, he attempts to intervene (in a superhuman manner) with the natural course of events.

Jeannette King, in *Tragedy in the Victorian Novel* (Cambridge, 1978) elaborates on the idea that in Michael Henchard character and Fate are inextricably linked:

> How can character avail against circumstances, the 'lot' which Fate allocates, if character is not itself independent of Fate? Out of work, impoverished, and burdened with a wife and child, Henchard sells his wife and child in an attempt to escape his 'lot'. He frees himself of his family and poverty, but remains burdened with the impulsiveness of character which made him commit so desperate an act, and immediately regret it. Fate is no longer an external, but an internal, concept.

Carrying his Fate with him in the form of his character, Henchard is doomed to repeat the same mistakes, and in the repetitious cycle of past events into the present, King sees the influence of Greek tragedy.

Not all critics, however, agree in construing *The Mayor of Casterbridge* within a tragic tradition. In a footnote to his commentary on the novel in *Thomas Hardy* (first published in 1967, reprinted 1985), Irving Howe rejects the idea of Henchard as a prototypical tragic hero and places him within the context of romanticism:

> ... He strikes me as a descendent of those stubborn figures in

romantic poetry and fiction who refuse to submit to their own limitations and demand more from the world than it can give them.

Jean Brooks, in *Thomas Hardy: The Poetic Structure* (London, 1971), summarises the novel's links with the archetypal, but also pinpoints what for Hardy's readers would have been an important contemporary issue – the 'self-made man' overthrown by the 'new order of big business':

> The ancient myth of the scapegoat-king meets the modern saga of the nineteenth-century self-made man deposed by the new order of big business, in a penetrating study of the alienation from self and natural harmony that follows the guilt of wilfully imposing conscious desires on the human condition.

The effect of economic change on the essentially agricultural community of Casterbridge is seen by many critics as a central theme of *The Mayor of Casterbridge*. Douglas Brown, in his valuable short study of Hardy, *Thomas Hardy* (first published in 1954), writes that the novel 'acknowledges the bitter situation of agriculture in contemporary England'. Henchard's story 'enacts forcefully the tension between the old rural world and the new urban one', with Henchard representing the old order and Farfrae 'the stranger within the gates':

> *The Mayor of Casterbridge*, then, is the tale of the struggle between the native countryman and the alien invader; of the defeat of dull courage and traditional attitudes by insight, craft, and the vicissitudes of nature; and of the persistence through that defeat of some deep layer of vitality in the country protagonist.

He concludes: '*The Mayor of Casterbridge* turns on the situation that led to the repeal of the Corn Laws. The consequences of that repeal to Victorian agricultural life are the centre of this book, provide the impulse that makes it what it is.'

Ian Gregor, however, argues that Brown's focus on the Corn Laws distorts his reading of the novel. In *The Great Web: The Form of Hardy's Major Fiction* (London, 1974), Gregor writes that when Hardy mentions the Corn Laws in his Preface:

> . . . he is not talking about the repeal of the Corn Laws as such; his emphasis is on 'the uncertain harvests which immediately preceded their repeal', and his emphasis will not really encourage a reading of the novel which sees it in terms of a polarising conflict between 'the native countryman' and 'the alien invader'.

He points out that an alternative reading is possible:

> . . . far from presenting an innocent agrarian economy undermined by new grasping business methods, Hardy shows in Henchard (if we really want to talk in these terms) the last of the old profiteers, existing by courtesy of a closed system of economic protection.

Gregor concludes:

> Clearly, it would be absurd to read the novel in such a way as to make it an indictment of Henchard and a vindication of Farfrae. I have put the counter-case simply to show that when concentration is made too directly on the historical implications of the novel, so that we see a precise agricultural crisis constituting its 'centre', then the move takes us further and further away from its imaginative life.

Laurence Lerner, in *Thomas Hardy's The Mayor of Caster-bridge: Tragedy or Social History?* (London, 1975), sees advantages in looking at literature from a social perspective: 'The social approach to Hardy. . . has undoubtedly drawn our attention to a good deal that other critics have missed.' In the case of Farfrae, it gives the reader valuable insights into his character:

> [T]here is no doubt that he brings new ways of thought into Casterbridge. For Farfrae represents economic rationalisation, in contrast to the highly personal way in which Henchard had previously done business. His way of dealing is less dramatic and more reliable, less temperamental and more easily detached from the individual situation . . . As a manager we see him treating Abel Whittle with cool good sense instead of Henchard's hot temper; later, as owner, he lowers wages but leaves the private lives of his men alone. He introduces into the agricultural world of Wessex the spirit of the industrial revolution, the depersonalising of labour relations; and so it is not surprising that he introduces the mechanisation of agriculture, by bringing the horse-drill to Casterbridge.

Farfrae is generally regarded as a somewhat unsympathetic character – the tepid man of business in contrast to Henchard's *Sturm und Drang*. However, he is a significant catalyst to the action of the novel, as is the other stranger in the community, Lucetta. In *Thomas Hardy: The Mayor of Casterbridge* (London, 1962), Douglas Brown revised his view of Farfrae as the Invader and allocated this role to Lucetta, whose arrival he sees as confirming two alternative themes in the novel: 'rising in the world', and 'education' and 'insight'.

Responses to Elizabeth-Jane, the other major female character in the novel, have sometimes been equivocal – one recalls the *Saturday Review*'s 'excellent' but 'more than a trifle dull'; however, as Michael Millgate points out in *Thomas Hardy: His Career as a Novelist* (London, 1971), she has a crucial role as onlooker:

> Elizabeth-Jane sits quietly, suffers quietly, watches, and learns. Like the Fanny Price of *Mansfield Park* she is, though not especially sympathetic, absolutely a person, essentially right-thinking, and very much to be taken seriously. Because of her position of onlooker, and because of her good sense, she gradually establishes herself for the reader as much the most acute and reliable intelligence within the novel, the one whose judgments are most to be trusted.

Two studies offer interesting insights into Michael Henchard. Albert J. Guerard, in *Thomas Hardy: The Novels and Stories* (Cambridge, Mass., 1949), places Henchard 'with certain towering and possessed figures of Melville, Hawthorne, and Dostoevsky: a man of character obsessed by guilt and so committed to his own destruction.' Hardy recognised, in advance of modern psychology, that accidents are not merely fortuitous and that the guilty create their own bad luck. 'Thus Hardy, who had seldom troubled himself with crime and punishment, at last explored the great nineteenth-century myth of the isolated, damned, and self-destructive individualist . . . conceived in terms as grand as the Wessex environment would allow'.

Guerard develops the theme of a life obsessed with atonement by comparing Henchard with Conrad's Lord Jim (*Lord Jim* was published in 1900):

> These two 'men of character' pursued strikingly similar destinies: forceful, conscientious, and proud, alike outcasts thanks to the unaccountable flarings of a moment's fear and anger, dedicating their lives to an impossible rehabilitation and a distant ideal of honor. They are isolated and obsessed by guilt even in their fat years of power and prestige; they are determined to bear yet face down the past. Both are men of character in a strangely double sense. They want to atone for the past through self-punishment; yet they resist, humanly, merely compulsive self-punishment. In the end both are paralyzed by 'chance' reminders from the past (Brown and the furmity-woman) – reminders which, in fact, they had never ceased to carry about with them. They achieve death in solitude, each having one dull-witted uncomprehending native who remains faithful to the last.

A rather different reading is offered by the feminist critic, Elaine

Showalter, in her essay 'The Unmanning of the Mayor of Casterbridge' (see Kramer volume in Suggestions for Further Reading). Showalter sees Hardy as understanding the androgyny of the human psyche: he 'understood the feminine self as the estranged and essential complement of the male self.' In the novel,

> Hardy gives the fullest nineteenth-century portrait of a man's inner life – his rebellion and his suffering, his loneliness and jealousy, his paranoia and despair, his uncontrollable unconscious. Henchard's efforts, first to deny and divorce his passional self, and ultimately to accept and educate it, involve him in a pilgrimage of 'unmanning' which is a movement towards both self-discovery and tragic vulnerability.

Showalter quotes Irving Howe's bold (and infamous?) introduction to his own commentary on the novel (*op. cit.*). Howe writes:

> To shake loose from one's wife; to discard that drooping rag of a woman, with her mute complaints and maddening passivity; to escape not by a slinking abandonment but through the public sale of her body to a stranger, as horses are sold at a fair; and thus to wrest, through sheer amoral willfulness, a second chance out of life – it is with this stroke, so insidiously attractive to male fantasy, that *The Mayor of Casterbridge* begins.

As Showalter points out, Howe appropriates the novel for a male audience. 'A woman's experience of this scene must be very different'. Further, Howe, as with the majority of Hardy's critics, ignores the sale of Elizabeth-Jane: a major oversight in a novel where paternity 'is a central subject . . . far more important than conjugal love.'

The sale of his family allows Henchard to commit himself to a masculine world; their return forces him towards 'a more complete humanity'. Showalter concludes:

> We might read the story of Henchard as a tragic taming of the heroic will, the bending and breaking of his savage male defiance in contest with a stoic female endurance . . . Yet this romantic and nostalgic reading would underestimate Hardy's generosity of imagination. Virginia Woolf, one of Hardy's earliest feminist critics, attributed the 'tragic power' of his characters to 'a force within them which cannot be defined, a force of love or of hate, a force which in the men is the cause of rebellion against life, and in the women implies an illimitable capacity for suffering.' [See 'The Novels of Thomas Hardy', *op. cit.*]

In Henchard the forces of male rebellion and female suffering ultimately conjoin; and in this unmanning Hardy achieves a tragic power unequalled in Victorian fiction . . . The skills which Henchard struggles finally to learn, skills of observation, attention, sensitivity, and compassion, are also those of the novelist; and they are feminine perhaps, if one contrasts them to the skills of the architect or the statesman. But it is because Hardy dares so fully to acknowledge this side of his own art, to pursue the feminine spirit in his man of character, that his hero, like the great heroines he would create in the 1890s, is more Shakespearean than Victorian.

SUGGESTIONS FOR FURTHER READING

BIOGRAPHY

Florence Emily Hardy, *The Life of Thomas Hardy 1840–1928* (London, 1962): mainly written by Hardy himself, and based on personal letters and notes. Originally published in two volumes: *The Early Life of Thomas Hardy* (London, 1928) and *The Later Years of Thomas Hardy* (London, 1930).

Robert Gittings, *Young Thomas Hardy* (London, 1975) and *The Older Hardy* (London, 1978): a sympathetic but clear-sighted exploration of the life by a gifted biographer and poet.

Michael Millgate, *Thomas Hardy: A Biography* (Oxford, 1982): the standard life, admirably thorough.

GENERAL REFERENCE

R. L. Purdy, *Thomas Hardy, A Bibliographical Study* (Oxford, 1954): classic bibliography of Hardy's writings.

R. G. Cox, ed., *Thomas Hardy: The Critical Heritage* (London, 1970): includes reprints of many contemporary reviews of the works.

F. B. Pinion, *A Hardy Companion* (London, 1968): reference guide to Hardy's writings, including a dictionary of people and places in the works.

Denys Kay-Robinson, *Hardy's Wessex Reappraised* (Newton Abbot, 1972): survey of all locations and buildings in Hardy's Wessex that are known or believed to be based on fact.

Ralph W. V. Elliot, *Thomas Hardy's English* (Oxford, 1984): exploration of Hardy's rich use of English, including his linguistic, literary and biblical sources.

CRITICAL TEXTS

*includes a section or chapter dealing with *The Mayor of Casterbridge*

Jean R. Brooks, *Thomas Hardy: The Poetic Structure* (London, 1971): an analysis of the centrality of the 'poetic vision' to Hardy's work.*

Douglas Brown, *Thomas Hardy: The Mayor of Casterbridge* (London, 1962): excellent brief study aimed at the student.

Lance St. John Butler, ed., *Thomas Hardy after Fifty Years* (London, 1977): wide-ranging series of essays by various contributors aimed at assessing Hardy's importance fifty years after his death; *includes David Lodge, 'Thomas Hardy as a Cinematic Novelist'.

David Cecil, *Hardy the Novelist: An Essay in Criticism* (London, 1943): a general introduction to Hardy's novels.

Ian Gregor, *The Great Web: The Form of Hardy's Major Fiction* (London, 1974): explores Hardy's aims and development in the major novels.*

Jeannette King, *Tragedy in the Victorian Novel: Theory and Practice in the Novels of George Eliot, Thomas Hardy and Henry James* (Cambridge, 1978): evaluates the relationship between the Victorian novel and tragic drama.*

Dale Kramer, ed., *Critical Approaches to the Fiction of Thomas Hardy* (London, 1979): essays on the novels by various contributors; *includes Elaine Showalter, 'The Unmanning of the Mayor of Casterbridge', an analysis of Hardy from the perspective of a feminist critic, with specific reference to Michael Henchard.

Laurence Lerner, *Thomas Hardy's The Mayor of Casterbridge: Tragedy or Social History?* (London, 1975): evaluates the novel in the contexts of Hardy's philosophy (and hence as tragedy) and of rural England on the edge of social change.

Michael Millgate, *Thomas Hardy: His Career as a Novelist* (London, 1971): takes 'a fresh look at both the texts and the contexts of his fiction'.*

Julian Moynahan, 'The Mayor of Casterbridge and the Old Testament's First Book of Samuel: A Study of Some Literary Relationships' in *PMLA*, 71 (1956), pp. 118–30: traces the parallels between the Saul/David relationship in *Samuel* with that between Henchard and Farfrae.

Norman Page, ed. *Thomas Hardy: The Writer and his Background* (London, 1980): essays by various contributors looking at aspects of Hardy's social, intellectual and literary/linguistic background.

John Paterson, 'The Mayor of Casterbridge as Tragedy' in *Victorian Studies*, 3 (December 1959), pp. 151–72: examines the novel as tragedy in the sense of Sophocles or Shakespeare.

Rosemary Sumner, *Thomas Hardy: Psychological Novelist* (London, 1981): explores the range and depth of Hardy's psychological insights, with reference to twentieth-century developments in the study of psychology.*

Virginia Woolf, 'The Novels of Thomas Hardy' in *The Common Reader*, Second Series (London, 1932): brief evaluation of Hardy's fiction, pinpointing his unique qualities.

SUMMARY OF THE TEXT

7 Elizabeth-Jane serves the young Scotsman, Donald Farfrae, his
   dinner. She and Susan overhear Farfrae explaining to Henchard how
   to improve the damaged wheat. He refuses Henchard's offer of a job
   as manager as he is en route for America.

8 Farfrae entertains the company at the Three Mariners with his
   nostalgic songs of home.

9 Susan sends Elizabeth-Jane to tell Henchard that his relative Susan is
   in town. A description of Casterbridge as Elizabeth-Jane walks along
   the High Street to his house. She finds Farfrae in the office: he has
   been persuaded to take the job of manager.

10 Henchard turns away Joshua Jopp, who had expected to be offered
    the manager's job. Elizabeth-Jane gives Henchard Susan's message
    and explains their history. He gives her a note and five guineas for
    Susan.

11 Susan and Henchard meet at the Ring, the Roman amphitheatre just
    outside the town. They agree to keep Elizabeth-Jane in ignorance of
    their true relationship. Susan will take a cottage in the town and
    Henchard will court and marry her.

12 Henchard tells Farfrae about Susan and his subsequent relationship
    with a young woman in Jersey. Farfrae composes a letter to the
    second woman on Henchard's behalf explaining why he can't marry
    her; later Henchard copies it and posts it with a cheque. Henchard
    rejects Farfrae's recommendation that he and Susan tell Elizabeth-
    Jane the truth.

13 Susan's courtship and marriage by Michael Henchard.

14 Elizabeth-Jane benefits from the opportunities offered by her more
    affluent life. Henchard's move to get her to change her name to his is
    abandoned. His business thrives under Farfrae's management and his
    close relationship with the young Scot is described. Elizabeth-Jane
    and Farfrae are mysteriously summoned by letter to a granary on
    Durnover Hill.

15 Elizabeth-Jane's budding beauty attracts admiration, including from
    Farfrae. The quarrel over Abel Whittle underlines Farfrae's
    ascendancy among Henchard's workers. A child confirms Farfrae's
    greater popularity. The rift is healed, but Henchard regrets telling
    Farfrae his secrets.

16 Henchard becomes more reticent towards Farfrae. The failure of
    Henchard's entertainment; the success of Farfrae's. Henchard again
    overhears gossip comparing him unfavourably with Farfrae and
    declares in front of senior townsmen that his manager will soon be
    leaving him.

17 Farfrae walks Elizabeth-Jane towards her home after the dancing, and hints at his attachment and his coming parting from Henchard. He buys a small corn and hay business, enraging Henchard despite Farfrae's attempts to avoid direct competition. The Mayor's popularity among the councillors has waned. Henchard forbids Elizabeth-Jane and Farfrae to meet. Farfrae's business is a success, and he and Henchard engage in a price war.

18 Susan's illness. Lucetta writes to request the return of her letters but fails to keep her appointment with Henchard. Susan writes a letter to Henchard to be opened on Elizabeth-Jane's wedding day. She tells her daughter that she had set up the Durnover granary rendezvous with Farfrae. Susan dies and Mother Cuxsom describes what she has learnt of the death from the nurse.

19 Henchard tells Elizabeth-Jane that she is his daughter and gets her to write to the local newspaper to announce she is changing her name to Henchard. He goes to look for documents to prove their relationship and reads Susan's poorly sealed letter: his own daughter is dead and Elizabeth-Jane is Newson's child. He gazes at the sleeping Elizabeth-Jane by candlelight and sees Newson's features in hers. Bitterly disappointed, he walks along the river past the gallows. The following morning, Elizabeth-Jane welcomes him as her father – but it is 'dust and ashes'.

20 Elizabeth-Jane is bewildered by Henchard's coldness and criticisms of her behaviour. Nance Mockridge reveals that Elizabeth-Jane had served at the Three Mariners: Henchard feels this has damaged his reputation and avoids the girl. Elizabeth-Jane studies incessantly. She sees a well-dressed woman by her mother's grave. Henchard learns he is not to be made an alderman when his term as Mayor expires; Farfrae is probably to join the Council. Henchard blames Elizabeth-Jane's serving-maid activities. Anxious to be rid of her, Henchard writes to Farfrae to say he can court Elizabeth-Jane after all. Elizabeth-Jane talks to the unknown woman, who suggests she should live with her as housekeeper/companion at High-Place Hall where she is moving that day.

21 Elizabeth-Jane goes to look at High-Place Hall. She leaves by the back entrance and fails to see Henchard enter by the same arched doorway. Later she tells Henchard of her plan to leave home. Unaware of the details, he agrees and offers her an annuity. Elizabeth-Jane meets the lady, Miss Templeman, again and arranges to move to her house the same evening. When Henchard sees the books and maps, etc, in her room, evidence of her attempts at self-improvement, he asks her to stay. It is too late. As she leaves, Elizabeth-Jane tells him she is going to High-Place Hall.

22 Lucetta had previously written to Henchard to tell him that she was coming to Casterbridge with a view to marrying him now that Susan was dead. Henchard's visit to High-Place Hall had been to enquire for Miss Le Sueur, as he knows Lucetta. Just after Elizabeth-Jane leaves, another letter arrives explaining that Lucetta has inherited property from her aunt and taken her name. The arrangement with Elizabeth-Jane will enable Henchard to visit. He calls the same evening, but is turned away. Elizabeth-Jane is welcomed by Lucetta who lets slip her connection with Jersey. Henchard does not call again and Elizabeth-Jane attributes this to her father's feelings against her. Lucetta gets rid of Elizabeth-Jane on errands and invites Henchard to call as if 'on business'. A male visitor is shown in.

23 It is Farfrae, visiting Elizabeth-Jane as a result of Henchard's letter and his own recent prosperity. He and Lucetta become acquainted and he is stimulated to hire a young man to save him from separation from his sweetheart. Farfrae leaves before Elizabeth-Jane returns; Lucetta turns away Henchard when he calls in response to her note.

24 Lucetta buys a cherry-coloured outfit. Elizabeth-Jane and Lucetta go out to look at the brightly hued horse-drill in the market-place. Elizabeth-Jane introduces Lucetta to Henchard, who ridicules the horse-drill; Farfrae recommends it. Elizabeth-Jane confesses to Lucetta her worries about lack of respectability. Elizabeth-Jane guesses that Lucetta is attracted to Farfrae. Lucetta sounds Elizabeth-Jane out about the predicament over Henchard and Farfrae, but gives no names.

25 Farfrae visits, but ignores Elizabeth-Jane. Henchard visits Lucetta, but she prevaricates over agreeing a wedding date. Elizabeth-Jane observes Lucetta with her two lovers, who ignore Elizabeth-Jane.

26 Henchard and Farfrae discuss Henchard's relationship with his unnamed second woman. They meet by chance at Lucetta's for tea; Elizabeth-Jane finds their behaviour ridiculous. Henchard hires Jopp as foreman and says Farfrae must be cut out. Jopp is aware of Lucetta and Henchard's Jersey connections. Elizabeth-Jane tries to persuade Henchard that Jopp is unsuitable. Henchard visits Mr Fall, the weather-prophet, and speculates unwisely on his predictions. He blames Jopp for his financial losses and sacks him.

27 Fall's predictions turn out to be accurate, but it is too late for Henchard to benefit. Farfrae's careful playing of the market wins him a substantial income. Farfrae and Henchard's waggons clash in the street. Henchard sees Lucetta go out with Farfrae to the night-harvesting and overhears their love-talk. He threatens Lucetta with public exposure of their former intimacy unless she agrees to marry him. She promises to do so with Elizabeth-Jane as witness.

28 The furmity-seller reveals in court that Henchard had auctioned his wife and child. Lucetta hears the story and is wretched. She goes on a visit to Port-Bredy.

29 Lucetta and Elizabeth-Jane are hemmed in by a bull in a barn. Henchard rescues them and walks on with Lucetta. He asks her to use their engagement to help him put off a creditor, but she is already married to Farfrae.

30 Farfrae moves into High-Place Hall; Elizabeth-Jane moves out to lodgings.

31 The furmity-woman's disclosure marks the downward turn in Henchard's fortunes. He is declared bankrupt, and moves to Jopp's cottage by Priory Mill; he refuses to see Elizabeth-Jane. Farfrae buys his business.

32 The two bridges. Jopp tells Henchard that Farfrae has bought his house and furniture. Farfrae suggests Henchard should live in his former house with himself and Lucetta, and offers him the pick of his furniture. Elizabeth-Jane visits Henchard when he is sick. He takes a job as journeyman hay-trusser. His oath is up and he 'busts out drinking'.

33 The Three Mariners after church: the scene of Henchard's first alcoholic drink for twenty-one years. He asks the choir to sing Psalm 109 and then applies it to Farfrae. Elizabeth-Jane takes him home. Henchard speaks threateningly against Farfrae. Elizabeth-Jane works with Henchard at Farfrae's yard. Farfrae is ignorant of the connection between Lucetta and Henchard. After Lucetta unexpectedly meets Henchard in the yard, she writes to ask him not to treat her uncivilly. Elizabeth-Jane sees Henchard's threatening gesture towards Farfrae at the top of the corn-stores.

34 Elizabeth-Jane warns Farfrae that Henchard may harm him. Farfrae gives up his plan to set Henchard up in a seed shop, which causes further bad feeling. Farfrae becomes Mayor. Henchard reads Lucetta's letters to Farfrae.

35 Lucetta overhears the reading. She meets Henchard at the Ring and he agrees to return her letters.

36 Jopp asks Lucetta for a recommendation; she refuses. Henchard gives Jopp the letters to return to Lucetta. The letters are read by the company at Peter's Finger in Mixen Lane: they plan a skimmity-ride. A stranger passes through en route to Casterbridge. Jopp delivers the letters to Lucetta.

37 The visit of the Royal Personage: Henchard's welcome is intercepted by Farfrae and he is spoken of disparagingly by Lucetta.

38 Henchard fights Farfrae in the corn-stores.

39 Well-wishers send Farfrae an anonymous letter to get him out of town; he diverts to Weatherbury instead of the Budmouth Road as originally planned. Lucetta sees the skimmington and collapses with a seizure. A messenger is sent to the Budmouth Road for Farfrae. The constables are unable to apprehend the skimmington revellers.

40 Henchard knows about Farfrae's change of plans and sets out to bring him home. Farfrae is suspicious and continues the second part of his journey, to Mellstock. Lucetta miscarries and dies. Henchard turns towards Elizabeth-Jane.

41 Having looked after Lucetta through the night, Elizabeth-Jane falls asleep at Henchard's lodgings. Newson arrives and Henchard tells him Elizabeth-Jane is dead. Henchard watches Newson take the coach out of Casterbridge. In his anxiety that Newson will return to reveal the deception to Elizabeth-Jane, Henchard walks out to the weir at the Ten Hatches. He sees himself floating in the water. Elizabeth-Jane returns with him and identifies the body as his effigy from the skimmington. She guesses his suicidal thoughts and asks to live with him.

42 The Town Council buy Henchard the small seed and root business, which he and Elizabeth-Jane run. Elizabeth-Jane takes long walks, and acquires a new muff and a quantity of books. Henchard divines Farfrae's renewed interest and fears losing her.

43 Henchard spies on Farfrae's meetings with Elizabeth-Jane on the Budmouth Road, and sees Newson waiting there. Elizabeth-Jane consults him about a letter: she is to go to a meeting that night at Farfrae's house. Henchard leaves Casterbridge in his former dress as hay-trusser. Elizabeth-Jane is reunited with Newson and her wedding to Farfrae is planned.

44 Henchard returns to Weydon-Priors. He takes up hay-trussing and learns news of Farfrae's wedding. He visits with a gift of a goldfinch in a cage, and watches the revelries unseen. Elizabeth-Jane reproaches him and he leaves without attempting to defend his behaviour.

45 Newson moves to Budmouth. Elizabeth-Jane discovers the dead goldfinch in its cage in her garden. Elizabeth-Jane and Farfrae set out to look for Henchard and see Abel Whittle go into an isolated cottage, where Henchard has just died. Henchard's will. Elizabeth-Jane's 'latitude of calm weather'.

ACKNOWLEDGEMENTS

The publishers would like to thank the following for permission to reproduce extracts in 'Hardy and His Critics':

Routledge & Kegan Paul: reviews of Thomas Hardy from the *Athenaeum, Nation, Saturday Review, Spectator* and *Westminster Review* reproduced in R. G. Cox, ed. *Thomas Hardy: The Critical Heritage* (London, 1970).

The Hogarth Press: Virginia Woolf, 'The Novels of Thomas Hardy' in *The Common Reader*, Second Series (London, 1932).

William Heinemann: D. H. Lawrence, 'Study of Thomas Hardy' in Edward D. McDonald, ed. *Phoenix: The Posthumous Papers of D. H. Lawrence* (London, 1936).

Constable and Co: David Cecil, *Hardy the Novelist: An Essay in Criticism* (London, 1943; 1965 edition).

Victorian Studies: John Paterson, 'The Mayor of Casterbridge as Tragedy' in *Victorian Studies*, 3 (December 1959).

Cambridge University Press: Jeannette King, *Tragedy in the Victorian Novel: Theory and Practice in the Novels of George Eliot, Thomas Hardy and Henry James* (Cambridge, 1978).

Macmillan: Irving Howe, *Thomas Hardy* (first published 1967; 1985 edition); Elaine Showalter, 'The Unmanning of the Mayor of Casterbridge' in Dale Kramer, ed. *Critical Approaches to the Fiction of Thomas Hardy* (London, 1979).

Elek Books: Jean R. Brooks, *Thomas Hardy: The Poetic Structure* (London, 1971).

Longmans, Green and Co: Douglas Brown, *Thomas Hardy* (first published 1954; 1961 edition).

Faber and Faber: Ian Gregor, *The Great Web: The Form of Hardy's Major Fiction* (London, 1974).

Chatto & Windus: Laurence Lerner, *Thomas Hardy's The Mayor of Casterbridge: Tragedy or Social History?* (London, 1975).

Edward Arnold: Douglas Brown, *Thomas Hardy: The Mayor of Casterbridge* (London, 1962).

The Bodley Head: Michael Millgate, *Thomas Hardy: His Career as a Novelist* (London, 1971).

Harvard University Press: Albert J. Guerard, *Thomas Hardy: The Novels and Stories* (Cambridge, Mass., 1949).

CLASSIC NOVELS
IN EVERYMAN

A SELECTION

The Way of All Flesh

SAMUEL BUTLER
A savagely funny odyssey from joy-
less duty to unbridled liberalism **£4.99**

Born in Exile

GEORGE GISSING
A rationalist's progress towards love
and compromise in class-ridden
Victorian England **£4.99**

David Copperfield

CHARLES DICKENS
One of Dickens' best-loved novels,
brimming with humour **£3.99**

The Last Chronicle of Barset

ANTHONY TROLLOPE
Trollope's magnificent conclusion
to his Barsetshire novels **£4.99**

He Knew He Was Right

ANTHONY TROLLOPE
Sexual jealousy, money and
women's rights within marriage –
a novel ahead of its time **£6.99**

Tess of the D'Urbervilles

THOMAS HARDY
The powerful, poetic classic of
wronged innocence **£3.99**

Wuthering Heights
and Poems

EMILY BRONTE
A powerful work of genius – one of
the great masterpieces of literature
£3.50

Tom Jones

HENRY FIELDING
The wayward adventures of one of
literatures most likable heroes **£5.99**

The Master of Ballantrae
and Weir of Hermiston

R. L. STEVENSON
Together in one volume, two great
novels of high adventure and family
conflict **£4.99**

£3.99

£2.99

£3.99

AVAILABILITY

All books are available from your local bookshop or direct from
**Littlehampton Book Services Cash Sales, 14 Eldon Way, LinesideEstate,
Littlehampton, West Sussex BN17 7HE.** PRICES ARE SUBJECT TO CHANGE.

To order any of the books, please enclose a cheque (in £ sterling) made payable to
Littlehampton Book Services, or phone your order through with credit card details (Access,
Visa or Mastercard) on 0903 721596 (24 hour answering service) stating card number and
expiry date. Please add £1.25 for package and postage to the total value of your order.

CLASSIC FICTION
IN EVERYMAN

A SELECTION

Frankenstein
MARY SHELLEY
A masterpiece of Gothic terror in its
original 1818 version **£3.99**

Dracula
BRAM STOKER
One of the best known horror stories
in the world **£3.99**

The Diary of A Nobody
GEORGE AND WEEDON
GROSSMITH
A hilarious account of suburban life
in Edwardian London **£4.99**

Some Experiences
and Further Experiences
of an Irish R. M.
SOMERVILLE AND ROSS
Gems of comic exuberance and
improvisation **£4.50**

Three Men in a Boat
JEROME K. JEROME
English humour at its best **£2.99**

Twenty Thousand Leagues
under the Sea
JULES VERNE
Scientific fact combines with
fantasy in this prophetic tale of
underwater adventure **£4.99**

The Best of Father Brown
G. K. CHESTERTON
An irresistible selection of crime
stories – unique to Everyman **£3.99**

The Collected Raffles
E. W. HORNUNG
Dashing exploits from the most glam-
orous figure in crime fiction **£4.99**

£2.99

£5.99

£5.99

WOMEN'S WRITING
IN EVERYMAN

A SELECTION

Female Playwrights of the Restoration
FIVE COMEDIES
Rediscovered literary treasures in a unique selection **£5.99**

The Secret Self
SHORT STORIES BY WOMEN
'A superb collection' *Guardian* **£4.99**

Short Stories
KATHERINE MANSFIELD
An excellent selection displaying the remarkable range of Mansfield's talent **£3.99**

Women Romantic Poets 1780-1830: An Anthology
Hidden talent from the Romantic era, rediscovered for the first time **£5.99**

Selected Poems
ELIZABETH BARRETT BROWNING
A major contribution to our appreciation of this inspiring and innovative poet **£5.99**

Frankenstein
MARY SHELLEY
A masterpiece of Gothic terror in its original 1818 version **£3.99**

The Life of Charlotte Brontë
MRS GASKELL
A moving and perceptive tribute by one writer to another **£4.99**

Vindication of the Rights of Woman and The Subjection of Women
MARY WOLLSTONECRAFT
AND J. S. MILL
Two pioneering works of early feminist thought **£4.99**

The Pastor's Wife
ELIZABETH VON ARNIM
A funny and accomplished novel by the author of *Elizabeth and Her German Garden* **£5.99**

£4.99

£2.99

£5.99

AVAILABILITY

All books are available from your local bookshop or direct from
Littlehampton Book Services Cash Sales, 14 Eldon Way, LinesideEstate,
Littlehampton, West Sussex BN17 7HE. PRICES ARE SUBJECT TO CHANGE.

To order any of the books, please enclose a cheque (in £ sterling) made payable to Littlehampton Book Services, or phone your order through with credit card details (Access, Visa or Mastercard) on 0903 721596 (24 hour answering service) stating card number and expiry date. Please add £1.25 for package and postage to the total value of your order.

SHORT STORY COLLECTIONS
IN EVERYMAN

A SELECTION

**The Secret Self
Short Stories by Women**
'A superb collection' *Guardian* **£4.99**

**Selected Short Stories
and Poems**
THOMAS HARDY
The best of Hardy's Wessex in a
unique selection **£4.99**

**The Best of
Sherlock Holmes**
ARTHUR CONAN DOYLE
All the favourite adventures in one
volume **£4.99**

**Great Tales of Detection
Nineteen Stories**
Chosen by Dorothy L. Sayers **£3.99**

Short Stories
KATHERINE MANSFIELD
A selection displaying the
remarkable range of Mansfield's
writing **£3.99**

Selected Stories
RUDYARD KIPLING
Includes stories chosen to reveal the
'other' Kipling **£4.50**

**The Strange Case of
Dr Jekyll and Mr Hyde
and Other Stories**
R. L. STEVENSON
An exciting selection of gripping
tales from a master of suspense **£3.99**

**Modern Short Stories 2:
1940-1980**
Thirty-one stories from the greatest
modern writers **£3.50**

**The Day of Silence and
Other Stories**
GEORGE GISSING
Gissing's finest stories, available for
the first time in one volume **£4.99**

Selected Tales
HENRY JAMES
Stories portraying the tensions
between private life and the outside
world **£5.99**

£4.99

£6.99

AVAILABILITY
All books are available from your local bookshop or direct from
**Littlehampton Book Services Cash Sales, 14 Eldon Way, LinesideEstate,
Littlehampton, West Sussex BN17 7HE.** PRICES ARE SUBJECT TO CHANGE.

To order any of the books, please enclose a cheque (in £ sterling) made payable to
Littlehampton Book Services, or phone your order through with credit card details (Access,
Visa or Mastercard) on 0903 721596 (24 hour answering service) stating card number and
expiry date. Please add £1.25 for package and postage to the total value of your order.

POETRY
IN EVERYMAN

A SELECTION

Silver Poets of the Sixteenth Century

EDITED BY
DOUGLAS BROOKS-DAVIES
A new edition of this famous
Everyman collection **£6.99**

Complete Poems

JOHN DONNE
The father of metaphysical verse in
this highly-acclaimed edition **£4.99**

Complete English Poems, Of Education, Areopagitica

JOHN MILTON
An excellent introduction to
Milton's poetry and prose **£6.99**

Selected Poems

JOHN DRYDEN
A poet's portrait of Restoration
England **£4.99**

Selected Poems

PERCY BYSSHE SHELLEY
'The essential Shelley' in one
volume **£3.50**

Women Romantic Poets 1780-1830: An Anthology

Hidden talent from the Romantic era,
rediscovered for the first time. **£5.99**

Poems in Scots and English

ROBERT BURNS
The best of Scotland's greatest lyric
poet **£4.99**

Selected Poems

D. H. LAWRENCE
A newly-edited selection spanning
the whole of Lawrence's literary
career **£4.99**

The Poems

W. B. YEATS
Ireland's greatest lyric poet
surveyed in this ground-breaking
edition **£6.50**

£5.99

£4.99

£3.50

AVAILABILITY

All books are available from your local bookshop or direct from
**Littlehampton Book Services Cash Sales, 14 Eldon Way, LinesideEstate,
Littlehampton, West Sussex BN17 7HE.** PRICES ARE SUBJECT TO CHANGE.

To order any of the books, please enclose a cheque (in £ sterling) made payable to
Littlehampton Book Services, or phone your order through with credit card details (Access,
Visa or Mastercard) on 0903 721596 (24 hour answering service) stating card number and
expiry date. Please add £1.25 for package and postage to the total value of your order.